AFTER THE END:
Recent Apocalypses

OTHER ANTHOLOGIES EDITED BY
PAULA GURAN

∼

Embraces
Best New Paranormal Romance
Best New Romantic Fantasy
Zombies: The Recent Dead
The Year's Best Dark Fantasy & Horror: 2010
Vampires: The Recent Undead
The Year's Best Dark Fantasy & Horror: 2011
Halloween
New Cthulhu: The Recent Weird
Brave New Love
Witches: Wicked, Wild & Wonderful
Obsession: Tales of Irresistible Desire
The Year's Best Dark Fantasy & Horror: 2012
Extreme Zombies
Ghosts: Recent Hauntings
Rock On: The Greatest Hits of Science Fiction & Fantasy
Season of Wonder
Future Games
Weird Detectives: Recent Investigations
The Mammoth Book of Angels & Demons

∼

AFTER THE END:
Recent Apocalypses

PRIME BOOKS

AFTER THE END: RECENT APOCALYPSES

Prime Books
www.prime-books.com

For more information, contact Prime Books:
prime@prime-books.com

ISBN: 978-1-60701-390-7

· CONTENTS ·

"It's the End of the World as We Know It (And I Feel Fine)"
—R. E. M. song title
(Written by Bill Berry, Michael Stipe, Mike Mills, Peter Buck)

• INTRODUCTION: BEFORE *AFTER THE END* •
Paula Guran

These are twenty-first century stories of what might happen after the end of the world as we know it: post-apocalyptic fiction.

In ancient Greek, *apocálypsis*, literally meant "uncovering." An apocalypse was like taking the lid off of a pot of previously hidden knowledge. It later came to mean, around the fourteenth century, "revelation," or the lifting of a veil to disclose mysteries. In Middle English, it also had a less specific meaning of "insight, vision" or even "hallucination."

Nowadays, outside of its prophetic meaning, we usually use *apocalypse* to mean a cataclysmic event or doomsday scenario in which the world suffers great or near-total devastation.

Of course, such scenarios can be revelatory, and post-apocalyptic tales often offer insight . . .

Homo sapiens have been expecting, predicting, and fearing the end of the world since they could conceive of such a thing.

Our close relations, the Neanderthals (just how we're related is too debatable to delve into here), became extinct around 30,000 years ago. At least some of our ancestors probably made note of that. Many of the theories of their demise match our own concepts of human apocalypse. To Neanderthals, *homo sapiens* might have equated with an alien race—one that may have killed with genocidal fervor, merely used their advanced technology to invade and conquer, or introduced new pathogens resulting in a species-ending pandemic. Climatic change and natural disasters could have played a role in bringing doom for the Neanderthals as well.

But, even now, modern humans share some nuclear DNA with the extinct Neanderthals. If there is such a thing as genetic memory, the story of their apocalypse might still be part of us all.

Since the extinction of the Neanderthals, humans have experienced, time and again, events that—at least for those involved—meant the end of their civilization, their cultures: their "world." There are numerous tales in many cultures of a great flood wiping out a civilization, and we know of various other verifiable cataclysmic natural disasters. Genocide reaches back at least to the first millennium BCE; draconian changes in climate have destroyed established ways of life or forced inhabitants to seek new territories over the millennia; countless pandemics have drastically reduced populations, altering social structures forever; mass panics have resulted in substantial ruin; and endless wars have led to numberless annihilations.

In the past, the end of the world for one tribe/country/continent may have been just an "extreme event" to those not affected. Today, all of humanity is far more closely linked, so we view apocalypse on a global scale. Some areas might survive better than others or retain more of a semblance of what once was, but the entire world as we know it would be affected to some extent.

There are still many who believe in a religious apocalypse brought about by the will of the divine, but science has given us plenty of new possibilities to be concerned with beyond holy wrath or predetermined prophecy: impacting asteroids, rogue planets, solar flares, overpopulation, Y2K (obviously we lived through that one), the Large Hadron Collider seeding a black hole, out-of-control nano-bots consuming stuff, AI displacing humans, intentional or accidental biological catastrophe . . . the more you know the more apprehensive you can be.

Speculation can also produce apocalyptic anxiety. The idea of aliens from another planet invading Earth or infiltrating among us was not a societal concern until we grasped the concept of our world as a planet, and then considered the possibility of life elsewhere and the means for them to reach us. Physics and electricity could fail, technology might cease to function altogether and we'd have to revert to a style of life we have not known for generations . . . or maybe magic would take the place of technology . . . or perhaps the end has already come and all of us are really only bits of binary code in a computer program.

Daily reality provides a lot of fearful fodder, too. Who worried much about nuclear warfare before 1945? The Cold War made worldwide destruction seem quite probable. In the sixties and seventies societal injustice and political upheaval brought rioting in the streets (it wasn't the first time). International energy crises, economic recessions, urban decay, and industrial collapse followed. The appearance of AIDS became both a moral watershed and a reminder of how quickly a deadly disease can change the world.

Although the Mideast always seems on the verge of explosion, how seriously did we concern ourselves with terrorism before 9/11? Did technological calamity bother us that much before events like the Gulf of Mexico oil spill? A hurricane like Katrina had long been anticipated for New Orleans, but when it happened, we wondered why we were so unprepared. When a "superstorm" devastates the Jersey Coast and shuts down New York City, we start considering how close to the brink society might be. The economic upheavals of the last few years have made cultural meltdown suddenly seem more probable. Senseless acts of mass violence against innocent victims shake us all.

Some feel our love/hate relationship with the apocalyptic is based in a collective anxiety about that which lies outside our individual control. Events like those above make us wonder if humankind even has the capacity to solve such overwhelming problems. We feel powerless.

Maybe that's where post-apocalyptic fiction, film, television, and gaming enter the picture. One researcher, Jerry Piven, has been quoted as saying he feels our consideration of doomsday almost embeds a tale of fantasy into reality and provides safe theater for exploring death. Robb Willer, an associate professor of sociology at the University of California, Berkeley, who studies apocalyptic political and religious psychology, thinks "end times" can be both a spectator sport and a reality show for some people.

Whatever the reasons, our pop cultural fascination with the end of the world is both ancient and current. Science fiction and fantasy critic Paul Goat Allen wrote, in 2011:

. . . the last few years have brought about a new Golden Age of apocalyptic and post-apocalyptic fiction. . . . What does this renaissance of apocalyptic fiction tell me? Readers—and writers—are, once again, becoming increasingly fascinated by various end-of-the-world scenarios: the causes, the implications, and the aftermath. The specific reasons readers are attracted to apocalyptic fiction releases varies from person to person but for me at least, I think it's all about comfort and hope. Reading these books and envisioning the nightmarish, end-of-days horrors described within makes me realize just how well off we have it. Yeah, I drive an 18-year-old car and sometimes it's a struggle to pay my bills but at least I have food to eat and a roof over my head. After reading about a world inhabited by masses of starving nomads . . . an America overrun by zombies . . . and a world where millions have simply disappeared after a Rapture-like event . . . my life seems pretty good! . . . I know it sounds paradoxical but reading apocalyptic fiction generally leaves me with a sense of hope—hope that we can somehow avoid the mistakes made in [this fiction] and right the wrongs before it is really too late.

There's also a simpler theory, one espoused by a character in one of the following stories:

I used to pretend the world had ended and that I was the only one who survived . . . I know your secret, you've fantasized about that too, everyone fantasizes that they're important enough to survive, more than survive, to be the last one left, right? [I]t's why you read those books or watched those Will Smith movies, you imagined how important the last one left would feel . . . you only indulged in the fantasy because it was safely impossible in your mind, sort of like daydream sex with somebody you're not supposed to be daydreaming about, you indulge in the danger until you start thinking about the consequences, until you start really thinking about the big what if, what if it *really* happened?

Although the twenty-first century has brought a plethora of media featuring zombies—both supernatural and "science"-based—you won't find that particular type of post-apocalyptic fiction in this anthology. I've edited one anthology, *Zombies: The Recent Dead* (Prime Books, 2011) that includes some of the best short zombie fiction from 2000-2011; another, *Zombies: More Recent Dead* is forthcoming in 2014. There's also *Extreme Zombies* (Prime Books, 2012)—not confined to only recent fiction and intended for those who enjoy more extreme explorations of the trope. In other words, I think I have zombies covered—apocalyptic and not.

I delighted in discovering the many non-zombie variations of post-apocalyptic futures depicted in the stories collected here. With one exception (first published in 2002), the stories in this volume first appeared from 2007 through 2012. I hope they demonstrate at least a few of our *current* ideations of what will bring the End and come after it. They vary in style from Anglo-Saxon epic verse to the near-surreal and, in tone, range from optimism and hope to the bleakest pessimism. What the stories all have in common, other than the theme, is that they are about people: their actions, reactions, interactions, and relationships; their hopes, dreams, strategies, and failures. More than one someone has survived. The world may have ended, but there is still life.

Paula Guran
9 March, 2013
(National Panic Day)

The End came perhaps a generation before the narrator of Kage Baker's story was born. His parents are members of a band of artisans and entertainers who once were a travelling "Renaissance fair." Now they use their "olden times" skills to make necessities of life, but they still provide much-needed entertainment too.

• THE BOOKS •
Kage Baker

We used to have to go a lot farther down the coast in those days, before things got easier. People weren't used to us then.

If you think about it, we must have looked pretty scary when we first made it out to the coast. Thirty trailers full of Show people, pretty desperate and dirty-looking Show people too, after fighting our way across the plains from the place where we'd been camped when it all went down. I don't remember when it went down, of course; I wasn't born yet.

The Show used to be an olden-time fair, a teaching thing. We traveled from place to place putting it on so people would learn about olden times, which seems pretty funny now, but back then . . . how's that song go? The one about mankind jumping out into the stars? And everybody thought that was how it was going to be. The aunts and uncles would put on the Show so space-age people wouldn't forget things like weaving and making candles when they went off into space. That's what you call irony, I guess.

But afterward we had to change the Show, because . . . well, we couldn't have the Jousting Arena anymore because we needed the big horses to pull the trailers. And Uncle Buck didn't make fancy work with dragons with rhinestone eyes on them anymore because, who was there left to buy that kind of stuff? And anyway, he was too busy making horseshoes. So all the uncles and aunts got together and worked it out like it is now, where we come into town with the Show and people come to see it and then they let us stay a while because we make stuff they need.

I started out as a baby bundle in one of the stage shows, myself. I don't remember it, though. I remember later I was in some play with a love story and I just wore a pair of fake wings and ran across the stage naked and shot at the girl with a toy bow and arrow that had glitter on them. And another time I played a dwarf. But I wasn't a dwarf, we only had the one dwarf and she was a lady, that was Aunt Tammy, and she's dead now. But there was an act with a couple of dwarves dancing and she needed a partner, and I had to wear a black suit and a top hat.

But by then my daddy had got sick and died so my mom was sharing the trailer with Aunt Nera, who made pots and pitchers and stuff, so that meant we were living with her nephew Myko too. People said he went crazy later on but it wasn't true. He was just messed up. Aunt Nera left the Show for a little while after it all went down, to go and see if her family—they were townies—had made it through okay, only they didn't, they were all dead but the baby, so she took the baby away with her and found us again. She said Myko was too little to remember but I think he remembered some.

Anyway we grew up together after that, us and Sunny who lived with Aunt Kestrel in their trailer which was next to ours. Aunt Kestrel was a juggler in the Show and Myko thought that was intense, he wanted to be a kid juggler. So he got Aunt Kestrel to show him how. And Sunny knew how already, she'd been watching her mom juggle since she was born and she could do clubs or balls or the apple-eating trick or anything. Myko decided he and Sunny should be a kid juggling act. I cried until they said I could be in the act too, but then I had to learn how to juggle and boy, was I sorry. I knocked out one of my own front teeth with a club before I learned better. The new one didn't grow in until I was seven, so I went around looking stupid for three years. But I got good enough to march in the parade and juggle torches.

That was after we auditioned, though. Myko went to Aunt Jeff and whined and he made us costumes for our act. Myko got a black doublet and a toy sword and a mask and I got a buffoon overall with a big spangly ruff. Sunny got a princess costume. We called ourselves the Minitrons. Actually Myko came up with the name. I don't know what he thought a Minitron was supposed to be but it sounded brilliant. Myko and I were both supposed to be in love with the princess and she couldn't decide between us so we had to do juggling tricks to win her hand, only she out-juggled us, so then Myko and I had a sword fight to decide things. And I always lost and died of a broken heart, but then the princess was sorry and put a paper rose on my chest. Then I jumped up and we took our bows and ran off, because the next act was Uncle Monty and his performing parrots.

By the time I was six we felt like old performers, and we swaggered in front of the other kids because we were the only kid act. We'd played it in six towns already. That was the year the aunts and uncles decided to take the trailers as far down the coast as this place on the edge of the big desert. It used to be a big city before it all went down. Even if there weren't enough people alive there anymore to put on a show for, there might be a lot of old junk we could use.

We made it into town all right without even any shooting. That was kind of amazing, actually, because it turned out nobody lived there but old people, and old people will usually shoot at you if they have guns, and these did. The other amazing thing was that the town was huge and I mean really huge, I just walked around with my head tilted back staring at these towers that went up and up, into the sky. Some of them you couldn't even see the tops because the fog hid them.

And they were all mirrors and glass and arches and domes and scowly faces in stone looking down from way up high.

But all the old people lived in just a few places right along the beach, because the further back you went into the city the more sand was everywhere. The desert was creeping in and taking a little more every year. That was why all the young people had left. There was nowhere to grow any food. The old people stayed because there was still plenty of stuff in jars and cans they had collected from the markets, and anyway they liked it there because it was warm. They told us they didn't have enough food to share any, though. Uncle Buck told them all we wanted to trade for was the right to go into some of the empty towers and strip out as much of the copper pipes and wires and things as we could take away with us. They thought that was all right; they put their guns down and let us camp, then.

But we found out the Show had to be a matinee if we were going to perform for them, because they all went to bed before the time we usually put on the Show. And the fire-eater was really pissed off about that because nobody would be able to see his act much, in broad daylight. It worked out all right, in the end, because the next day was dark and gloomy. You couldn't see the tops of the towers at all. We actually had to light torches around the edges of the big lot where we put up the stage.

The old people came filing out of their apartment building to the seats we'd set up, and then we had to wait the opening because they decided it was too cold and they all went shuffling back inside and got their coats. Finally the Show started and it went pretty well, considering some of them were blind and had to have their friends explain what was going on in loud voices.

But they liked Aunt Lulu and her little trained dogs and they liked Uncle Manny's strongman act where he picked up a Volkswagen. We kids knew all the heavy stuff like the engine had been taken out of it, but they didn't. They applauded Uncle Derry the Mystic Magician, even though the talkers for the blind shouted all through his performance and threw his timing off. He was muttering to himself and rolling a joint as he came through the curtain that marked off Backstage.

"Brutal crowd, kids," he told us, lighting his joint at one of the torches. "Watch your rhythm."

But we were kids and we could ignore all the grownups, in the world shouting, so we grabbed our prop baskets and ran out and put on our act. Myko stalked up and down and waved his sword and yelled his lines about being the brave and dangerous Captainio. I had a little pretend guitar that I strummed on while I pretended to look at the moon, and spoke my lines about being a poor fool in love with the princess. Sunny came out and did her princess dance. Then we juggled. It all went fine. The only time I was a little thrown off was when I glanced at the audience for a split second and saw the light of my juggling torches flickering on all those glass lenses or blind eyes. But I never dropped a torch.

Maybe Myko was bothered some, though, because I could tell by the way his eyes glared through his mask that he was getting worked up. When we had the sword duel near the end he hit too hard, the way he always did when he got worked up, and he banged my knuckles so bad I actually said "Ow" but the audience didn't catch it. Sometimes when he was like that his hair almost bristled, he was like some crazy cat jumping and spitting, and he'd fight about nothing.

Sometimes afterward I'd ask him why. He'd shrug and say he was sorry. Once he said it was because life was so damn boring.

Anyway I sang my little sad song and died of a broken heart, *flumpf* there on the pavement in my buffoon suit. I felt Sunny come over and put the rose on my chest and, I will remember this to my dying day, some old lady was yelling to her old man " . . . and now the little girl gave him her rose!"

And the old man yelled "What? She gave him her nose?"

"Damn it, Bob! Her *ROSE*!"

I corpsed right then, I couldn't help it, I was still giggling when Myko and

Sunny pulled me to my feet and we took our bows and ran off. Backstage they started laughing too. We danced up and down and laughed, very much getting in the way of Uncle Monty, who had to trundle all his parrots and their perches out on stage.

When we had laughed ourselves out, Sunny said, "So . . . what'll we do now?" That was a good question. Usually the Show was at night, so usually after a performance we went back to the trailers and got out of costume and our moms fed us and put us to bed. We'd never played a matinee before. We stood there looking at each other until Myko's eyes gleamed suddenly.

"We can explore the Lost City of the Sands," he said, in that voice he had that made it sound like whatever he wanted was the coolest thing ever. Instantly, Sunny and I both wanted to explore too. So we slipped out from the backstage area, just as Uncle Monty was screaming himself hoarse trying to get his parrots to obey him, and a moment later we were walking down an endless street lined with looming giants' houses.

They weren't really, they had big letters carved up high that said they were this or that property group or financial group or brokerage or church, but if a giant had stepped out at one corner and peered down at us, we wouldn't have been surprised. There was a cold wind blowing along the alleys from the sea, and sand hissed there and ran before us like ghosts along the ground, but on the long deserted blocks between there was gigantic silence. Our tiny footsteps only echoed in doorways.

The windows were mostly far above our heads and there was nothing much to see when Myko hoisted me up to stand on his shoulders and look into them.

Myko kept saying he hoped we'd see a desk with a skeleton with one of those headset things on sitting at it, but we never did; people didn't die that fast when it all went down. My mom said they could tell when they were getting sick and people went home and locked themselves in to wait and see if they lived or not.

Anyway Myko got bored finally and started this game where he'd charge up the steps of every building we passed. He'd hammer on the door with the hilt of his sword and yell, "It's the Civilian Militia! Open up or we're coming in!" Then he'd rattle the doors, but everything was locked long ago. Some of the doors were too solid even to rattle, and the glass was way too thick to break.

After about three blocks of this, when Sunny and I were starting to look at each other with our eyebrows raised—meaning "Are you going to tell him this game is getting old or do I have to do it?"—right then something amazing happened: one of the doors swung slowly inward and Myko swung with it. He staggered into the lobby or whatever and the door shut behind him. He stood staring at us through the glass and we stared back and I was scared to death, because I thought we'd have to run back and get Uncle Buck and Aunt Selene with their hammers to get Myko out, and we'd all be in trouble.

But Sunny just pushed on the door and it opened again. She went in so I had to go in too. We stood there all three and looked around. There was a desk and a dead tree in a planter and another huge glass wall with a door in it, leading deeper into the building. Myko began to grin.

"This is the first chamber of the Treasure Tomb in the Lost City," he said. "We just killed the giant scorpion and now we have to go defeat the army of zombies to get into the second chamber!"

He drew his sword and ran yelling at the inner door, but it opened too, soundlessly, and we pushed after him. It was much darker in here but there was still enough light to read the signs.

"It's a libarary," said Sunny. "They used to have paperbacks."

"*Paperbacks*," said Myko gloatingly, and I felt pretty excited myself. We'd seen lots of paperbacks, of course; there was the boring one with the mended cover that Aunt Maggie made everybody learn to read in. Every grownup we knew had one or two or a cache of paperbacks, tucked away in boxes or in lockers under beds, to be thumbed through by lamplight and read aloud from, if kids had been good.

Aunt Nera had a dozen paperbacks and she'd do that. It used to be the only thing that would stop Myko crying when he was little. We knew all about the Last Unicorn and the kids who went to Narnia, and there was a really long story about some people who had to throw a ring into a volcano that I always got tired of before it ended, and another really long one about a crazy family living in a huge castle, but it was in three books and Aunt Nera only had the first two. There was never any chance she'd ever get the third one now, of course, not since it all went down. Paperbacks were rare finds, they were ancient, their brown pages crumbled if you weren't careful and gentle.

"We just found all the paperbacks in the *universe*!" Myko shouted.

"Don't be dumb," said Sunny. "Somebody must have taken them all away years ago."

"Oh yeah?" Myko turned and ran further into the darkness. We followed, yelling at him to come back, and we all came out together into a big round room with aisles leading off it. There were desks in a ring all around and the blank dead screens of electronics. We could still see because there were windows down at the end of each aisle, sending long trails of light along the stone floors, reflecting back on the long shelves that lined the aisles and the uneven surfaces of the things on the shelves. Clustering together, we picked an aisle at random and walked down it toward the window.

About halfway down it, Myko jumped and grabbed something from one of the shelves. "Look! Told you!" He waved a paperback under our noses. Sunny leaned close to look at it. There was no picture on the cover, just the title printed big.

"Roget's. The. Saurus," Sunny read aloud.

"What's it about?" I asked.

Myko opened it and tried to read. For a moment he looked so angry I got ready to run, but then he shrugged and closed the paperback. "It's just words. Maybe it's a secret code or something. Anyway, it's mine now." He stuck it inside his doublet.

"No stealing!" said Sunny.

"If it's a dead town it's not stealing, it's salvage," I told her, just like the aunts and uncles always told us.

"But it isn't dead. There's all the old people."

"They'll die soon," said Myko. "And anyway Uncle Buck already asked permission to salvage." Which she had to admit was true, so we went on. What we didn't know then, but figured out pretty fast, was that all the other things on the shelves were actually big hard books like Uncle Des's *Barlogio's Principles of Glassblowing*.

But it was disappointing at first because none of the books in that aisle had stories. It was all, what do you call it, reference stuff. We came out sadly thinking we'd been gypped, and then Sunny spotted the sign with directions.

"Children's Books, Fifth Floor," she announced.

"Great! Where's the stairs?" Myko looked around. We all knew better than to ever, ever go near an elevator, because not only did they mostly not work, they could kill you. We found a staircase and climbed, and climbed for what seemed forever, before we came out onto the Children's Books floor.

And it was so cool. There were racks of paperbacks, of course, but we stood there with our mouths open because the signs had been right—there were books here. Big, hard, solid books, but not about grownup stuff. Books with bright pictures on the covers. Books for us. Even the tables and chairs up here were our size.

With a little scream, Sunny ran forward and grabbed a book from a shelf. "It's Narnia! Look! And it's got different pictures!"

"What a score," said Myko, dancing up and down. "Oh, what a score!"

I couldn't say anything. The idea was so enormous: all these were ours. This whole huge room belonged to us . . . at least, as much as we could carry away with us.

Myko whooped and ran off down one of the aisles. Sunny stayed frozen at the first shelf, staring with almost a sick expression at the other books. I went close to see.

"Look," she whispered. "There's *millions*. How am I supposed to choose? We need as many stories as we can get. " She was pointing at a whole row of books with color titles: *The Crimson Fairy Book. The Blue Fairy Book. The Violet Fairy Book. The Orange Fairy Book.* I wasn't interested in fairies, so I just grunted and shook my head.

I picked an aisle and found shelves full of flat books with big pictures. I opened one and looked at it. It was real easy to read, with big letters and the pictures were funny, but I read right through it standing there. It was about those big animals you see sometimes back up the delta country, you know, elephants.

Dancing, with funny hats on. I tried to imagine Aunt Nera reading it aloud on winter nights. It wouldn't last even one night; it wouldn't last through one bedtime. It was only one story. Suddenly I saw what Sunny meant. If we were going to take books away with us, they had to be full of stories that would *last*. What's the word I'm looking for? *Substance.*

Myko yelled from somewhere distant "Here's a cool one! It's got pirates!" It was pretty dark where I was standing, so I wandered down the aisle toward the window. The books got thicker the farther I walked. There were a bunch of books about dogs, but their stories all seemed sort of the same; there were books about horses too, with the same problem. There were books to teach kids how to make useful stuff, but when I looked through them they were all dumb things like how to weave potholders for your mom or build things out of Popsicle sticks.

I didn't even know what Popsicle sticks were, much less where I could get any.

There were some about what daily life was like back in olden times, but I already knew about that, and anyway those books had no *story*.

And all the while Myko kept yelling things like "Whoa! This one has guys with spears and shields and *gods*!" or "Hey, here's one with a flying carpet and it says it's got a thousand stories!" Why was I the only one stuck in the dumb books shelves?

I came to the big window at the end and looked out at the view—rooftops, fog, gray dark ocean—and backed away, scared stiff by how high up I was. I was turning around to run back when I saw the biggest book in the world.

Seriously. It was half as big as I was, twice the size of *Barlogio's Principles of Glassblowing*, it was bound in red leather and there were gold letters along its back. I crouched down and slowly spelled out the words.

The Complete Collected Adventures of Asterix the Gaul.

I knew what "Adventures" meant, and it sounded pretty promising. I pulled the book down—it was the heaviest book in the world too—and laid it flat on the floor. When I opened it I caught my breath. I had found the greatest book in the world.

It was full of colored pictures, but there were words too, a lot of them, they were the people in the story talking but you could *see them talk*. I had never seen a comic before. My mom talked sometimes about movies and TV must have been like this, I thought, talking pictures. And there was a story. In fact, there were lots of stories. Asterix was this little guy no bigger than me but he had a mustache and a helmet and he lived in this village and there was a wizard with a magic potion and Asterix fought in battles and traveled to all these faraway places and had all these adventures!!! And I could read it all by myself, because when I didn't know what a word meant I could guess at it from the pictures.

I settled myself more comfortably on my stomach, propped myself up on my elbows so I wouldn't crunch my starched ruff, and settled down to read.

Sometimes the world becomes a perfect place.

Asterix and his friend Obelix had just come to the Forest of the Carnutes when I was jolted back to the world by Myko yelling for me. I rose to my knees and looked around. It was darker now; I hadn't even realized I'd been pushing my nose closer and closer to the pages as the light had drained away. There were drops of rain hitting the window and I thought about what it would be like running through those dark cold scary streets and getting rained on too.

I scrambled to my feet and grabbed up my book, gripping it to my chest as I ran. It was even darker when I reached the central room. Myko and Sunny were having a fight when I got there. She was crying. I stopped, astounded to see she'd pulled her skirt off and stuffed it full of books, and she was sitting there with her legs bare to her underpants.

"We have to travel light, and they're too heavy," Myko was telling her. "You can't take all those!"

"I have to," she said. "We *need* these books!" She got to her feet and hefted the skirt. *The Olive Fairy Book* fell out. I looked over and saw she'd taken all the colored fairy books. Myko bent down impatiently and grabbed up *The Olive Fairy Book*. He looked at it.

"It's stupid," he said. "Who needs a book about an olive fairy?"

"You moron, it's not about an olive fairy!" Sunny shrieked. "It's got all kinds of stories in it! Look!" She grabbed it back from him and opened it, and shoved it out again for him to see. I sidled close and looked. She was right: there was a page with the names of all the stories in the book. There were a lot of stories, about knights and magic and strange words. Read one a night, they'd take up a month of winter nights. And every book had a month's worth of stories in it? Now, that was *concentrated* entertainment value.

Myko, squinting at the page, must have decided the same thing. "Okay," he said. "But you'll have to carry it. And don't complain if it's heavy."

"I won't," said Sunny, putting her nose in the air. He glanced at me and did a double-take.

"You can't take that!" he yelled. "It's too big and it's just one book anyway!"

"It's the only one I want," I said. "And anyhow, you got to take all the ones you wanted!" He knew it was true, too. His doublet was so stuffed out with loot, he looked pregnant.

Myko muttered under his breath, but turned away, and that meant the argument was over. "Anyway we need to leave."

So we started to, but halfway down the first flight of stairs three books fell out of Sunny's skirt and we had to stop while Myko took the safety pins out of all our costumes and closed up the waistband. We were almost to the second floor when Sunny lost her hold on the skirt and her books went cascading down to the landing, with the loudest noise in the universe. We scrambled down after them and were on our knees picking them up when we heard the other noise.

It was a hissing, like someone gasping for breath through whistly dentures, and a jingling, like a ring of keys, because that's what it was. We turned our heads.

Maybe he hadn't heard us when we ran past him on the way up. We hadn't been talking then, just climbing, and he had a lot of hair in his ears and a pink plastic sort of machine in one besides. Or maybe he'd been so wrapped up, the way I had been in reading, that he hadn't even noticed us when we'd pattered past. But he hadn't been reading.

There were no books in this part of the library. All there was on the shelves was old magazines and stacks and stacks of yellow newspapers. The newspapers weren't crumpled into balls in the bottoms of old boxes, which was the only way we ever saw them, they were smooth and flat. But most of them were drifted on the floor like leaves, hundreds and hundreds of big leaves, ankle-deep, and on every, single one was a square with sort of checkered patterns and numbers printed in the squares and words written in pencil.

I didn't know what a crossword puzzle was then but the old man must have been coming there for years, maybe ever since it all went down, years and years he'd been working his way through all those magazines and papers, hunting down every single puzzle and filling in every one. He was dropping a stub of a pencil now as he got to his feet, snarling at us, showing three brown teeth. His eyes behind his glasses were these huge distorted magnified things, and full of crazy anger. He came over the paper-drifts at us fast and light as a spider.

"Fieves! Ucking kish! Ucking fieving kish!"

Sunny screamed and I screamed too. Frantically she shoved all the books she could into her skirt and I grabbed up most of what she'd missed, but we were taking too long. The old man brought up his cane and smacked it down, crack, but he missed us on his first try and by then Myko had drawn his wooden sword and put it against the old man's chest and shoved hard. The old man fell with a crash, still flailing his cane, but he was on his side and striking at us faster than you'd believe, and so mad now he was just making noises, with spittle flying from his mouth. His cane hit my knee as I scrambled up. It hurt like fire and I yelped.

Myko kicked him and yelled, "Run!"

We bailed, Sunny and I did, we thundered down the rest of the stairs and didn't stop until we were out in the last chamber by the street doors. "Myko's still up there," said Sunny. I had an agonizing few seconds before deciding to volunteer to go back and look for him. I was just opening my mouth when we spotted him running down the stairs and out toward us.

"Oh, good," said Sunny. She tied a knot in one corner of her skirt, for a handle, and had already hoisted it over her shoulder onto her back and was heading for the door as Myko joined us. He was clutching the one book we'd missed on the landing. It was *The Lilac Fairy Book* and there were a couple of spatters of what looked like blood on its cover.

"Here. You carry it." Myko shoved the book at me. I took it and wiped it off. We followed Sunny out. I looked at him sidelong. There was blood on his sword too.

It took me two blocks, though, jogging after Sunny through the rain, before I worked up the nerve to lean close to him as we ran and ask: "Did you kill that guy?"

"Had to," said Myko. "He wouldn't stop."

To this day I don't know if he was telling the truth. It was the kind of thing he would have said, whether it was true or not. I didn't know what I was supposed to say back. We both kept running. The rain got a lot harder and Myko left me behind in a burst of speed, catching up to Sunny and grabbing her bundle of books.

He slung it over his shoulder. They kept going, side by side. I had all I could do not to fall behind.

By the time we got back the Show was long over. The crew was taking down the stage in the rain, stacking the big planks. Because of the rain no market stalls had been set up but there was a line of old people with umbrellas standing by Uncle Chris's trailer, since he'd offered to repair any dentures that needed fixing with his jeweler's tools. Myko veered us away from them behind Aunt Selene's trailer, and there we ran smack into our moms and Aunt Nera. They had been looking for us for an hour and were really mad.

I was scared sick the whole next day, in case the old people got out their guns and came to get us, but nobody seemed to notice the old man was dead and missing, if he was dead. The other thing I was scared would happen was that Aunt Kestrel or Aunt Nera would get to talking with the other women and say something like, "Oh, by the way, the kids found a library and salvaged some books, maybe we should all go over and get some books for the other kids too" because that was exactly the sort of thing they were always doing, and then they'd find the old man's body. But they didn't. Maybe nobody did anything because the rain kept all the aunts and kids and old people in next day. Maybe the old man had been a hermit and lived by himself in the library, so no one would find his body for ages.

I never found out what happened. We left after a couple of days, after Uncle Buck and the others had opened up an office tower and salvaged all the good copper they could carry. I had a knee swollen up and purple where the old man had hit it, but it was better in about a week. The books were worth the pain.

They lasted us for years. We read them and we passed them on to the other kids and they read them too, and the stories got into our games and our dreams and the way we thought about the world. What I liked best about my comics was that even when the heroes went off to far places and had adventures, they always came back to their village in the end and everybody was happy and together.

Myko liked the other kind of story, where the hero leaves and has glorious adventures but maybe never comes back. He was bored with the Show by the time he was twenty and went off to some big city up north where he'd heard they had their electrics running again. Lights were finally starting to come back on in the towns we worked, so it seemed likely. He still had that voice that could make anything seem like a good idea, see, and now he had all those fancy words he'd gotten out of *Roget's Thesaurus* too. So I guess I shouldn't have been surprised that he talked Sunny into going with him.

Sunny came back alone after a year. She wouldn't talk about what happened, and I didn't ask. Eliza was born three months later.

Everyone knows she isn't mine. I don't mind.

We read to her on winter nights. She likes stories.

⌒

Best known for her "Company" series, **Kage Baker**'s other notable works include the novel *Mendoza In Hollywood* and "The Empress of Mars," a 2003 novella that won the Theodore Sturgeon Award and was nominated for a Hugo Award. In 2009, her short story "Caverns of Mystery" and her novel *House of the Stag* were both nominated for World Fantasy Awards. Baker died on January 31, 2010. Later that year, her novella *The Women of Nell Gwynne's* was nominated for both Hugo and World Fantasy Awards, and won the Nebula Award. Based on extensive notes left by the author, Baker's unfinished novel, *Nell Gwynne's On Land and At Sea*, was completed by her sister Kathleen Bartholomew and published in 2012.

⌒

After the End—the Great Change—the laws of physics no longer apply, barriers between worlds have disintegrated, and children (called meta-humans) are born with strange abilities. Dikéogu, a sixteen-year-old Nigerian and a fledging rainmaker who can control the weather, has escaped slavery and is in Timia, a city in Niger, the country directly north of Nigeria.

• TUMAKI •
Nnedi Okorafor

Dikéogu Audio File Series
begun April 8, 2074

Current Location: Unknown Region, Niger
Weather: 36° C (98° F), N.I.U.F. (Not Including Unpredictable Factors)

This audio file has been automatically translated from the Igbo language.

Tumaki

I found the electronics shop two blocks from my hotel. All I needed to do was go in the opposite direction of the market.

The small store was packed with all sorts of appliances and devices. A few were from Ginen, like the solar powered e-legba that was part machine and part plant and the very small unhealthy-looking glow lily. Most everything else was very much from earth. Thin laptops, standard e-legbas, all kinds of coin drives, batteries, and hardware like bundles of wiring, piles of microprocessors, digicards, and every kind of tool imaginable. It was a tinker's dream. It was my nightmare. Way too cramped. I planned to be quick.

To make things worse, the place was air-conditioned. The minute I walked in, my skin instantly started to protest. I wrapped my hands around my arms as I stepped up to the counter. A woman stood behind it. At least I thought it was a woman. I'll never get used to burkas. Maybe it's the southeastern Nigerian in me but those things are creepy.

About fifty percent of the women in Niger wore them. Most are made out of stiff cotton and a cotton screen covers the women's faces. You can barely see their eyes. These women, especially when you see them walking down the street at dusk or dawn, scare the hell out of me. They look like ghosts, all silent and mysterious. No, I've never liked burkas.

"Yes?" she asked. Okay, so I had been standing there staring. I never knew whether I was supposed to speak to these women or not. And since I couldn't see their faces, I was even less sure.

"I . . ."

She sighed loudly, rolled her eyes and held out a hand. It was a careful hand. My mother would have described it as the hand of a surgeon. Her nails were cut very short, the palm of her hand slightly calloused. Her fingers were long and they moved with a precise care that reminded me of a snail's antenna.

"Hand it here," she said.

I gave her my broken e-legba.

She turned it over, tapping the "on" button. The damn thing only whimpered. Never have I been so embarrassed. All e-legbas do that when they're broken. There are different whimpers, weeps, moans, or groans depending on the type of breakage. What kind of obnoxious engineer programmed them to do that? It's bad enough that the thing is broken. Why should a machine act like a whiny child?

"What'd you do to it?" she asked. As if my e-legba was some living creature.

"It's a long story," I said.

She turned it over some more between her antenna-like fingers and laughed. "This is practically a toy," she said. "This is your only personal device?"

"It's a prime e-legba," I insisted, indignant. "An electrical god of the best kind."

She laughed her condescending laugh again. "A lesser god, if a god at all. With a weak solar sucker, sand grains in the fingerboard, a faulty *and* cracked screen, and probably a smashed-up microprocessor."

It gave a sad pained groan as if to stress her points. I wanted to grab and hurl it across the room. *What do I need it for anyway?* I thought. But in the back of my head, I knew I wanted to watch my mother's news program. And I had a copy of *My Cyborg Manifesto* on it, a much-needed Hausa/Arabic dictionary, and it picked up a fairly decent hip-hop station whose signal seemed to remain strong wherever I went.

"I can fix it, though," she said after a while.

"You?"

She looked up, her dark brown eyes full of pure irritation. I stepped back, holding my hands up. "I'm sorry," I said. "I . . . my mouth is what it is."

"It's not your mouth that bothers me," she said. "It's your brain. My *mother* owns this shop. Not my father. Does that surprise you, too?"

I didn't respond. It did surprise me.

She nodded. "At least you're honest." She paused cocking her head as she looked at me. Then she brought my e-legba to her face for a closer look. As she inspected it, she talked to me. "My mother's an electrician. She taught me everything I know. My father's an imam. He tries to teach me all he knows, but there are some things that I cannot digest." She laughed to herself and looked up at me. "You're not Muslim, are you?"

"No."

She grunted something that sounded like, "Good."

"But you are, right?" I asked.

"Sort of," she said. "But not really."

"Then why do you wear that damn sheet?" I asked.

"Why shouldn't I?"

"Because you don't want to," I said.

"You don't even know me."

"Do I need to? A sheet is a sheet." I saw her eyes flash with anger. I kept talking anyway. "Doesn't matter if you look like a giant toad with sores oozing puss. You shouldn't . . . "

She pointed a long finger in my face like a knife. "You have got to be . . . " She stopped. I saw where her eyes flicked to. The black tattoos on the bridge of my nose from my time as a slave on the coca farms. I could tell she got it. She understood my obsession with free will.

"My mother and I are electricians and this town is dominated by patriarchal New Tuareg ways and even stronger patriarchal Hausa, Old Tuareg, and Fulani ways. People here still . . . expect things. My mother and I play along. My father, well, he prefers us to play along, too. Everyone's happy."

"Except you have to live under a sheet."

"Business is business," she said with a shrug. "It's not so bad. I get to be an electrician who is female." She looked me in the eye. "Plus, sometimes I don't want people looking at me."

That was the excuse my close friend Ejii often gave whenever she wore her burka. I didn't buy it from Ejii and I didn't buy it from this girl.

"Well, other people's problems should be their business, not yours."

"In an ideal world, certainly," she said. "So can you pay?"

"Yes."

"In full?"

"Yes."

She paused, obviously deciding whether she could trust me. She brought out a black case and opened it. Her tools were shiny like they were made for surgery on humans not machines. She started to repair my e-legba right there. It was a simple gesture, but it meant a lot to me. She'd noticed my tattoos, considered them, yet she trusted me. She trusted me.

Minutes later, a woman came in also draped in a black burka. Her mother. I was about two feet away from her daughter. It was too late to step back from the counter.

"*As-salaamu Alaikum*," the woman said to me, after a moment's pause.

"*Wa 'Alaykum As-Salām*," I responded, surprised. She glanced at my tattoos but that was all.

People came in and out of the store. Her mother helped customers, sold items, chatted with them. But I was focused on the electrician fixing my e-legba. I ignored my claustrophobia and the freeze of the air-conditioning. I didn't want to leave. I didn't want to move.

She had my e-legba in pieces within three minutes. She tinkered, fiddled, replaced and tinkered some more. After about a half hour, she looked up at me and said, "Give me a day with this. I need to buy two new parts."

"Okay," I said. "I'll see you tomorrow then."

From that day on, that store became my second home. Her name was Tumaki.

Poetry

My e-legba was nothing to Tumaki. She could take apart and rebuild the engine of a truck, a capture station, a computer! She could even fix some of the Ginen technology. You should have seen what she did to that pathetic glow lily that I saw the first day I was in the shop. She got that plant to do the opposite of die. Once, she tried to explain to me her theory of why nuclear weapons and bullets no longer worked on earth. She started talking physics and chemistry. I remember nothing but the intense look on her face.

She was a year older than me and planned to eventually attend university. I wasn't sure if she liked or just tolerated me. When I was around her, I couldn't stop talking.

"We just use pumpkin seeds," she told me one day while she worked on an e-legba. We were talking about how to make egusi soup.

"See. That's where you people go wrong when you make the soup," I said.

"Us people?" she said, as she unscrewed some tiny screw.

"You people. Yeah. You know, those of you who live here in Timia," I said. I shrugged. "Anyway, Nigerians call it egusi soup for a *reason*. Because we use egusi seeds. Goat meat, chicken, stock fish, fresh greens, peppers, spices, and ground *egusi* seeds. What they serve in the restaurants here is a disgrace."

"Fine, we'll call it pumpkin soup, then," she mumbled, as she placed another screw. "Makes no difference to me."

"Ah ah, I miss the real thing, *o*," I said, thinking of home. "With pounded yam and a nice glass of Sprite. Goddamn. You people don't know what you're missing." I wished I could shut up. I didn't want her asking me any new questions about home. All I'd told her was that I was from Nigeria.

She only glared at me and loudly sucked her teeth. I grinned sheepishly. I was just talking, totally drunk on her presence. No matter how much rubbish I talked, though, she never got distracted enough to lose track of what she was doing. She could listen to me and work on a computer like she had two brains. Tumaki was genius smart. But she was also very lonely, I think. I figured this might have been why she didn't tell me to get lost. Maybe it was also why only two weeks after I met her, she did something very unlike her.

I was half asleep when I heard the banging at my hotel room door. It was around two a.m. I don't know how I heard it, as I was outside in deep REM sleep on the balcony. It was rare for me to sleep this well.

When the banging on the door didn't stop, I got up, stumbled across the room, no shirt on, mouth all gummy, crust in my eyes, smelling of outside and my own night sweat, barely coherent. I opened the door and came face to face with a black ghost. Death had come to finally take me. That thing from the fields outside the cocoa farms I'd escaped was back.

My eyes widened, my heart slammed in my chest. If my mind hadn't finally kicked in and my eyes hadn't adjusted, I'd have summoned an entire storm into the hotel room to fight for my life. Then Tumaki would have learned the secret I'd kept from her just before that secret killed her.

"Tumaki?" I whispered, stepping back. I ran my hand over my dreadlocks. They were probably smashed to the side. I must have looked like a mad man.

She laughed. "How'd you guess?"

A thousand emotions went through me. Delight, pleasure, excitement, horror, fear, confusion, worry, irritation, fatigue. I slammed the door in her face.

"Shit!" I hissed, staring at the closed door, instantly knowing it was the wrong reaction.

She banged on the door. She was going to wake my neighbors. I quickly opened it. "What the hell are you doing?" she snapped.

"Trying to save my neck," I said.

She sucked her teeth loudly. "Let me in," she demanded.

Oh my God, I have no shirt on, I realized. My heart pounded faster. I looked down both ends of the hallway. I saw no one. But who knew who might have been listening or peeking out. I grabbed her arm and pulled her in. "You could get me killed by coming here," I whispered. I didn't know what to do with myself. Tumaki's family was highly respected. She was the imam's daughter! No girl went to a guy's hotel room in the middle of the night! Period. Especially not to meet a guy like me. Especially if anyone suspected that I was a meta-human.

"Nah," she said. "They'll just chop off one of your hands."

"Not funny," I said, as I looked for a shirt. My room was tidy as I barely had use for it. I don't like messes, either. My clothes were neatly folded on one of the beds. Four shirts, one caftan, three pairs of pants. I grabbed a semi-clean cotton shirt. "What are you doing here?"

She shrugged and walked past me to my balcony. The scent of the incense she liked to burn in the shop touched my nose. Nag champa. I loved that scent, though when I bought some and burned it in my room, it didn't smell as good. She stepped over the mat I'd been sleeping on and took in the view. She inhaled and exhaled. "Nice," she said.

"Tumaki . . ."

"You sleep out here?"

I sighed loudly. "Yes."

"Why?"

"I like to," I said.

"You don't like the indoors."

"No."

She looked back out. "Makes sense."

There was a cool breeze. This was probably what allowed me to sleep so well. Despite her presence, my head still felt a little fuzzy. It had been a while since I'd slept that deeply and to be ripped from that kind of sleep was jarring. "Tumaki, your parents are going to . . . "

She laughed and whirled around, her eyes grabbing mine. "Let's go to the desert!"

"Eh!?"

"Just out of town," she said. "For a little while. I never get to do anything."

I opened my mouth to protest.

"I'm often in my library late into the night. Sometimes I sleep there," she said. "They assume that's where I am if I'm not in my bed. They can't imagine me being *anywhere* else but alone in my library. Trust me."

We could have taken her scooter, but we walked. I didn't know how to drive one and, even at this time of night, too many people would remember a woman driving a man on a scooter. It was *always* the other way around

For once, I was glad she was wearing her black burka. In the night, you could barely see her. But I didn't have to see her to be aware of her close proximity. It was the first time we were completely alone together— no mother in the back room or customers looming. But it wasn't the first time I felt this strong attraction to her. It didn't make sense. I didn't even know what she looked like! But the sound of her voice, the scent of her nag champa, the dance of her graceful hands, just being close to her, I've never felt anything so real.

Each time I stepped into that shop, my heart started hammering. I'd get all sweaty. My mouth dried up. When talking to her and she had to leave for one second, I'd feel so impatient. She was my last thought before I went to sleep and my first thought when I woke up. Tumaki, Tumaki, Tumaki. I hated feeling like this. No, I didn't trust it.

I was sixteen with no experience with women. Well, there was Ejii. I definitely liked Ejii, who'd been a shadow speaker. But that had really never taken off. Two meta-humans? That probably would have been a little much. But this thing with Tumaki came out of nowhere. I didn't like things that just came out of nowhere. I didn't like surprises.

"I wanted to go see that spontaneous forest so badly," she said as we walked in the moonlight.

I laughed and shook my head.

"I did," she insisted. "But I didn't have anyone to go with."

Tumaki had told me that all of her friends had been married off. Now she barely ever heard from them except for baby announcements. It was as if they entered a different world. They had, in a way. The Married Woman World. In Timia, that world had no place for friends.

"Spontaneous forests can be dangerous as hell," I said. "Especially when you don't know what you're doing."

"Not all the time."

"You want to take that risk?"

"Yep."

I almost laughed. She sounded kind of like me. I was glad that damn forest was long gone. I think she'd have gone in there and I'd have had to go after her. As we passed the last building, a man on the camel slowly passed us on his way into town.

"*As-salaamu Alaikum*," he said to me.

"*Wa 'Alaykum As-Salām*," I responded, trying not to meet his eyes. Tumaki stayed quiet. Every part of my body was a sharp edge. How must we have looked heading into the desert with nothing but ourselves? *Oh Allah, they are going to lynch me, o*, I thought.

"Relax," Tumaki said when the man was gone. "He didn't know it was me."

"You knew that guy?"

"He was my uncle."

Before I could start cursing and going ballistic, she grabbed my hand. It was warm but not soft. I stared down at her hand in mine. I had no clue what to say or do. I considered snatching it away. She was the kind of girl who would slap the hell out of you if you did something to her that she didn't like. Don't let the burka fool you. I'd heard her tell off a man who'd tried to cheat her on the cost of an e-legba repair. She'd handed the man his masculinity on a silver platter.

"Dikéogu," she said. The sound of my name on her lips . . . *let them cut off both my hands,* I thought. I wasn't letting go of her hand for anything. "Come on," she said pulling me along. "No time for you to start losing it."

We didn't go out far. About a mile. Timia was still within shouting distance. Between the luminance of the half moon and the dim light from Timia, it wasn't very dark here. By this time, the thought of having a foot or hand chopped off or being publicly whipped for fornication, attempted rape, or some other fabricated camelshit had faded completely. Tumaki filled my mind like a rainstorm.

And I knew she liked me, too.

The cool breeze was still blowing and she opened her arms as if to hug it. Her burka fluttered. She looked like a giant bat. I laughed at the thought.

"I *love* the wind," she said, her eyes closed, at least I thought they were.

I suddenly had an idea. I focused on the breeze and the rhythm of my breathing. The breeze picked up. Tumaki laughed with glee, her burka flapping hard now.

"When I was a little girl, before I had to start wearing this thing, I used to run outside on windy days," she said. "There was this one day in the school yard where suddenly this giant dust devil whipped up! Everyone went running away from it. I went running *to* it."

She laughed and whooped, whirling around. I increased the breeze to a wind.

"I managed to get in the middle of it," she said, raising her voice over the wind. "It twirled me around and around and around. I felt as if it would suck me into the sky! My skirt lifted way up and everything." She turned to me, her burka billowing around her. "My father beat the hell out of me that day. For shaming Allah. I have a scar on my face from it."

A ripple of anger swept through me at the thought of this. And I lost control of the wind. *Whooosh!* It swept from the desert floor to her ankles and blasted upwards, taking her burka with it.

We both stood there watching it flutter back down many yards away. Then slowly our eyes fell on each other.

Almond-shaped eyes. Skin dark like the night. Lips like two orange segments. The African nose of a warrior queen. She was taller than me and lanky in her red T-shirt with a yellow flower in the center and an orange-patterned skirt that went past her knees. She wore her thick hair in two long cornrowed braids, the moon made it black but I suspected it was closer to brownish red. She had a long scar on her left cheek. Her hand went right to it.

Now she knew what I was and I knew what she looked like.

There was a flash of lightning from above. I could feel it in every part of my body and soul. It started to rain. We were soaked. But we didn't care. We ran around in the sandy mud and lighting and rain. We threw mud at the sky. We laughed and screamed and it rained and rained. Was it because or me of the will of the skies? Both, I'd say.

I grabbed her wet hand and pulled her to me. The first time I ever kissed a girl was accompanied by a chorus of simultaneous lightning, thunder and a torrential rain and tasted like the wind and aquatic roses.

The moment was poetry.

Glow Lily

Tumaki wore her brown-red hair cornrowed at the shop and at school. Basically whenever it was under a burka. When she was at home or with me, she let it out into the big bushy tangled afro that it wanted to be. I liked it best when it was out. So did she.

Her parents knew little about us. They only saw me in their shop, when I'd come around. I wasn't stupid. Her parents were progressive, but they were still Muslim. I was lucky that they allowed me in the store at all.

Her parents named her well. "Tumaki" meant "books" in Hausa, which her father was extremely fond of. During those wonderful six months, I spent most of my time in two places, in Tumaki's arms and in her library, which I learned was an underground room behind their house. It was a place that she had made hers. Her space. That was the only reason I could stand being in a small underground room. The room was like Tumaki's soul.

She'd even reinforced the walls with concrete all by herself three years ago. She'd also installed a winding metal staircase. She said she hired some guys to help with it, so I guess the library wasn't *completely* secret. "About four years ago, this room just appeared," she told me. "My mother believes it was made by one of those giant underground worms. It might have dug the hole for eggs and then decided that it didn't like the land or being too close to humans."

"I believe it," I said. Ejii had once told me about "reading" the mind of one of those weird giant worms. She said it was obsessed with the number eight or something. The creatures definitely had strong opinions about stuff.

Tumaki had tons of books stacked down there. Books on physics, geometry, geology, biomimicry, African history, nuclear weapons, novels, biographies, how-to books, old magazines. She didn't discriminate. She loved information. She had an old beat-up couch and two tables and gold satiny pillows with tassels. Glow lilies that she'd cultivated lit the room. The place was always cool even during the day. It smelled like the nag champa she loved to burn and the curry she liked to eat. And there was always soft Arabic music playing.

We didn't go back out to the desert but we did explore the more progressive parts of Timia. We went to late-night tea shops where people spoke freely, tea cups in hand, about whatever was on their minds. Once in a while people talked about meta-humans, mostly as if they were the scourge of the earth.

Usually when there was meta-human bashing, we'd stay for a long while. I really wanted to understand the root of their hatred of people like myself. Fear, arrogance, ignorance, you take your pick, those people suffered from all those. But eventually, I'd start getting really steamed. The way those guys would talk (always guys, women never spoke in the tea shop discussions), it was like they weren't on earth during the Great Change. Like they were untouched by it. They thought they were so "pure." It was ridiculous. More than once, Tumaki had to drag me out before I threw hot tea in someone's face. The last thing I needed was for people to know I was a meta-human.

Tumaki and I were quiet as I walked her home on these nights. After that night in the desert, we didn't speak of my abilities. She didn't ask about them and I didn't really want to talk about them. She knew I was a rainmaker, what more did we need to discuss?

We went to secret poetry slams held by students, usually in empty or abandoned buildings. Here I heard some of the worst poetry ever. But Tumaki seemed to enjoy it and none of these people bashed meta-humans. So, though I made it a point to tell her the poets stunk, we kept going to them. She knew most of the students here and again her burka protected her, as it did the identity of most of the women there. If word ever got back to her father about her being out at night *and* with me, she'd have more than just a scar to show for it.

"But my father isn't the monster you're imagining," she insisted during one of our conversations about her scar.

"Any father who puts a mark on his child is a monster," I said. "I don't care if he's an imam."

I'd never spoken to her father. Tumaki had tried to introduce me once but I wasn't up for it. He was one of those "big chief" men in Timia. The kind that struts around followed by guys who will admire even the toilet paper he wipes his ass with. His expensive embroidered thick cotton robes were always a heavenly white—how do you keep your clothes that white in a place where there is so much dust, eh? His long beard was bushy and dark black, his hair cut short, not one gray hair on his head. You could tell he was a proud, proud man. I didn't like him.

"You don't know him," Tumaki said.

"I beg to differ," I mumbled. I'd known many like him, including Chief Ette, including *my* father.

That afternoon, she asked her mother if she could take the day off from the shop. Then she took me to the market square to see her father speak. We stood out of his sight, beside the booth of a man selling dried grasshoppers. The seller absentmindedly munched at a grasshopper leg as he listened to Tumaki's father speak.

Her father sat on a table before about a hundred young men who sat on the ground. He had their full attention. Every single one. I wished I could command that kind of attention . . . in a positive way.

Around them, the market went about its business, but people were obviously preoccupied, listening to Tumaki's father. I spotted her mother on the other side of the square. She was trying to be inconspicuous as she stood, fully veiled, in the shade of a cloth shop. Even the shadows couldn't hide the pride in her stance.

"And then whoooosh! The sweetest smelling wind ever imaginable," her father said. "Everyone agrees the smell of the Great Change was like billions of blooming roses. It made your skin feel new, soft like a baby's backside. Allah is great, *quo*. If you were not there to witness the Great Change you will never be able to fully imagine it. The Great Change was Allah's return. All its results are Allah's will."

He paused dramatically, then his eyes widened and he pointed his index finger up beside his head. "Now you have these *foreigners* who know nothing about us. Who do not respect local traditions. They slaughter cows indiscriminately. They consume goat milk." He spat to the side; several men in the audience did the same. "And have you ever shared tea with these people? They take one cup and then get up and leave when there is a whole pot left! What kind of nonsense is that?" Several people in the audience sucked their teeth and grumbled. I noticed more, however, were starting to look around, uncomfortable.

"They openly disrespect Islamic tradition. Look at all the addicts addicted to that . . . that drug, that mystic moss they brought with them. How many die from eating other people's personal peppers? A whole family died from them a month ago when a woman mistook one for a normal pepper and used it to make stew."

"And the worst thing," he stressed, his voice rising. "The worst thing is that they come here from their world and think they can tell us that we have gone wrong. They say the Great Change has made the Earth and its people unnatural. They doubt the will of Allah. They take their own lives for granted." He narrowed his eyes and looked at his audience and then around the market. "You know who you are. You know who you are."

My mouth practically hung open. Beside me, Tumaki gave me a small smile and nodded. Tumaki had insisted that her scar had been an accident. A stupid mistake of an overprotective father. I'd scoffed. "Why do you protect him?" I'd asked. I was sure he'd done it on purpose, because he didn't want her to be too beautiful. I assumed he was the usual non-progressive ego-driven type of guy that I was used to seeing. Okay, so I had to revise how I felt about Tumaki's father.

He was a traditional imam, certainly, but this man was open-minded. And the man had balls. The "foreigners" he was griping about were Ginenians, people from the world of Ginen. No one did that! The people of Timia practically worshipped Ginenians. And though he didn't openly say it, the meaning was clear: he was *defending* meta-humans. Can you imagine? In a town where meta-humans where treated like, well, cockroaches, here he was saying that meta-humans were the "will of Allah." Maybe Tumaki's scar *was* an accident caused by the hand of a scared father. Maybe. Even people who do good things can still do terrible things once in a while. He should have never scarred his daughter's face. I don't care what was going through his damn head.

More people gathered. Women, veiled, unveiled, gathered at the periphery of the all male audience. There was a young girl standing not far from me whom I think was a metal worker, as Tumaki's necklace was softly pulled in the girl's direction.

There was some booing. A few Ginenians had come to listen, too, and some local people simply didn't like what they were hearing. But mostly there was silence and attention and a deep sense of fear. His words were obviously inflammatory but many agreed with him. He was tapping into Timia's quietly festering disease. That thing that was on everyone's mind that no one dared to speak of.

He spoke with a casual eloquence that made you listen, consider, and fear for his life and your own for being there. You could see where Tumaki got her humanity. I felt my heart in my throat when I glanced at her as she looked at her father. I knew I had to deal with my parents eventually, my parents who had sold me into slavery because I was a meta-human. *Not yet*, I thought. I couldn't imagine leaving Tumaki. *Will she come with me?* I couldn't imagine that, either.

When her father finished speaking, I still refused to meet him. No one wants to meet that kind of man while knowing you've more than kissed his daughter. No way.

Not long after that, invigorated by his speech, Tumaki and I went into the part of Timia where drug deals, prostitution, and other illegal transactions took place. It was her idea. I'd seen such places plenty of times since escaping the cocoa farms. I knew damn well that they existed and thrived. But I guess, Tumaki was pretty sheltered.

"I need to see it," she told me.

So we went. One thing I noticed about Timia's ghettos is that you didn't see one Ginenian. You saw them at the poetry slams and always in the tea shops but never ever in ghettos. I guess that was sinking too low for them.

Sometimes Tumaki and I just walked the streets at night. Because we could. And I knew Tumaki liked the risk of it, though deep down she knew that I'd never let anything happen to her.

Nonetheless, we spent the most time down in her library. We didn't have to wait until night to go here. I'd meet her here after she finished school, when she didn't have to work or on her days off on the weekends. We'd simply read and enjoy each other's company. It was the first time I'd really had a chance to sit down and educate myself since my abilities had begun to manifest. Back home, school was not a good place for me. I was "The Boy That God Was Angry With," "The Kid Who Kept Getting Struck by Lightning," the butt of everyone's jokes.

"This book was amazing," Tumaki would say, shoving a thick book in my hand. Or she'd say, "You've got to read this! It'll change your life!" I couldn't not listen to her. I was in love with her, I guess . . . if I want to use that cliché overused damn-near-meaningless word.

Anyway, I must have read hundreds of books in those months. Reading kept thoughts of my parents at bay. And it helped me make sense of the strong anti-meta-human discrimination I saw in Timia. I was slowly running out of money but I'd cross that bridge when I got to it. I wasn't thinking about my future at all.

I read about witch hunts, persecution, racism, tribalism, infanticide. I read about the genocides that had taken place in the world so many decades ago. In Germany, Rwanda, Bosnia, Sudan, Kosovo. I memorized the eight stages; classification, symbolization, dehumanization, organization, polarization, preparation, extermination, and denial. I, of course, read extensively about slavery and those who fought for freedom. I read about the pollution and eventual nuclear destruction of the environment.

I read about camels. I read *The Autobiography of Malcolm X* (I usually don't care for super-old books like that when it's not history but I liked this book very, very much). Tumaki made me read some of those novels about Muslim women . . . not bad, except for the ones that were mostly about perfumed and oiled girls dodging eager men and landing a rich princely husband.

My brain must have doubled in size.

Rainmaker

Tumaki didn't wear make-up. Even without the burka she had no need for it. She only lied when she had to. Like when her mother asked about me. She told her that I was just a friend and that I was harmless. Her mother would have had me beheaded if she knew that I knew every part of Tumaki. Every part.

Tumaki wasn't deceptive and because she grew up around trust, it was easy to learn to trust me. She quietly worked hard to earn mine. At first, I couldn't see past her looks. Then, as time passed, yes, I began to trust her, too. Bit by bit.

You think of the times in your life where you actual accomplish something useful and good. Where you create love and beauty. Then when you reach the bad ugly place, where everything is a rainy prison, you understand that life is meant to be lived. We are meant to go on.

That's what I tell myself here. Each day we get closer and each day those good days with Tumaki get farther and farther away. Soon it will be as if they never happened at all. It will be as if none of this happened. It will only be the wind, the rain, the lightning, this great storm.

Paradise Lost

Now, listen.

I'm not telling the story of my relationship with Tumaki. That was gloriously normal. Textbook stuff. She and I were good together, when you didn't count all the outside stuff—like her being from a Muslim, fairly well-off family, and me being a meta-human ex-slave who'd been rejected from his basically Catholic stinking-rich family. I told Tumaki a little about my past. And she didn't ask much more. She knew the basics. My secrets were not her preoccupation.

The story I'm trying to tell started when Tumaki's father disappeared.

Recall the incident I saw with the little boy shadow speaker. I saw so much of that in Timia. Meta-humans treated like radioactive cancer-causing evil infidel waste. Meta-humans were threats to small children and wholesome family values. They caused women to become sterile. They were the cause of all that had gone wrong. It was the Ginen folk spreading these stupid rumors.

But local people took to it like fish to water. They loved the Ginen folk like people love superstars and the wealthy. You could see it in their eyes. Women would swoon over the young Ginen men. Men would chase after Ginen women like they'd lost their damn minds. I have to hand it to the Ginenians, they had style. Their clothes were always the most fashionable. They had a way of speaking that sounded like music to your ears—I think some of this had to do with the magic involved in their language. And they always had money from selling their rare items.

It was the people, the natives of Niger, who took to calling meta-humans (and anyone who sympathized with or gave birth to them) "cockroaches."

It was a slow disease in Timia. I might have left that city if it weren't for Tumaki. Hiding away in her library, I didn't realize how bad it was getting. Not until the day she came running down the winding staircase, shaking, eyes wide and wet. I'd been waiting down there for an hour.

I jumped up and ran to her. "Tumaki! What . . . "

She snatched her hand from mine as she threw off her dark blue burka and let loose a string of obscenities that even impressed me.

"What?" I asked again. "What happened?"

"My papa!" she shouted. Her left eye was twitching as she sat down on the couch. She stood up and started pacing. Then she made to go up the staircase. "I have to make sure . . . "

I grabbed her hand. "Will you tell me—"

She whirled around. The look on her face made me back away. I thought she was about to punch me. Her panicked rage practically burst from her skin. "They took him!"

"Who?"

"Some men." She shook her head. "And one woman. All of them strong like oxen. People were cheering! How can that be? People of his own home!"

"But why?"

"People are suddenly disappearing all over Timia," she snapped. "Haven't you noticed?

I shook my head.

"Oh Allah! They took my papa, *o*!" she wailed. She screamed and moaned. I didn't dare touch her. Eventually, minutes later, she knelt down and was silent. She shut her eyes. When she opened them, she was calm. She stood and grabbed my hand. "Come, Dikéogu," she said, her voice steady, her eyes blank. "I don't care what my mother says."

We went up the stairs, across the yard, into her house.

Her mother didn't care, either. She didn't ask why I was with her daughter alone or why I was in her house. It was the house of wealthy folks. It reminded me of my home in Arondizuogu, but not as obnoxious. The floors were wooden, not marble. The furniture was plush, sturdy, and well-made, but probably not black leather imported from Italy.

There was a large picture with a white silk veil over it. I assumed this was a portrait of Tumaki's father. The house reeked of burned rice and Tumaki had to run to the kitchen to turn the heat off the pot. Her mother just sat there on the couch. She wore no burka and she stared blankly ahead. It was my first time seeing her face. Tumaki was the spitting image of her mother.

"It was only a matter of time," her mother whispered. "Of course they'll take the imams first. Right there in the mosque. They have no respect."

Tumaki brought her a glass of water. Her mother took it absentmindedly. Tumaki looked at me and then back at her mother. "He should have kept quiet," her mother said. She whimpered. "He used to watch windseekers fly about at night when the bats were out; when they thought no one would see them." She set the water on the rug beneath her feet.

That day, I moved my things from the hotel into Tumaki's home.

I walked the streets, letting people assume I was a slave. The slave of Tumaki and her mother. I went shopping for them. I helped Tumaki in their electronics shop. I went to tea shops to listen to gossip. The government was finally doing what "needed to be done," some drunken blockhead said. Everyone, including me, mumbled assent.

"Soon this city will be free of meta-humans and troublemakers." More mumbled agreement, this time a bit livelier.

"Good riddance," a woman muttered.

It was all happening so fast.

Within one week, I stopped seeing meta-humans with obvious characteristics in Timia. No windseekers; they brought wind wherever they went. No metal workers; they attracted things like earrings, necklaces, and keys just by standing near people. No shadow speakers with their weird eyes. Professors started disappearing. And certain students, many of whom we'd seen at the poetry slams, disappeared, too.

Two weeks later, Tumaki's mother's shop was ransacked, then burned down. Two days after that, her mother disappeared from her own bedroom.

The streets were busy and, dare I say, jubilant. Something was very wrong with these people. It was as if they'd been programmed and then the program had been turned on.

Tumaki and I dragged as much food and water as we could into the library and hid there. We read books and enjoyed each other, but avoided talking about anything serious. Especially about the fact that I was a rainmaker and she was a female electrician and student.

We were down there for three days.

By the third, we were smelly, hungry and angry. And that was when we heard people rushing down the stairs.

Now, when you've been cooped up for that long in a small room, you become concentrated. You know every sound. You know every angle. And you're a bundle of nerves. We'd been waiting for three days for something to happen.

Tumaki had her mother's best hammer. I had myself. But nothing could have prepared us for what came down those stairs. There were four of them. Tall, dark-skinned, bald, even the woman. They wore white long kaftans, the woman a white flowing dress made of the same flawless material. They moved swiftly down the winding stairs and they made not a sound. I mean, not . . . a . . . sound. Silent as ghosts. Once in the room, they zoomed right at Tumaki and me.

I shoved Tumaki behind me. She tried to shove me behind her. It didn't matter. With my peripheral vision I saw one of them zip right at Tumaki, grabbing her in his clutches. It all seemed to happen in slow motion. I turned, my mouth open. He slammed Tumaki against a bookcase. She winced, mournfully glancing at me. He had teeth like a snake, fangs. *Vampire?*

"Let her g . . . " I was grabbed from behind.

But I saw it sink its teeth into Tumaki's neck as she raked her nails across its face. Its skin tore away but there was no blood. It didn't let go. Tumaki's eyes went blank.

I was grappling with the woman, trying to get back to Tumaki. She said into my ear, "Where do you think you're going, cockroach?" Two more of them grabbed me.

I didn't hear a sound from Tumaki. But I heard the sound of her hammer dropping to the floor. In all that scuffling, I heard that.

I'd had enough. I stopped fighting. I focused. I let burst the most powerful surge of electricity I could produce. It made a low deep deep *thud*!

Screeches like you would not believe.

Like rabid rats trapped in a tiny tiny cage.

Spitting and hissing and high-pitched screeching.

They fled up the stairs. I don't know if they flew or ran or oozed or what. All I knew was that they took Tumaki. She was gone. They must have picked her up like a sack of dried dates. They'd sucked the life from her and then they took her.

"Oh Allah, what is this, *o*?" I screamed. Then I just screamed and screamed until a darkness fell over my mind.

The only gift my father really ever gave me was a thick book about an Igbo poet named Christopher Okigbo.

A line from his poetry: "For the far removed, there is wailing."

It was several things about Tumaki.

It was her books. It was the fact that she *hid* her books. Maybe one of the men who'd helped her install the staircase that led down to her library had told on her. It was her tinkering. It was how she knew to wear her burka despite all this. It was her pride. It was her wanting to attend university. And it was probably her parents.

I have no doubts about why they killed her.

I went mad.

Darkness crowded in on me. Down there in her library, all alone. I barely noticed. Tumaki was gone. I'd seen one of those creatures bite her. Her eyes had gone out. Like a light. I loved her. I was consumed by terror, shock, rage, shame. I tore at the neck of my caftan. I had no one left. A breeze lifted up around me.

It oozed up though the library floor like some ancient crude oil. It pooled around me, whispering and sighing. It was nothing but a breeze. It was opportunistic, searching for a way into me. I could feel something else bubbling up in me, just as I could feel the darkness oozing around my feet: The Destruction. I wanted to destroy all things. Murder, mayhem, havoc. Crush, Kill, Destroy. "Yessssss," the darkness whispered to me, like the sound of whirling sand. "Sssssssssss."

Only my utter grief made me flee deep into myself instead of taking it out on what was outside myself, and maybe a tiny shred of humanity, too. I was lucky . . . in a way. In another way, I wonder if I'd have been better off succumbing to the thing from outside the cocoa farm that seemed to have followed me into Tumaki's library, like some lethal black smoky snake that had waited for the right moment to strike.

A large chunk of my life remains mostly a blank and the few short moments that I remember was just more badness. I do not recall leaving the library, or the city of Timia. I briefly recall some idiot of a man grabbed me and told me I was going with his family to Agadez. He needed someone to help him with his camels. He read my tattoos as the mark of a slave, though they were of a slave and rainmaker. I let him. In Agadez, I slipped away in the dead of night two days later. My memory is blank for weeks after this. In the following months, I'd mentally surface for an hour or two, finding myself in this town or that town. So much blank memory. I'll not talk about the worst of it.

My mind was unhinged. I forgot Tumaki. I forgot myself.

Somehow I ended up nearly dead in the desert squinting up at that curious tall man whose face was covered by an indigo veil. He stood feet away from me, unmoving like some djinni. I think it was being nearly dead that finally woke me up. The closeness of death has a way of awakening even the most damaged senses.

⌐⌐

Nnedi Okorafor (nnedi.com) is an author of Nigerian descent. In a profile of her work, the *New York Times* called her imagination "stunning." Okorafor's novels include *Zahrah the Windseeker* (winner of the Wole Soyinka Prize for African Literature), *The Shadow Speaker* (winner of the CBS Parallax Award), and *Long Juju Man* (winner of the Macmillan Writer's Prize for Africa). Her latest novel is *Who Fears*. Her first short story collection—*Kabu Kabu*—will be published this fall. Okorafor holds a PhD in English and currently is a professor of creative writing at Chicago State University.

Global warming and other factors have left Mexico better off than the US. After the End, America is slowly eroding and some portions—like the Southwest—have become no-man's-lands. Mexico sends some help to its northern neighbor, but one aid-giver has more than humanitarian reasons to travel there.

• THE EGG MAN •
Mary Rosenblum

Zipakna halted at midday to let the Dragon power up the batteries. He checked on the chickens clucking contentedly in their travel crates, then went outside to squat in the shade of one fully deployed solar wing in the 43 centigrade heat. Ilena, his sometimes-lover and poker partner, accused him of reverse snobbery, priding himself on being able to survive in the Sonoran heat without air conditioning. Zipakna smiled and tilted his water bottle, savoring the cool, sweet trickle of water across his tongue.

Not true, of course. He held still as the first wild bees found him, buzzed past his face to settle and sip from the sweat-drops beading on his skin. Killers. He held very still, but the caution wasn't really necessary. Thirst was the great gentler here. Every other drive was laid aside in the pursuit of water.

Even love?

He laughed a short note as the killers buzzed and sipped. So Ilena claimed, but she just missed him when she played the tourists without him. It had been mostly tourists from China lately, filling the underwater resorts in the Sea of Cortez. Chinese were rich and tough players and Ilena had been angry at him for leaving. But he always left in spring. She knew that. In front of him, the scarp he had been traversing ended in a bluff, eroded by water that had fallen here eons ago. The plain below spread out in tones of ochre and russet, dotted with dusty clumps of sage and the stark upward thrust of saguaro, lonely sentinels contemplating the desiccated plain of the

Sonoran and in the distance, the ruins of a town. Paloma? Zipakna tilted his wrist, called up his position on his link. Yes, that was it. He had wandered a bit farther eastward than he'd thought and had cut through the edge of the Pima preserve. Sure enough, a fine had been levied against his account. He sighed. He serviced the Pima settlement out here and they didn't mind if he trespassed. It merely became a bargaining chip when it came time to talk price. The Pima loved to bargain.

He really should let the nav-link plot his course, but Ilena was right about that, at least. He prided himself on finding his way through the Sonora without it. Zipakna squinted as a flicker of movement caught his eye. A lizard? Maybe. Or one of the tough desert rodents. They didn't need to drink, got their water from seeds and cactus fruit. More adaptable than *Homo sapiens,* he thought, and smiled grimly.

He pulled his binocs from his belt pouch and focused on the movement. The digital lenses seemed to suck him through the air like a thrown spear, gray-ochre blur resolving into stone, mica flash, and yes, the brown and gray shape of a lizard. The creature's head swiveled, throat pulsing, so that it seemed to stare straight into his eyes. Then, in an eyeblink, it vanished. The Dragon chimed its full battery load. Time to go. He stood carefully, a cloud of thirsty killer bees and native wasps buzzing about him, shook free of them and slipped into the coolness of the Dragon's interior. The hens clucked in the rear and the Dragon furled its solar wings and lurched forward, crawling down over the edge of the scarp, down to the plain below and its saguaro sentinels.

His sat-link chimed and his console screen brightened to life. *You are entering unserviced United States territory.* The voice was female and severe. *No support services will be provided from this point on. Your entry visa does not assure assistance in unserviced regions. Please file all complaints with the US Bureau of Land Management. Please consult with your insurance provider before continuing.* Did he detect a note of disapproval in the sat-link voice? Zipakna grinned without humor and guided the Dragon down the steep slope, its belted treads barely marring the dry surface as he navigated around rock and thorny clumps of mesquite. He was a citizen of the Republic of Mexico and the US's sat eyes would certainly track his chip. They just wouldn't send a rescue if he got into trouble.

Such is life, he thought, and swatted an annoyed killer as it struggled against the windshield.

He passed the first of Paloma's plantings an hour later. The glassy black disks of the solar collectors glinted in the sun, powering the drip system that fed the scattered clumps of greenery. Short, thick-stalked sunflowers turned their dark faces to the sun, fringed with orange and scarlet petals. Zipakna frowned thoughtfully and videoed one of the wide blooms as the Dragon crawled past. Sure enough, his screen lit up with a similar blossom crossed with a circle-slash of warning.

An illegal pharm crop. The hairs on the back of his neck prickled. This was new. He almost turned around, but he liked the folk in Paloma. Good people; misfits, not sociopaths. It was an old settlement and one of his favorites. He sighed, because three diabetics lived here and a new bird flu had come over from Asia. It would find its way here eventually, riding the migration routes. He said a prayer to the old gods and his mother's *Santa Maria* for good measure and crawled on into town.

Nobody was out this time of day. Heat waves shimmered above the black solar panels and a lizard whip-flicked beneath the sagging Country Market's porch. He parked the Dragon in the dusty lot at the end of Main Street where a couple of buildings had burned long ago and unfurled the solar wings again. It took a lot of power to keep them from baking here. In the back Ezzie was clucking imperatively. The oldest of the chickens, she always seemed to know when they were stopping at a settlement. That meant fresh greens. "You're a pig," he said, but he chuckled as he made his way to the back to check on his flock.

The twenty hens clucked and scratched in their individual cubicles, excited at the halt. "I'll let you out soon," he promised and measured laying ration into their feeders. Bella had already laid an egg. He reached into her cubicle and cupped it in his hand, pale pink and smooth, still warm and faintly moist from its passage out of her body. Insulin nano-bodies, designed to block the auto-immune response that destroyed the insulin producing Beta cells in diabetics. He labeled Bella's egg and put it into the egg fridge. She was his highest producer. He scooped extra ration into her feeder.

Intruder, his alarm system announced. The heads-up display above the front console lit up. Zipakna glanced at it, brows furrowed, then smiled. He slipped to the door, touched it open. "You could just knock," he said.

The skinny boy hanging from the front of the Dragon by his fingers as he tried to peer through the windscreen let go, missed his footing and landed on his butt in the dust.

"It's too hot out here," Zipakna said. "Come inside. You can see better."

The boy looked up, his face tawny with Sonoran dust, hazel eyes wide with fear.

Zipakna's heart froze and time seemed to stand still. *She* must have looked like this as a kid, he thought. Probably just like this, considering how skinny and androgynous she had been in her twenties. He shook himself. "It's all right," he said and his voice only quivered a little. "You can come in."

"Ella said you have chickens. She said they lay magic eggs. I've never seen a chicken. But Pierre says there's no magic." The fear had vanished from his eyes, replaced now by bright curiosity.

That, too, was like her. Fear had never had a real hold on her.

How many times had he wished it had?

"I do have chickens. You can see them now." He held the door open. "What's your name?"

"Daren." The boy darted past him, quick as one of the desert's lizards, scrambled into the Dragon.

Her father's name.

Zipakna climbed in after him, feeling old suddenly, dry as this ancient desert. *I can't have kids*, she had said, so earnest. *How could I take a child into the uncontrolled areas? How could I leave one behind? Maybe later. After I'm done out there.*

"It's freezing in here." Daren stared around at the control bank under the wide windscreen, his bare arms and legs, skin clay-brown from the sun, ridged with goosebumps.

So much bare skin scared Zipakna. Average age for onset of melanoma without regular boosters was twenty-five. "Want something to drink? You can go look at the chickens. They're in the back."

"Water?" The boy gave him a bright, hopeful look. "Ella has a chicken. She lets me take care of it." He disappeared into the chicken space.

Zipakna opened the egg fridge. Bianca laid steadily even though she didn't have the peak capacity that some of the others did. So he had a good stock of her eggs. The boy was murmuring to the hens who were clucking greetings at him. "You can take one out," Zipakna called back to him. "They like to be held." He opened a packet of freeze-dried chocolate soy milk, reconstituted it, and whipped one of Bianca's eggs into it, so that it frothed tawny and rich. The gods knew if the boy had ever received any immunizations at all. Bianca provided the basic panel of nanobodies against most of the common pathogens and cancers. Including melanoma.

In the chicken room, Daren had taken Bella out of her cage, held her cradled in his arms. The speckled black and white hen clucked contentedly, occasionally pecking Daren's chin lightly. "She likes to be petted," Zipakna said. "If you rub her comb she'll sing to you. I made you a milkshake."

The boy's smile blossomed as Bella gave out with the almost-melodic squawks and creaks that signified her pleasure. "What's a milkshake?" Still smiling, he returned the hen to her cage and eyed the glass.

"Soymilk and chocolate and sugar." He handed it to Daren, found himself holding his breath as the boy tasted it and considered.

"Pretty sweet." He drank some. "I like it anyway."

To Zipakna's relief he drank it all and licked foam from his lip.

"So when did you move here?" Zipakna took the empty glass, rinsed it at the sink.

"Wow, you use water to clean dishes?" The boy's eyes had widened. "We came here last planting time. Pierre brought those seeds." He pointed in the general direction of the sunflower fields.

Zipakna's heart sank. "You and your parents?" He made his voice light.

Daren didn't answer for a moment. "Pierre. My father." He looked back to the chicken room. "If they're not magic, why do you give them water? Ella's chicken warns her about snakes, but you don't have to worry about snakes in here. What good are they?"

The cold logic of the Dry, out here beyond the security net of civilized space. "Their eggs keep you healthy." He watched the boy consider that. "You know Ella, right?" He waited for the boy's nod. "She has a disease that would kill her if she didn't eat an egg from that chicken you were holding every year."

Daren frowned, clearly doubting that. "You mean like a snake egg? They're good, but Ella's chicken doesn't lay eggs. And snake eggs don't make you get better when you're sick."

"They don't. And Ella's chicken is a banty rooster. He doesn't lay eggs." Zipakna looked up as a figure moved on the heads-up. "Bella is special and so are her eggs." He opened the door. "Hello, Ella, what are you doing out here in the heat?"

"I figured he'd be out here bothering you." Ella hoisted herself up the Dragon's steps, her weathered, sun-dried face the color of real leather, her loose sun-shirt falling back from the stringy muscles of her arms as she reached up to kiss Zipakna on the cheek. "You behavin' yourself, boy? I'll switch you if you aren't."

"I'm being good." Daren grinned. "Ask him."

"He is." Zipakna eyed her face and briefly exposed arms, looking for any sign of melanoma. Even with the eggs, you could still get it out here with no UV protection. "So, Ella, you got some new additions to town, eh? New crops, too, I see." He watched her look away, saw her face tighten.

"Now don't you start." She stared at the south viewscreen filled with the bright heads of sunflowers. "Prices on everything we have to buy keep going up. And the Pima are tight, you know that. Plain sunflower oil don't bring much."

"So now you got something that can get you raided. By the government or someone worse."

"You're the one comes out here from the city where you got water and power, go hiking around in the dust with enough stuff to keep raiders fat and happy for a year." Ella's leathery face creased into a smile. "You preachin' risk at me, Zip?"

"Ah, but we know I'm crazy, eh?" He returned her smile, but shook his head. "I hope you're still here, next trip. How're your sugar levels? You been checking?"

"If we ain't we ain't." She lifted one bony shoulder in a shrug. "They're holding. They always do."

"The eggs do make you well?" Daren looked at Ella.

"Yeah, they do." Ella cocked her head at him. "There's magic, even if Pierre don't believe it."

"Do you really come from a city?" Daren was looking up at Zipakna now. "With a dome and water in the taps and everything?"

"Well, I come from Oaxaca, which doesn't have a dome. I spend most of my time in La Paz. It's on the Baja peninsula, if you know where that is."

"I do." He grinned. "Ella's been schooling me. I know where Oaxaca is, too. You're Mexican, right?" He tilted his head. "How come you come up here with your eggs?"

Ella was watching him, her dark eyes sharp with surmise. Nobody had ever asked him that question openly before. It wasn't the kind of question you asked, out here. Not out loud. He looked down into Daren's hazel eyes, into *her* eyes. "Because nobody else does."

Daren's eyes darkened and he looked down at the floor, frowning slightly.

"Sit down, Ella, let me get you your egg. Long as you're here." Zipakna turned quickly to the kitchen wall and filled glasses with water. While they drank, he got Bella's fresh egg from the egg fridge and cracked it into a glass, blending it with the raspberry concentrate that Ella favored and a bit of soy milk.

"That's a milkshake," Daren announced as Zipakna handed Ella the glass. "He made me one, too." He looked up at Zipakna. "I'm not sick."

"He didn't think you were." Ella lifted her glass in a salute. "Because nobody else does." Drank it down. "You gonna come eat with us tonight?" Usually the invitation came with a grin that revealed the gap in her upper front teeth, and a threat about her latest pequin salsa. Today her smile was cautious. Wary. "Daren?" She nodded at the boy. "You go help Maria with the food. You know it's your turn today."

"Aw." He scuffed his bare feet, but headed for the door. "Can I come pet the chickens again?" He looked back hopefully from the door, grinned at Zipakna's nod, and slipped out, letting in a breath of oven-air.

"Ah, Ella." Zipakna sighed and reached into the upper cupboard. "Why did you plant those damn sunflowers?" He pulled out the bottle of aged mescal tucked away behind the freeze-dried staples. He filled a small, thick glass and set it down on the table in front of Ella beside her refilled water glass. "This can be the end of the settlement. You know that."

"The end can come in many ways." She picked up the glass, held it up to the light. "Perhaps fast is better than slow, eh?" She sipped the liquor, closed her eyes and sighed. "Luna and her husband tried for amnesty, applied to get a citizen-visa at the border. They've canceled the amnesty. You live outside the serviced areas, I guess you get to stay out here. I guess the US economy faltered again. No more new citizens from Outside. And you know Mexico's policy about US immigration." She shrugged. "I'm surprised they even let you come up here."

"Oh, my government doesn't mind traffic in this direction. It likes to rub the US's nose in the fact that we send aid to its own citizens," he said lightly. Yeah, the border was closed tight to immigration from the north right now, because the US was being sticky about tariffs. "I can't believe they've made the Interior Boundaries airtight." That was what *she* had been afraid of, all those years ago.

"I guess they have to keep cutting and cutting." Ella drained the glass, probing for the last drops of amber liquor with her tongue. "No, one is enough." She shook her head as he turned to the cupboard. "The folks that live nice want to keep it that way, so you got to cut somewhere. We all know the US is slowly eroding away. It's not a superpower anymore. They just pretend." She looked up at Zipakna, her eyes like flakes of obsidian set into the nested wrinkles of her sun-dried face. "What is your interest in the boy, Zip? He's too young."

He turned away from those obsidian-flake eyes. "You misunderstand."

She waited, didn't say anything.

"Once upon a time there was a woman." He stared at the sun-baked emptiness of the main street on the vid screen. A tumbleweed skeleton turned slowly, fitfully across dust and cracked asphalt. "She had a promising career in academics, but she preferred field work."

"Field work?"

"She was a botanist. She created some drought-tolerant GMOs and started field testing them. They were designed for the drip irrigation ag areas, but she decided to test them . . . out here. She . . . got caught up in it . . . establishing adaptive GMOs out here to create sustainable harvests. She . . . gave up an academic career. Put everything into this project. Got some funding for it."

Ella sat without speaking as the silence stretched between them. "What happened to her?" She asked it, finally.

"I don't know." The tumbleweed had run up against the pole of a rusted and dented *No Parking* sign and quivered in the hot wind. "I . . . lost contact with her."

Ella nodded, her face creased into thoughtful folds. "I see."

No, you don't, he thought.

"How long ago?"

"Fifteen years."

"So he's not your son."

He flinched even though he'd known the question was coming. "No." He was surprised at how hard it was to speak that word.

Ella levered herself to her feet, leaning hard on the table. Pain in her hip. The osteo-sarcoma antibodies his chickens produced weren't specific to her problem. A personally tailored anti-cancer panel might cure her, but that cost money. A lot of money. He wasn't a doctor, but he'd seen enough osteo out here to measure her progress. It was the water, he guessed. "I brought you a present." He reached up into the cupboard again, brought out a flat plastic bottle of mescal with the Mexico state seal on the cap. Old stuff. Very old.

She took it, her expression enigmatic, tilted it, her eyes on the slosh of pale golden liquor. Then she let her breath out in a slow sigh and tucked the bottle carefully beneath her loose shirt. "Thank you." Her obsidian eyes gave nothing away.

He caught a glimpse of rib bones, faint bruising, and dried, shrunken flesh, revised his estimate. "You're welcome."

"I think you need to leave here." She looked past him. "We maybe need to live without your eggs. I'd just go right now."

He didn't answer for a moment. Listened to the chuckle of the hens. "Can I come to dinner tonight?"

"That's right. You're crazy. We both know that." She sighed.

He held the door for her as she lowered herself stiffly and cautiously into the oven heat of the fading day.

She was right, he thought as he watched her limp through the heat shimmer, back to the main building. She was definitely right.

He took his time with the chickens, letting them out of their cages to scratch on the grass carpet and peck at the vitamin crumbles he scattered for them. While he was parked here, they could roam loose in the back of the Dragon. He kept the door leading back to their section locked and all his hens were good about laying in their own cages, although at this point, he could tell who had laid which egg by sight. By the time he left the Dragon, the sun was completely down and the first pale stars winked in the royal blue of the darkening sky. No moon tonight. The wind had died and he smelled dust and a whiff of roasting meat as his boots grated on the dusty asphalt of the old main street. He touched the small hardness of the stunner in his pocket and climbed the sagging porch of what had once been a store, back when the town had still lived.

They had built a patio of sorts out behind the building, had roofed it from the sun with metal sheeting stripped from other derelict buildings. Long tables and old sofas clustered inside the building, shelter from the sun on the long hot days where residents shelled sunflower seed after harvest or worked on repair jobs or just visited, waiting for the cool of evening. He could see the yellow flicker of flame out back through the old plate-glass windows with their taped cracks.

The moment he entered he felt it—tension like the prickle of static electricity on a dry, windy day. Paloma was easy, friendly. He let his guard down sometimes when he was here, sat around the fire pit out back and shared the mescal he brought, trading swallows with the local stuff, flavored with cactus fruit, that wasn't all that bad, considering.

Tonight, eyes slid his way, slid aside. The hair prickled on the back of his neck, but he made his smile easy. "Hola," he said, and gave them the usual grin and wave. "How you all makin' out?"

"Zip." Ella heaved herself up from one of the sofas, crossed the floor with firm strides, hands out, face turning up to kiss his cheeks. Grim determination folded the skin at the corners of her eyes tight. "Glad you could eat with us. Thanks for that egg today, I feel better already."

Ah, that was the issue? "Got to keep that blood sugar low." He gave her a real hug, because she was so *solid*, was the core of this settlement, whether the others realized it or not.

"Come on." Ella grabbed his arm. "Let's go out back. Rodriguez got an antelope, can you believe it? A young buck, no harm done."

"Meat?" He laughed, made it relaxed and easy, from the belly. "You eat better than I do. It's all vat stuff or too pricey to afford, down south. Good thing maize and beans are in my blood."

"Hey." Daren popped in from the firelit back, his eyes bright in the dim light. "Can my friends come see the chickens?"

My friends. The shy, hopeful pride in those words was so naked that Zipakna almost winced. He could see two or three faces behind Daren. That same tone had tainted his own voice, back when he had been a government scholarship kid from the wilds beyond San Cristobal, one of those who spoke Spanish as a second language. *My friends*, such a precious thing when you did not belong.

"Sure." He gave Daren a "we're buddies" grin and shrug. "Any time. You can show 'em around." Daren's eyes betrayed his struggle to look nonchalant.

A low chuckle circulated through the room, almost too soft to be heard, and Ella touched his arm lightly. Approvingly. Zipakna felt the tension relax a bit as he and Ella made their way through the dusk of the building to the firelit dark out back. One by one the shadowy figures who had stood back, not greeted him, thawed and followed. He answered greetings, pretending he hadn't noticed anything, exchanged the usual pleasantries that concerned weather and world politics, avoided the real issues of life. Like illegal crops. One by one, he identified the faces as the warm red glow of the coals in the firepit lit them. She needed the MS egg from Negro, he needed the anti-malaria from Seca and so did she. Daren had appeared at his side, his posture taut, a mix of proprietary and anxious.

"Meat, what a treat, eh?" Zipakna grinned down at Daren as one of the women laid a charred strip of roasted meat on a plate, dumped a scoop of beans beside it and added a flat disk of tortilla, thick and chewy and gritty from the bicycle-powered stone-mill that the community used to grind maize into masa.

"Hey, you be careful tomorrow." She nodded toward a plastic bucket filled with water, a dipper and cups beside it. "Don't you let my Jonathan hurt any of those chickens. He's so clumsy."

"I'll show 'em how to be careful." Daren took the piled plate she handed him, practically glowing with pride.

Zipakna smiled at the server. She was another diabetic, like Ella. Sanja. He remembered her name.

"Watch out for the chutney." Sanja grinned and pointed at a table full of condiment dishes. "The sticky red stuff. I told Ella how to make it and she made us all sweat this year with her pequins."

"I like it hot." He smiled for her. "I want to see if it'll make me sweat."

"It will." Daren giggled. "I thought I'd swallowed coals, man." He carried his plate to one of the wooden tables, set it down with a possessive confidence beside Zipakna's.

Usually he sat at a crowded table answering questions, sharing news that hadn't yet filtered out here with the few traders, truckers, or wanderers who risked the unserviced Dry. Not this time. He chewed the charred, overdone meat slowly, aware of the way Daren wolfed his food, how most of the people here ate the same way, always prodded by hunger. That was how they drank, too, urgently, always thirsty.

Not many of them meant to end up out there. He remembered her words, the small twin lines that he called her "thinking dimples" creasing her forehead as she stared into her wine glass. *They had plans, they had a future in mind. It wasn't this one.*

"That isn't really why you come out here, is it? What you said before—in your big truck?"

Zipakna started, realized he was staring into space, a forkful of beans poised in the air. He looked down at Daren, into those clear hazel eyes that squeezed his heart. She had always known when he wasn't telling the truth. "No. It isn't." He set the fork down on his plate. "A friend of mine . . . a long time ago . . . went missing out here. I've . . . sort of hoped to run into her." At least that was how it had started. Now he looked for her ghost. Daren was staring at his neck.

"Where did you get that necklace?"

Zipakna touched the carved jade cylinder on its linen cord. "I found it diving in an old cenote—that's a kind of well where people threw offerings to the gods centuries ago. You're not supposed to dive there, but I was a kid—sneaking in."

"Are the cenotes around here?" Daren looked doubtful. "I never heard of any wells."

"No, they're way down south. Where I come from."

Daren scraped up the last beans from his plate, wiped it carefully with his tortilla. "Why did your friend come out here?"

"To bring people plants that didn't need much water." Zipakna sighed and eyed the remnants of his dinner. "You want this? I'm not real hungry tonight."

Daren gave him another doubting look, then shrugged and dug into the last of the meat and beans. "She was like Pierre?"

"No!"

The boy flinched and Ziapakna softened his tone. "She created food plants so that you didn't need to grow as much to eat well." And then . . . she had simply gotten too involved. He closed his eyes, remembering that bitter, bitter fight. "Is your mother here?" He already knew the answer but Daren's head shake still pierced him. The boy focused on wiping up the last molecule of the searing sauce with a scrap of tortilla, shoulders hunched.

"What are you doing?"

At the angry words, Daren's head shot up and he jerked his hands away from the plate as if it had burned him.

"I was just talking with him, Pierre." He looked up, sandy hair falling back from his face. "He doesn't mind."

"I mind." The tall, skinny man with the dark braid and pale skin frowned down at Daren. "What have I told you about city folk?"

"But . . . " Daren bit off the word, ducked his head. "I'll go clean my plate." He snatched his plate and cup from the table, headed for the deeper shadows along the building.

"You leave him alone." The man stared down at him, his gray eyes flat and cold. "We all know about city folk and their appetites."

Suddenly the congenial chatter that had started up during the meal ended. Silence hung thick as smoke in the air. "You satisfied my appetite quite well tonight." Zipakna smiled gently. "I haven't had barbecued antelope in a long time."

"You got to wonder." Pierre leaned one hip against the table, crossed his arms. "Why someone gives up the nice air conditioning and swimming pools of the city to come trekking around out here handing out free stuff. Especially when your rig costs a couple of fortunes."

Zipakna sighed, made it audible. From the corner of his eye he noticed

Ella, watching him intently, was aware of the hard lump of the stunner in his pocket. "I get this every time I meet folk. We already went through it here, didn't anyone tell you?"

"Yeah, they did." Pierre gave him a mirthless smile. "And you want me to believe that some non-profit in Mexico—Mexico!—cares about us? Not even our own government does that."

"It's all politics." Zipakna shrugged. "Mexico takes quite a bit of civic pleasure in the fact that Mexico has to extend aid to US citizens. If the political situation changes, yeah, the money might dry up. But for now, people contribute and I come out here. So do a few others like me." He looked up, met the man's cold, gray eyes. "Haven't you met an altruist at least once in your life?" he asked softly.

Pierre looked away and his face tightened briefly. "I sure don't believe you're one. You leave my son alone." He turned on his heel and disappeared in the direction Daren had taken.

Zipakna drank his water, skin prickling with the feel of the room. He looked up as Ella marched over, sat down beside him. "We know you're what you say you are." She pitched her voice to reach everyone. "Me, I'm looking forward to my egg in the morning, and I sure thank you for keeping an old woman like me alive. Not many care. He's right about that much." She gave Zipakna a small private wink as she squeezed his shoulder and stood up. "Sanja and I'll be there first thing in the morning, right, Sanja?"

"Yeah." Sanja's voice emerged from shadow, a little too bright. "We sure will."

Zipakna got to his feet and Ella rose with him. "You should all come by in the morning. Got a new virus northwest of here. It's high mortality and it's moving this way. Spread by birds, so it'll get here. I have eggs that will give you immunity." He turned and headed around the side of the building.

A thin scatter of replies drifted after him and he found Ella walking beside him, her hand on his arm. "They change everything," she said softly. "The flowers."

"You know, the sat cams can see them." He kept his voice low as they crunched around the side of the building, heading toward the Dragon. "They measure the light refraction from the leaves and they can tell if they're legit or one of the outlaw strains. That's no accident, Ella. You don't realize how much the government and the drug gangs use the same tools. One or the other will get you." He shook his head. "You better hope it's the government."

"They haven't found us yet."

"The seeds aren't ready to harvest are they?"

"Pierre says we're too isolated."

Zipakna turned on her. "Nowhere is isolated any more. Not on this entire dirt ball. You ever ask Pierre why he showed up here? Why didn't he stay where he was before if he was doing such a good job growing illegal seeds?"

Ella didn't answer and he walked on.

"It's a mistake to let a ghost run your life." Ella's voice came low from the darkness behind him, tinged with sadness.

Zipakna hesitated as the door slid open for him. "Good night, Ella." He climbed into its cool interior, listening to the hens' soft chortle of greeting.

They showed up in the cool of dawn, trickling up to the Dragon in ones and twos to drink the frothy blend of fruit and soymilk he offered and to ask shyly about the news they hadn't asked about last night. A few apologized. Not many.

Neither Daren nor Pierre showed up. Zipakna fed the hens, collected the day's eggs, and was glad he'd given Daren his immunization egg the day before. By noon he had run out of things to keep him here. He hiked over to the community building in the searing heat of noon, found Ella sewing a shirt in the still heat of the interior, told her goodbye.

"Go with God," she told him and her face was as seamed and dry as the land outside.

This settlement would not be here when he next came this way. The old gods wrote that truth in the dust devils dancing at the edge of the field. He wondered what stolen genes those seeds carried. He looked for Daren and Pierre but didn't see either of them. Tired to the bone, he trudged back to the Dragon in the searing heat. Time to move on. Put kilometers between the Dragon and the dangerous magnet of those ripening seeds.

You have a visitor, the Dragon announced as he approached.

He hadn't locked the door? Zipakna frowned, because he didn't make that kind of mistake. Glad that he was still carrying the stunner, he slipped to the side and opened the door, fingers curled around the smooth shape of the weapon.

"Ella said you were leaving." Daren stood inside, Bella in his arms.

"Yeah, I need to move on." He climbed up, the wash of adrenaline through his bloodstream telling him just how tense it had been here. "I have other settlements to visit."

Daren looked up at him, frowning a little. Then he turned and went back into the chicken room to put Bella back in her traveling coop. He scratched her comb, smiled a little as she chuckled at him, and closed the door. "I think maybe . . . this is yours." He turned and held out a hand.

Zipakna stared down at the carved jade cylinder on his palm. It had been strung on a fine steel chain. She had worn it on a linen cord with coral beads knotted on either side of it. He swallowed. Shook his head. "It's yours." The words came out husky and rough. "She meant you to have it."

"I thought maybe she was the friend you talked about." Daren closed his fist around the bead. "She said the same thing you did, I remember. She said she came out here because no one else would. Did you give it to her?"

He nodded, squeezing his eyes closed, struggling to swallow the pain that welled up into his throat. "You can come with me," he whispered. "You're her son. Did she tell you she had dual citizenship—for both the US and Mexico? You can get citizenship in Mexico. Your DNA will prove that you're her son."

"I'd have to ask Pierre." Daren looked up at him, his eyes clear, filled with a maturity far greater than his years. "He won't say yes. He doesn't like the cities and he doesn't like Mexico even more."

Zipakna clenched his teeth, holding back the words that he wanted to use to describe Pierre. Lock the door, he thought. Just leave. Make Daren understand as they rolled on to the next settlement. "What happened to her?" he said softly, so softly.

"A border patrol shot her." Daren fixed his eyes on Bella, who was fussing and clucking in her cage. "A chopper. They were just flying over, shooting coyotes. They shot her and me."

She had a citizen chip. If they'd had their scanner on, they would have picked up the signal. He closed his eyes, his head filled with roaring. Yahoos out messing around, who was ever gonna check up? Who cared? When he opened his eyes, Daren was gone, the door whispering closed behind him.

What did any of it matter? He blinked dry eyes and went forward to make sure the thermosolar plant was powered up. It was. He released the brakes and pulled into a tight turn, heading southward out of town on the old, cracked asphalt of the dead road.

He picked up the radio chatter in the afternoon as he fed the hens and let the unfurled panels recharge the storage batteries. He always listened, had paid a lot of personal money for the top decryption chip every trek. He wanted to know who was talking out here and about what.

US border patrol. He listened with half an ear as he scraped droppings from the crate pans and dumped them into the recycler. He knew the acronyms, you mostly got US patrols out here. *Flower-town.* It came over in a sharp, tenor voice. He straightened, chicken shit spilling from the dustpan in his hand as he listened. Hard.

Paloma. What else could "Flower-town" be out here? They were going to hit it. Zipakna stared down at the scattered gray and white turds on the floor. Stiffly, slowly, he knelt and brushed them into the dustpan. This was the only outcome. He knew it. Ella knew it. They'd made the choice. *Not many of them meant to end up out there.* Her voice murmured in his ear, so damn earnest. *They had plans, they had a future in mind. It wasn't this one.*

"Shut up!" He bolted to his feet, flung the pan at the wall. "Why did you have his kid?" The pan hit the wall and shit scattered everywhere. The hens panicked, squawking and beating at the mesh of their crates. Zipakna dropped to his knees, heels of his hands digging into his eyes until red light webbed his vision.

Flower-town. It came in over the radio, thin and wispy now, like a ghost voice.

Zipakna stumbled to his feet, went forward and furled the solar panels. Powered up and did a tight one-eighty that made the hens squawk all over again.

The sun sank over the rim of the world, streaking the ochre ground with long, dark shadows that pointed like accusing fingers. He saw the smoke in the last glow of the day, mushrooming up in a black flag of doom. He switched the Dragon to infrared navigation, and the black and gray images popped up on the heads-up above the console. He was close. He slowed his speed, wiped sweating palms on his shirt. They'd have a perimeter alarm set and they'd pick him up any minute now. If they could claim he was attacking them, they'd blow him into dust in a heartbeat. He'd run into US government patrols out here before and they didn't like the Mexican presence one bit. But his movements were sat-recorded and recoverable and Mexico would love to accuse the US of firing on one of its charity missions in the world media. So he was safe. If he was careful. He slowed the Dragon even more although he wanted to race. Not that there would be much he could do.

He saw the flames first and the screen darkened as the nightvision program filtered the glare. The community building? More flames sprang to life in the sunflower fields.

Attention Mexican registry vehicle N45YG90. The crudely accented Spanish filled the Dragon. *You are entering an interdicted area. Police action is in progress and no entry is permitted.*

Zipakna activated his automatic reply. "I'm sorry. I will stop here. I have a faulty storage bank and I'm almost out of power. I won't be able to go any farther until I can use my panels in the morning." He sweated in the silence, the hens clucking softly in the rear.

Stay in your vehicle. The voice betrayed no emotion. *Any activity will be viewed as a hostile act. Understand?*

"Of course." Zipakna broke the connection. The air in the Dragon seemed syrupy thick, pressing against his eardrums. They could be scanning him, watching to make sure that he didn't leave the Dragon. All they needed was an excuse. He heard a flurry of sharp reports. Gunshots. He looked up at the screen, saw three quick flashes of light erupt from the building beyond the burning community center. No, they'd be looking there. Not here.

Numbly he stood and pulled his protective vest from its storage cubicle along with a pair of night goggles. He put the Dragon on standby. Just in case. If he didn't reactivate it in forty-eight hours, it would send a mayday back to headquarters. They'd come and collect the hens and the Dragon. He looked once around the small, dimly lit space of the Dragon, said a prayer to the old gods and touched the jade at his throat. Then he touched the door open, letting in a dry breath of desert that smelled of bitter smoke, and slipped out into the darkness.

He crouched, moving with the fits and starts of the desert coyotes, praying again to the old gods that the patrol wasn't really worrying about him. Enough clumps of mesquite survived here in this long ago wash to give him some visual cover from anyone looking in his direction and as he remembered, the wash curved north and east around the far end of the old town. It would take him close to the outermost buildings.

It seemed to take a hundred years to reach the tumbledown shack that marked the edge of the town. He slipped into its deeper shadow. A half moon had risen and his goggles made the landscape stand out in bright black and gray and white. The gunfire had stopped. He slipped from the shed to the fallen ruins of an old house, to the back of an empty storefront across from the community building. It was fully in flames now and his goggles damped the light as he peered cautiously from the glassless front window. Figures moved in the street, dressed in military coveralls. They had herded a dozen people together at the end of the street and Zipakna saw the squat, boxy shapes of two big military choppers beyond them.

They would not have a good future, would become permanent residents of a secure resettlement camp somewhere. He touched his goggles, his stomach lurching as he zoomed in on the bedraggled settlers. He recognized Sanja, didn't see either Ella or Daren, but he couldn't make out too many faces in the huddle. If the patrol had them, there was nothing he could do. They were searching the buildings on this side of the street. He saw helmeted figures cross the street, heading for the building next to his vantage point.

Zipakna slipped out the back door, made his way to the next building, leaned through the sagging window opening. "Daren? Ella? It's Zip," he said softly. "Anyone there?" Silence. He didn't dare raise his voice, moved on to the next building, his skin tight, expecting a shouted command. If they caught him interfering they'd arrest him. It might be a long time before Mexico got him freed. His bosses would be very unhappy with him.

"Ella?" He hurried, scrabbling low through fallen siding, tangles of old junk. They weren't here. The patrol must have made a clean sweep. He felt a brief, bitter stab of satisfaction that they had at least caught Pierre. One would deserve his fate, anyway.

Time to get back to the Dragon. As he turned, he saw two shadows slip into the building he had just checked—one tall, one child short. Hope leaped in his chest, nearly choking him. He bent low and sprinted, trying to gauge the time . . . how long before the patrol soldiers got to this building? He reached a side window, its frame buckled. As he did, a slight figure scrambled over the broken sill and even in the black and white of nightvision, Zipakna recognized Daren's fair hair.

The old gods had heard him. He grabbed the boy, hand going over his mouth in time to stifle his cry. "It's me. Zip. Be silent," he hissed.

Light flared in the building Daren had just left. Zipakna's goggles filtered it and crouching in the dark, clutching Daren, he saw Pierre stand up straight, hands going into the air. "All right, I give up. You got me." Two uniformed patrol pointed stunners at Pierre.

Daren's whimper was almost but not quite soundless. "Don't move," Zipakna breathed. If they hadn't seen Daren . . .

"You're the one who brought the seeds." The taller of the two lowered his stunner and pulled an automatic from a black holster on his hip. "We got an ID on you."

A gun? Zipakna stared at it as it rose in seeming slow motion, the muzzle tracking upward to Pierre's stunned face. Daren lunged in his grip and he yanked the boy down and back, hurling him to the ground. The stunner seemed to have leaped from his pocket to his hand and the tiny dart hit the man with the gun smack in the center of his chest. A projectile vest didn't stop a stunner charge. The man's arms spasmed outward and the ugly automatic went sailing, clattering to the floor. Pierre dived for the window as the other patrol yanked out his own weapon and pointed it at Zipakna. He fired a second stun charge but as he did, something slammed into his shoulder and threw him backward. Distantly he heard a loud noise, then Daren was trying to drag him to his feet.

"Let's go." Pierre yanked him upright.

"This way." Zipakna pointed to the distant bulk of the Dragon.

They ran. His left side was numb but there was no time to think about that. Daren and Pierre didn't have goggles so they ran behind him. He took them through the mesquite, ignoring the thorn slash, praying that the patrol focused on the building first before they started scanning the desert. His back twitched with the expectation of a bullet.

The Dragon opened to him and he herded them in, gasping for breath now, the numbness draining away, leaving slow, spreading pain in its wake. "In here." He touched the hidden panel and it opened, revealing the coffin-shaped space beneath the floor. The Dragon was defended, but this was always the backup. Not even a scan could pick up someone hidden here. "You'll have to both fit. There's air." They managed it, Pierre clasping Daren close, the boy's face buried against his shoulder. Pierre looked up as the panel slid closed. "Thanks." The panel clicked into place.

Zipakna stripped off his protective vest. Blood soaked his shirt. They were using piercers. That really bothered him, but fortunately the vest had slowed the bullet enough. He slapped a blood-stop patch onto the injury, waves of pain washing through his head, making him dizzy. Did a stimtab from the med closet and instantly straightened, pain and dizziness blasted away by the drug. Didn't dare hide the bloody shirt, so he pulled a loose woven shirt over his head. *Visitor*, the Dragon announced. *US Security ID verified.*

"Open." Zipakna leaned a hip against the console, aware of the heads-up that still showed the town. The building had collapsed into a pile of glowing embers and dark figures darted through the shadows. "Come in." He said it in English with a careful US accent. "You're really having quite a night over there." He stood back as two uniformed patrol burst into the Dragon while a third watched warily from the doorway. All carrying stunners.

Not guns, so maybe, just maybe, they hadn't been spotted.

"What are you up to?" The patrol in charge, a woman, stared at him coldly through the helmet shield. "Did you leave this vehicle or let anyone in?"

The gods had come through. Maybe. "Goodness, no." He arched his eyebrows. "I'm not that crazy. I'm still stunned that Paloma went to raising pharm." He didn't have to fake the bitterness. "That's why you're burning the fields, right? They're a good bunch of people. I didn't think they'd ever give in to that."

Maybe she heard the truth in his words, but for whatever reason, the leader relaxed a hair. "Mind if we look around?" It wasn't a question and he shrugged, stifling a wince at the pain that made it through the stimulant buzz.

"Sure. Don't scare the hens, okay?"

The two inside the Dragon searched, quickly and thoroughly. They checked to see if he had been recording video and Zipakna said thanks to the old gods that he hadn't activated it. That would have changed things, he was willing to bet.

"You need help with your battery problem?" The cold faced woman—a lieutenant, he noticed her insignia—asked him.

He shook his head. "I'm getting by fine as long as I don't travel at night. They store enough for life support."

"I'd get out of here as soon as the sun is up." She jerked her head at the other two. "Any time you got illegal flowers you get raiders. You don't want to mess with them."

"Yes, ma'am." He ducked his head. "I sure will do that." He didn't move as they left, waited a half hour longer just to be sure that they didn't pop back in. But they did not. Apparently they believed his story, hadn't seen their wild dash through the mesquite. He set the perimeter alert to maximum and opened the secret panel. Daren scrambled out first, his face pale enough that his freckles stood out like bits of copper on his skin.

Her freckles.

Zipakna sat down fast. When the stim ran out, you crashed hard. The room tilted, steadied.

"That guy shot you." Daren's eyes seemed to be all pupil. "Are you going to die?"

"You got medical stuff?" Pierre's face swam into view. "Tell me quick, okay?"

"The cupboard to the left of the console." The words came out thick. Daren was staring at his chest. Zipakna looked down. Red was soaking into the ivory weave of the shirt he'd put on. So much for the blood-stop. The bullet must have gone deeper than he thought, or had hit a small artery. Good thing his boarders hadn't stuck around longer.

Pierre had the med kit. Zipakna started to pull the shirt off over his head and the pain hit him like a lightning strike, sheeting his vision with white. He saw the pale green arch of the ceiling, thought, *I'm falling* . . .

He woke in his bed, groping drowsily for where he was headed and what he had drunk that made his head hurt this bad. Blinked as a face swam into view. Daren. He pushed himself up to a sitting position, his head splitting.

"You passed out." Daren's eyes were opaque. "Pierre took the bullet out of your shoulder while you were out. You bled a lot but he said you won't die."

"Where's Pierre?" He swung his legs over the side of the narrow bed, fighting dizziness. "How long have I been out?"

"Not very long." Daren backed away. "The chickens are okay. I looked."

"Thanks." Zipakna made it to his feet, steadied himself with a hand on the wall. A quick check of the console said that Pierre hadn't messed with anything. It was light out. Early morning. He set the video to sweep, scanned the landscape. No choppers, no trace of last night's raiders. He watched the images pan across the heads-up; blackened fields, the smoldering pile of embers and twisted plumbing that had been the community center, still wisping smoke. The fire had spread to a couple of derelict buildings to the windward of the old store. Movement snagged his eye. Pierre. Digging. He slapped the control, shut off the vid. Daren was back with the chickens. "Stay here, okay? I'm afraid to leave them alone."

"Okay." Daren's voice came to him, hollow as an empty eggshell.

He stepped out into the oven heat, his head throbbing in time to his footsteps as he crossed the sunbaked ground to the empty bones of Paloma. A red bandana had snagged on a mesquite branch, flapping in the morning's hot wind. He saw a woman's sandal lying on the dusty asphalt of the main street, a faded red backpack. He picked it up, looked inside. Empty. He dropped it, crossed the street, angling northward to where he had seen Pierre digging.

He had just about finished two graves. A man lay beside one. The blood that soaked his chest had turned dark in the morning heat. Zipakna recognized his grizzled red beard and thinning hair, couldn't remember his name. He didn't eat any of the special eggs, just the ones against whatever new bug was out there. Pierre climbed out of the shallow grave.

"You shouldn't be walking around." He pushed dirty hair out of his eyes.

Without a word, Zipakna moved to the man's ankles. Pierre shrugged, took the man's shoulders. He was stiff, his flesh plastic and too cold, never mind the morning heat. Without a word they lifted and swung together, lowered him into the fresh grave. It probably wouldn't keep the coyotes out, Zipakna thought. But it would slow them down. He straightened, stepped over to the other grave.

Ella. Her face looked sad, eyes closed. He didn't see any blood, wondered if she had simply suffered a heart attack, if she had had enough as everything she had worked to keep intact burned around her. "Did Daren see her die?" He said it softly. Felt rather than saw Pierre's flinch.

"I don't know. I don't think so." He stuck the shovel into the piled rocks and dirt, tossed the first shovel full into the hole.

Zipakna said the right words in rhythm to the grating thrust of the shovel. First the Catholic prayer his mother would have wanted him to say, then the words for the old gods. Then a small, hard prayer for the new gods who had no language except dust and thirst and the ebb and flow of world politics that swept human beings from the chessboard of the earth like pawns.

"You could have let them shoot me." Pierre tossed a last shovelful of dirt onto Ella's grave. "Why didn't you?"

Zipakna tilted his gaze to the hard blue sky. "Daren." Three tiny black specks hung overhead. Vultures. Death called them. "I'll make you a trade. I'll capitalize you to set up as a trader out here. You leave the pharm crops alone. I take Daren with me and get him Mexican citizenship. Give him a future better than yours."

"You can't." Pierre's voice was low and bitter. "I tried. Even though his mother was a US citizen, they're not taking in offspring born out here. Mexico has a fifteen year waiting list for new immigrants." He was staring down at the mounded rock and dust of Ella's grave. "She was so angry when she got pregnant. The implant was faulty, I guess. She meant to go back to the city before he was born but . . . I got hurt. And she stuck around." He was silent for a while. "Then it was too late, Daren was born and the US had closed the border. We're officially out here because we want to be." His lips twisted.

"Why did you come out here?"

He looked up. Blinked. "My parents lived out here. They were the rugged individual types, I guess." He shrugged. "I went into the city, got a job, and they were still letting people come and go then. I didn't like it, all the people, all the restrictions. So I came back out here." He gave a thin laugh. "I was a trader to start with. I got hit by a bunch of raiders. That's when . . . I got hurt. Badly. I'm sorry." He turned away. "I wish you could get him citizenship. He didn't choose this."

"I can." Zipakna watched Pierre halt without turning. "She . . . was my wife. We married in Oaxaca." The words were so damn hard to say. "That gave her automatic dual citizenship. In Mexico, only the mother's DNA is required as proof of citizenship. We're pragmatists," he said bitterly.

For a time, Pierre said nothing. Finally he turned, his face as empty as the landscape. "You're the one." He looked past Zipakna, toward the Dragon. "I don't like you, you know. But I think . . . you'll be a good father for Daren. Better than I've been." He looked down at the dirty steel of the shovel blade. "It's a deal. A trade. I'll sell you my kid. Because it's a good deal for him." He walked past Zipakna toward the Dragon, tossed the shovel into the narrow strip of shade along one of the remaining buildings. The clang and rattle as it hit sounded loud as mountain thunder in the quiet of the windless heat.

Zipakna followed slowly, his shoulder hurting. Ilena would be pissed, would never believe that Daren wasn't his. His mouth crooked with the irony of that. The old gods twisted time and lives into the intricate knots of the universe and you could meet yourself coming around any corner. As the Dragon's doorway opened with a breath of cool air, he heard Pierre's voice from the chicken room, low and intense against the cluck and chortle of the hens, heard Daren's answer, heard the brightness in it.

Zipakna went forward to the console to ready the Dragon for travel. As soon as they reached the serviced lands again he'd transfer his savings to a cash card for Pierre. Pierre could buy what he needed on the Pima's land. They didn't care if you were a Drylander or not.

Ilena would be doubly pissed. But he was a good poker partner and she wouldn't dump him. And she'd like Daren. Once she got past her jealousy.

Ilena had always wanted a kid, just never wanted to take the time to *have* one.

He wondered if she had meant to contact him, tell him about Daren, bring the boy back to Mexico. She would have known, surely, that it would have been all right.

Surely. He sighed and furled the solar wings.

Maybe he would keep coming out here. If Daren wanted to. Maybe her ghost would find them as they traveled through this place she had loved. And then he could ask her.

~

Mary Rosenblum's (www.newwritersinterface.com) first story came out in 1990 and her first novel, *The Drylands*, which won the Compton Crook Award for Best First Novel, in 1993. Her career began in, and has now largely returned to, science fiction, but from 1999 to 2002, she wrote the Gardening Mysteries novel series under the name "Mary Freeman." The author of more than sixty works of short fiction, Rosenblum won the Sidewise Award for Alternate History Short Form for her story "Sacrifice" in 2009. An accomplished cheesemaker who teaches the craft at selected workshops, Rosenblum earned her pilot's license at age fifty-seven. She lives in Oregon.

~

The End has come, but for someone like Simon Thomas St. Martinborough it takes a bit to realize what role the over-privileged and entitled type should play in the new world order.

• CHISLEHURST MESSIAH •
Lauren Beukes

It wasn't the blood seas that got to him. Or the dead birds that fell out of the sky and rotted on the lawn in crumpled bundles of feathers. Or the plague of flying ants crusting themselves up against the windowpanes. Or even Marlowe dying in agony as her organs liquidized inside her and gushed out all over the carpet so Simon had to rip the damn thing out. You'd be surprised how much the smell of spleen will permeate a room. Especially when you can't open the windows because of the ants.

That was all Very Upsetting, make no mistake. Even though he had been about to divorce the silly bitch and nail her for half her estate and the account in Jersey that she thought he didn't know about. And even though her death was messy and ugly and awkward—embarrassed, he'd left her to it, going into the den to play that jewel-swapping game on Facebook while she screamed and writhed and spat up black strings of blood—frankly, her dying saved him a lot of time and effort because the dumb cunt hadn't changed her will yet. Easier to inherit than squeeze a decent alimony out of a shit-hot investment banker with a shit-hot investment banker's lawyer.

Not that all that cash was any use to him at the moment. That was the supreme fucker of it. The banks were locked up. The bankers were either dead or hiding out in holiday houses in Spain and France, fortified in a hurry, private security guards patrolling the perimeters with automatic weapons. At least, that's what he'd seen on the news before the news cut out.

He missed television. He missed the stock ticker running along the bottom of the business report. Missed the explosions in dusty Third World deserts and the Women Who Kill and plastic surgery reality shows and especially the scruffy animals being rescued from nasty abusive owners by trained task teams of dedicated volunteers. He felt a bit like one of those pathetically mangy pets himself, trapped in Marlowe's Chislehurst block of flats all alone, with nothing to eat except cans of foie gras and baked beans. (Marlowe had thrown out anything with "organic" on the label back in the early days when rumors about terrorists targeting the food markets was still the prevailing theory.)

And surely it'd be Only A Matter of Time before the government restored order and his satellite TV and sent an elite unit, CO19 maybe, to the rescue? He just needed to outlast the hoodie scum running rampant in the streets.

At least the building still had electricity. After last year's riots, the body corporate had passed a motion to install generators in the building. (Couldn't have warm Stoli!) Simon reckoned there was at least a few weeks' worth of diesel stashed in the basement.

So far he hadn't had to leave home for supplies. He went shopping in the neighboring apartments, with a handkerchief doused in Issey Miyake pressed over his mouth and nose to try to obscure the smell. The bodies left him strangely unmoved. It was all very abstract, like some grotesque modern art exhibition, all black puddled insides and swarms of flies that lifted off the bloated gray corpses in a halo when he stepped into the room.

He was much more interested in snooping around, reaffirming the suspicions he'd long fostered about their friends and neighbors. The Pepoys, for example, had a lifetime supply of prescription uppers in their medicine cabinet, which would explain the delirious cheer Alice had brought to dinner parties. He'd never liked her or her over-eager speculative conversation starters: "If you could go to anywhere on holiday where would it be?" Right where I've just been, you stupid bint. That's the whole point of marrying into money. The only pick-me-up Alice Pepoys needed now was a spatula, he thought, grinning spitefully.

He cleaned out her stash of pharmaceuticals just in case. He didn't mind feeling a bit sorry for himself with Everything He'd Been Through, but he didn't want to get stuck in wallowing self-pity. Especially if CO19 got delayed.

The Bennetts were even more pathetic. Four of the five bedrooms were lavishly appointed straight from a bespoke decorator's catalogue: pinstripe walls and inoffensive abstract prints. The fifth was kitted out with a king size bed with a black rubber sheet and a closet containing a parking attendant's outfit and a camera rigged in the mirrored door.

He took the tapes home with him, along with four tins of sardines, sun-dried heritage tomatoes imported from Italy, water biscuits, a loaf of rye bread, frozen and, an even dirtier secret than the half-hearted sex dungeon: three months' worth of Sainsbury's microwave meals.

On the way back, he thought he heard a baby screaming from the house a block over. But cats fighting make almost exactly the same noise. And he wasn't going to risk his life for a bloody cat. It wasn't that he was a man of no conscience. He'd seen that heart-breaking documentary on the pets left behind after 9/11. It had reduced even that cold bitch Marlowe to a sobbing, snotty bundle tucked under his arm on the couch. Even worse than that dolphin movie. He'd be sure to tell CO19 about poor little kitty when they got here, and they could sort it out.

The Bennetts' sex videos were tedious. He'd seen way better on the Internet. Which was the only thing still running. All the major networks were down. No TV. No radio. No mobile phone reception. He'd picked up some radio chatter in the beginning; government broadcasts advising people to stay in their homes: pip, pip, keep calm and carry on, which segued into increasingly panicky emergency services reports asking people to report to local medical centers as soon as possible. Then it petered off into static. Occasionally, bizarrely, he'd pick up heavy metal music, as if some radio engineer had walked out and left *Shouty Goth Freaks Greatest Hits Volume 13* playing at full blast.

And yet, somehow, by some mechanism he didn't understand, probably learned from dodgy Arab protestors, the Internet was still working. And the bloody chavs were in control of it.

He's been glued to Marlowe's laptop, trawling YouTube, his only link to the outside world. He spent hours bouncing from clip to clip, compulsively shoving cashew nuts into his mouth. If the footage was anything to go by, the looting was still in full swing.

Occasionally he heard the roar of engine noise in the distance, which inspired him to keep the curtains closed at night. But Marlowe's neighbors weren't the type who coveted designer trainers and iPods and the other shit the kids on the clips were still going after. And anyway, why would they bother with the suburbs when the little scum had the whole city as their playground?

He spent the next couple of days mainlining Colombian coffee and Ardbeg and popping Alice Pepoys' uppers and a course of expired antibiotics, because he'd seen enough zombie movies to know that the only thing worse than rampaging hordes of dead-eyed creatures is dying of something embarrassing like an infected toenail (And he *had* stubbed his toe on the doorframe, when he dragged Marlowe's corpse, wrapped in twelve layers of garbage bags, out onto the front lawn where it wouldn't be so very much in the way, no doubt exposing himself to all kinds of horrible bacteria in the process.)

Mostly he stayed in bed, the laptop balanced on his stomach, which was admittedly a little more padded than normal. He needed to get to the gym; his abs were turning into jelly. Too much stale bruschetta and salty snack foods. But the one in the building's basement stank like an abattoir and the Stairmaster was practically alive with maggots.

He scrolled through the comments sections of the videos. "The yoof shall inherit the earth" was the most common slogan, outnumbering the diehard spam streams ten to one. He clicked on a link titled "Chelsea Deth Rap," spooning duck pâté into his mouth with his fingers while he waited for it load.

A grainy image of a teenaged moron cruising along in a black BMW SUV, arm lolling out the window, miming along to out-of-sync lyrics, mediocre bass tinny in the background. The yoof shall inherit the earth, all right. Pity they can't fucking rhyme. Or spell, Simon thought, checking out the mangled language superimposed on the screen: "When the birds is dieng/the peoples is crying/when the rich are fuked/they ain't got no luck/ our time is here/yeah, our time is here/is right fukin now."

Christ.

He clicked the link to another one, ("apacolypse now innit"), the Gherkin burning in the background, a kid wearing a balaclava dancing in front of it, a Sprite bottle filled with what had to be petrol in one raised hand. Simon couldn't hear what the kid was shouting at the camera or iPhone or whatever; the sound of exploding glass and screaming smothered his voice.

Another clip showed a group of kids roaring through Harvey Nichols on dirt bikes, casually swiping perfume and make-up displays off the shelves with golf clubs. Marlowe had practically lived at Harvey Nicks. Her closets heaved with Vivienne Westwood corsets that were decades too young for her.

The only survivors seemed to be the kind of kids you saw shambling around the sink estates. Hollow-eyed yobs with acne-faced girlfriends cluttering up the pavements with pushchairs and streaming-nosed toddlers. "Underprivileged," my arse, Simon thought, bitterly. Not exactly starving African children. Living off benefits, leeches on society. Breeding like cockroaches and sucking the life out of the country. Human scum, the lot of them. Taking the piss.

Parasites like them were the reason he voted Conservative. That and tax cuts.

He did find some diversity, hidden deep in the results pages: a young Nigerian or Somali girl or something (who can tell, honestly?) with a shaved head and metal shit in her face, demonstrating first aid techniques and basic water filtration in a series of clips. In another video, a gloating young Eastern European lunatic with a husky voice and a pony-tail and a grease-stained T-shirt, sitting in his basement, ranting into his webcam in a *hilarious* accent about "viral Ragnarok" and "zis is vot happens ven you don't vaccinate your children."

Simon realized that he hadn't seen a single person over thirty on any of the recent clips. He hoped this was because people his age couldn't be arsed. But he was beginning to doubt it.

Feverishly, he clicked on clip after clip, desperate to find someone—anyone—who looked like his sort of person. His age. His type. Nothing. And that's when he had The Epiphany.

CO19 were never coming.

He, Simon Thomas St. Martinborough, was the last of his kind.

He half-skidded, half-ran to the full-length mirror in the walk-in-closet, taking a moment to admire himself before searching out the truth in his reflection. You'd never say he was thirty-eight. (A wannabe silver fox, Marlowe had called him. At twenty-three years his senior, she could fucking talk.) His scruffy beard was peppered with silver. His hair was dirty and sticking up in places. But his skin glowed with oily pink health and his eyes were wild, full of intensity and fire. He looked like a man who had survived a Terrible Thing. He looked Enlightened. He looked, in short, like The Chosen One.

His reverie was interrupted by roaring engines. Aston Martins, if he was any judge of fine luxury motor vehicles (and he was). He quickly reached for the light to turn it off. No point letting them know he was here. He poured the last slug of whisky into his glass and sat waiting in the dark for the damn yoof to fuck right off. Which is when they lobbed the Molotov through the downstairs window into the study, where it just so happened he'd been storing all the liquor he'd rescued from the neighboring apartments. It went down, or rather up, like a bomb.

The house filled with churning clouds of hot black smoke faster than he could have imagined was possible. He grabbed the closet thing to hand—one of Marlowe's trendy terrorist-chic scarves that had been all the rage several years back—and wrapped it round his face and scrambled for the exit.

He launched himself down the stairs, hearing the crack and pop as the glass buckled in the study, feeling the white heat against his skin. He almost got lost in the hallway, disoriented by the smoke and, yes, all right, the whisky too. But all the way through the dreadful choking gauntlet he felt himself buoyed by a sense of invincibility. And yes, even a kind of inner peace.

He fell out the front door, gasping great big lungfuls of the cool night air (mixed in with the sweet stench of Marlowe on the grass half a foot away) and turned to see her two-million-quid love nest alive with flames. He felt a surge of exhilaration. He was alive. He was It. The Guy. Untouchable! And watching the flat spewing great gobs of greasy smoke out of its faux-Tudor windows, Simon had his second epiphany of the day. There was a Master Plan at work. A Grand Design. Simon had a destiny to fulfill.

Eyes gritty from smoke and lack of sleep, he wandered out into the morning, making for the high street, passing a dead horse from the nearby riding stables lying in the center of the road, its skin undulating with maggots.

Obviously, it was intended for him to walk. He'd smashed the window of every luxury car for three blocks (the Messiah—yes, Messiah—couldn't be expected to show up driving a Toyota) but not a single one had the keys in it. He wondered if Miss Nigeria's instructional YouTube videos included how-to-hot-wire-a-car. Too late now. The laptop was long gone, together with his previous life. Besides, the roads were clogged with burned-out buses and overturned cars.

He couldn't believe Chislehurst High Street was the same place. The storefront windows were jagged dark holes; the delicatessen's doorway was blocked by fallen debris; the Waitrose a burnt-out, stinking shell. An Audi R8 had rammed through the estate agent's window; he could make out the shadowy figure of the driver crumpled over the wheel. And everywhere, bodies inflated with rot.

He crunched over the desiccated corpses of a flock of swallows smeared across the road. A designer dog—some kind of Chihuahua—covered in sores and burrs, trotted after him for a while, but he shooed it away. He felt for it, of course, but he had More Important Things to do right now. The future of England depended on him.

The people needed him. He could show them how to put society back together again. He would explain why looting was wrong, why a good university education mattered and why having too many children too young was short-sighted and wholly untenable. (Although he realized that they would probably need to start in on repopulating the planet fairly soon and his seed would be an absolute requirement. He'd already resigned himself to having sex with only the most beautiful and promising young chav girls, with their big hair and over-abundance of make-up and their Juicy velour-tracksuited bottoms.)

He headed towards Orpington, then Mottingham—he remembered seeing the high street on one of the clips, and it looked fairly intact. The kids would be tired of looting and rampaging by now. They'd want someone to tell them what to do. Too many years living in a nanny state would mean that eventually they'd welcome a forward-thinking leader to Show Them The Way.

It took him most of the day to make it into Mottingham. He'd had to wrap his shirt around his mouth to block out the stink of burning plastic and putrefying bodies that filled the air in the Bromley town center. He'd almost made it past the smoldering wreck of Marks & Spencer when he heard the grumble of an engine and the squeal of tires. He whirled around in time to see a motorbike—a Ducati for fuck's sake—roaring towards him. He ran into the center of the street, almost tripping over the seeping body of a policeman in riot gear, and waved his arms over his head. The bike screamed straight past him, its riders turning back briefly. Then he heard the crash of splintering glass. He ducked instinctively, nostrils filled with the reek of petrol, heat crisping the hairs on his arms. Bastard had chucked a petrol bomb at him. But at least he knew he was getting closer. This was it. He gobbled another fistful of Alice Pepoy's pills, just to take the edge off.

He followed the sound of drum 'n' bass through a labyrinth of council houses and narrow alleyways, weirdly free of rubbish. Then he saw the first one: A black kid wearing an ill-fitting Armani suit and smoking a cigar, leaning up against the bonnet of a black BMW parked at an angle and blocking the street. Simon heard the sound of children's laughter. Smelled the delicious odor of some kind of roasting meat. He could hear music pumping out of the nearby houses. It looked like business as usual. He felt his heart soar. Soon he would take his Rightful Place.

"What do you want, man?" the kid said. Behind him, a group of kids emerged from the houses. Some had children slung casually on their hips. Simon felt heat spread through his stomach like a good single malt. His people. His heart went out to them. He thought about how they would look back on this moment, tell the story over and over again. All part of his legend. The Coming of Simon.

A plump girl wearing a white miniskirt in defiance of the cold stepped up next to the black kid. Her arms dripped with gold jewelry, her blue-white legs were mottled with cellulite. She had a really big gun, drooping casually from her fingers with their luminous orange nail polish. Simon kept up his beatific smile. He should have expected a little resistance. Change is hard.

The girl with the firearm spoke first. "What's 'e want, then?"

"Dunno. Ask him," the black kid said.

"I'm here to save you," Simon said. No one was returning his smile.

"Yeah?" The girl looked unimpressed. A spike of doubt pierced Simon's happy glow. He wasn't used to feeling out of his depth. He remembered how he'd hooked up with Marlowe. How he'd read the situation the second he saw her. Knew what she needed. It was almost a sixth sense. A skill. And he knew what these kids needed. Someone to Bring Them Out of Darkness. They just didn't know it yet. He should probably keep it simple.

"I know this is going to be hard for you to understand. But I need you to trust me. I'm the Messiah."

The black kid rolled his eyes.

"Right." The girl said. Then she raised the gun at his heart.

"No, really," Simon stammered. "I can help. I'm—"

He didn't get to finish the sentence. A bright ball of light exploded in his head. He couldn't breathe. It felt like a bloody great rhinoceros had ploughed into his chest. He suddenly felt very heavy and woozy, perversely all at the same time. His knees folded up under him like one of those balloon men outside cheap car dealerships.

The girl looked down at him blankly. "Had quite enough of you lot," she said and turned on her heel, dismissing him. The black kid shook his head. He looked a bit sad. Then he dropped the cigar and walked away after her. The kids in the houses followed suit, vanishing back through the doorways like ghosts. Nothing to see here.

These were the last things Simon St. Martinborough, Messiah, thought before he died. First: *This isn't right.* And, then, as the smoke from the still smoldering Hamlet cigar got up his nose: *Stupid fucking chavs. Couldn't even loot a decent brand.*

Lauren Beukes is a South African author, comics writer, scriptwriter, documentary filmmaker, and former journalist. She is the author of novels *Moxyland*, *Zoo City*, and, most recently, *The Shining Girls*. *Zoo City* won the 2011 Arthur C. Clarke Award. She also authored *Fairest: The Hidden Kingdom*, a six-part series for Vertigo. Beukes has written extensively for TV and is currently writing the *Zoo City* screenplay for producer Helena Spring.

Paul Park tells his story of an Iceland after the End in the (quite appropriate) form of an ancient verse Edda in Anglo-Saxon style. The opening lines provide a brief scenario of the End as well as the lineage of its hero, Eirik the African.

· RAGNAROK ·
Paul Park

There was a man, Magnus's son,
Ragni his name. In Reykjavik
Stands his office, six stories,
Far from the harbor in the fat past.
Birds nest there, now abandoned.
The sea washes along Vesturgata,
As they called it.
                    In those days
Ragni's son, a rich man,
Also a scholar, skilled in law,
Thomas his name, took his wife
From famished Boston, far away.
Brave were her people, black-skinned,
Strong with spear, with shield courageous,
Long ago.
                    Lately now
The world has stopped. It waits and turns.
Fire leaps along the hill.
Before these troubles, Thomas took her,
    Black Naomi, belly big,
To Hvolsvollur where he had land,
A rich farm before the stream,
Safe and strong.

In the starving years,
There was born, Thomas's son,
Eirik the African, as they called him.
Hard his heart, heavy his hand
Against the wretches in the ruined towns,
Bandits and skraelings beyond the wall,
Come to plunder, kill and spoil,
Over and over.
Every night,
Thomas stands watch, wakeful and sure,
Guarding the hall with his Glock Nine.
Forty men, farmers by day,
Cod-fishermen from the cold coast,
Pledge to shelter, shield from harm
What each man loves, alone, together
Through the winter.
When spring thaws
The small boughs, buds unpack
From the red earth. Eirik passes
Into the fields. The fire weeds
Move around him, arctic blooms
And purple bells. Below the ricks,
He finds Johanna, Johan's daughter,
Guests at the farm.
At his father's house
He'd sometimes seen her, slim and fair,
Ripening too, a tall primrose.
He draws her down with dark hands,
Meaning no harm, but honor only.
Rich is her father, in Reykjavik,
Rich is her cousin, with cod boats
In Smoke Harbor.
Happy then,
Proud Naomi offers her hall
For the wedding feast, but she's refused
For no reason. Rather instead
Johanna chooses the little church
At Karsnes, close to home,

South of the city along the shore.
High-breasted,
                    Snake-hearted,
Sick with pride, she predicts
No trouble. Near that place,
In Keflavik airport, cruel Jacobus
Gathers his men, gap-toothed Roma,
Thieves and Poles, pock-marked and starving.
The skraeling king calls for silence
In the shattered hall.
                    Shards of glass,
Upturned cars, chunks of concrete
Make his throne. There he sits
With his hand high. "Hear me," he says
In the Roma language, learned from his father
In distant London. "Long we've fought
Against these killers. Ghosts of friends
Follow us here."
                    Far to the east,
Black Eirik, in the same hour,
Walks by the water in Hvolsvollur.
By the larch tree and the lambing pens,
Thomas finds him, takes his sleeve,
Brings his gift, the Glock Nine
With precious bullets, powder and brimstone
From his store.
                    Father and son
Talk together, until Naomi
Comes to find them. "Fools," she calls them.
(Though she loves them.) "Late last night
I lay awake. When do you go
To meet this woman, marry her
Beyond our wall? Why must you ride
To far Karsnes?"
                    Cruel Jacobus
Waits to answer, in Keflavik,
Hand upraised. "These rich men
Goad us to act. Am I the last

To mourn my brother, mourn his murder?
The reckless weakling, Thomas Ragnisson,
Shot him down, shattered his skull
Outside the wall
          In Hvolsvollur,
With his Glock Nine. Now I hear
About this wedding. His black son,
Scorning us, splits his strength,
Dares us to leave him alone in Karsnes
In the church. Christ Jesus
Punishes pride, pays them back
My brother's murder!"
          At that moment
Black Naomi bows her head,
Tries to agree. Eirik turns toward her,
Groping to comfort. "God will protect
The holy church. Hear me, Mother,
Jesus will keep us, Johanna and me."
Then he strips the semi-automatic
From its sheath.
          Some time later
Embracing her, he unbolts, unlocks
The steel door, draws its bars,
Rides north beneath the barrier,
Built of cinderblocks and barbed wire,
Twenty feet tall. With ten men
He takes the road toward Reykjavik,
West to Karsnes
          On the cold sea.
There the pastor prepares the feast,
Lights the lamp in the long dusk.
In the chapel porch, pacing and ready,
Eirik waits, wonders and waits.
Where's the bride, the wedding party?
Where's her father, fat Johan?
No one knows.
          Night comes.
Checking his watch, counting the hours,

Eirik frets. At first light
He rides north through the ruined towns,
Empty and burned, broken and looted.
Abandoned cars block his path.
The hill rises to Hallgrimskirkja
At the city's heart.
                    Here at the summit
Above the harbor, the high tower
Jabs the sky. Johan's hall,
Rich and secure, is silent now.
The dogs slink out the door,
Baring their teeth, biting at bones.
At Leif's statue we leave our horses,
Wait for something,
                    Sounds from the hall.
The concrete porch piles to heaven.
The door's wrenched open, all is still.
No one shouts, issues a challenge
As we approach. Eirik the African
Draws his pistol. The danger's past.
No one's left. We know for certain
On the threshold.
                    There inside
Lies Thorgeir Grimsson, throat cut.
We find the others, one by one
Among the benches in their marriage clothes.
The bleached wool, black with blood,
Polished stones, stained with it.
Windows broken, birds fly
In the tall vault.
                    Eirik, distraught,
Watches the birds wind above him,
Strives to find her, fair Johanna
Where she lies. Ladies and bridesmaids
Died in a heap, huddled together,
Peeled and butchered at the pillar's base.
She's not there; he searches farther
Up the aisle.

Underneath
The high altar, he uncovers
Fat Johan, father-in-law,
But for this. There's his body,
Leaked and maimed below the organ,
The wooden cross. Cruel Jacobus
Tortured and killed him, kidnapped his daughter
Twelve hours previous.
Proud Eirik
Turns to listen in the long light.
Out in the morning, his men call
Beyond the door. Desperate to leave
The stinking hall, holding his gun,
He finds them there. Fridmund, his friend,
Shows what they caught outside in the plaza,
A wretched skraeling
Skulking on Njalsgata,
A teen-aged boy, bald already
Back bent, black-toothed,
Hands outstretched. Stern and heavy,
Eirik stands over him, offering nothing
But the gun's mouth. Meanwhile the boy
Lowers his head, laughs at his anger,
Spits out blood.
"I expect you know
All that happened. Here it was
That King Jacobus carried the girl,
Stole her away, struggling and screaming,
Kicking and cursing when he kissed her.
Now he's punished, proud Johan,
Who took this church, chased us away,
Made it his hall.
Who among us
Steals such a thing, thieves though we are,
Jesus' house, Hallgrimskirkja?
Now you threaten me, though I'm helpless,
With your Glock Nine. Go on, shoot me.
Cunt-mouth, coward—I dare you.

Jesus loves me. Laughing, I tell you.
Fuck you forever."
                        Fridmund Bjarnsson
Pulls back his head, bares his throat.
But the African offers a judgment.
"Murder's too kind. Cut him loose.
Let him crawl to his king, Jacobus the Gypsy.
If he touches her, tell him I'll kill him.
Bring him this message . . . "
                        But the skraeling
Spits on his boots. "Say it yourself,"
The boy scolds. "Better from you.
Besides, you'll see him sooner than me
If you ride home to Hvolsvollur!"
Furious now, fearing the worst,
Eirik Thomasson turns from him,
Shouts for his horse,
                        A shaggy gelding,
Stout and faithful. Sturla's his name.
Climbing up, calling the others,
Eirik sets off, out of the plaza,
Down the hill. Dark are his thoughts
As he rides east, hurrying home
Under Hekla, the hooded mountain,
Steaming and boiling.
                        Sturla toils
Along the asphalt, eighty kilometers,
All that day. Dark is the sky
When Eirik and Sturla, outstripping the rest,
Reach the farm. The fire burns
Under the clouds. Clumps of ash
Fall around them. Furious and empty,
Eirik dismounts.
                        Without moving,
He stands a minute by Sturla's flank
And the split wall. Waiting, he listens
To the strife inside. Soon he unlimbers
The precious gun, the Glock Nine,

Checks the slide, checks the recoil,
Stacks the clip with steel bullets.
Gusts of rain
                    Gather around him.
Thunder crashes. Then he begins.
A storm out of nothing strikes the gate.
Men die among the horses,
Shot in the head with hollow-points,
Shot in the mouth for maximum damage.
They shake their spears, scythes and axes,
Swords and brands.
                    In the burning rooms,
Eirik kills them. By the cold stream,
The crumbling barns, he kills more.
Howling they turn in the hot cinders.
Clip empty, he cannot reload,
Seizes instead a skraeling axe.
They circle around him, certain of triumph,
Not for long.
                    Near the porch
Of his father's hall, he finds their leader,
Pawel the Bull, a Polack giant.
Stripped to the waist, he stands his ground.
Sword in hand, he swears and bellows.
Tattooed and painted, he paws the mud.
Now he charges, cuts and falters,
Falls to his knees,
                    Face split,
Lies full-length. Lightning strikes
On Hekla's side. Howling with rage,
The skraelings escape, scatter in darkness.
Come too late, we can't catch them,
Let them go. Gathering hoses,
We pump water, wet the timbers
In the rain.
                    Or we roam
Among the dead, drag them out
From the burned hall. Here they lie

On the wet ground, wives and children,
Old men. Naomi stands
Among the living, leans away,
Turns her face. Thomas is there,
Blood spilled,

          Body broken,
With the others. Eirik lays him
By the fire. Fridmund Bjarnsson
Finds the gun, the Glock Nine
Buried in mud, by the stream.
"Here," he says, holding it up.
"I was scared the skraelings took it.
Thank Jesus—"

          There by the fire,
Eirik rebukes him. "Bullshit," he says.
"Close your mouth." He climbs the porch,
Raises his hands. Red are the doorposts,
The frame behind him, hot with sparks.
"God," he repeats, "God be thanked.
You know Johan, for Jesus' sake,
Took for his house

          Hallgrimskirkja,
On the hill. He thought Jesus
Could sustain him, could preserve him,
Save his daughter—don't you see?
I also, Eirik the African,
Sank my faith in something empty—
Thomas's gun, the Glock Nine,
Chrome barreled,

          Bone grip.
But look now. Neither Jesus
Nor my Glock is good enough.
The rich hide behind their walls
In Hvolsvollur. Who comes to help?
But I will hike to Hekla's top,
Hurl my gun, heave it down
Into the steam,

          And the steel bullets

After it. In the afternoon
I'll wreck this wall, winch it apart.
Safety is good, grain in the fields,
Greenhouse vegetables; vengeance is better.
This I tell you: Time was,
We were happy, here in Iceland.
Cod in the sea,
                    Snow on the mountain,
Hot water in every house,
Cash in our pockets, planes and cars,
The world outside, waiting and close.
Old men remember, mumble and mutter—
That time's gone, turned forever.
The pools are drained, dams breached,
Turbines wrecked,
                    Ruined engines
Starved for oil. The sea rises
Beyond Selfoss. You have seen
Thousands die, tens of thousands—
The mind rebels, breaks or bends.
Days ahead, the dim past,
Forward, backward, both the same,
Wound together.
                    At the world's end,
Jormungand, the great worm,
Holds his tail between his jaws.
Ragnarok rages around us
Here, tonight, now, forever,
Or long ago. Good friends,
Remember it: men and skraelings
Fought together
                    Ages past.
So—tomorrow we'll march west
To Keflavik. Jacobus waits.
We'll scour the coast, search for fighters,
Heroes to help us, guide us home.
Left behind, you'll learn of us,
Tell our legend, teach the truth

Or invent it

       The old way.

Parse our lines upon the page:

Two beats, then pause.

Two more. Thumping heart,

Chopping axe, and again.

Not like the skraelings, with their long lines

Of clap-trap, closing rhymes—

Not for us.

       No more.

Johanna's alive. How I know,

I don't know. Don't ask.

But I swear I'll bring her here,

Avenge this." Then he's silent,

Standing near the spitting fire,

Under Hekla, in the rain.

Paul Park's first novel, *Soldiers of Paradise*, was published in 1987; his next two novels, *Sugar Rain* (1989) and *The Cult of Loving Kindness* (1991) share the same setting, a world on which the seasons last for generations. His most recent novels are a sequence set in a Ruritanian-flavored parallel world where magic works: *A Princess of Roumania* (2005), *The Tourmaline* (2006), *The White Tyger* (2007), and *The Hidden World* (2008). Park's short stories have appeared in *Omni, Interzone, The Magazine of Fantasy and Science Fiction,* and other venues. His short story "The Persistence of Memory, or This Space for Sale" was nominated for a World Fantasy Award and his novella *Ghosts Doing the Orange Dance* was nominated for a Nebula Award. He lives in Massachusetts with his wife and two children and teaches a course in reading and writing science fiction at Williams College.

Biowarfare brought plague and we bombed our own cities to contain it. The End came a decade ago, but automated planes still fly overhead— providing an unusual rhythm section to the only band left in the world.

· BEAT ME DADDY (EIGHT TO THE BAR) ·
Cory Doctorow

We were the Eight-Bar Band: there was me and my bugle; and Timson, whose piano had no top and got rained on from time to time; and Steve, the front-man and singer. And then there was blissed-out, autistic Hambone, our "percussionist" who whacked things together, more-or-less on the beat. Sometimes, it seemed like he was playing another song, but then he'd come back to the rhythm and *bam*, you'd realize that he'd been subtly keeping time all along, in the mess of clangs and crashes he'd been generating.

I think he may be a genius.

Why the Eight-Bar Band? Thank the military. Against all odds, they managed to build automated bombers that *still fly*, roaring overhead every minute or so, bomb-bay doors open, dry firing on our little band of survivors. The War had been over for ten years, but still, they flew.

So. The Eight-Bar Band. Everything had a rest every eight bars, punctuated by the white-noise roar of the most expensive rhythm section ever imagined by the military-industrial complex.

We were playing through "Basin Street Blues," arranged for bugle, half-piano, tin cans, vocals, and bombers. Steve, the front-man, was always after me to sing backup on this, crooning a call-and-response. I blew a bugle because I didn't *like* singing. Bugle's almost like singing, anyway, and I did the backup vocals *through* it, so when Steve sang, "Come along wi-ith me," I blew, "Wah wah wah wah-wah wah," which sounded dynamite. Steve hated it. Like most front-men, he had an ego that could swallow the battered planet, and didn't want any lip from the troops. That was us. The troops. Wah-wah.

The audience swayed in time with the music, high atop the pile of rubble we played on in the welcome cool of sunset, when the workday was through. They leaned against long poles, which made me think of gondoliers, except that our audience used their poles to pry apart the rubble that the bombers had created, looking for canned goods.

Steve handed Hambone a solo cue just as a bomber flew by overhead, which was his idea of a joke. He didn't like Hambone much. "Take it, Hambone!" he shouted, an instant before the roar began. It got a laugh. Hambone just grinned his blissed-out smile and went gonzo on the cans. The roar of the bomber faded, and he played on, and then settled into a kicky lick that set me on an expedition on the bugle, that left me blue in the face. Steve gave us dirty looks.

Then a stranger started dancing.

It was pretty shocking: not the dancing; people do that whenever they find some booze or solvents or whatever; it was the stranger. We didn't get a lot of strangers around there. Lyman and his self-styled "militia" took it upon themselves to keep wanderers out of our cluster of rubble. She was dirty, like all of us, but she had good teeth, and she wasn't so skinny you could count her ribs. Funny how that used to be sexy when food was plentiful.

And she could dance! Steve skipped a verse, and Timson looked up from the book he keeps on his music stand and gawped. I jammed in, and Hambone picked up on it, and Steve didn't throw a tantrum, just scatted along. She danced harder, and we didn't break for the next bomber, kept playing, even though we couldn't hear ourselves, and when we could, we were still in rhythm.

We crashed to an ending, and before the applause could start, we took off on "Diggin' My Potatoes," which Steve sang as dirty and lecherous as he could. We *hopped* and the stranger danced and the audience joined in and the set went twice as long as it normally would have, long after the sun set. Man!

Steve made a beeline for her after the set, while I put away the bugle and Timson tied a tarp down over his piano. Hambone kept banging on his cans, making an arrhythmic racket. He only did that when he was upset, so I helped him to his feet.

"C'mon, Ham," I said. "Let's get you home."

Hambone smiled, but to a trained Hambone-ologist like me, it was a worried grin. The stranger was staring at Hambone. Hambone was looking away. I led him to his cave, guiding him with one hand at the base of his skull, where he had a big knot of scar tissue—presumably, whatever had given him that lump had also made him into what he was. I made sure he went in, then went back, nervous. Hambone was a barometer for trouble, and when he got worried, I got worried, too.

The stranger had peeled Steve off of her, and was having an animated conversation with Timson. Uh-oh. That meant that she was a reader. It's all Timson ever talked about. He was a world-class bookworm. He'd moved into the basement of what was left of a bookstore-café, and was working his way through their stock. You never saw Timson without a book.

"Anemic Victorian girlybook—that's all that was," he was saying, when I caught up with him.

The stranger shoved his shoulder, playfully. Timson is a big one, and not many people are foolhardy enough to shove him, playfully or otherwise. "You've got to be kidding me! Are you some kind of *barbarian*? *Emma* is a classic, you bunghole!" My sainted mother would have said that she had a mouth on her like a truck driver. It turned me on.

"Hi!" I said.

Timson's retort was derailed as he turned to look at me. He said, "Brad, meet Jenna. Jenna, meet Brad."

I shook her hand. Under the dirt, she was one big freckle, and the torchlight threw up red highlights from her hair. Mmmm. Redheads. I had it bad.

"You blow good," the stranger—Jenna—said.

"Hell," Timson said, slapping me on the back hard enough to knock a whoosh of air out of my lungs. "Brad is the best trumpet player for a hundred klicks!" Jenna raised a dubious eyebrow.

"I'm the *only* trumpet player for a hundred klicks," I explained. Talking to a stranger was a novel experience: we got to recycle all the band jokes. She smiled.

I don't know where she slept that night. She was pretty good at taking care of herself—there weren't hardly any wanderers around anymore, and I'd never seen a solo woman. When I retired to my shack, I was pretty sure that she'd found herself shelter.

"This is how *all of you* survive?" she asked me the next day. I'd taken her out prospecting with me, going after a mountain of concrete rubble that had recently shifted after a baby quake. I had a good feeling about it.

"Yeah," I said, wedging my pole in and prying down hard. If you do it just right, you start a landslide that takes off a layer of the pile, revealing whatever's underneath. Do it wrong, you break your pole, give yourself a hernia, or bury yourself under a couple tons of rebar and cement. I'd seen a movie where people used the technique after some apocalypse or another. A plane went by overhead and stopped the conversation.

"But it's not bloody *sustainable*," she said. Her face was red with exertion, as she pried down hard.

I stopped prying and looked around pointedly. Mountains of rubble shimmered in the damp heat, dotting the landscape as far as the eye could see.

She followed my gaze around. "Okay, fine. You've got a good supply. But not everyone else does. Sooner or later, someone, somewhere, is going to run out. And then what? Turf wars? The last thing we need around here is another fucking war."

It wasn't the first time I'd heard that theory. Lyman and his buddies were particular proponents of it. They drilled half-ass military maneuvers in their spare time, waiting for the day when they'd get to heroically repel an invasion. I told her what I told them. "There's plenty of rubble to go around."

Another plane went by. She went back to her rock with renewed vigor and I went back to mine. After several moments of grunting and sweating, she said, "For this generation, maybe. What'll your kids eat?"

I leaned against my pole. "Who said anything about kids? I don't plan on having any."

She leaned against hers. Actually, it was my spare—two-and-a-half meters of one-inch steel gas-pipe—but I'd let her use it for the day. "So that's it for the human race, as far as you're concerned? The buck stops here?"

I got the feeling that she had this argument a lot. "Other people can do whatever they want. I'm not gonna be anyone's daddy."

Another plane passed. "That's pretty damned selfish," she said.

I rose to the bait. "It's selfish not to have kids I can't look after in a world that's gone to hell?"

"If you took an interest in the world, you could make it a livable place for your kids."

"Yeah, and if I wanted to have kids, I'd probably do that. But since I don't, I won't. QED."

"And if my grandma had wheels, she'd be a friggin' roller-skate. Come on, Brad. Live like a savage if you must, but let's at least keep the rhetoric civilized."

She sounded like Timson, then. I hate arguing with Timson. He always wins. I pushed against my pole and the chunk I'd been working on all morning finally shifted and an ominous rumbling began from up the hill. "Move!" I shouted.

We both ran downslope like nuts. That was my favorite part of any day, the rush of pounding down an uneven mountain face with tons of concrete chasing after me. I scrambled down and down, leaping over bigger obstacles, using all four limbs and my pole for balance. Jenna was right behind me, and then she was overtaking me, grinning hugely. We both whooped and dove into the lee of another mountain. The thunder of the landslide was temporarily drowned out by the roar of another plane.

I turned around quick, my chest heaving, and watched my work. The entire face of the mountain was coming down in stately march. Lots of telltale glints sparkled in the off-pour. Canned goods. Fossil junkfood from more complex times.

"Tell me that that's not *way* funner than gardening," I panted at Jenna.

She planted her hands on her thighs and panted.

I loved going out prospecting with other people. Some folks liked to play it safe, nicking away little chunks of a mountain. I liked to make a *big* mess. It's more dangerous, more cool, and more rewarding. I'm a big show-off.

I went back and started poking at the newly exposed stratum, popping cans into my sack. The people who'd lived in this city before it got plagued and dresdenned had been ready for a long siege, every apartment stuffed with supplies. I kept my eyes open for a six-pack of beer or a flask of booze, and I found both. The beer would be a little skunky after a decade of mummification, but not too bad. The tequila would be smooth as silk. I found it hard not to take a long swallow, but it was worth too much in trade for me to waste it on my liver.

Jenna joined me, scooping up the cans and stashing them in her pack. I didn't begrudge her the chow: there was more than I could carry home before the day was through in this load, and whatever I didn't take would get snapped up by some entrepreneur before morning. I wandered off, selecting the best of the stuff for my larder. I heard Jenna throwing up on the other side of the mountain. I scampered over to her.

It was what I'd expected: she'd turned up some corpses. Ten years of decomposition had cleaned them up somewhat, but they weren't pretty by any stretch. The plague bombs they dropped on this town had been full of nasty stuff. It killed fast, and left its victims twisted into agonized hieroglyphs. I turned, and pulled Jenna's hair out of the way of her puke.

"Thanks," she said, when she was done, five planes later. "Sorry, I can't get used to dead bodies, even after all this."

"Don't apologize," I said. "Plague victims are worse than your garden variety corpse."

"Plague victims! Damn!" she said, taking several involuntary steps backward. I caught her before she fell.

"Whoa! They're not contagious anymore. That plague stuff was short-lived. The idea was to kill everyone in the city, wait a couple months, then clean out the bodies and take up residence. No sense in destroying prime real estate."

"Then how did all this—" she waved at the rubble "—happen?"

"Oh, that was our side. After the city got plagued, they dresdenned the hell out of it so that the enemy wouldn't be able to use it." After the War, I'd hooked up for a while with a crazy guy who wouldn't tell me his name, who'd been in on all the dirty secrets of one army or another. From all he knew, he must've been in *deep*, but even after two years of wandering with him, I never found out much about him. He died a month before I found my current home. Lockjaw. Shitty way to go.

"They bombed their own fucking city?" she asked, incredulous. I was a little surprised that she managed to be shocked by the excesses of the War. Everyone else I knew had long grown used to the idea that the world had been trashed by some very reckless, immoral people. As if to make the point, another plane buzzed us.

"Well, everyone was already dead. It was their final solution: if they couldn't have it, no one else could. What's the harm in that?" I said. Whenever my nameless companion had spilled some dirty little secret, he'd finish it with *What's the harm in that?* and give a cynical chuckle. He was a scary guy.

She didn't get the joke.

"Come on," I said. "We gotta get this stuff back home."

That evening, the band played again. Our audience was bigger, maybe a hundred people. Steve liked a big crowd. He jumped around like bacon in a pan, and took us through all our up-tempo numbers: "South America, Take It Away," "All the Cats Join In," "Cold Beverages," "Atomic Dog," and more. The crowd loved it, they danced and stomped and clapped, keeping the rhythm for us during the long rests when the planes went by.

We played longer than usual. When we were done, I was soaked with sweat, my lips and cheeks were burning, and the sun had completely set. Some enterprising soul had built a bonfire. We used to do that all the time, back when booze was less scarce: build a big fire and party all night. Somewhere along the line, we'd stopped, falling into a sunup-to-sundown rhythm.

That night, though, I lay on my back beside the fire and watched the constellations whirl overhead. The planes counterpointed the soft crackling noises the fire made, and I felt better than I had in a long time.

The crowd had mostly gone home, but the band was still out, as were Lyman and his boys, and a few other die-hards. And Jenna. She'd led the dancing all night.

"That was *fun*," she said, hunkering down with me and Timson and Hambone. Steve was fondling one of his groupies, a skinny girl with bad teeth named Lucy. In my nastier moods, I called her "Loose." She was dumb enough not to get the joke.

Jenna passed Timson the canteen and he swigged deeply. "It sure was," he said. "We haven't been that tight in a while."

"You know, I've been all through the southland, but you guys are the only band I've seen. Everyone else is just scratching out a living. How'd you guys get together?"

"Hambone," I said. He was rappity-tappiting some firewood.

"*Hambone?*" she said. "I gotta hear this."

"I got here about seven years ago," I said, taking a pull from the canteen. "I'd been wandering around for a while, but for some reason, I thought I'd stay here for a while. Hambone was already here—near as anyone can tell, he's been here since the War. He managed to keep himself alive, just barely.

"I'd been here for a couple of weeks, and I'd spent most of that time building my house. I spent a lot of time hanging around out front of my place, blowing my horn, thinking. I didn't have any friends around here: I didn't want any. I just wanted to blow and watch the flies." I paused while a plane howled by.

"Then, one morning, I was blowing 'Reveille' and watching the sun come up, and I heard this crazy beat behind me. I looked around, and it was Hambone, sitting on top of the hill out back of my place, keeping time. I didn't know about him, then, so I figured he was just one of the locals. I waved at him, but he just kept on pounding, so I picked up my horn and we jammed and jammed.

"It became a regular morning gig. Once I ran out of steam, he'd get up and wander away. After a while, he was playing right on my doorstep, and I noticed how skinny he was. I tried to talk to him, and that's when I figured out he was *special*. So after we finished, I gave him a couple cans of Spam." A plane flew past.

"After a month of this, I decided I'd follow him when he left. He didn't seem to mind. We came to a ladder that led down into a big, bombed-out basement, all full of books. And this big asshole was playing a piano, just pounding on it."

I nodded at Timson, who picked up the tale. "It'd been tough to get the piano down there, but when I found it, I knew I needed to have it. I'd been going nuts, looking for a chance to play. Hambone had been coming by regular to jam around, and I tried to make sure he got fed. I figured he was shell-shocked and needed a hand. Then, one day, he shows up with this guy and his horn. Next thing you know, we're all playing our asses off. It was the most fun I'd ever had." He waited for a plane to pass, and built up the fire.

"The rest, as they say, is history," he continued. "Steve heard us jamming and invited himself along. He kept after us to play publicly."

Jenna looked over at Steve, who was lying on his back with Lucy twined around him. "Well, he can sing, anyway," she said, and grinned wickedly.

We all nodded.

"So," she said, stretching casually. "What are you guys gonna do when you run out of cans?"

I groaned. She'd been picking at the subject all day.

Timson poked at the fire, and Lyman sauntered over. He said, "Our supply will hold out a while yet," he said, "if we keep interlopers out." He loomed threateningly over her. Timson stood up and loomed back. Lyman retreated a little.

"How about gardens?" she said. "A decent garden could really stretch out your food supply."

"Who," I said, lazily, "is going to work on a garden when there's all this food just lying around?"

"I will, for one. Think about it: fresh vegetables! Fruit! When was the last time you had a tomato, a big fat red one?"

My mouth watered. Lyman said, "When we run out of cans, we'll just move along. Gardens'll only tie us down here." His boys all nodded, the way they did when he made a pronouncement.

Jenna glared at him. "That's pretty goddamn short-sighted. How long can you live off the past? When are you going to start living for the future?"

Lyman's rebuttal was cut off by another plane.

Timson slapped her on the back. "'When are you going to start living for the future?' You've practiced that, right?"

She pretended she didn't hear him. "How come the planes don't run out of fuel?" she said.

I said, "They've got an automated maintenance station somewhere around here. They land there for scheduled repairs and refueling. It's supposed to re-stock their ammo, too, but it looks like they've run out. Lucky for us."

Jenna's ears pricked up. "You know where this station is? They'd have power? Radios? Maybe we could call for help."

Everyone looked at her like she was nuts. "Where, exactly, are you going to call?" Timson asked.

"New Zealand. They didn't get into the War at all. They're probably sitting pretty. Maybe they could help us out."

"*On the Beach*, Neville Shute," Timson said. "You've been reading too much science fiction, girl."

She slapped his shoulder. "It was *The Chrysalids* actually. John Wyndham. Kiwis and Aussies *always* come out okay. Seriously," she continued, "what else are you doing around here? Aren't you getting bored of slipping back into savagery?"

"We've got plenty to do," Lyman called from across the fire. "We've got to drill the militia!"

"Band's gotta practice," Steve called, from under Lucy.

"Sure you do!" Jenna retorted. "If you're gonna play the Sydney Opera House, you're gonna need a whole *shitload* of practice!"

Steve glared at her, and Timson pounded her on the back. I produced my mickey of tequila and magnanimously shared it all around, even letting Lyman and his thugs have a swig.

She dropped in the next morning while I was blowing 'Reveille.' I hadn't had the energy the night before to take Hambone back to his cave, so he'd crashed on the floor of my shack. It's a pretty good shack: three of the walls are concrete, there from before the War. I'd put together a roof of tin and cardboard and whatever else I could find, and added another wall the same way. Be it ever so humble.

"You gonna help me dig a garden?" she asked.

I squinted at her. She'd gotten some water somewhere to clean up. Timson had a big reservoir in his basement, a flooded sub-basement. I had thought I'd seen them go off together.

Pink and scrubbed, with her hair tied back tight, she was, well, pneumatic. Sweat beaded on her forehead, and on her pink eyebrows. She was wearing a T-shirt and cutoffs, and the prospect of passing a day beside her while she bent over a garden was very tempting. But if she and Timson had something going on, I'd best put myself out of temptation's way. Besides, I was sure that the hill I'd been working on still had some good stuff in it.

"Got a full dance-card today, sorry," I said.

"Well, don't get caught under any rockslides," she said, giving me a slightly pissed-off look.

I spent the day undermining the mountain, but I couldn't get it to come down. Finally, exhausted, I staggered to the hill where we played and warmed up on the horn.

Jenna and Timson arrived together, eating olives and stewed tomatoes with their fingers. Timson set up an architecture book on his stand and tapped at the piano. Hambone ambled up. Steve showed up with Lucy clinging to him like a limpet, and then we played our asses off.

Jenna danced and so did lots of other people, and then Steve waded out into the crowd and danced with them, and I joined him, and then the crowd and the band were all mixed up, and it was *fine*.

It turned out I was wrong about Jenna and Timson. She used his water but that was it. He *was* feeding her, though. Now, he can do whatever he wants with his food, it's his, but the two of us had always fed Hambone, and Timson couldn't afford to feed both of them, so I ended up running my larder down to dangerous levels over the next couple months.

I started to get a little grumpy about it, but that all ended when Jenna and Timson showed up at Hambone's cave one night while I was feeding him. They had three big sacks, filled right to the top with fresh vegetables: tomatoes, string beans, squash, rutabaga, cabbage, and onions. There was even lemon grass, parsley, and basil. And strawberries! My eyes nearly fell out of my head.

"Holy crap!" I said.

Timson pounded me on the back, then popped a cherry tomato into my gaping mouth. I bit down involuntarily and gasped. "That is the best thing I've ever tasted," I said.

"Tell me something I don't know," Jenna said. "We've noticed you sulking around the last couple months. I figured that I could bribe you and you'd quit pissing around."

"Did you *grow these*?" I said.

"No, I pulled them out of my ass," Jenna said, and ate a big, fat strawberry.

Timson fed Hambone a few strawberries, and that signaled the beginning of a chowdown that went on and on until we could hardly move. My hands stank of a wondrous cocktail of strawberries and herbs and onions. It had been a long time since I'd put fresh vegetables inside my body. I felt like I was sweating *green*.

"Sun's going down," Timson said. "Showtime. I'll catch up."

Jenna and Hambone and I climbed slowly up the hill, luxuriating in satiety. Hambone's smile was a new one, pure joy.

Timson met up, lugging more sacks. He shelled them out before we started playing, and I never saw more snaggle-toothed grins. Even Steve had some. He made a crack about the wisdom of handing out fruit to an audience before a show, but no one was going to waste any of that beautiful food by throwing it.

Between sets, Timson stood up. "Jenna's been growing this food for the last couple months. I think you'll agree that it's pretty goddamn good." There were hoots of agreement. "So here's the deal. We've got some plots over on the south, ready to be hoed and planted. We've got seeds. But we need people to work the plots and gather water. Anyone who's interested can meet us tomorrow morning."

Well, that kind of put a damper on the celebration. I felt a little down, realizing that this wonderful chow meant stooping in fields, hoeing and planting like some kind of Dark Ages peasant. In the back of my mind, I still thought that I could just keep on prospecting for cans until someone rebuilt civilization and started making more cans. Rebuilding civilization was going to take a long, long time. Then I burped up an onion-basil-tomato-tasting burp, and knew that I'd be out the next morning, anyway.

We kept on playing, and people kept dancing, and I may have been the only one who noticed Lyman and his boys shaking their heads and stalking off into the night.

Nearly everyone showed up the next morning and collected a precious handful of Jenna's seeds. She explained that she'd been hoarding them for years, looking for a place to plant them. The way she said it, you got the feeling that she was trusting you with her children.

We attacked the plots. They were rocky and rubble-strewn, and the poles were poorly suited to hoeing. People improvised: empty bottles became scoops, flattened cans, blades.

We worked, and Jenna came by and kibbitzed, pointing out rocks that we'd missed, and generally being a pain in the ass. Eventually, enough grumbling got grumbled, and she went and tended her own garden, so to speak.

The work got hypnotic after that. The roar of the planes, the sounds of digging, it all blended into a deep rhythm. Hambone meandered by and idly tapped out a beat, and I found myself singing "Minnie the Moocher," and everyone joined in on the call-and-response. It was great, until I realized that I was singing for a crowd and shut my mouth. I didn't like singing for other people.

Not everyone was cut out to be a farmer. Good thing, too, or we would've starved to death waiting for the harvest. Still, there were people down at the gardens from sunup to sundown, clucking over their veggies.

The shit hit the fan one night as we were setting up to play. Lyman was sitting on Timson's piano, grinning wide enough to show us all his rotten chiclets. Three of his boys hung around close, and another four or five stood at a distance, sniggering.

Timson gave him a long, considering look. It was the kind of look I'd seen him give a humongous hunk of concrete in his plot one day, before he squatted down and hauled it out of the earth, like a hundred-kilo spud.

Lyman grinned bigger. "I wanna talk to you," he said.

Timson nodded slowly. Hambone rapped out a nervous tatter with his fingernails on a beer bottle he'd been carrying around, but I didn't need his help to know that things were getting bad.

"This gardening thing is getting out of hand," Lyman said. "People are neglecting their duties."

"What duties?" Timson asked, in a low tone.

"Drilling with us. We got to be ready to defend our land."

Timson gave a little shake of his head.

Lyman jumped in with more: "People're getting too attached to this place. We'll have to move when the food runs out, and we can't take no garden with us."

Timson's look got more considering. He cocked his head. "Why do they have to defend it and get ready to leave? That seems like a bit of a contradiction to me."

Lyman's brow furrowed. If I'm making him sound a little dim, that's only because he was. "We'll defend it until the food runs out, then we'll move on."

Jenna snickered. One of Lyman's boys reached out to smack her. Hambone drummed louder, Jenna batted his hand away.

I found myself saying, "What if the food doesn't run out? What if we grow enough of our own to stay alive?"

Lyman glared at me. "Is that how you want to live?"

I said, "Sooner or later, all the cans will be gone."

Lyman waved a dismissive hand. "Someone will take care of that. I'm worried about *this* group. *This* city."

"So why not let us make sure we've got enough to eat?"

Lyman started forward and I jumped. "I told you! We need to defend the place! And we need to be ready to go if we can't!"

Timson interceded. "What does this have to do with me?"

Lyman spread his hands out. "I want you to shut down the garden. We were doing just fine without it. I don't like to see people wasting their time."

Timson said, "It's not mine to shut down." He nodded at Jenna, who was glaring daggers at the goon who'd tried to smack her.

"Not mine, either," she said, with barely controlled fury. "It's everyone's."

Lyman said, "Well, you just tell everyone that the garden's got to be shut down."

He slid off the piano and took off, goons in tow. One of them contrived to bump into me hard enough to make me drop my horn, and I had to snag it up quick before he stomped it.

Steve showed up, looking pissed, which meant that he was worried. "What was that all about?" he said.

"What was what all about?" Timson said, and propped a book up on his music-stand.

They trashed the gardens two nights later, while we played. I wouldn't have thought that pack of lazy bastards had it in them to haul enough gravel to cover all the beds, especially not at night, but that's what they did. They kicked up the plants, and smashed the makeshift tools that the gardeners had left.

They didn't even have the smarts to steer clear of us the next day. Instead, they waited until a shocked crowd had gathered, and then showed up with big grins. Lyman had a pistol shoved in his waistband. I'd seen it before, and I didn't think it worked, but you never knew.

"Good morning!" Lyman said, stomping across the murdered beds. "How's everybody doing today?"

Timson hefted his pole and looked significantly at the militia. A number of people in the crowd got the idea. Lyman's boys looked uneasy.

Lyman said, "We've been chasing off rovers to the north every day and more are coming. Things are getting rough. We'll need volunteers for the militia. You've all got spare time now."

I'd never even harvested a single tomato from my plot. I could see the smashed green buds that I'd been nurturing.

Jenna said, "Who's got any spare time? It's going to take us *days* to clean up this mess." She stooped and picked up a stone and tossed it away from the beds. "Lucky I got more seeds."

I bent and picked up a rock of my own and tossed it. I wanted to toss it at Lyman, but Jenna had set an example.

Not everyone followed it. A lot wandered off, to prospect or go with Lyman. I couldn't blame them—I felt like giving up.

Over the next week or two, the plots started to get back into shape. Occasionally, Lyman would cruise by and glare, and we'd try to ignore him. He and his boys would walk across the plots, talking loudly about running off wanderers. Some of his boys had been planting gardens not long before. It made me boil.

I got it out at nights, when we played. The crowd had diminished. Anyone who had anything to do with Lyman stayed away. Those left behind were more into it than ever. A lot of them sang along, to Steve's chagrin. Some of them were pretty good.

Lyman hadn't trashed the beds again. I knew he hadn't given up. I waited, nervously, for the other shoe to drop.

It didn't take long. One night, our set ended early because of rain, which always made Hambone nervous. I led him back to his cave and was met on the trail by Lyman, dripping and grinning.

There was no small talk. He put a hand on my chest. "When you going to stop pussying around and help us defend ourselves?"

"I'm a little busy right now. Why don't you ask me again in a couple of centuries?" Hambone started doing a little shuffle.

Lyman gave him a fist in the ear. His head spun around, and I saw the knot of scar at the base of his skull strain. He turned back around and started shuffling. Lyman drew his arm back.

"Jesus, Lyman, what the hell is your problem?" I said.

He turned and popped me right in the mouth, splitting my lip and loosening one of my teeth. I'm proud of my teeth: I brushed 'em every morning and every night, and they were in better shape than most. I clutched my mouth. Lyman kicked me down, then walked away, stepping hard on my chest as he walked past me.

I led Hambone back up to his cave, and slept there.

I felt so bad the next morning, I almost didn't go back to the gardens. My face ached, and I couldn't blow a single note.

But I dragged myself down anyway. I was feeling stubborn.

Timson had a black eye and a limp, but he grinned like a pirate when he saw me. "How many?" he said.

"Just Lyman," I said.

He snorted. "They sent six for me. None of 'em are feeling too good this morning, I bet. Couple of them won't be walking for a while." He showed me his hands. His knuckles were raw.

"Can you play?" I asked, wincing in sympathy.

"Probably." He yanked a weed out of a plot. "I can garden."

Jenna got away unscathed. No one, not even Timson, was sure where she slept. I'd thought it was a weird quirk, but I realized that she knew what she was doing.

We worked together in the garden that day, the three of us and Hambone. No one else showed up. Some of the early berries were ripe, so we ate them. "Hey," I said, pointing at a plane. "You still plan on making that long-distance call? New Zealand?"

Jenna wiped the sweat off her forehead. "Once we've got this crop in. I don't know that we'd be let back in if we left."

I conceded the point.

That night, Timson played as best as he could, and I confined myself to the occasional sour blat on the horn. The crowd was subdued, and grew more so when Lyman and his boys showed up.

Steve called the set over early, then went and chatted with Lyman. Pretty soon they were whooping it up. Timson and I shared disgusted looks. "Fuck this," he said, and stalked away.

Jenna and me and Hambone went and sat in the gardens, where Hambone played a soft racket with my pole.

"I don't think we'll play again," I said.

"Come on," she said, dismissively. "This'll blow over. You guys are good, you should play."

"Who gives a damn if we're good or not? It's just a band."

She stared at Hambone for a while. "You ever wonder why I stayed here?" she said, finally.

"Tired, I guess. Same as me."

"I'd been looking for a place to grow a garden for a long time. A place where they were starting over, not just doing the same old stuff. And one day, I'm wandering along, and I heard you guys. I thought I'd found civilization. Before I could figure out exactly where the sound was coming from, I spotted some of Lyman's boys and hid. I hid out until I heard the music the next day, and then I snuck in. And I said, 'Girl, here's a place where they still have something besides eating and killing and screwing.' So I settled. I let you use my precious seeds. I think if you guys give up playing, this place will dry up and fly away in a couple of years."

"Unless we get rescued by Kiwis first," I said, playfully. I grinned, and my lip started bleeding again. "Ow," I said.

She laughed, and I laughed.

Steve avoided the band for a week. We didn't play, even after my lip had healed. Everyone was tense, ready to blow.

Then the gardens got trashed again. This time, they did it in broad daylight, while Timson and Jenna and I glared at them. It wasn't just Lyman and his pals, either: almost everyone came out, including a number of former gardeners. And Steve.

Timson walked away. Even Lyman's boys had the sense not to taunt him. Jenna and I stared as our beds were murdered again. They did a thorough job, sowing the soil with gravel and crap like nails and glass. Some of the former gardeners avoided our gaze, but other than that, there was no remorse. I shook.

Jenna led me away, with Hambone in tow. They weren't too scared to taunt *us*, and someone hit me with a dirt clod.

Jenna took me to a little cave whose entrance was hidden by an overhang from an I-beam. Jenna cleared some debris from the doorway, then led me inside.

It was claustrophobic and dark inside, and a bedroll was spread out on the floor beside a giant internal-frame pack.

The three of us sat in silence. Jenna's shoulders shook. Tentatively, I reached out for her and she hugged tight to me. Hambone clapped the buckles of her pack's straps together.

I held her there for a long time. Eventually, she tried to pull away, but I held on, and she relaxed into me. It had been a long time since I'd held a woman like that, and I found myself clutching her tighter. A warm, fluttery feeling filled my belly. I tried to kiss her.

She shoved me away abruptly. "Fuck off!" she said.

"What?" I said.

"Jesus, put it back in your pants!"

"What's your problem?" I said.

"My problem is I thought you were my *friend*. All of a sudden, you start grab-assing. Get out, you goddamned letch!" She shoved at me. I scrambled out and slogged home.

I stayed in bed until noon, wallowing in self-pity. Then I cracked a bottle of vodka out of my larder and killed it. It had been a while since my last bender, but it all came back just fine. Before I knew it, I was huffing from a rag soaked in solvent, reeling and dazed. I stayed stoned until I fell asleep, then got up and felt so rotten that I started over again.

I knew I was sulking, but I didn't see any reason to stop. The band was gone, the gardens were gone, Jenna was gone.

I realized that I'd spent the decade since the War waiting for someone to rebuild civilization, and that it wasn't going to happen. It was just going to get worse, every single year. Even if we planted a million gardens, the best I could hope for was to die of old age in a cave, surrounded by my illiterate offspring.

It was enough to make me want to join the militia.

Eventually, I staggered out into the blinding light. I went to work on a hill, and that's where Timson found me.

He was flustered and angry, showing more emotion than he usually did. "Have you seen her?" he said.

"Who?" I said, blearily.

"Jenna. You haven't seen her?"

"No," I said, guiltily, "not since Lyman—"

"Shit!" he said, and spun on his heel, taking off.

His urgency penetrated my fog and I chased after him. "You think something's up?" I said.

He nodded grimly. "Lyman's been too smug lately, like the cat that ate the cream. I think he's got her."

"Where would he keep her?" I said. There wasn't much standing that you could keep a person locked up inside of.

"Those assholes have an 'armory' where they keep all their goddamn weapons. He's said as much to me, when he was bragging. I want to find it."

"Hang on a sec," I said. "Have you checked her place?"

"You know where it is?" he asked, surprised.

"Come on," I said, feeling perversely proud that he didn't.

She wasn't at her place, but there were signs of a struggle. Her pack was shredded, her seeds ground into the concrete floor.

Timson took one look and tore off. I followed his long strides as best as I could. I knew where he was headed: Steve's.

Steve lived in part of a half-buried underground shopping mall. Timson pummeled down the stairs with me close behind.

Steve and Lucy were twined on a pile of foam rubber. Timson hauled him up by the arm and slammed his head against a wall.

"Where's the armory?" he roared.

Steve held his head. "Fuck you," he sneered.

Timson slammed his head again. Lucy rushed him from behind and I tripped her.

"Where is it?" Timson said. "Don't make me any angrier."

Steve dangled, nude, from Timson's meaty paws. Terror and anger warred on his features. Terror won. He spilled his guts. "They'll kill you," he said. "They've been fighting off wanderers all week. They're in a bad mood."

Timson snorted and dropped him.

Lyman was expecting us. He blocked the entrance to the armory, a bomb-shelter with a heavy, counterweighted steel door. I'd seen a few doors like it in my travels, but I'd never managed to get one open.

Timson got ready to rush him, then checked himself. Lyman had his gun hanging lazily off one hand.

"Afternoon, boys," he said, grinning.

"Are you going to shoot me?" Timson said.

Lyman held up his gun with an expression of mock-surprise. "Probably not," he said. "Not unless you give me a reason to. I'm here to protect."

"Well, I'm about to give you a reason to. I'm going in there to get Jenna. I'll kill you if you try to stop me."

Lyman stuck his gun back into his waistband. "You're too late," he said.

I saw red and started forward, but he held a hand up.

"She got away. We only wanted to scare her off and get rid of her seeds, but she went nuts. It's a good thing she got away, or I would've forgotten my manners."

Timson *growled*.

Lyman took a step backwards. "Look, if you don't believe me, go on in and take a look around, be my guest."

Jenna wasn't inside, but they weren't kidding when they called it an arsenal. I hadn't seen that many weapons since the War. It made me faintly sick.

Then I spotted something that froze me in my tracks. Beneath one of the long tables, a dented silver canister with ugly biohazard decals. You saw fragments of them sometimes, exploded in the midst of plague-wracked corpses. A plague-bomb.

Lyman strutted around like a proud papa. "Lots of these were here when I found the place, but we've picked up a few here and there along the way. Nobody's chasing us out of here." He followed my horrified gaze.

"You like it?" he said. "That's just in case someone *does* manage to run us off: it won't do them any good! Our Final Solution." He patted the bomb with a proprietary air.

All of a sudden, it got to me. I started laughing. "Nobody's chasing you out!" I gasped. "This is your rubble, and nobody's chasing you out!" Timson started laughing, too. Lyman and his boys reddened. We left.

We found Jenna with Hambone, in his cave. She had the remains of her pack with her, and was shoveling Hambone's things into it.

She startled when we came in, but once she'd seen us, she went back to packing. "Getting outta Dodge," she said, in answer to our unspoken question.

"Are you all right?" I asked, feeling guilty and awful.

"They killed my seeds," she said, in a hopeless voice. I started to reach for her, then stopped and stared at the floor.

She finished packing and grabbed Hambone. "You coming?"

Timson shouldered her pack, answering for both of us.

I'd settled seven years before. I thought I'd stayed in good shape, but I'd forgotten how punishing life on the road could be.

Jenna set a brutal pace. She wouldn't talk to me any more than necessary. We ate sparingly, from what she scrounged on the way. She knew a lot about what was edible and what wasn't, skills I'd never picked up, but my belly still growled.

"Where are we going?" I said, after a week. My feet had toughened, but my legs felt like they'd been beaten by truncheons.

Instead of answering, she pointed up at a plane overhead. Of course, I thought, time to make a long-distance call.

A week later, I said, "Have you thought this thing through? I mean, the station may be automated, but it'll have defenses. Locks, at least. How do you plan on getting in?"

Timson, who'd been silent the whole morning, said, "I'm curious, too. I've been thinking: this Australia thing is kind of far-fetched, isn't it? If they wanted to rescue us, they would've done it a long time ago, don't you think?"

"Screw Australia," she said impatiently. "Any station capable of maintaining those jets is bound to have lots of things we can use. I want a fence for my garden."

"But how are we going to get in?" I said.

"Hambone," she said, with a smug smile.

Hambone grinned affably. "Guh?" I said.

"He's a *pilot*. High ranking one, too."

"Not to repeat myself," I said, "but, guh?"

She spun Hambone around and pulled his shaggy hair away from the collar of his grimy T-shirt. "Look." I did. She dug at the knot of scar tissue at the base of his skull. Horrified, I watched as the scar flapped back, revealing a row of plugs, ringed with cracked and blackened skin.

"Brainstem interface. I noticed it the first time I saw you guys. You never noticed?"

"I noticed the scar, sure—"

"Scar?" she said. She flapped it around. "It's a dustcover! Hambone's wired! We'll just point his retinas at the scanner and voila, instant entry. Damn, you didn't think I was going to try and hop the fence, did you?"

Timson grinned sheepishly. "Well, *actually* . . . "

We reached the station the next day. The familiar roar of the jets was joined by the ear-shattering sound of them landing and taking off, like clockwork.

The airfield was fenced in by a lethal wall, ten meters tall and ringed with aged corpses. A lot of slow learners had found out the hard way about the station's defenses.

We wandered the perimeter for several kilometers before we came to a gate. It had a retinal scanner, like I sometimes found when I unearthed the remains of a bank machine. Hambone grew more and more agitated as we neared it.

"Go on," Jenna whispered. "Come on, you can do it."

His nervous drumming became more and more pronounced, until he was waving his arms, flailing wildly.

Jenna caught his hands and held them tightly. "That's all right," she cooed. "It's all right, come on."

Centimeter by slow centimeter, Jenna coaxed Hambone to the scanner. Finally, he put his eyes against the battered holes. Red light played over his features, and the gates sighed open.

We were all still standing around and grinning like idiots before we noticed that Hambone was running across the airfield.

He was already halfway to a jet. We caught up with him as he was vaulting the extruded ladder. An armored cart that had been attached to the fuselage reeled in its umbilicus and rolled away.

Hambone was already seated in the pilot's chair, punching at the buttons. A cable snaked from the back of his seat into the plugs on his neck. I had time to think, *That's weird*, and then the plane lurched forward. The cockpit had seats for a copilot and a bombardier, and we all crammed in like sardines, Jenna on my lap, and we crushed together when the plane jolted.

"Holy shit!" Jenna shouted.

Hambone drummed his fingers against an instrument panel while he pulled back on a joystick. "Strap in!" Timson shouted.

I did, pulling crash-webbing across us.

"Hambone, what the hell are you doing?" Jenna shouted.

He grinned affably, and the plane lifted off.

Hambone flew the plane confidently, with small, precise movements. Jenna, Timson and I stared at each other helplessly. The jet had taken off at a screaming climb that flattened us back against our seats—I noted with curious detachment that Hambone's seat had a recessed niche so that the cables depending from his skull weren't compressed.

In an instant, we were above the clouds, with only tiny patches of scorched earth visible.

The silence inside the cockpit rang inside my ears. For the first time in seven years, I couldn't hear jets crashing overhead.

"Hey, Hambone?" I said, cautiously.

Jenna shushed me. "Don't distract him," she whispered.

It was good advice. Timson stared at the instrument panels.

"I think," he whispered, "that we're headed out to sea."

Jenna and I groaned. Hambone reached out with one hand and unlatched a compartment that spilled out freeze-dried rations.

"At least we won't starve to death," Timson whispered.

"Why are we whispering?" I said.

"So Hambone doesn't get panicked," Jenna said.

"He never gets panicked," I said in a normal tone. Hambone unwrapped a bar of fruit leather and munched thoughtfully at it, while his fingers danced over the controls.

"He never flies planes, either," she hissed.

"We're over the ocean now. Pacific, I think," Timson said. He'd done something with the seat that caused it to slide back into a crawlspace. We were still cramped, but at least we weren't in each other's laps. I looked out the window. Yup, ocean.

I started shivering.

"We're going to die," I said.

"Probably," Jenna said. She giggled.

I punched her playfully and my panic receded.

Timson started playing with one of the panels.

"What are you doing?" I said, alarmed.

"Trying to figure out where we're going. Don't worry, this is the co-pilot's seat. I don't think I can screw up the navigation from here unless he turns it over to me." Ragged and filthy, he looked like a caveman next to the sleek controls.

"You don't think?" I said.

He waved impatiently at me, poked some more. "Okay," he said. "Hambone's taking us to Australia."

I always knew that Hambone had heard the things we'd said. Still, it was easy to forget. We took turns trying to convince him to head back. After a few hours, we gave up. Timson said that we'd crossed the halfway mark, anyway. We were closer to Australia than home.

Then there was nothing to do but eat and wait.

Eventually, some of the instruments lit and I thought, *This is it, we're dead.* Curiously, I wasn't scared. I'd been scared so long, and now I was bored, almost glad that it was ending.

"Bogeys," Timson said, staring out the window.

I looked up. Two sleek, new fighters were paralleling us. Inside their cockpits, I could see pilots in what looked like spacesuits. I waved to one. He tapped his headset.

Jenna said, "They're trying to radio us."

Timson picked up a lightweight headset from a niche above his seat. He screwed it into his ear and held up a finger.

"Hello?" he said. We held our breath.

"Yes, that's us," he said.

"What?" I said. He shushed me.

"All right," he said.

"*What?*" I shouted, startling Hambone. Jenna clapped a hand over my mouth.

"I'm sorry, I don't know how. Do you know which button I push? I see. All right, I think this is it. I'm going to push it. Is that all right? Okay, thanks. Bye."

I peeled Jenna's hand off my mouth. "What?" I demanded.

"That's the Panoceanic Air Force. They're landing us at Sydney. We'll be quarantined when we get there, but I think it's just a formality."

The lights in the cockpit dimmed and the cable zipped out of Hambone's neck. Absently, he reached back and smoothed the dustcover over the plugs. "They're landing us," Timson said.

I leaned back and sighed. I like Hambone a lot, but I'd rather not have an autistic flying my plane, thank you very much.

I was reaching for another bar of fruit-leather when the plane took a tremendous lurch that pressed Jenna and me against the crash-webbing hard enough to draw blood on our exposed skin. I heard a sickening crack and looked around wildly, terrified that it was someone's skull. In the juddering chaos, I saw Timson, face white, arm hanging at a nauseating, twisted angle.

We jolted again, and I realized that I was screaming. I closed my mouth, but the screaming continued. Out of the bombardier's porthole, I saw the air convecting across the shuddering wings, and realized that the screaming was the air whistling over the fuselage. The ground rushed towards us.

Jenna's head snapped back into my nose, blinding me with pain, and then we were tumbling through the cockpit. Jenna had released the crash-webbing altogether and was ping-ponging around Hambone. I saw her claw at the dustcover on his neck before she was tossed to the floor.

I pried my fingers loose from the armrests on my chair and came forward to Hambone. I straddled him, legs around his waist, and suppressed my gorge as I scrabbled at what I still thought of as his "scar" until it peeled back. My fingertips skated over the plugs and the knots of skin around them, and then I did toss up, spraying vomit and losing my grip on Hambone.

I ended up atop Jenna. The plane screamed down and down and I locked eyes with Hambone, silently begging him to do something. His gaze wandered, and my eyes stopped watering long enough to see Hambone do something to his armrest, which caused the cabling on his seat to snake out and mate with his brainstem. The plane leveled off and he smiled at us.

It couldn't have taken more than thirty seconds, but it seemed like a lifetime. Timson cursed blue at his arm, which was swollen and purple, and Jenna cradled her bumped head in arms that streamed blood from dozens of crisscrossed webbing cuts. I got us strapped in as we touched down.

We got escorted off the ship by a bunch of spacemen with funny accents. They didn't take us to the hospital until they'd scrubbed us and taken blood. They wanted to take Hambone away, but we were very insistent. The spacemen told us that he was very "high functioning," and that the plugs in the back of his neck were only rated for about five years.

"They'll have to come out," one of them explained to us. "Otherwise, he'll only get worse."

Jenna said, "If you take them out, will he get better?"

The spaceman shrugged. "Maybe. It's a miracle that he's still bloody alive, frankly. Bad technology."

They de-quarantined us a month later. I'd never been cleaner. Those Aussies are pretty worried about disease.

The four of us took a flat near Bondi Beach. Timson found a job in a bookstore, and Jenna spends most of her time working with Hambone. Some days, I think she's getting through to him.

I'm on the Dole and feeling weird about it. I can't get used to the idea of just showing up at someone else's place and taking handouts. But the Aussies don't seem to mind. Very progressive people. They ran our story on the news and a music store in Canberra donated a bugle and an electric piano.

I'm teaching Jenna to blow. It's not that I don't like playing anymore, but it's hard to sing and play at the same time. All four of us practice every night, out in our garden. We still flinch every eight bars, waiting for the roar of a jet to interrupt us, then smile sheepishly when it doesn't come. The important thing is, we're playing.

Even an interloper like me knows how you get to Sydney Opera House: practice.

‿

Cory Doctorow (craphound.com) is a science fiction author, activist, journalist, blogger, the co-editor of Boing Boing (boingboing.net), and the author of young adult novels like *Pirate Cinema*, *Little Brother*, and *Homeland* and novels for adults like *Rapture of the Nerds* and *Makers*. He is the former European director of the Electronic Frontier Foundation and cofounded the UK Open Rights Group. Born in Toronto, Canada, he now lives in London.

‿

The End came gradually: rolling brownouts, a dirty bomb in Disney World, the economy really tanking. The US is failing, but it's worse in Mexico. There are rumors of a camp for the homeless outside of Toronto, so people are heading there. Jane and her thirteen-year-old daughter, Franny, have made it—mostly on foot—to somewhere in Missouri.

• AFTER THE APOCALYPSE •
Maureen F. McHugh

Jane puts out the sleeping bags in the backyard of the empty house by the tool shed. She has a lock and hasp and an old hand drill that they can use to lock the tool shed from the inside, but it's too hot to sleep in there, and there haven't been many people on the road. Better to sleep outside. Franny has been talking a mile a minute. Usually by the end of the day she is tired from walking—they both are—and quiet. But this afternoon she's gotten on the subject of her friend Samantha. She's musing on if Samantha has left town like they did. "They're probably still there, because they had a really nice house in, like, a low-crime area, and Samantha's father has a really good job. When you have money like that, maybe you can totally afford a security system or something. Their house has five bedrooms and the basement isn't a basement, it's a living room, because the house is kind of on a little hill, and although the front of the basement is underground, you can walk right out the back."

Jane says, "That sounds nice."

"You could see a horse farm behind them. People around them were rich, but not like, on-TV rich, exactly."

Jane puts her hands on her hips and looks down the line of backyards.

"Do you think there's anything in there?" Franny asks, meaning the house, a '60s suburban ranch. Franny is thirteen, and empty houses frighten her. But she doesn't like to be left alone, either. What she wants is for Jane to say that they can eat one of the tuna pouches.

"Come on, Franny. We're gonna run out of tuna long before we get to Canada."

"I know," Franny says sullenly.

"You can stay here."

"No, I'll go with you."

God, sometimes Jane would do anything to get five minutes away from Franny. She loves her daughter, really, but Jesus. "Come on, then," Jane says.

There is an old square concrete patio and a sliding glass door. The door is dirty. Jane cups her hand to shade her eyes and looks inside. It's dark and hard to see. No power, of course. Hasn't been power in any of the places they've passed through in more than two months. Air conditioning. And a bed with a mattress and box springs. What Jane wouldn't give for air conditioning and a bed. Clean sheets.

The neighborhood seems like a good one. Unless they find a big group to camp with, Jane gets them off the freeway at the end of the day. There was fighting in the neighborhood, and at the end of the street, several houses are burned out. Then there are lots of houses with windows smashed out. But the fighting petered out. Some of the houses are still lived in. This house had all its windows intact, but the garage door was standing open and the garage was empty except for dead leaves. Electronic garage door. The owners pulled out and left and didn't bother to close the door behind them. Seemed to Jane that the overgrown backyard with its toolshed would be a good place to sleep.

Jane can see her silhouette in the dirty glass, and her hair is a snarled, curly, tangled rat's nest. She runs her fingers through it, and they snag. She'll look for a scarf or something inside. She grabs the handle and yanks up, hard, trying to get the old slider off track. It takes a couple of tries, but she's had a lot of practice in the last few months.

Inside, the house is trashed. The kitchen has been turned upside-down, and silverware, utensils, drawers, broken plates, flour, and stuff are everywhere. She picks her way across, a can opener skittering under her foot with a clatter.

Franny gives a little startled shriek.

"Fuck!" Jane says. "Don't do that!" The canned food is long gone.

"I'm sorry," Franny says. "It scared me!"

"We're gonna starve to death if we don't keep scavenging," Jane says.

"I know!" Franny says.

"Do you know how fucking far it is to Canada?"

"I can't help it if it startled me!"

Maybe if she were a better cook, she'd be able to scrape up the flour and make something, but it's all mixed in with dirt and stuff, and every time she's tried to cook something over an open fire it's either been raw or black or, most often, both—blackened on the outside and raw on the inside.

Jane checks all the cupboards anyway. Sometimes people keep food in different places. Once they found one of those decorating icing tubes and wrote words on each other's hands and licked them off.

Franny screams, not a startled shriek but a real scream.

Jane whirls around, and there's a guy in the family room with a tire iron.

"What are you doing here?" he yells.

Jane grabs a can opener from the floor, one of those heavy jobbers, and wings it straight at his head. He's too slow to get out of the way, and it nails him in the forehead. Jane has winged a lot of things at boyfriends over the years. It's a skill. She throws a couple of more things from the floor, anything she can find, while the guy is yelling, "Fuck! Fuck!" and trying to ward off the barrage.

Then she and Franny are out the back door and running.

Fucking squatter! She hates squatters! If it's the homeowner they tend to make the place more like a fortress, and you can tell not to try to go in. Squatters try to keep a low profile. Franny is in front of her, running like a rabbit, and they are out the gate and headed up the suburban street. Franny knows the drill, and at the next corner she turns, but by then it's clear that no one's following them.

"Okay," Jane pants. "Okay, stop, stop."

Franny stops. She's a skinny adolescent now—she used to be chubby, but she's lean and tan with all their walking. She's wearing a pair of falling-apart pink sneakers and a tank top with oil smudges from when they had to climb over a truck tipped sideways on an overpass. She's still flat-chested. Her eyes are big in her face. Jane puts her hands on her knees and draws a shuddering breath.

"We're okay," she says. It is gathering dusk in this Missouri town. In a while, streetlights will come on, unless someone has systematically shot them out. Solar power still works. "We'll wait a bit and then go back and get our stuff when it's dark."

"No!" Franny bursts into sobs. "We can't!"

Jane is at her wit's end. Rattled from the squatter. Tired of being the strong one. "We've got to! You want to lose everything we've got? You want to die? Goddamn it, Franny! I can't take this anymore!"

"That guy's there!" Franny sobs out. "We can't go back! We can't!"

"Your cell phone is there," Jane says. A mean dig. The cell phone doesn't work, of course. Even if they still somehow had service, if service actually exists, they haven't been anywhere with electricity to charge it in weeks. But Franny still carries it in the hope that she can get a charge and call her friends. Seventh graders are apparently surgically attached to their phones. Not that she acts even like a seventh grader anymore. The longer they are on the road, the younger Franny acts.

This isn't the first time that they've run into a squatter. Squatters are cowards. The guy doesn't have a gun, and he's not going to go out after dark. Franny has no spine, takes after her asshole of a father. Jane ran away from home and got all the way to Pasadena, California, when she was a year older than Franny. When she was fourteen, she was a decade older than Franny. Lived on the street for six weeks, begging spare change on the same route that the Rose Parade took. It had been scary, but it had been a blast, as well. Taught her to stand on her own two feet, which Franny wasn't going to be able to do when she was twenty. Thirty, at this rate.

"You're hungry, aren't you?" Jane said, merciless. "You want to go looking in these houses for something to eat?" Jane points around them. The houses all have their front doors broken into, open like little mouths.

Franny shakes her head.

"Stop crying. I'm going to go check some of them out. You wait here."

"Mom! Don't leave me!" Franny wails.

Jane is still shaken from the squatter. But they need food. And they need their stuff. There is seven hundred dollars sewn inside the lining of Jane's sleeping bag. And someone has to keep them alive. It's obviously going to be her.

Things didn't exactly all go at once. First there were rolling brownouts and lots of people unemployed. Jane had been making a living working at a place that sold furniture. She started as a salesperson, but she was good at helping people on what colors to buy, what things went together, what fabrics to pick for custom pieces. Eventually they made her a service associate, a person who was kind of like an interior decorator, sort of. She had an eye. She'd grown up in a nice suburb and had seen nice things. She knew what people wanted. Her boss kept telling her a little less eye makeup would be a good idea, but people liked what she suggested and recommended her to their friends even if her boss didn't like her eye makeup.

She was thinking of starting a decorating business, although she was worried that she didn't know about some of the stuff decorators did. On TV they were always tearing down walls and redoing fireplaces. So she put it off. Then there was the big Disney World attack where a kazillion people died because of a dirty bomb, and then the economy really tanked. She knew that business was dead and she was going to get laid off, but before that happened, someone torched the furniture place where she was working. Her boyfriend at the time was a cop, so he still had a job, even though half the city was unemployed. She and Franny were all right compared to a lot of people. She didn't like not having her own money, but she wasn't exactly having to call her mother in Pennsylvania and eat crow and offer to come home.

So she sat on the balcony of their condo and smoked and looked through her old decorating magazines, and Franny watched television in the room behind her. People started showing up on the sidewalks. They had trash bags full of stuff. Sometimes they were alone; sometimes there would be whole families. Sometimes they'd have cars and they'd sleep in them, but gas was getting to almost ten dollars a gallon, when the gas stations could get it. Pete, the boyfriend, told her that the cops didn't even patrol much anymore because of the gas problem. More and more of the people on the sidewalk looked to be walking.

"Where are they coming from?" Franny asked.

"Down south. Houston, El Paso, anywhere within a hundred miles of the border." Pete said. "Border's gone to shit. Mexico doesn't have food, but the drug cartels have lots of guns, and they're coming across to take what they can get. They say it's like a war zone down there."

"Why don't the police take care of them?" Franny asked.

"Well, Francisca," Pete said—he was good with Franny, Jane had to give him that—"sometimes there are just too many of them for the police down there. And they've got kinds of guns that the police aren't allowed to have."

"What about you?" Franny asked.

"It's different up here," Pete said. "That's why we've got refugees here. Because it's safe here."

"They're not *refugees*," Jane said. Refugees were, like, people in Africa. These were just regular people. Guys in T-shirts with the names of rock bands on them. Women sitting in the front seats of Taurus station wagons, doing their hair in the rearview mirrors. Kids asleep in the back seat or running up and down the street shrieking and playing. Just people.

"Well, what do you want to call them?" Pete asked.

Then the power started going out, more and more often. Pete's shifts got longer although he didn't always get paid.

There were gunshots in the street, and Pete told Jane not to sit out on the balcony. He boarded up the French doors and it was as if they were living in a cave. The refugees started thinning out. Jane rarely saw them leaving, but each day there were fewer and fewer of them on the sidewalk. Pete said they were headed north.

Then the fires started on the east side of town. The power went out and stayed out. Pete didn't come home until the next day, and he slept a couple of hours and then when back out to work. The air tasted of smoke—not the pleasant, clean smell of wood smoke, but a garbagey smoke. Franny complained that it made her sick to her stomach.

After Pete didn't come home for four days, it was pretty clear to Jane that he wasn't coming back. Jane put Franny in the car, packed everything she could think of that might be useful. They got about 120 miles away, far enough that the burning city was no longer visible, although the sunset was a vivid and blistering red. Then they ran out of gas, and there was no more to be had.

There were rumors that there was a refugee camp for homeless outside of Toronto. So they were walking to Detroit.

Franny says, "You can't leave me! You can't leave me!"

"Do you want to go scavenge with me?" Jane says.

Franny sobs so hard she seems to be hyperventilating. She grabs her mother's arms, unable to do anything but hold onto her. Jane peels her off, but Franny keeps grabbing, clutching, sobbing. It's making Jane crazy. Franny's fear is contagious, and if she lets it get in her, she'll be too afraid to do anything. She can feel it deep inside her, that thing that has always threatened her, to give in, to stop doing and pushing and scheming, to become like her useless, useless father puttering around the house vacantly, bottles hidden in the garage, the basement, everywhere.

"GET OFF ME!" she screams at Franny, but Franny is sobbing and clutching.

She slaps Franny. Franny throws up, precious little, water and crackers from breakfast. Then she sits down in the grass, just useless.

Jane marches off into the first house.

She's lucky. The garage is closed up and there are three cans of soup on a shelf. One of them is cream of mushroom, but luckily, Franny liked cream of mushroom when she found it before. There are also cans of tomato paste, which she ignores, and some dried pasta, but mice have gotten into it.

When she gets outside, some strange guy is standing on the sidewalk, talking to Franny, who's still sitting on the grass.

For a moment she doesn't know what to do, clutching the cans of soup against her chest. Some part of her wants to back into the house, go through the dark living room with its mauve carpeting, its shabby blue sofa, photos of school kids and a cross-stitch flower bouquet framed on the wall, back through the little dining room with its border of country geese, unchanged since the eighties. Out the back door and over the fence, an easy moment to abandon the biggest mistake of her life. She'd aborted the first pregnancy, brought home from Pasadena in shame. She'd dug her heels in on the second, it's-my-body-fuck-you.

Franny laughs. A little nervous and hiccupy from crying, but not really afraid.

"Hey," Jane yells. "Get away from my daughter!"

She strides across the yard, all motherhood and righteous fury. A skinny, dark-haired guy holds up his hands, palms out, no harm, ma'am.

"It's okay, Mom," Franny says.

The guy is smiling. "We're just talking," he says. He's wearing a red plaid flannel shirt and T-shirt and shorts. He's scraggly, but who isn't.

"Who the hell are you," she says.

"My name's Nate. I'm just heading north. Was looking for a place to camp."

"He was just hanging with me until you got back," Franny says.

Nate takes them to his camp—also behind a house. He gets a little fire going, enough to heat the soup. He talks about Alabama, which is where he's coming from, although he doesn't have a Southern accent. He makes some excuse about being an army brat. Jane tries to size him up. He tells some story about when two guys stumbled on his camp north of Huntsville, when he was first on the road. About how it scared the shit out of him but about how he'd bluffed them about a buddy of his who was hunting for their dinner but would have heard the racket they made and could be drawing a bead on them right now from the trees, and about how something moved in the trees, some animal, rustling in the leaf litter, and they got spooked. He's looking at her, trying to impress her, but being polite, which is good with

Franny listening. Franny is taken with him, hanging on his every word, flirting a little the way she does. In a year or two, Franny was going to be guy crazy, Jane knew.

"They didn't know anything about the woods, just two guys up from Biloxi or something, kind of guys who, you know, manage a copy store or a fast-food joint or something, thinking that now that civilization is falling apart they can be like the hero in one of their video games." He laughs. "I didn't know what was in the woods, neither. I admit I was kind of scared it was someone who was going to shoot all of us, although it was probably just a sparrow or a squirrel or something. I'm saying stuff over my shoulder to my 'buddy,' like, 'Don't shoot them or nothing. Just let them go back the way they came.' "

She's sure he's bullshitting. But she likes that he makes it funny instead of pretending he's some sort of Rambo. He doesn't offer any of his own food, she notices. But he does offer to go with them to get their stuff. Fair trade, she thinks.

He's not bad looking in a kind of skinny way. She likes them skinny. She's tired of doing it all herself.

The streetlights come on, at least some of them. Nate goes with them when they go back to get their sleeping bags and stuff. He's got a board with a bunch of nails sticking out of one end. He calls it his mace.

They are quiet, but they don't try to hide. It's hard to find the stuff in the dark, but luckily, Jane hadn't really unpacked. She and Franny, who is breathing hard, get their sleeping bags and packs. It's hard to see. The backyard is a dark tangle of shadows. She assumes it's as hard to see them from inside the house—maybe harder.

Nothing happens. She hears nothing from the house, sees nothing, although it seems as if they are all unreasonably loud gathering things up. They leave through the side gate, coming nervously to the front of the house, Nate carrying his mace and ready to strike, she and Franny with their arms full of sleeping bags. They go down the cracked driveway and out into the middle of the street, a few gutted cars still parked on either side. Then they are around the corner and it feels safe. They are all grinning and happy and soon putting the sleeping bags in Nate's little backyard camp made domestic—no, civilized—by the charred ash of the little fire.

In the morning, she leaves Nate's bedroll and gets back to sleep next to Franny before Franny wakes up.

They are walking on the freeway the next day, the three of them. They are together now, although they haven't discussed it, and Jane is relieved. People are just that much less likely to mess with a man. Overhead, three jets pass going south, visible only by their contrails. At least there are jets. American jets, she hopes.

They stop for a moment while Nate goes around a bridge abutment to pee.

"Mom," Franny says. "Do you think that someone has wrecked Pete's place?"

"I don't know," Jane says.

"What do you think happened to Pete?"

Jane is caught off guard. They left without ever explicitly discussing Pete, and Jane just thought that Franny, like her, assumed Pete was dead.

"I mean," Franny continues, "if they didn't have gas, maybe he got stuck somewhere. Or he might have gotten hurt and ended up in the hospital. Even if the hospital wasn't taking regular people, like, they'd take cops. Because they think of cops as one of their own." Franny is in her adult-to-adult mode, explaining the world to her mother. "They stick together. Cops and firemen and nurses."

Jane isn't sure she knows what Franny is talking about. Normally she'd tell Franny as much. But this isn't a conversation she knows how to have. Nate comes around the abutment, adjusting himself a bit, and it is understood that the subject is closed.

"Okay," he says. "How far to Wallyworld?" Fanny giggles.

Water is their biggest problem. It's hard to find, and when they do find it, either from a pond or, very rarely, from a place where it hasn't all been looted, it's heavy. Thank God Nate is pretty good at making a fire. He has six disposable lighters that he got from a gas station, and when they find a pond, they boil it. Somewhere Jane thinks she heard that they should boil it for eighteen minutes. Basically they just boil the heck out of it. Pond water tastes terrible, but they are always thirsty. Franny whines. Jane is afraid that Nate will get tired of it and leave, but apparently as long as she crawls over to his bedroll every night, he's not going to.

Jane waits until she can tell Franny is asleep. It's a difficult wait. They are usually so tired it is all she can do to keep from nodding off. But she is afraid to lose Nate.

At first she liked that at night he never made a move on her. She always initiates. It made things easier all around. But now he does this thing where she crawls over and he's pretending to be asleep. Or is asleep, the bastard, because he doesn't have to stay awake. She puts her hand on his chest, and then down his pants, getting him hard and ready. She unzips his shorts, and still he doesn't do anything. She grinds on him for a while, and only then does he pull his shorts and underwear down and let her ride him until he comes. Then she climbs off him. Sometimes he might say, "Thanks, Babe." Mostly he says nothing and she crawls back next to Franny feeling as if she just paid the rent. She has never given anyone sex for money. She keeps telling herself that this night she won't do it. See what he does. Hell, if he leaves them, he leaves them. But then she lies there, waiting for Franny to go to sleep.

Sometimes she knows Franny is awake when she crawls back. Franny never says anything, and unless the moon is up, it is usually too dark to see if her eyes are open. It is just one more weird thing, no weirder than walking up the highway, or getting off the highway in some small town and bartering with some old guy to take what is probably useless US currency for well water. No weirder than no school. No weirder than no baths, no clothes, no nothing.

Jane decides she's not going to do it the next night. But she knows she will lie there, anxious, and probably crawl over to Nate.

They are walking, one morning, while the sky is still blue and darkening near the horizon. By midday the sky will be white and the heat will be flattening. Franny asks Nate, "Have you ever been in love?"

"God, Franny," Jane says.

Nate laughs. "Maybe. Have you?"

Franny looks irritable. "I'm in eighth grade," she says. "And I'm not one of those girls with boobs, so I'm thinking, no."

Jane wants her to shut up, but Nate says, "What kind of guy would you fall in love with?"

Franny looks a little sideways at him and then looks straight ahead. She has the most perfect skin, even after all this time in the sun. Skin like that is wasted on kids. Her look says, "Someone like you, stupid." "I don't know," Franny says. "Someone who knows how to do things. You know, when you need them."

"What kind of things?" Nate asks. He's really interested. Well, fuck, there's not a lot interesting on a freeway except other people walking and abandoned cars. They are passing a Sienna with a flat tire and all its doors open.

Franny gestures toward it. "Like fix a car. And I'd like him to be cute, too." Matter of fact. Serious as a church.

Nate laughs. "Competent and cute."

"Yeah," Franny says. "Competent and cute."

"Maybe you should be the one who knows how to fix a car," Jane says.

"But I don't," Franny points out reasonably. "I mean maybe, someday, I could learn. But right now, I don't."

"Maybe you'll meet someone in Canada," Nate says. "Canadian guys are supposed to be able to do things like fix a car or fish or hunt moose."

"Canadian guys are different than American guys?" Franny asks.

"Yeah," Nate says. "You know, all flannel shirts and Canadian beer and stuff."

"You wear a flannel shirt."

"I'd really like a Canadian beer about now," Nate says. "But I'm not Canadian."

Off the road to the right is a gas station/convenience store. They almost always check them. There's not much likelihood of finding anything in the place, because the wire fence that borders the highway has been trampled here so people can get over it, which suggests that the place has long since been looted. But you never know what someone might have left behind. Nate lopes off across the high grass.

"Mom," Franny says, "carry my backpack, okay?" She shrugs it off and runs. Amazing that she has the energy to run. Jane picks up Franny's backpack, irritated, and follows. Nate and Franny disappear into the darkness inside.

She follows them in. "Franny, I'm not hauling your pack anymore."

There are some guys already in the place, and there is something about them, hard and well fed, that signals they are different. Or maybe it is just the instincts of a prey animal in the presence of predators.

"So what's in that pack?" one of them asks. He's sitting on the counter at the cash register window, smoking a cigarette. She hasn't had a cigarette in weeks. Her whole body simultaneously leans toward the cigarette and yet magnifies everything in the room. A room full of men, all of them staring.

She just keeps acting like nothing is wrong, because she doesn't know what else to do. "Dirty blankets, mostly," she says. "I have to carry most of the crap."

One of the men is wearing a grimy hoodie. Hispanic yard workers do that sometimes. It must help in the sun. These men are all Anglos, and there are fewer of them than she first thought. Five. Two of them are sitting on the floor, their backs against an empty dead ice cream cooler, their legs stretched out in front of them. Everyone on the road is dirty, but they are dirty and hard. Physical. A couple of them grin, feral flickers passing between them like glances. There is understanding in the room, shared purpose. She has the sense that she cannot let on that she senses anything, because the only thing holding them off is the pretense that everything is normal. "Not that we really need blankets in this weather," she says. "I would kill for a functioning Holiday Inn."

"Hah," the one by the cash register says. A bark. Amused.

Nate is carefully still. He is searching, eyes going from man to man. Franny looks as if she is about to cry.

It is only a matter of time. They will be on her. Should she play up to the man at the cash register? If she tries to flirt, will it release the rising tension in the room, allow them to spring on all of them? Will they kill Nate? What will they do to Franny? Or she can use her sex as currency. Go willingly. She does not feel as if they care if she goes willingly or not. They know there is nothing to stop them.

"There's no beer here, is there," she says. She can hear her voice failing.

"Nope," says the man sitting at the cash register.

"What's your name?" she asks.

It's the wrong thing to say. He slides off the counter. Most of the men are smiling now.

Nate says, "Stav?"

One of the guys on the floor looks up. His eyes narrow.

Nate says, "Hey, Stav."

"Hi," the guy says cautiously.

"You remember me," Nate says. "Nick. From the Blue Moon Inn."

Nothing. Stav's face is blank. But another guy, the one in the hoodie, says, "Speedy Nick!"

Stav grins. "Speedy Nick! Fuck! Your hair's not blond anymore!"

Nate says, "Yeah, well, you know, upkeep is tough on the road." He jerks a thumb at Jane. "This is my sister, Janey. My niece, Franny. I'm taking 'em up to Toronto. There's supposed to be a place up there."

"I heard about that," the guy in the hoodie says. "Some kind of camp."

"Ben, right?" Nate says.

"Yeah," the guy says.

The guy who was sitting on the counter is standing now, cigarette still smoldering. He wants it, doesn't want everybody to get all friendly. But the moment is shifting away from him.

"We found some distilled water," Stav says. "Tastes like shit but you can have it if you want."

Jane doesn't ask him why he told her his name was Nate. For all she knows, "Nate" is his name and "Nick" is the lie.

They walk each day. Each night she goes to his bedroll. She owes him. Part of her wonders is maybe he's gay? Maybe he has to lie there and fantasize she's a guy or something. She doesn't know.

They are passing by water. They have some, so there is no reason to stop. There's an egret standing in the water, white as anything she has seen since this started, immaculately clean. Oblivious to their passing. Oblivious to the passing of everything. This is all good for the egrets. Jane hasn't had a drink since they started for Canada. She can't think of a time since she was sixteen or so that she went so long without one. She wants to get dressed up and go out someplace and have a good time and not think about anything, because the bad thing about not having a drink is that she thinks all the time and, fuck, there's nothing in her life right now she really wants to think about. Especially not Canada, which she is deeply but silently certain is only a rumor. Not the country, she doesn't think it doesn't exist, but the camp. It is a mirage. A shimmer on the horizon. Something to go toward but which isn't really there.

Or maybe they're the rumors. The three of them. Rumors of things gone wrong.

At a rest stop in the middle of nowhere they come across an encampment. A huge number of people, camped under tarps, pieces of plastic, and tatters, and astonishingly, a convoy of military trucks and jeeps including a couple of fuel trucks and a couple of water trucks. Kids stop and watch as they walk in and then go back to chasing each other around picnic tables. The two groups are clearly separate. The military men have control of all the asphalt and one end of the picnic area. They stand around or lounge at picnic tables. They look so equipped, from hats to combat boots. They look so clean. So much like the world Jane has put mostly out of her mind. They awake in her the longing that she has put down. The longing to be clean. To have walls. Electric lights. Plumbing. To have order.

The rest look like refugees, the word she denied on the sidewalks outside the condo. Dirty people in T-shirts with bundles and plastic grocery bags and even a couple of suitcases. She has seen people like this as they walked. Walked past them sitting by the side of the road. Sat by the side of the road as others walked past them. But to see them all together like this . . . this is what it will be like in Canada? A camp full of people with bags of wretched clothes waiting for someone to give them something to eat? A toddler with no pants and curly hair watches solemnly like one of those children in those "save a child" commercials. He's just as dirty. His hair is blond.

She rejects it. Rejects it all so viscerally that she stops and for a moment can't walk to the people in the rest stop. She doesn't know if she would have walked past, or if she would have turned around, or if she would have struck off across the country. It doesn't matter what she would have done, because Nate and Franny walk right on up the exit ramp. Franny's tank top is bright, insistent pink under its filth and her shorts have a tear in them, and her legs are brown and skinny and she could be a child on a news channel after a hurricane or an earthquake, clad in the loud synthetic colors so at odds with the dirt or ash that coats her. Plastic and synthetics are the indestructibles left to the survivors.

Jane is ashamed. She wants to explain that she's not like this. She wants to say, she's an American. By which she means she belongs to the military side, although she has never been interested in the military, never particularly liked soldiers.

If she could call her parents in Pennsylvania. Get a phone from one of the soldiers. Surrender. You were right, Mom. I should have straightened up and flown right. I should have worried more about school. I should have done it your way. I'm sorry. Can we come home?

Would her parents still be there? Do the phones work just north of Philadelphia? It has not until this moment occurred to her that it is all gone.

She sticks her fist in her mouth to keep from crying out, sick with understanding. It is all gone. She has thought herself all brave and realistic, getting Franny to Canada, but somehow she didn't until this moment realize that it all might be gone. That there might be nowhere for her where the electricity is still on and there are still carpets on the hardwood floors and someone still cares about damask.

Nate has finally noticed that she isn't with them and he looks back, frowning at her. *What's wrong?* his expression says. She limps after them, defeated.

Nate walks up to a group of people camped around and under a stone picnic table. "Are they giving out water?" he asks, meaning the military.

"Yeah," says a guy in a Cowboys football jersey. "If you go ask, they'll give you water."

"Food?"

"They say tonight."

All the shade is taken. Nate takes their water bottles—a couple of two-liters and a plastic gallon milk jug. "You guys wait, and I'll get us some water," he says.

Jane doesn't like being near these people, so she walks back to a wire fence at the back of the rest area and sits down. She puts her arms on her knees and puts her head down. She is looking at the grass.

"Mom?" Franny says.

Jane doesn't answer.

"Mom? Are you okay?" After a moment more. "Are you crying?"

"I'm just tired," June says to the grass.

Franny doesn't say anything after that.

Nate comes back with all the bottles filled. Jane hears him coming and hears Franny say, "Oh, wow. I'm so thirsty."

Nate nudges her arm with a bottle. "Hey, Babe. Have some."

She takes a two-liter from him and drinks some. It's got a flat, faintly metal/chemical taste. She gets a big drink and feels a little better. "I'll be back," she says. She walks to the shelter where the bathrooms are.

"You don't want to go in there," a black man says to her. The whites of his eyes are yellow.

She ignores him and pushes in the door. Inside, the smell is excruciating, and the sinks are all stopped and full of trash. There is some light from windows up near the ceiling. She looks at herself in the dim mirror. She pours a little water into her hand and scrubs at her face. There is a little bit of paper towel left on a roll, and she peels it off and cleans her face and her hands, using every bit of the scrap of paper towel. She wets her hair and combs her fingers through it, working the tangles for a long time until it is still curly but not the rat's nest it was. She is so careful with the water. Even so, she uses every bit of it on her face and arms and hair. She would kill for a little lipstick. For a comb. Anything. At least she has water.

She is cute. The sun hasn't been too hard on her. She practices smiling.

When she comes out of the bathroom, the air is so sweet. The sunlight is blinding.

She walks over to the soldiers and smiles. "Can I get some more water, please?"

There are three of them at the water truck. One of them is a blond-haired boy with a brick-red complexion. "You sure can," he says, smiling back at her.

She stands, one foot thrust out in front of her like a ballerina, back a little arched. "You're sweet," she says. "Where are you from?"

"We're all stationed at Fort Hood," he says. "Down in Texas. But we've been up north for a couple of months."

"How are things up north?" she asks.

"Crazy," he says. "But not as crazy as they are in Texas, I guess."

She has no plan. She is just moving with the moment. Drawn like a moth.

He gets her water. All three of them are smiling at her.

"How long are you here?" she asks. "Are you like a way station or something?"

One of the others, a skinny Chicano, laughs. "Oh, no. We're here tonight and then headed west."

"I used to live in California," she says. "In Pasadena. Where the Rose Parade is. I used to walk down that street where the cameras are every day."

The blond glances around. "Look, we aren't supposed to be talking too much right now. But later on, when it gets dark, you should come back over here and talk to us some more."

"Mom!" Franny says when she gets back to the fence, "You're all cleaned up!"

"Nice, Babe," Nate says. He's frowning a little.

"Can I get cleaned up?" Franny asks.

"The bathroom smells really bad," Jane says. "I don't think you want to go in there." But she digs her other T-shirt out of her backpack and wets it and washes Franny's face. The girl is never going to be pretty, but now that she's not chubby, she's got a cute thing going on. She's got the sense to work it, or will learn it. "You're a girl that the boys are going to look at," Jane says to her.

Franny smiles, delighted.

"Don't you think?" Jane says to Nate. "She's got that thing, that sparkle, doesn't she?"

"She sure does," Nate says.

They nap in the grass until the sun starts to go down, and then the soldiers line everyone up and hand out MREs. Nate gets Beef Ravioli, and Jane gets Sloppy Joe. Franny gets Lemon Pepper Tuna and looks ready to cry, but Jane offers to trade with her. The meals are positive cornucopias—a side dish, a little packet of candy, peanut butter and crackers, fruit punch powder. Everybody has different things, and Jane makes everybody give everyone else a taste.

Nate keeps looking at her oddly. "You're in a great mood."

"It's like a party," she says.

Jane and Franny are really pleased by the moist towelette. Franny carefully saves her plastic fork, knife, and spoon. "Was your tuna okay?" she asks. She is feeling guilty now that the food is gone.

"It was good," Jane says. "And all the other stuff made it really special. And I got the best dessert."

The night comes down. Before they got on the road, Jane didn't know how dark night was. Without electric lights it is cripplingly dark. But the soldiers have lights.

Jane says, "I'm going to go see if I can find out about the camp."

"I'll go with you," Nate says.

"No," Jane says. "They talk to a girl more than they'll talk to a guy. You keep Franny company."

She scouts around the edge of the light until she sees the blond soldier. He says, "There you are!"

"Here I am!" she says.

They are standing around a truck where they'll sleep this night, shooting the shit. The blond soldier boosts her into the truck, into the darkness. "So you aren't so conspicuous," he says, grinning.

Two of the men standing and talking aren't wearing uniforms. It takes her a while to figure out that they're civilian contractors. They aren't soldiers. They are technicians, nothing like the soldiers. They are softer, easier in their polo shirts and khaki pants. The soldiers are too sure in their uniforms, but the contractors, they're used to getting the leftovers. They're *grateful.* They have a truck of their own, a white pickup truck that travels with the convoy. They do something with satellite tracking, but Jane doesn't really care what they do.

It takes a lot of careful maneuvering, but one of them finally whispers to her, "We've got some beer in our truck."

The blond soldier looks hurt by her defection.

⌒

She stays out of sight in the morning, crouched among the equipment in the back of the pickup truck. The soldiers hand out MREs. Ted, one of the contractors, smuggles her one.

She thinks of Franny. Nate will keep an eye on her. Jane was only a year older than Franny when she lit out for California the first time. For a second she pictures Franny's face as the convoy pulls out.

Then she doesn't think of Franny.

She doesn't know where she is going. She is in motion.

⌒

Maureen F. McHugh has published four novels and two collections of short stories. She's won a Hugo and a Tiptree award. Her most recent collection, *After the Apocalypse*, was named a *Publishers Weekly* Top Ten Best Book of 2011, was a Philip K. Dick Award finalist, a Story Prize Notable Book, and named to the io9 Best SF&F Books of 2011 list and the Tiptree Award Honor List. McHugh lives in Los Angeles, where she is attempting to sell her soul to the entertainment industry.

⌒

Before the End, Todd was a geeky uncool teenager running a lame ride at an amusement park. But he survived. And, along with others—mostly teens—he occupies the remains of a theme amusement park. Even after The End, growing up is still traumatic and there are consequences of isolation.

• WE WILL NEVER LIVE IN THE CASTLE •
Paul Tremblay

Polar Coaster

Mr. Matheson lives over in Heidi's Hill, we confab every three days in the old mist tent between the World Pavilion and my Slipshod Safari Tour, but today he's late for our date, he scurries and hurries into the tent, something's up.

Mr. Matheson says, She took over the Polar Coaster, he says, I don't know if Kurt just up and left or if she chased him off or killed him but he's gone and now she's there.

I thought we'd never be rid of that retarded kid, he used to eat grass and then puke it all up.

I say, Who is she, what's she look like, does she have a crossbow?

He says, She's your age of course, medium-size, bigger than my goat anyway, and quiet, I didn't get a great look at her, but I know she's there, she wears a black cap, she just won't talk to me.

Why would she say anything to him, I only talk to him out of necessity, necessity is what rules my life, necessity is one of the secrets to survival, I'll give other secrets later, maybe when we take the tour.

Mr. Matheson and me have a nice symbiosis thing going, he gets to stay alive and enjoy a minimum base of human contact, he keeps an eye on my Slipshod Safari Tour's rear flank, last year he saw these two bikers trying to ambush me via Ye Olde Mist Tent, Mr. Matheson gave me that goat's call of his, he is convincing, I took care of the burly thunderdome bikers, they tried to sneak down the tracks and past the plastic giraffe, the one with a crick in its neck and the missing tail, typical stupid New Hampshire rednecks, not that there's a New Hampshire anymore, live free or die bitches, their muscles and tattoos didn't save them, little old me, all 132 pounds of me, me and necessity.

Mr. Matheson is clearly disappointed she won't talk to him, whoever she is, he's probably taken stupid risks to his own skin, and by proxy mine, trying to get her attention, it's so lame and predictable, because of the fleeting sight of a mysterious girl the old man would jeopardize my entire operation here, Mr. Matheson is down to his last goat, the house on Heidi's Hill is a small one-room dollhouse with a mini-bed, mini-table, mini-chair, no future there, it's a good place for a geezer with a white beard going yellow, straw on his face, getting ready to die, no place for a girl, she needs space, the Polar Coaster is a decent spot, back when Fairy Tale Land was up and running the Polar Coaster was one of the most popular rides, I never got to work it, they kept me over on the Whirling Whales, a toddler ride.

At the Polar Coaster the fiberglass igloo and icebergs are holding up okay, they make good hidey holes, warmth and shelter in the winter, shade in the summer, some reliable food stores, wild blueberry bushes near the perimeter of its northern fence, birds nest in the tracks, free pickings of eggs and young, small duck pond in the middle of it all and with ample opportunity to trap smaller critters, the Polar Coaster might be the third best spot in the park behind my Slipshod Safari Tour and Cinderella's Castle, of course, third because it's a little too out in the open for my tastes, everyone who comes to Fairy Tale Land always goes to the Castle and then the Polar Coaster.

I ask, Do you know her name?

Mr. Matheson says, She won't talk to me, remember.

Yeah, I remember, but sometimes it's hard when every day is the same.

Tour: North

I'm not using magnetic north, I know how to use it, gridlines and a map and a steady hand, I'm using the entrance as due south, so in the park's north you've got the Crazy Barn, Farm Follies Show, and Turtle Twirl, no one's lived in those areas since the big freeze last winter, too much damage from the initial lootings for there to be enough shelter, the Crazy Barn used to lift off the ground and spin real slow, too slow, like the rotation of the world slow before that changed, before it stopped.

There was the panic, the Crazy Barn was uprooted off the hydraulic and picked apart, lots of rides suffered similar fates even if they didn't deserve it.

Going in order walking back toward my Slipshod Safari Tour, the Whirling Whales, which I keep cleared out of any potential residents, purely an egomania kind of gesture on my part, everyone needs a hobby, the Oceans of Fun Sprayground with its submarine that was destroyed by three feuding squatters to be, then the Great Balloon Chase, which is a Ferris wheel of hot air balloons, empty now, early on there was a guy named Mr. Philips living in one of the balloons, I called him Dick behind his back, it was late spring and I don't think he was planning on staying there because it would've been too cold in the winter, with the mountains shooting up directly behind the park we always remembered winter, Dick would tell me stuff about his life, not that I cared, he used to sell lawn mowers and motorcycles on the weekends and was twice divorced from the same woman, that's all I remember, that and he had big yellow horse teeth, he didn't breathe, he chewed on the air, I didn't trust him one bit with how he climbed up into the highest balloons to spy on me, there was how he talked too, he always had something to say about how short and skinny and pale I was, he bragged about being a fisherman and hunter and how he used to watch those survivalist shows and he could still do one-hundred push ups easy, even if he was on the sunny side down of forty, Dick was all talk and no chalk, he didn't know anything about his surroundings, he didn't know magnetic north, he didn't listen to what the park and the forest and the mountains had to say, you need to stop and listen, he was a total ass, he listened to me though, he asked how I knew about all the edible wild plants, I give him fiddleheads first, then he ate *amanita phalloides*, death cap mushrooms, next.

Polar Coaster

I belly crawl from the mist tent to what used to be the waiting area in front of the Polar Coaster, Mr. Matheson is probably taking a nap, the old fool always plans eight days in advance, not seven days, he doesn't do anything by the old ways which I do kind of admire, Mr. Matheson leaves me his plan inside one of the Dutch Shoes, a kiddie ride just north of the Polar Coaster and its pond, the plan is usually written in crayon, he wrote his latest plan in burnt sienna.

I don't care if he's taking a nap, I didn't make any sort of pact with him that I would keep away from the new girl, even if we did, I'd break it, I just want to make contact, see what her deal is, see if she presents a danger to my Slipshod Safari Tour.

I say, Hello? Is there anybody out there in the Polar Coaster? Or is it just some funny walking penguins?

I should've probably worn my best threads for the introduction, underneath my jacket is a vest of bamboo that I clipped and ripped from The Bamboo Chute, a water flume ride that took a picture of you before you plummeted down, would never want to work that ride, the line moved too fast, but I liked that the ride exposed a truth, in those pictures where everyone was screaming at the big drop, everyone looked so happy when they were scared, the bamboo vest should stop any arrows or other projectiles that might be flung at me.

I say, Just want to say hi, and that me and Mr. Matheson over there in the Heidi House are friendly, we're not like those monkeys in the south of the park, by the castle, those frauds aren't in it for the long haul, like us, they'll all be gone in a week and then be replaced by other marauders and barbarians, a never-ending cycle, and for what? stupid Cinderella's Castle, it's nothing but a status symbol, no practical reason for surviving there, you'd think we'd be beyond that now, right? will people never learn!

I stop, drop, and listen, she doesn't say anything, yells and screams and other battle noises float up from the park's south, it's like a low cloud that's drawn in, tucked away in Mr. Matheson's crayon-blue sky.

I cup my hands as if that ever makes them stronger, and say, We're living fine in these parts, we help each other out up here, I say, I've killed three bad guys over at The Bamboo Chute with my bamboo spring traps, they shoot bamboo spears out of a panda bear's eyes and clean through the victim's chest, I mean, I've never seen it triggered live, but I've heard it go off, and there were these sick blood trails going away from the chute after, so cool.

A small rectangular chunk of the igloo pops out, so does the tip of an arrow, or a spear, then her voice, the sound of it makes me want to put the old act back on, makes me remember the kid I used to be at the Whirling Whales.

She says, What do you want?

That's a good question, didn't think I'd get this far, really, or, I just haven't admitted to myself what it is I do want.

I say, Just want to make friends, be neighborly, borrow a cup of sugar or something every once in a while, right? I can help, give you information, a tour of the park, what to know what to avoid what to eat where to sleep, you can probably help me too, I live there, Slipshod Safari Tour, we can watch each other's backs.

She says, I don't need help.

I say, Fair enough, how about I give you the Slipshod Tour, the works, haven't done it in a while, we can fix it up for tomorrow, still got some gasoline for the tractor, it'll be fun, Mr. Matheson can drive us around, be our chaperone.

I'm done talking and my hands don't know what to do, they snap and slap into each other like triggered snares.

Tour: Boulder

There's this one-ton sphere made of granite right outside my mist tent and the World Pavilion next door, the World Pavilion is where everyone got their overpriced burgers, fries, and sodas, there's no food left there, the boulder sits on a thick, square base a few feet off the ground, when Fairy Tale Land was up and running the base filled with water and a kindergartner could spin the boulder with his kinder-hands in the thin layer of *agua*, all that weight supported by a puddle less than a quarter-inch thick, I used to visit the boulder on my breaks, nudged kids out of the way so I could put my hands on the wet rock and spin it in any direction I wanted, I'd get all wet, there was nowhere else to get that sensation, the power of moving all that impossible weight with my pencil fingers, I liked to stop that rock from turning too, pushing against all those other little hands until it was still, that was more exciting, daring, felt like I was doing something spectacularly deliciously wrong.

Of course, that big old rock doesn't move now, but you knew that.

Whirling Whales

Truth is, before everything happened, I wouldn't have wanted to work the Polar Coaster, the gig was boring, people on and off too fast, no time to talk to anyone, not like the Whirling Whales where I took my time checking the kiddies' seat belts, making jokes about how whales weren't supposed to fly, no one laughed, the other joke I used all the time was something I'd say to whoever was supposed to sit in whale number nine, you see, there was no whale number nine, only eight whales, get it? when kids and parents filled the eight whales I had to shut off the waiting line with a thin white chain that only came up to a toddler's chin or just above a parent's kneecap, it was small but no one dared to cross.

Whoever missed out on whale nine and had to watch the whales fly from right behind that chain I'd say to them, It's not your lucky day, is it? I knew by looking at you, you weren't lucky.

It wasn't much of a joke, I thought it was back then, funny I realize how awkward I used to be when there were all these people around but now that almost everyone's gone I know better, okay it's not funny, it's odd, they all thought I was odd Todd, they were right, I was, I didn't have much back then to hold onto so I made the Whirling Whales my domain, I was the star, I strutted around that ride when I checked the seat belts, sometimes I'd push a whale up and down pretending that I was performing some structural integrity test, I always pushed the fly button with flair, then I'd pretend to not watch the ride and chat up the parents in line, talk tough with the dads, flirt up the moms using my odd looks and leers, arching my barely-there eyebrows into the craziest spots on my forehead, with the kids I tried be the cool teenager, the one they looked up to, wanted to be even if they were too young to know what cool was, but that isn't right, they knew what cool was, just wouldn't be able to articulate it, right? none of them ever took me seriously, and why should they have? I was a short skinny bleached white kid with curly orangey-yellow hair and probably the physically weakest and geekiest teenager in the state, I didn't play football or go hunting or fishing, I got harassed all the time, I was the runt of the state's litter, my Fairy Tale Land shirt never did fit right, always so baggy, made me look thinner than I was, couldn't wear a wristwatch because it'd slide off my wrist, I wore Dickies that were too tight and too small for me because Mom wouldn't buy me new ones, some of the older kids at the park used to ask where the flood was, they don't ask that anymore, do they?

I knew, even then, my act wasn't working, but I committed to it, you have to commit, always, it's how I survived then and how I survive now, you see, I've come a long way since then and really, it didn't matter if no one bought my act back then because it only mattered that I believed in it myself.

Slipshod Safari

She creeps under the entrance canopy that I've worked hard to maintain, I had to replace some of the plastic palm leaves with fir and maple branches, the effect is almost the same, it stays dark in here.

I say, Hi, Joyce, welcome to the Slipshod Safari Tour! go bananas on your trek through the jungles of Africa! please do not feed or pet the animals, same goes for the tour leader.

I bow, take off my safari hat, my blond curls bounce and rebound, Slinkys on escalators, my hair isn't all that blond anymore, more like the color of the diluted Tang Mr. Matheson is always trying to get me to drink, no thanks, she stares at my hair, my Tang, so I put my hat back on, I look ridiculous either way, but in this new world, the one that doesn't turn or spin, what I look like is irrelevant.

She says, I'm supposed to sit in there? with you, in there? with you?

The tractor coughs out turds of black smoke, Mr. Matheson is at the wheel of the open air rig, wearing a white T-shirt with yellow pit stains and overalls that are three sizes too big for him, I know what I said already about looks being irrelevant but I can't help but be embarrassed for him, the tractor pulls a cage on wheels with damp hay bales as seats, the cage is the punch line, it was supposed to protect everyone in the park from the safari animals.

I say, I know it's a lot, it'll be fun, an escape from the daily survival grind.

Joyce takes it all in and says, Do we really need to waste the gasoline on this?

Not sure what she means by *we* but I like it and don't like it at the same time, my palms are sweating like they did when I saw a girl anywhere near my age in line at the Whirling Whales, then it got that much harder to press the fly button with my practiced and patented button flair, hiding those old feelings is impossible sometimes, even as useless as they are to me now.

I assure Joyce that we, *we*, we can spare a gallon, and I make a joke about my unlimited supply.

Mr. Matheson was right for a change, she is my age, give or take a grade, she wears an olive-green shirt and jeans, she's lost somewhere inside of both, black wool cap mushrooms her head, I don't know where hat ends and black hair begins, her crossbow is slung across the back of her shoulders, she talks real fast about this being dumb and it'll attract attention from all the assholes in the south end of the park, and she's right, it's true, the sound of the tractor might raise some curiosity in our little neighborhood, but we're in my area, I've made sure we're safe here.

She says, I'm Korean.

I say, What?

Her confession is abrupt and I'm caught, guardless, I don't know if she's making fun of me, or not, I used to be used to that feeling.

She says, I'm Korean, just wanted to get that out of the way, this morning our chaperone asked if my parents were Chinese or Japanese, or from Vietnam or something, to quote him directly, I figured you and he might share the same brain.

I say, We don't share that lame brain or anything like that, and besides, it doesn't matter to me what you are, or were, I just see a person like me.

She says, Glad that you're able to dismiss my personal identity and thousands of years of cultural experience so easily, how big of you.

Hey, sorry, I didn't mean it like that, really.

How did you mean it?

I shrug and say, You're right, I'm sorry and should've been more sensitive, I've been spending too much time around Mr. Matheson, my discourse skills are rusty not trusty, my tongue is all feet, left feet, club-footed left feet, with painful corns and bunions.

I turn away, not sure if she'll follow me, I duck inside the cage and sit, the hay bale is a bit damp and tied too loosely together, falling apart, it'll do for now, there's a machete and a field knife underneath mine in case I need them, the hunting blade is almost as long as my forearm, serrated, lots of nasty little teeth, across from me on the most level bale is an old red tray that I scrounged from the wreckage of the World Pavilion, two plates of wild greens, apples, and charred goose meat covered in some of the shake-n-a-bag spice I rationed, only three bags left now, two canteens with sugarless lemonade mix, some good and bad mushrooms in my pocket if I need them.

I say, Are you coming? the tour leaves with or without, and soon.

The Great Balloon Chase

Mr. Matheson thought Mr. Philips died of a heart attack despite the clear physical evidence to the contrary, he only sees what he wants to see, that's true of almost everyone, you too.

Oh, I found Mr. Philips, I found Dick leaning up against one of his grounded balloons, it was red and he was dying, drool spilled out between those horse teeth of his, it was gross and he was gross, there was no one else around, I was going to cut off his feet with my machete and use them as bait in a bear trap, but I wouldn't know what to do with a bear if I caught one.

Dick saw me and said some gibberish then he closed his eyes, his puffy eyes, then gathered himself for a clear moment, he said, you and me are a lot different.

He was right but I think he meant it as some sort of insult, implicating my moral character or lack thereof, whatever, fuckface, he was wrong and I told him so, I told him we are different, I told him about a road deemed worthy of the label *scenic route*, it was near my house, near where I grew up, that scenic route had a chunk of it washed out into a sink hole during a rainstorm, they closed a half-mile section of route to all through-traffic in both directions, confusing detours branched out for miles, that simple patch of washed-out blacktop was like an octopus, it had a reach in every direction, my mother swore about it all the time, how it would never be fixed, how they might need to have an emergency town vote on a budget override but not everyone would vote for it, how inconvenient getting around town was, she never got how cool it was, and you would never have got how cool it was either, that's part of the difference, our difference, listen, whenever I could, usually during the day, during working hours, I rode my bike to the route and past the *road is closed* signs and barriers, breaking the law, right? there were homes on the road but the driveways were usually empty, if they weren't empty no one seemed to be out, I rode my bike up and down the closed stretch until my legs shook, riding in the middle of the busy thirty-five mph route, that stretch had no more rules, I traced the yellow lines with my tires, it was so quiet and empty, I listened to the birds, that's all I would hear, I used to pretend the world had ended and that I was the only one who survived, that's not why we're different though, I know your secret, you've fantasized about that too, everyone fantasizes that they're important enough to survive, more than survive, to be the last one left, right? it's why you read those books or watched those Will Smith movies, you imagined how important the last one left would feel, but here's how we're different, I actually wished and wanted that fantasy to come true, and you, you only indulged in the fantasy because it was safely impossible in your mind, sort of like daydream sex with somebody you're not supposed to be daydreaming about, you indulge in the danger until you start thinking about the consequences, until you start really thinking about the big what if, what if it *really* happened? the difference between me and you, you and me, the only one that matters now, is that I wanted it, I wasn't as strong as you were, I wasn't stronger than anyone, I was a frail little ridiculous-looking boy riding a bike, all elbows and knees and nose and bad skin and stupid curly hair but I wanted it, I knew it would happen too, I'm not lying, not a revisionary Larry, that stuff is for you, I figured that if a little rain washing out a small square of road could mess up the everyday lives of the town and commerce routes and anyone else who needed to use that road, well then, it really would take a whole lot less than most people thought to trip up everything, put an end to it all, I knew it was just a matter of time before everything stopped turning.

I was right, I wanted it, I was ready for it, you weren't.

Tour: Slipshod Safari

She's very distrustful of me, but we eat, the goose is as good as goose gets, I don't think I'll need the mushrooms, things are going well, she's cooperating, tolerating, the tractor struggles and muggles through the overgrown tour path, the tall grass whispers on the bottom of our cage, sometimes I dream about being on a small wooden boat, a life raft, a dinghy, I'm by myself, everyone in the world is below the water, all those fingernails tapping and scratching on my hull, the grass sounds like a ghost version of that, it's creepy, it's perfect.

I eat fast, finish before her, then give the tour, talking into the dead handheld microphone receiver, props are important for a successful tour, I tell her, Over there, in the creek bed, that alligator with the shit-eating smile had big pink sunglasses, a beach hat, and an umbrella drink in his claw, tore that stuff out when I moved in, found uses for them, you know, that giraffe who's supposed to be singing in the shower over there, his neck got bent in an attack I fended off a few years ago, now don't tell anyone but that giant fiberglass elephant is my winter bedroom, it's very well insulated, very well supplied, I sleep in its belly and made lookouts and breathe holes through its trunk and asshole, yin and yang, baby, the elephant entrance is hidden, just below its pink skirt, warmer months I sleep in the cage or inside the baseball playing bear, more breezy in there, I can show you the elephant if you'd like? moving too soon, too much too fast? I know, ha ha! okay, I let this next area grow over a bit, the Ol' Fishin' Hole (with the ƒ backwards and in kid-script), nothing but a few frogs and crawdaddies in there, and the kiddie statues are kind of creepy looking, and annoying, Huck Finn kind of caricatures in unbuttoned overalls, straw hats, and big smiles, so I just let it grow over.

She says, Why didn't you take them down?

Tour interrupted! She keeps on about if it bothered me so much, why didn't I take the statues down, take them apart and reuse them like I did with the alligator parts.

There's a string tucked behind my hay bale, I reach back, pull on it twice, the other end is tied around Mr. Matheson's ankle, he stops the tractor like he's supposed to, I say, That's a good idea, come on, let's go, you can help me knock them over and perform a field autopsy, not that I mean to make that sound so grim, think of them as piñatas instead, who knows what we'll find inside when we crack them open, I'll let you take their fishing poles, I don't need them, they're made out of bamboo, bamboo is real strong stuff, very useful.

Joyce puts down the charred flank from a goose that never laid any golden eggs, that attraction is in the south of the park, she says, You want me to go into that thick brush with you? why would I go in there with you? I'd probably get ticks too.

Come on, it'll be fun.

I don't find wanton destruction fun.

No, not wanton, we're destroying to create, that's the big idea, like you suggested, we're harvesting parts to help us survive, we will survive! we'll be Gloria Gaynor! as long as we know how to love we'll always be alive! I sing/ say to her, which was likely a too bold too goofy too weird thing to say, but I'm feeling good.

She says, Oh, gross.

Come on, I'm just kidding, pulling your leg, pull pull pull.

Stay away from my leg!

Let's go, let's chop 'em down and chop 'em up.

No.

Okay, all right, I drop my chummy tone, there's too much of my charisma and charm to handle, so I get formal, soothing, I say, Tell me, Joyce, from whence did you come? how'd you get to the yonder Polar Coaster?

She rolls her eyes at me, and that's all good, of course, she says, Does it matter? I'm new, that's it, I'm new here.

Completely new to the park, are you? I say, and then I cross my legs proper.

She says, No, I tried a couple nights in the south end of the park, in Miss Muffet's Market, but I was displaced.

She's answering my questions, finally, she's digging my formalized speak, I say, Displaced? how fascinating, do continue.

She says, Thrown out, a mob of jerks wearing football pads and helmets chased me out, broke up and stole what little stuff I'd collected.

Mr. Matheson shuts off the tractor engine, sighs loudly, I flash mad, feel hot blood pooling in my cheeks, red, ruddy, we might not get that tractor started again, composure, though, must compose, I say, That's what those football guys do, they try to clear out and claim that area, they're a joke, an annoying one for sure, they never come up here, though, never.

She says, I know that now, but it doesn't make sense, Muffet's Market is at the very southwestern tip of the park, still a good distance away from the Castle, probably as far away from the Castle as this place is, whatever, the south end was too crowded, too loud, and not good enough for me anyway, I could've fought off those assholes if I really wanted to.

I say, I know you could've, you're a bad mo fo, whoops! shut my mouth.

Joyce eyes me up and down and sideways, she's not sure whether to laugh or stab my thigh, whether she needs to take me seriously or not, she says, I left the market of my own free will but I'm heading back to that area soon, I deserve the Castle, I want the Castle.

I'm disappointed, it's always about the Castle, always, about, the, Castle, I don't know why, everyone goes there, they sleep and fuck and fight on the front lawn if they can't get in and if they do get in the stay is never long, I haven't had word trickle up here of a permanent resident, the Castle is always under siege, stuck in a permanent coup loop.

I say, I thought you were better than the Castle, you wanting to live there, I have to say, is so cliché, thought there was more to you than that, Joyce, really.

She says, Fuck you, don't even pretend to know me, so typical, I want what I want and I have my own reasons for what I want.

Okay, I'm sorry, I take it back, I say and pretend to catch the words out from the air and stuff them in my mouth, I say, Mmm, tastes like goose, let's talk later about the Castle, maybe we can work something out, now, don't be freaked out but I have a machete on board with us, we can use it to clear us a little path to the fishing hole, right there, I only keep the machete here because I'm always prepared, prepared always.

Joyce stands and doesn't have to crouch in the cage, pulls her hat down tighter, unsheathes her own machete hidden inside her pant leg, strapped around her calf, she says, Fine, we'll do this, but after you and me are going to talk about the Castle, seriously talk.

We jump out of the cage and hack two separate paths in the brush, Mr. Matheson pretends not to watch us like a good chaperone, maybe I'll forgive his shutting off the tractor, I swing the machete wildly, freely, and all the other ly-ies, I'm losing control, it's a good feeling, I catch the back of my knuckle on the recoil and open up a bright cut, skin opens as easily as the brush, the shrubbery, the lean green, I'm at the fishin' hole's edge, so is Joyce, she pushes her sleeves up, smiles at me, she says, We could do this over near the Castle, make a path, sneak in the back, it would work.

She takes a mighty hack at the freckle-faced all a-okay usa fisherboy, loosening the right arm at the shoulder, I know she's pretending the kid is one of those footballers who chased her off, I hack away at his buddy, punch through the plaster chest, cave in his always happy face, Joyce and I are daydreaming about what we can do, together, it feels good, it feels more like practice than daydreaming.

Professor Wigglesteps's Loopy Lab

Mr. Matheson couldn't start the tractor again, we ditched him there, his head inside the engine trying to figure out why everything falls apart, breaks down, good luck with that, I invited her back to my elephant, show her my supplies, I think Joyce sensed how nervous I was, I am, that neither of us were ready for that, she declined, I was relieved, instead we jogged out of the Slipshod Safari, past the Great Balloon Chase.

Joyce was a self-described average student but very intelligent, there's a difference of course, she was quiet, no friends, accepted school as her great trial, a personal gulag she said, then when it all ended she lost her parents during the great panic, all of the state became a refugee camp pressing up against the canadian border, it was epic and sad, maybe her parents were trampled during a border rush, Joyce remembers being squeezed so tight, face pressed into someone's sweaty back, her feet didn't touch the ground, her movements determined by the tide of humanity coming in from every direction, it was no way to die, it was no way to live, she swam out, kicked punched clawed out, climbed on top, walked on heads and scalps, away from the border, she hiked back down through the state to Fairy Tale Land, she doesn't really know for sure if her parents died under a million desperate heels, it feels true, it's what she fears but at the same time it makes living here by herself easier, wondering if they were alive or if they missed her would be too difficult to bear, care bear, or maybe the truth is that Joyce's parents were overbearing snot-jobs she couldn't kick to the curb fast enough, for her the great panic was the day she was born, the great panic was an opportunity, like it was and is for me.

I'm not sure, I don't really know anything, Joyce doesn't tell me any of this, but the border-scenario is what I imagine for her as we walk to Professor Wigglestep's Lab.

The lab is an empty but cavernous building that has been stripped, just a few hunks of two-by-fours lying around, and stray red-blue-green-yellow plastic balls from the ball pit, we rustle up the stray balls, corral them into the pit, less a pit than a depression in the floor, the balls are hard and brittle, and deflate easily into hard shapes with uncomfortable nubs and corners but we sit on them anyway, Joyce puts her hands behind her head and closes her eyes, I just start talking, tell her everything I know about the park, give her an oral tour of the north section, tell her about the stilled boulder at the World Pavilion near the Polar Coaster, she's seen it but hasn't tried to spin it, I tell her about me and my mom, about the Whirling Whales, about the washed out road, about how I took care of Dick.

She says, Stop it, the kids down near Muffet's Market told me about Mr. Philips, how he died of a heart attack.

That's the story Mr. Matheson told them, I'm giving you the real deal, I say, and I pout, blood filling my cheeks again, blood always wants to break out from beneath the surface, that's what I think about while picking at the splintered edge of the ball depression with my pocket knife.

Joyce must feel bad for calling me out like that and finally starts telling me stuff, she talks about some books and blogs she used to read, Jungian treatises on the nature of reality, stuff on cultural appropriation and radical politics, she tells me her utopian visions for the park, she makes it all sound so cool, I'm mostly listening and she uses the word *opportunity*, I do envy her big social ideas, her ability to include everyone who deserves to be included, but I can't go fooling myself or anyone else, not anymore, I'm in this for me and no one else, then I think about Mr. Matheson and wonder if he's still working on the tractor, working on it by himself.

I'm still picking at the frame, twisting the knife, turning the wood dust, still more than a little sore that she'd dismiss my dispatching of Dick story so quickly, and just when I'm thinking that maybe she doesn't understand me at all, we're somehow back on the subject of Cinderella's Castle, she has a plan on how the two of us could take it over, not for personal glory, no never, we claim it so we could lead the park, instill some order, the right kind of order, a new golden age of civilization, a pax Fairy Tail Land-a, Joyce doesn't use those exact words but it's what she means.

I say, Okay, what's the plan, Stan? I'll be your Achilles to your Helen of

Troy, I'll be your Rasputin to your Anastasia, she doesn't laugh until I say, I never was any good at history, we should just re-write it all now anyway, no one cares.

Joyce digs underneath her legs and pulls out a red pit-ball, it's not in ball shape anymore, caved in, a half-moon, a half-eaten rotted poisoned fruit, she says, Okay, this is the Castle.

Tour: South

It's early dark, the dark before, everything covered in dew, I walk by Muffet's Market, there are two dudes in football or lacrosse gear, asleep, maybe drunk or stoned, toad or leaf lickers, snores echo in their helmets, cleated feet stick out the market front door, too bad it wasn't that someone dropped a house on them, wish I was that strong, my machete is out, I think about having some pre-Castle-coup fun, a little hacky hacky, but I'm not working alone today, stick to the plan, a two-pronged attack, with me walking to the Castle's front door and Joyce sneaking in through the back, it'll never work.

Down by the south end of the park, by the old entrance, I hate it down here, it's easy to get sick, it's commoner than the cold, thick in the air here, like pollen, common, the want the need, to be seen with everyone else, to be park popular, park important, to live in the Castle, or settle near it, to be in its shadow, as if that's enough, I mouse it past the Old Woman in the Shoe, Humpty Dumpty, Three Bear's House, and Granny's Cottage and weak, curled-up thoughts of relocation fill my head, oh my poor little head, no, I'm staying where I am, we will never live in the Castle, I'm only helping Joyce get to where she wants to go and then I'm going back, recede into the background, a man behind the curtain is something to be.

Past the Cuckoo Glockenspiel, the empty Storybook Animals pen, the petting zoo, to the Swan Boats, and there, across the bridge and up the hill is the Castle, I sit at the foot of the bridge, I could be the grumpy old troll who lives under the bridge, I really don't care about other people answering my questions three, it's hours past midnight, waiting for the sun to rise from the east, waiting for the sign.

Cinderella's Castle

Something went wrong, Joyce must've got caught, failed, bailed, I don't see her anywhere, everyone on the grass hill is awake, this was a mistake, what was our plan exactly, anyway? a mistake I'm going to make worse, I run across the footbridge, the hero who knows he's going to die, a Grimm or Aesop hero, not fucking fraud Disney, I run in slow motion, show my import, the weight of the hero's every step, machete raised and sharpened, hungry, greedy, the tip cuts off chunks of sunlight that fall to the ground, everything dies, the green hill ahead of me is a hive, crawls with people, everyone fights each other, every person for himself, they'll be ready for my army of one.

At the other end of the bridge, my first combatants, a tall girl wearing a plastic but reinforced Viking helmet and brandishing a wooden chair leg versus a short hamburger of a dude in a suit of armor made of duct tape, he swings a metal fence post, I yell and offer some manic machete swings that connect with no one, nothing, the two combatants join forces to face and fend my attack, she whacks my arm with the chair leg, fucking ow! I drop the machete, it clangs like a gong, get the hook, the hamburger dude is slow with his bulky fence post, he doesn't swing so much as he pushes, he nudges, nudges me aside so they can finish the serious fighting, I've been dismissed as a threat so easily, it's because I'm out of my element, out of my elephant? why am I here?

I'll have to do this without my weapon, the machete gone, someone swooped in and took it already, damn, a costly casualty I wasn't expecting, I run up the hill and don't stop for the plethora of battle engagement invites thrown my way like casual insults, I run past warriors sporting the everyday household items as shields, as weapons, blunt instruments most of them, but there's one person waving around a whisk-spatula combo that looks sharp enough to pierce through pseudo duct tape armor.

Word of my gauntlet-run passes through the epic unending battle scene, the word is a virus, a worm, I sense it more than hear it, everyone here is here every day, fighting the same person or the same people, they're a group, a whole, an entity, they know when there's an intruder, interloper, outsider, a me making a go at them.

Near the top of the hill, almost off the grass, just ahead is the rotunda where Cinderella's pumpkin cart pulled a *u*-ey, turned around and went back down the hill, I'm close, the front door isn't far, the Castle is a cartoon capping on a hill, gleaming white with purple and teal spires and turrets, it's shaped like a crown with a swirl of marble staircase leading to its great wooden doors, the doors are closed, I'll open them, I will.

I'm still on the grass, haven't made the swirl, the front stairs where the fighting is the most intense, a blur of the thwarted and the thwartees, a cluster of jousters and their tree-branch or golf-club lances demand that I halt who goes there, these masked riders riding piggy-back on their masked rides block my path, circle me, shepherd me backwards, lost sheep, I'm blinded by someone's pocket laser pointer, I stumble and bumble, then broadsided by two park-issued baby carriages, the trundling plastic wheels take my legs out at the knees, I'm down, I lose my breath, I'm effectless useless and all the other-lesses, this might be it, everyone moves in, picks me up, swallows me whole, spits me out, rejected, I roll down the hill, I roll down forever and into the pond, I can't swim, it's only knee-deep.

I limp home, the battle renews behind me.

Heidi's Hill

He let me in but this place isn't big enough for the two of us, he let me in but he isn't talking to me, he pretends to be busy whittling something, a goat maybe, what is it with fucking goats?

I sit at the mini table, my chin plays the bongos on my knees, I say, She never showed, she's not at the Polar Coaster either, she must've made it without me.

Mr. Matheson sits on his bed, it's small enough to be a couch cushion, he shrugs and almost hits his head on the ceiling, he says, I'm sure she's fine, you should probably just leave her alone, you're going to have to leave, I'm sorry, but I'm busy.

I'm a cast of a thousand questions, I say, Maybe I was enough of a distraction out there on the hill for her to get into the Castle, I mean, don't get me wrong, I don't really care about the Castle, the Castle can suck it, those damn dirty apes can have it, but I hope she made it, maybe she's still waiting for me to show up, should I try coming in from behind like she did?

Mr. Matheson is wearing his park-issued Heidi's grandfather outfit, his brown hat is too small, his legs too white and veiny, he says, Visiting hours are over, kid, scram.

Mr. Matheson gets in moods, funky funks, he probably has his lederhosen in a bunch because I left him with the broken-down tractor in the middle of the Slipshod Safari, I say, You blew it by shutting the tractor off, don't even remind me.

I stand up, tall as Paul Bunyan, and lurch around the place, I say, What if Joyce ditched me, used me? if I let that happen, if I allowed that happen to me, it's so stock, cliché, right out of a middle-schooler's YA novel of the week, it's like Jill pushing Jack down the hill, or something.

He says, Just go.

I'm still soaking wet from the dunk in the pond, I lost my machete, he has one tacked onto the wall, a real big knife sitting there on the replicated and miniaturized wall, Heidi's wall, Heidi was a story about an orphaned girl being taken care of by her grandfather, a grandfather who lives like a recluse in the Swiss Alps, Mr. Matheson isn't the grandfather, he just plays one in the park, he told me the story once about Heidi's grandfather learning to love her and there's other crap about Heidi helping some girl in a wheelchair walk because of goat milk and the mountain air, but I stopped listening, stopped caring about Heidi, the story was as stupid and small as the Heidi House, everything is so stupid and so small.

I say, All right, Mr. Happy Pappy, I'll go, I know what to do now anyway.

It's true, I do, I know what to do, I say, Thanks for helping with the tour earlier, really, I appreciate it, I brought you a bounty, more a snack than a bounty to be honestly honest, your favorite kind of snack, picked just for you.

I empty my pockets onto the mini-table, my pockets were full of mushrooms, a mix with a fix, a medley of mushrooms, it takes all kinds, a bit soggy and loggy but he'll eat them, even the ones he shouldn't eat, the ones with the great green caps, big as garbage-can covers.

End of the Tour: Boulder safari castle boulder

I'm back here, outside my mist tent and the World Pavilion, opposite the Polar Coaster, I'm back here, at the center of the park, its core, the heart, the one-ton heart, this here granite boulder is my crystal ball, in it I see my past, the past is passed.

The past, I left Heidi's Hill and went back to my the Slipshod Safari, avoided the booby traps and snares and crawled inside my elephant, it's the elephant in the park, inside the elephant was my room, darker than any closet, inside were the supplies, and the surprise, inspired by Mr. Matheson I put on my old Fairy Tale Land uniform, the one I had worn when I was that little shit working the Whirling Whales, it all still fit, the baggy blue shirt was still baggy, the tight pants were still tight, I walked to the Castle, my arms loaded with barrels and bullets, fingers itching triggers, I walked to the Castle as determined as an earthquake.

Even through the lens of my handy-dandy boulder crystal ball, my assault on the hill and the Castle is fuzzy, it was like that scene in the cartoon movie about a secret society of rabbits, cartoon movie but not a kid's movie, not some anesthetized fairy tale that you'd find here or in other parks, this movie was real, there was this scene near the beginning of the movie, the end of it all came at the beginning, the farmers ploughed the rabbits and their warren all under, there was rabbit screaming, wide bulging rabbit eyes, rabbit terror, frozen rabbit expressions gone all swirly in a flood of torn throats and blood and dirt and bodies, my ears ringing afterward, just like after my run up the Castle hill, and after, it was all quiet, the park cleared, I was alone, I was alone, dripping the rabbit blood, standing outside the great wooden doors, at the top of the swirled marble staircase, I was alone, dripping the movie blood, knocking on the great wooden doors, no one answered my knocks or my calls, Cinderella wasn't home, she didn't live there, I knew this, standing there alone and outside the great doors yelling *let me in* felt like the end to a different story, a different fairy tale, the wrong one, so I opened the doors even if I wasn't supposed to, inside the castle everything was small, it made me angry to think that this is what everyone was fighting over, it was only one room with mirrored walls, some fake suits of armor, a dingy red carpet, a shoddy throne, Joyce was there, huddled and hiding behind the throne along with the pumpkin driver dressed in service orange and a phony Cinderella with painted-on apple cheeks and a few other kids that used to work the park, Joyce was wearing her old Polar Coaster outfit, the one with the penguins, she wouldn't look at me, but tried to talk me out of whatever it was I was trying to do, she tried to tell me it was okay that we could still live in the castle like she promised, I knew better, and I made like that movie again, I ploughed her and the rest of them rabbits under, the end came so quickly, and then I just left, I've learned it works that way sometimes, I came back here and covered the boulder with the blood from my hands and my clothes and my hair, there was enough blood so that I could turn and spin the boulder again, it's a wheel and has always been greased with blood.

The boulder, the one-ton boulder is my mirror mirror on the wall, it's showing me the future now, I will survive, no one will care or come after me for what I did because there's no one left, I told you that already, there's no one left, I'm the last one, it has to be that way, what I'll do is this, I'll dig out my bike from out behind the employees shack out behind the World Pavilion, the bike is beat up, a little small for me, the spokes and chain will have some rust but the gears will still work, still turn, it'll be the only thing that still turns, I'll get my bike out from behind the shed and ride it around Fairy Tale Land, ride it around the park for a lark, to wherever I want, and it'll be just like when I was riding my bike up and down that closed road, you and no one else will be there.

⌐⌐

Paul Tremblay is the author of the novels *The Little Sleep*, *No Sleep Till Wonderland,* and *Swallowing a Donkey's Eye,* and the short story collections *Compositions for the Young and Old* and *In the Mean Time*. He has published two novellas, and his essays and short fiction have appeared in the *Los Angeles Times*, *Five Chapters.com*, and *Best American Fantasy 3*. He is the co-editor of four anthologies including *Creatures: Thirty Years of Monster Stories* (with John Langan). Tremblay is the president of the board of directors for the Shirley Jackson Awards. He lives outside of Boston, Massachusetts and has a master's degree in Mathematics.

⌐⌐

The End has come and in England most people are trying to get to London—not that just anyone is going to be allowed in. Just getting there is a challenge, but for a blind man and a woman in a wheelchair it is more difficult than for most.

• NEVER, NEVER, THREE TIMES NEVER •
Simon Morden

Somewhere outside of Cheltenham, her automatic car had run out of petrol. No one wanted to give her any more, and she couldn't buy so much as a teaspoon. Pounds sterling were only good for keeping warm at night, either by burning the banknotes or by stuffing them under a coat for an extra layer. Coins, properly sharpened, could be thrown or used in a sling.

Eventually, an army Land Rover had come along. The soldiers let her get herself out and collect some of her belongings from the boot, before rolling the car into the ditch. Their orders were to keep the roads clear. They sympathized, but they couldn't take passengers.

She had known, too. How many hard-luck cases had they come across that day, that week? She had let them leave with her dignity intact. She hadn't begged or pleaded, just worked out what she could carry in her lap and started down the road in her wheelchair.

A day and a night later, she was still making progress down the minor roads of Gloucestershire when a car, a sofa tied recklessly to its roof, careered around the corner. She would either die, or throw herself aside. Despite everything, she chose to live.

The car didn't stop. It left her lying in a muddy entrance to a field of wheat that no-one would ever harvest. Her chair had tipped, righted itself and run on out of sight down the slight incline. She heard its squeaky wheel fade, then stop abruptly. Having resolved to drag herself along the wet tarmac by her fingernails, she was just inching herself and her useless stiff leg round when she heard a rhythmic tapping.

A man was walking towards her, a long white cane in his right hand. He swept the road like a metronome, tapping the hard black surface at one extreme, touching the silent verge at the other. He wore a hat down over his face, and a raincoat buttoned up to the chin. She could see nothing of him.

He wore a satchel over his back, which she could see clearly as he passed her by, feeling out the unfamiliar route with the tip of his stick.

She finally remembered to shout to him.

"Hey!"

He stopped and turned his head. Perhaps he thought he had heard the cry of a rook, and made to walk on.

"Please, can you help me?" she said.

"I don't know," he replied simply. "Can I?"

"My wheelchair ran away without me. I think it stopped further down the hill."

"And you'd like me to bring it to you?" He didn't move, but listened intently.

"I would be grateful. I don't have much to share, but," and she shrugged, and felt stupid for doing so, since he would never see the gesture.

"I think I can do better than that." He walked over to near where she was, probing the ground as he went. When he touched her, she flinched. Why, she wasn't sure.

"That's me."

"Of course it is." He folded the stick away, click-click-click, and felt for her knees and her shoulders. Before she could object, he had picked her up in his arms. It felt strange, comfortable yet vulnerable, like she was a little child again. Despite the bulk of the full leg cast, he said: "You weigh nothing at all. Are you an angel?"

"No." She was close to his face, what she could see of it. His dark stubble, the marks on his face from spattered mud. He wore blacked-out glasses perched on a strong, narrow nose.

"All the same, you'll have to guide me."

She told him which way to walk, which potholes to avoid. It was only twenty yards, but for the first time in months she felt safe. He set her down on the road gently, and brushed the seat down for her before she pulled herself up his coat and into the chair again.

They went back for the rest of her belongings, few though they were: a blanket, a sleeping bag, a cup, some clothes.

"When did you last eat?" he asked her.

"Monday? I think it was Monday. I had some food in my house."

"And today is?"

"Wednesday."

He opened his satchel, and gave her a bread bun. It was stale. She didn't care.

While she ate, he pushed her, and after being reminded how hungry she really was, she asked him to stop.

"What's wrong?"

"Where were you going?" She lowered her head. She had been independent, successful, and she wanted that again. "I don't want to be a burden to you."

"Let us bear one another's burdens gladly. It's in the Bible. So I'm glad. Where shall I take you?"

"I wanted to get to London. It's where everyone's going."

"I've heard it's about the only place which is still open. What will you do when you get there?"

"Find work. There must be work."

"Of course there must. Shall we go?" He started pushing her again.

"Diane. My name's Diane."

"Owen."

They worked as a team. As she had said, everyone was heading towards London, and they had left almost everything behind. Looting was illegal, punishable by death; but all the lawgivers had gone to the capital, too.

They only took what they needed. Vegetables from a garden, eggs still warm from a chicken's feathers, paraffin from an unguarded tank in a farmyard. They ate, without fear. If they had been whole and able and scared of contamination, they might have hesitated. But they both knew that hunger or infections would kill them quicker than cancer might.

One night, drinking bottled beer around Owen's ridiculously small paraffin cooker, she offered him her sleeping bag.

"I'm fine," he said, cupping his hands closer to the meager heat.

"That's not quite what I meant." She looked around her, at the tiny pool of light they inhabited inside a vast, empty warehouse.

"I . . . Diane."

"You do love me, don't you?"

"Yes. Dear God, yes."

"Then come and lie down with me. There's nothing on telly tonight."

He laughed a quiet sad laugh, because she reminded him of everything that was momentarily lost but feared forever gone.

"I'll hurt you."

"It's only my leg." She reached out and touched his arm. Through the layers of rough, dirty fabric, she could feel him trembling for her. "I know you'll be gentle with me."

"I'm filthy."

"Then let me wash you." She took off his hat, which was the last thing he did at night—putting it on was the first thing he did in the morning—and pressed her fingers into his thick black greasy hair. With careful maneuvering, she sat behind him and, with a pair of tiny nail scissors, started to trim along the collar line, above the ears.

She blew the shorn hair away, and he shivered at her breath.

She reached around in front of him, and unbuttoned his topcoat, unzipped the fleece he wore underneath. He shrugged them off, slowly. They fell behind him and she pulled them away.

He had a thick sweater on, and two T-shirts. Owen seemed to make up his mind. He took his glasses from his blind eyes and gave them to Diane to put somewhere safe. While she did so, he crossed his arms at the waist and pulled the rest of his top garments off in a single pull.

He smelled of the road, just like she did, but he had the bruises to prove it. His back was marked with a dozen circular bruises, fat and purple, obvious even in the dim light.

"What are these?" She touched one with the tip of one finger, more a caress than an examination.

"Stones. They didn't break my bones, but they drove me off. I don't know where I was when it happened: I don't even know who threw them. Children, I think. There seem to be so many children, and not enough adults to go around."

She bent over awkwardly and kissed his bruised back, once for every injury. There was hot water in Owen's little kettle. She mixed it with cold until she could stand to dip a piece of cloth in it and wring it out. She started to wash him, just as she had promised. When she had done his back, he turned towards her.

His fingers found her hair, her ear, her cheek, her neck, and lower, lower.

They made love, slow and serious, to the sound of the wind catching the high warehouse roof, and the murmuring of pigeons sheltering from the night.

They moved on, traveling a little at a time, taking bites out of the distance so that it wouldn't seem so far. His shoes were worn through, and she found him some new ones. She hesitated to ask him how far he had walked, because his life had started when he had met her, and before that moment there was nothing.

Of course, there were other people on the road, too. Some, like them, were travelers with a purpose; they had either a destination or a loved one to find. They clutched their maps or their photographs like life itself.

Others just drifted, following this rumor or that. There was food and water in a town. There were trucks going to a transit camp. There was a train taking refugees all the way to London. They wandered, despondent, becoming tired and ill for no discernible benefit.

Still more were mad. It was difficult to tell whether they had been driven insane by the things they had seen since the start of Armageddon, or whether they had always been that way. They had nuclear dreams, and shouted and screamed whilst awake.

And then there was Fox.

He was already waiting for them in the prefabricated hut they had chosen for the night. It was in the grounds of a village school, and had been bought as an extra classroom. It was full of little wooden desks and chairs, still set out in orderly rows.

None of the windows had been broken. It was perfect.

Owen carried Diane carefully up the steps to the door. She opened it with her free hand, and guided him in. He felt her stiffen.

"What? What's wrong?"

"There's someone else here."

Fox lit a cigarette, and leaned back in the teacher's chair. "Plenty of room. I don't mind sharing."

"You weren't here earlier."

"True, true. Not when you first came in, but what about the night before, or the night before that? I've almost been here forever. Not quite true, but places like this, and this place in particular for the past week. But welcome anyway."

"I'll get your chair inside," said Owen. "Is the floor clear?"

"It's fine. Put me down."

Owen lowered her gently to the floor, and went back outside to retrieve her wheelchair and their latest scavengings.

"You've been in the wars," said Fox. "But haven't we all, in the most literal sense?" He leaned forward and opened some drawers at random, riffling through the contents of papers, books, and pencils. He produced a fat black marker pen, and strode down the central aisle towards her. He wore a long weather-beaten leather coat, and brown leather driving gloves, and dusty brown boots.

"What are you doing?" she asked.

He knelt down before her, and scribbled "Fox" on her leg cast, just above the bulge of her knee, on the inside of her thigh.

"There," he said. "It's done properly, now."

She looked at him, and pushed his hand away. "You could help Owen."

He snapped the lid back on the pen. "I could," he said, tapping his chin, "but that would make you think you owed me something. Do you want to feel obligated to me?"

"No," she said, and was surprised about how small her voice sounded.

Owen struggled in through the door with her chair. He set it down on its wheels and felt for the brake, to make sure it was properly on.

Fox wandered slowly back up to the head of the class, spinning the pen between his fingers like a majorette's baton, and Diane hauled herself back into her chair.

He waited until Owen had gone back outside for the bags. "He'll never see how beautiful you are. Doesn't that make you sad?"

She looked at her leg, to remind herself of the name. "Fox. Shut up."

"It makes me sad. A beauty like yours ought to be admired, cherished, worshipped even." He put the pen back in its drawer. "I'd worship you."

"You're a madman."

"Touched by the heat of a man-made sun? I know perfection when I see it." He put his finger to his eye. "I see."

Owen came back up the stairs, carrying two bags. He might not have offered if he could have seen Diane's body language. "We've food enough for three. Will you join us?"

"I'd be delighted to, old chap. Just like the days of the Savoy and the Ritz; we shall have silver service and a bottle of the finest premier cru champagne. Candles will light our faces, and a string quartet will discreetly play Schubert."

"I . . . don't think so. Diane says it's meatballs in some sort of sauce, and some potatoes we dug up."

"Then meatballs it shall be. Put the champagne back on ice and crack open a bottle of Bordeaux. Instead of Schubert, we'll have some robust Romany songs."

Diane peeled the potatoes, while Owen opened the cans and slopped the contents into one of the integral pans that came with the cooker. She wanted to tell him about Fox, and his strangeness. Every time she thought they were alone, she started to warn him, but Fox would reappear suddenly, startling her and making her clam up.

It transpired that they were never alone for the rest of the evening. She was quiet, almost to the point of rudeness. Owen asked Fox about news of the rest of the country.

"It's gone to hell in a hand basket, my good man. The stout yeomen of England have abandoned ship, and the stink of fear spreads like a contagious disease. Our blessed government has fenced in London, all the way around the M25. Every soldier who can carry a gun—cooks, bandsmen, the lot—stand shoulder to shoulder behind the wire. There would be a queue from Heathrow to Cardiff, if there was still a Cardiff to queue to, just to get through the gates they've built."

"How do you know this?"

"Know it? This isn't some third-hand scuttlebucket. I've seen it myself. There are three ways into London: the interchanges of the M25 with the M4, the M11, and the M2, and they're all guarded like they expect Satan himself to try and break through. They strip you, X-ray you, search everything you own, go through every seam of your clothing. They check your identity so thoroughly that some people have confessed to crimes forgotten for half a century. It takes hours, and not everyone gets in. Oh no."

"Well, we're heading for London."

"The whole country, south of Sheffield, is going to London. I wish you luck. I prefer the open road, the clear sky, and the freedom of being at no-one's beck and call."

"What about water contamination? And the food will run out eventually."

"The politicians don't have a country to run anymore, but they still need subjects to order around and give their lives meaning. So they cram as many as they can behind the barbed wire and the guns—which are there not to keep the Armageddonists out, but to keep their slave population in. They tell you that there will be no police, no hospitals, no bins emptied, no streets swept, no festivals or flower shows, no shops or offices or pubs outside of the M25, and we like sheep follow them as if we can't exist without such things. People lived off this land for ten thousand years without someone wiping their nose. There'll always be people outside, people like me, who won't do as they're told."

"Well, I for one like hot baths and penicillin." Owen yawned, and rested his head in Diane's lap. She pulled off his hat and stroked his hairline, and soon he was asleep.

Fox sat opposite them, staring.

"They won't let him in, you know."

"You don't know that."

"I do. He's a burden to them. Someone who won't give, but will get. He'll take food and shelter away from someone who can see. He'll be turned away at the gates."

"And what about me? You think they'll turn me away too?" Her voice was defiant.

"Not you. You've broken your leg. It's in a cast. It's probably set by now, strong enough to take your weight. You're a professional, aren't you? You'll be on their favored occupations list. You'll get in. Easy. You'll start a new life in London."

"But not Owen."

"He's blind. Or hadn't you noticed?"

"He's a physiotherapist. He's got a better chance of getting in than me, a mere teacher. So you're wrong, Fox. And in any event, I'd never leave him. We're going to London together, and we're going to get in together. I'd do anything for him."

"Would he do anything for you?"

"I'm sure of it."

"Best thing he could do is just walk off into the night and disappear. He knows you'll never leave him. He knows he'll be turned back at the gates and you'll go with him. He wouldn't want that. He wants you safe. He'll tell you, even as they're pushing him away with the barrels of their guns, that he doesn't love you, that he used you to try and get him in. Your love for him will finish you both."

"How can you say such things? That's hateful."

"He wants you to live. How long do you think you'll last outside, away from your hot baths and your penicillin?"

"I'm not going to listen to any more of this. I will never leave Owen. We didn't find each other by chance. It was destiny. As if the whole of Armageddon had been arranged to throw us together. And now we are together, we won't let go."

Fox rubbed the palms of his gloved hands together, then spread them wide.

"I'm just telling you how it is down at the gates. He'll be the death of you. That would be a not just a shame, but a crime."

"We'll be fine. Whatever you say." She looked down at Owen, his head cradled in her lap. "We'll be better than fine."

"You'll learn," said Fox, and wrapping his coat around him, he retreated back to the teacher's desk.

Softly, she whispered to Owen. "I'll never leave you. Never, never, never."

When she woke up, Owen was gone. Her head pounded with pain as she sat up. Her vision was blurred and her tongue so thick in her mouth that she could only croak out his name.

He was gone. His bag was gone. Her first thought was that he had been awake during her conversation with Fox, and had been taken in by his ridiculous argument.

He must have heard her say she would stay with him no matter what.

She found a bottle of water, and drank half of it.

"Fox? Fox? Where's Owen? He's gone."

But Fox had gone too.

"Owen?" she shouted, her voice cracking with panic. She pulled herself over to the windows where the bright sunlight streamed in. The sun was well up. She stared at her watch. It was late morning. A fresh surge of anxiety rose up in her throat.

There was no one outside either.

Diane crawled to her chair and clambered in. She'd have to negotiate the steps herself. She'd open the door, push herself out onto the wide landing, then hang on to the guardrails and cast the chair down the steps. She'd follow, easing herself down on her bottom. That's what she'd do.

She got to the door, and it opened before she could put her hand to the knob.

"Owen!"

It was Fox. "What? I heard a commotion, and I came as fast as I could."

She swallowed hard on her disappointment. "Owen's gone, and it's because of you."

"Me? I didn't do anything? How can you blame this on me?"

"Shut up and help me find him. He can't have gone far."

"Yes, yes of course. I'll bounce you down the steps."

It felt wrong to have Fox behind her, and not Owen. He didn't know how to handle the chair, his heavy-handed touch betraying his inexperience. He rushed her to the road outside the school. Owen wasn't there, tapping his way with his white cane.

"How did I sleep so long? He could be a mile away, or more by now." She took a deep breath and shouted for him again.

"Let's try left first," said Fox. "That's the way to London."

"No. Go the other way. Go right. If Owen doesn't think he's going to get in, he'll turn back."

Fox swung the chair around and started north and west at a brisk pace. She kept on calling his name, hoping that he would answer, and she could explain and cling to him with all her might and make him come with her.

They rolled all the way through the short village, and there was no sign of him. They came up hard against "Westbury welcomes careful drivers," and she put her head down in despair and wept.

"He's gone. It's so stupid, but he's gone."

"Gone? No. Stupid? Not that either. It takes someone with brains to pull something like this off. I'm not stupid. I'm cunning. Just like a fox."

She almost heard him, couldn't quite make out what he had said through her gasps and sobs. "Why did I have to sleep so late?"

"Because I poisoned the pair of you, you silly cow, that's why. A bit of ground-up Mogadon in the evening repast, and you slept like babies. Him first, because he was tired, you later because you weren't."

"What's that? Fox?"

"God almighty, don't you get it? Aren't you listening? You're just like the men on the gate. You're just not listening to me. Your precious Owen's not gone anywhere except to the toilets at the school. I promised him a real flush loo, and he was so bloody grateful. I imagine he's washing and shaving, and he'll wait for me to come and find him."

Her tears dried on her cheeks. "What have you done?"

"Done? Nothing yet, except get you out of the way. You could scream until your throat bled and he wouldn't hear you from down here. Why do you think I was in such a hurry to get you away from the school? But when I get back, that's when I'll do it. I'll tell Owen you've gone. To London. On your own. That you've abandoned him. Oh, he'll be upset, he'll want to follow you. I'll point him down the right road, maybe even go with him for a while. But you won't be there. You'll be back here."

Fox's voice was hardly his own. He spoke in a harsh growl that was more animal than human. His eyes burned, his skin flushed, his fingers clawed at the air and his feet crushed the ground.

"But I love him."

"I hate love! I hate it. I can't bear to see it, sickly sweet, foul and base and vile." He pulled off one glove and pressed his tainted palm into her face, forcing her head back until her neck ached with the strain. "Do you see that? Do you see? I was turned away at the gate. Rejected, spat out, vomited and shat upon. If you're rejected, they stain you with an indelible blue dye. That's it. You're out. Never coming back. You won't waste their time again."

He kept pushing, and the front wheels of the chair tipped off the ground. She tried to balance, failed, and went over. Her head went *crack* on the tarmac, no matter that she tried to protect it with her hands.

He wrenched the chair away, and flung it as hard as he could. It screeched and scraped and slid into a ditch. He was panting, his hands on his knees, trying to catch his breath.

"Do you see why? Why I have to do this? They turned me away to die. I can't touch them. They're too strong. But I can make them weak by destroying those they want to let in. That's why. It's fair, don't you think? Fair?" He stumbled as he bent to retrieve his glove. "Back for Owen now. I've been long enough."

Diane felt she could move again after a few minutes. The blood was still oozing from the cut at the back of her head, but the sharp sting cleared her mind rather than befuddled her.

She raised herself up on her arms. She'd been here before. She'd survived. Now she had to go and get Owen.

Slowly, painfully, she began to crawl her way back down the road to the school.

⌇

Gateshead-based **Simon Morden**'s writing career includes an eclectic mix of short stories, novellas, and novels that blend science fiction, fantasy, and horror, a five-year stint as an editor for the British Science Fiction Association, and as a judge for the Arthur C. Clarke Awards. The first three books of the Metrozone (*Equations of Life, Theories of Flight, Degrees of Freedom*) were published in 2011, and collectively won the Philip K. Dick Award. The fourth Metrozone novel, *The Curve of the Earth*, and *Arcanum*, a doorstep-sized alternate history set a millennium after the fall of Rome, will be published in 2013.

⌇

Stupidity and immediate gratification could be a whimpering End to the world as we know it—and with the right pharmaceuticals, we might not even realize it was happening. But when the remaining technology that still works starts failing—like sewage Pump Six—at least some people will start noticing they are in, literally, deep shit.

• PUMP SIX •
Paolo Bacigalupi

The first thing I saw Thursday morning when I walked into the kitchen was Maggie's ass sticking up in the air. Not a bad way to wake up, really. She's got a good figure, keeps herself in shape, so a morning eyeful of her pretty bottom pressed against a black mesh nightie is generally a positive way to start the day.

Except that she had her head in the oven. And the whole kitchen smelled like gas. And she had a lighter with a blue flame six inches high that she was waving around inside the oven like it was a Tickle Monkey revival concert.

"Jesus Christ, Maggie! What the hell are you doing?"

I dove across the kitchen, grabbed a handful of nightie and yanked hard. Her head banged as she came out of the oven. Frying pans rattled on the stovetop and she dropped her lighter. It skittered across the tuffscuff, ending up in a corner. "Owwwwww!" She grabbed her head. "Oooowwww!"

She spun around and slapped me. "What the fuck did you do that for?" She raked her nails across my cheek, then went for my eyes. I shoved her away. She slammed into the wall and spun, ready to come back again. "What's the matter with you?" she yelled. "You pissed off you couldn't get it up last night? Now you want to knock me around instead?" She grabbed the cast-iron skillet off the stovetop, dumping NiftyFreeze bacon all over the burners. "You want to try again, trogwad? Huh? You want to?" She waved the pan, threatening, and started for me. "Come on then!"

I jumped back, rubbing my cheek where she'd gouged me. "You're crazy! I keep you from getting yourself blown up and you want to beat my head in?"

"I was making your damn breakfast!" She ran her fingers through her black tangled hair and showed me blood. "You broke my damn head!"

"I saved your dumb ass is what I did." I turned and started shoving the kitchen windows open, letting the gas escape. A couple of the windows were just cardboard curtains that were easy to pull free, but one of the remaining whole windows was really stuck.

"You sonofabitch!"

I turned just in time to dodge the skillet. I yanked it out of her hands and shoved her away, hard, then went back to opening windows. She came back, trying to get around in front of me as I pushed the windows open. Her nails were all over my face, scratching and scraping. I pushed her away again and waved the skillet when she tried to come back. "You want me to use this?"

She backed off, eyes on the pan. She circled. "That's all you got to say to me? 'I saved your dumb ass'?" Her face was red with anger. "How about 'Thanks for trying to fix the stove, Maggie,' or 'Thanks for giving a damn about whether I get a decent breakfast before work, Maggie.' " She hawked snot and spat, missing me and hitting the wall, then gave me the finger. "Make your own damn breakfast. See if I try to help you again."

I stared at her. "You're dumber than a sack of trogs, you know that?" I waved the skillet toward the stove. "Checking a gas leak with a lighter? Do you even have a brain in there? Hello? Hello?"

"Don't talk to me like that! You're the trogwad—" She choked off mid sentence and sat, suddenly, like she'd been hit in the head with a chunk of concrete rain. Just plopped on the yellow tuffscuff. Completely stunned.

"Oh." She looked up at me, wide-eyed. "I'm sorry, Trav. I didn't even think of that." She stared at her lighter where it lay in the corner. "Oh, shit. Wow." She put her head in her hands. "Oh . . .Wow."

She started to hiccup, then to cry. When she looked up at me again, her big brown eyes were full of tears. "I'm so sorry. I'm really really sorry." The tears started rolling, pouring off her cheeks. "I had no idea. I just didn't think. I . . . "

I was still ready to fight, but seeing her sitting on the floor, all forlorn and lost and apologetic took it out of me.

"Forget it." I dropped the pan on the stove and went back to jamming open the windows. A breeze started moving through, and the gas stink faded. When we had some decent air circulation, I pulled the stove out from the wall. Bacon was scattered all over the burners, limp and thawed now that it was out of its NiftyFreeze cellophane, strips of pork lying everywhere, marbled and glistening with fat. Maggie's idea of a homemade breakfast. My granddad would have loved her. He was a big believer in breakfasts. Except for the NiftyFreeze. He hated those wrappers.

Maggie saw me staring at the bacon. "Can you fix the stove?"

"Not right now. I've got to get to work."

She wiped her eyes with the palm of her hand. "Waste of bacon," she said. "Sorry."

"No big deal."

"I had to go to six different stores to find it. That was the last package, and they didn't know when they were going to get more."

I didn't have anything to say to that. I found the gas shutoff and closed it. Sniffed. Then sniffed all around the stove and the rest of kitchen.

The gas smell was almost gone.

For the first time, I noticed my hands were shaking. I tried to get a coffee packet out of the cabinet and dropped it. It hit the counter with a water balloon plop. I set my twitching hands flat on the counter and leaned on them, hard, trying to make them go still. My elbows started shaking instead. It's not every morning you almost get yourself blown up.

It was kind of funny, though, when I thought about it. Half the time, the gas didn't even work. And on the one day it did, Maggie decided to play repairman. I had to suppress a giggle.

Maggie was still in the middle of the floor, snuffling. "I'm really sorry," she said again.

"It's okay. Forget it." I took my hands off the counter. They weren't flapping around anymore. That was something. I ripped open the coffee packet and chugged its liquid cold. After the rest of the morning, the caffeine was calming.

"No, I'm really sorry. I could have got us both killed."

I wanted to say something nasty but there wasn't any point. It just would have been cruel. "Well, you didn't. So it's okay." I pulled out a chair and sat down and looked out the open windows. The city's sky was turning from yellow dawn smog to a gray-blue morning smog. Down below, people were just starting their day. Their noises filtered up: Kids shouting on their way to school. Hand carts clattering on their way to deliveries. The grind of some truck's engine, clanking and squealing and sending up black clouds of exhaust that wafted in through the window along with summer heat. I fumbled for my inhaler and took a hit, then made myself smile at Maggie. "It's like that time you tried to clean the electric outlet with a fork. You just got to remember not to look for gas leaks with a fire. It's not a good idea."

Wrong thing to say, I guess. Or wrong tone of voice.

Maggie's waterworks started again: not just the snuffling and the tears, but the whole bawling squalling release thing, water pouring down her face, her nose getting all runny and her saying, "I'm sorry, I'm sorry, I'm sorry," over and over again, like a Ya Lu aud sample, but without the subsonic thump that would have made it fun to listen to.

I stared at the wall for a while, trying to wait it out, and thought about getting my earbug and listening to some real Ya Lu, but I didn't want to wear out the battery because it took a while to find good ones, and anyway, it didn't seem right to duck out while she was bawling. So I sat there while she kept crying, and then I finally sucked it up and got down on the floor next to her and held her while she wore herself out.

Finally she stopped crying and started wiping her eyes. "I'm sorry. I'll remember."

She must have seen my expression because she got more insistent. "Really. I will." She used the shoulder of her nightie on her runny nose. "I must look awful."

She looked puffy and red-eyed and snotty. I said, "You look fine. Great. You look great."

"Liar." She smiled, then shook her head. "I didn't mean to melt down like that. And the frying pan . . . " She shook her head again. "I must be PMS-ing."

"You take a Gynoloft?"

"I don't want to mess with my hormones. You know, just in case . . . " She shook her head again. "I keep thinking maybe this time, but . . . " She shrugged. "Never mind. I'm a mess." She leaned against me again and went quiet for a little bit. I could feel her breathing. "I just keep hoping," she said finally.

I stroked her hair. "If it's meant to happen, it will. We've just got to stay optimistic."

"Sure. That's up to God. I know that. I just keep hoping."

"It took Miku and Gabe three years. We've been trying, what, six months?"

"A year, month after next." She was quiet, then said, "Lizzi and Pearl only had miscarriages."

"We've got a ways to go before we start worrying about miscarriages." I disentangled and went hunting for another coffee packet in the cabinets. This one I actually took the time to shake. It heated itself and I tore it open and sipped. Not as good as the little brewer I found for Maggie at the flea market so she could make coffee on the stove, but it was a damn sight better than being blown to bits.

Maggie was getting herself arranged, getting up off the floor and starting to bustle around. Even all puffy faced, she still looked good in that mesh nightie: lots of skin, lots of interesting shadows.

She caught me watching her. "What are you smiling at?"

I shrugged. "You look nice in that nightie."

"I got it from that lady's estate sale, downstairs. It's hardly even used."

I leered. "I like it."

She laughed. "Now? You couldn't last night or the night before, but now you want to do it?"

I shrugged.

"You're going to be late as it is." She turned and started rustling in the cabinets herself. "You want a brekkie bar? I found a whole bunch of them when I was shopping for the bacon. I guess their factory is working again." She tossed one before I could answer. I caught it and tore off the smiling foil wrapper and read the ingredients while I ate. Fig and Nut, and then a whole bunch of nutrients like dextroforma-albuterolhyde. Not as neat as the chemicals that thaw NiftyFreeze packets, but what the hell, it's all nutritional, right?

Maggie turned and studied the stove where I'd marooned it. With hot morning air blowing in from the windows, the bacon was getting limper and greasier by the second. I thought about taking it downstairs and frying it on the sidewalk. If nothing else, I could feed it to the trogs. Maggie was pinching her lip. I expected her to say something about the stove or wasting bacon, but instead she said, "We're going out for drinks with Nora tonight. She wants to go to Wicky."

"Pus girl?"

"That's not funny."

I jammed the rest of the brekkie bar into my mouth. "It is to me. I warned both of you. That water's not safe for anything."

She made a face. "Well nothing happened to me, smarty pants. We all looked at it and it wasn't yellow or sludgy or anything—"

"So you jumped right in and went swimming. And now she's got all those funny zits on her. How mysterious." I finished the second coffee packet and

tossed it and the brekkie bar wrapper down the disposal and ran some water
to wash them down. In another half hour, they'd be whirling and dissolving
in the belly of Pump Two. "You can't go thinking something's clean, just
because it looks clear. You got lucky." I wiped my hands and went over to
her. I ran my fingers up her hips.

"Yep. Lucky. Still no reaction."

She slapped my hands away. "What, you're a doctor, now?"

"Specializing in skin creams . . . "

"Don't be gross. I told Nora to meet us at eight. Can we go to Wicky?"

I shrugged. "I doubt it. It's pretty exclusive."

"But Max owes you—" she broke off as she caught me leering at her
again. "Oh. Right."

"What do you say?"

She shook her head and grinned. "I should be glad, after the last couple
nights."

"Exactly." I leaned down and kissed her.

When she finally pulled back, she looked up at me with those big brown
eyes of hers and the whole bad morning just melted away. "You're going to
be late," she said.

But her body was up against mine, and she wasn't slapping my hands
away anymore.

Summer in New York is one of my least favorite times. The heat sits down
between the buildings, choking everything, and the air just . . . stops. You
smell everything. Plastics melting into hot concrete, garbage burning, old
urine that effervesces into the air when someone throws water into the
gutter; just the plain smell of so many people living all packed together.
Like all the skyscrapers are sweating alcoholics after a binge, standing there
exhausted and oozing with the evidence of everything they've been up to.
It drives my asthma nuts. Some days, I take three hits off the inhaler just to
get to work.

About the only good thing about summer is that it isn't spring so at least
you don't have freeze-thaw dropping concrete rain down on your head.

I cut across the park just to give my lungs a break from the ooze and
stink, but it wasn't much of an improvement. Even with the morning heat
still building up, the trees looked dusty and tired, all their leaves drooping,
and there were big brown patches on the grass where the green had just
given up for the summer, like bald spots on an old dog.

The trogs were out in force, lying in the grass, lolling around in the dust and sun, enjoying another summer day with nothing to do. The weather was bringing them out. I stopped to watch them frolicking—all hairy and horny without any concerns at all.

A while back someone started a petition to get rid of them, or at least to get them spayed, but the mayor came out and said that they had some rights, too. After all, they were somebody's kids, even if no one was admitting it. He even got the police to stop beating them up so much, which made the tabloids go crazy. They all said he had a trog love child hidden in Connecticut. But after a few years, people got used to having them around. And the tabloids went out of business, so the mayor didn't care what they said about his love children anymore.

These days, the trogs are just part of the background, a whole park full of mash-faced monkey people shambling around with bright yellow eyes and big pink tongues and not nearly enough fur to survive in the wild. When winter hits, they either freeze in piles or migrate down to warmer places. But every summer there's more of them.

When Maggie and I first started trying to have a baby, I had a nightmare that Maggie had a trog. She was holding it and smiling, right after the delivery, all sweaty and puffy and saying, "Isn't it beautiful? Isn't it beautiful?" and then she handed the sucker to me. And the scary thing wasn't that it was a trog; the scary thing was trying to figure out how I was going to explain to everyone at work that we were keeping it. Because I loved that little squash-faced critter. I guess that's what being a parent is all about.

That dream scared me limp for a month. Maggie put me on perkies because of it.

A trog sidled up. It—or he or she, or whatever you call a hermaphrodite critter with boobs and a big sausage—made kissy faces at me. I just smiled and shook my head and decided that it was a him because of his hairy back, and because he actually had that sausage, instead of just a little pencil like some of them have. The trog took the rejection pretty well. He just smiled and shrugged. That's one nice thing about them: they may be dumber than hamsters, but they're pleasant-natured. Nicer than most of the people I work with, really. Way nicer than some people you meet in the subway.

The trog wandered off, touching himself and grunting, and I kept going across the park. On the other side, I walked down a couple blocks to Freedom Street and then down the stairs into the command substation.

Chee was waiting for me when I unlocked the gates to let myself in.

"Alvarez! You're late, man."

Chee's a nervous skinny little guy with suspenders and red hair slicked straight back over a bald spot. He always has this acrid smell around him because of this steroid formula he uses on the bald spot, which makes his hair grow all right for a while, but then he starts picking at it compulsively and it all falls out and he has to start all over with the steroids, and in the meantime, he smells like the Hudson. And whatever the gel is, it makes his skull shine like a polished bowling ball. We used to tell him to stop using the stuff, but he'd go all rabid and try to bite you if you kept it up for long.

"You're late," he said again. He was scratching his head like an epileptic monkey trying to groom himself.

"Yeah? So?" I got my work jacket out of my locker and pulled it on. The fluorescents were all dim and flickery, but climate control was running, so the interior was actually pretty bearable, for once.

"Pump Six is broken."

"Broken how?"

Chee shrugged. "I don't know. It's stopped."

"Is it making a noise? Is it stopped all the way? Is it going slowly? Is it flooding? Come on, help me out."

Chee looked at me blankly. Even his head-picking stopped, for a second.

"You try looking at the troubleshooting indexes?" I asked.

Chee shrugged. "Didn't think of it."

"How many times have I told you, that's the first thing you do? How long has it been out?"

"Since midnight?" He screwed up his face, thinking. "No, since ten."

"You switch the flows over?"

He hit his forehead with the palm of his hand. "Forgot."

I started to run. "The entire Upper West Side doesn't have sewage processing since LAST NIGHT? Why didn't you call me?"

Chee jogged after me, dogging my heels as we ran through the plant's labyrinth to the control rooms. "You were off duty."

"So you just let it sit there?"

It's hard to shrug while you're running full-out, but Chee managed it. "Stuff's broken all the time. I didn't figure it was that bad. You know, there was that bulb out in tunnel three, and then there was that leak from the toilets. And then the drinking fountain went out again. You always let things slide. I figured I'd let you sleep."

I didn't bother trying to explain the difference. "If it happens again, just remember, if the pumps, any of them, die, you call me. It doesn't matter where I am, I won't be mad. You just call me. If we let these pumps go down, there's no telling how many people could get sick. There's bad stuff in that water, and we've got to stay on top of it, otherwise it bubbles up into the sewers and then it gets out in the air, and people get sick. You got it?"

I shoved open the doors to the control room, and stopped.

The floor was covered with toilet paper, rolls of it, all unstrung and dangled around the control room. Like some kind of mummy striptease had gone wrong. There must have been a hundred rolls unraveled all over the floor. "What the hell is this?"

"This?" He looked around, scratching his head.

"The paper, Chee."

"Oh. Right. We had a toilet paper fight last night. For some reason they triple delivered. We didn't have enough space in the storage closet. I mean, we haven't had ass wipes for two months, and then we had piles and piles of it—"

"So you had a toilet paper fight while Pump Six was down?"

Something in my voice must have finally gotten through. He cringed. "Hey, don't look at me that way. I'll get it picked up. No worries. Jeez. You're worse than Mercati. And anyway, it wasn't my fault. I was just getting ready to reload the dispensers and then Suze and Zoo came down and we got into this fight." He shrugged. "It was just something to do, that's all. And Suze started it, anyway."

I gave him another dirty look and kicked my way through the tangle of t.p. to the control consoles.

Chee called after me, "Hey, how am I going to wind it back up if you kick it around?"

I started throwing switches on the console, running diagnostics. I tried booting up the troubleshooting database, but got a connection error. Big surprise. I looked on the shelves for the hard copies of the operation and maintenance manuals, but they were missing. I looked at Chee. "Do you know where the manuals are?"

"The what?"

I pointed at the empty shelves.

"Oh. They're in the bathroom."

I looked at him. He looked back at me. I couldn't make myself ask. I just turned back to the consoles. "Go get them, I need to figure out what these flashers mean." There was a whole panel of them winking away at me, all for Pump Six.

Chee scuttled out of the room, dragging t.p. behind him. Overhead, I heard the Observation Room door open: Suze, coming down the stairs. More trouble. She rustled through the t.p. streamers and came up close behind me, crowding. I could feel her breathing on my neck.

"The pump's been down for almost twelve hours," she said. "I could write you up." She thumped me in the back, hard. "I could write you up, buddy." She did it again, harder. *Bam.*

I thought about hitting her back, but I wasn't going to give her another excuse to dock pay. Besides, she's bigger than me. And she's got more muscles than an orangutan. About as hairy, too. Instead, I said, "It would have helped if somebody had called."

"You talking back to me?" She gave me another shove and leaned around to get in my face, looking at me all squinty-eyed. "Twelve hours down-time," she said again. "That's grounds for a write-up. It's in the manual. I can do it."

"No kidding? You read that? All by yourself?"

"You're not the only one who can read, Alvarez." She turned and stomped back up the stairs to her office.

Chee came back lugging the maintenance manuals. "I don't know how you do this," he puffed as he handed them over. "These manuals make no sense at all."

"It's a talent."

I took the plastirene volumes and glanced up at Suze's office. She was just standing there, looking down at me through the observation glass, looking like she was going to come down and beat my head in. A dimwit promo who got lucky when the old boss went into retirement.

She has no idea what a boss does, so mostly she spends her time scowling at us, filling out paperwork that she can't remember how to route, and molesting her secretary. Employment guarantees are great for people like me, but I can see why you might want to fire someone; the only way Suze was ever going to leave was if she fell down the Observation Room stairs and broke her neck.

She scowled harder at me, trying to make me look away. I let her win. She'd either write me up, or she wouldn't. And even if she did, she might still get distracted and forget to file it. At any rate, she couldn't fire me. We were stuck together like a couple of cats tied in a sack.

I started thumbing through the manuals' plastic pages, going back and forth through the indexes as I cross-referenced all the flashers. I looked up again at the console. There were a lot of them. Maybe more than I'd ever seen.

Chee squatted down beside me, watching. He started picking his head again. I think it's a comfort thing for him. But it makes your skin crawl until you get used to it. Makes you think of lice.

"You do that fast," he said. "How come you didn't go to college?"

"You kidding?"

"No way, man. You're the smartest guy I ever met. You totally could have gone to college."

I glanced over at him, trying to tell if he was screwing with me. He looked back at me, completely sincere, like a dog waiting for a treat. I went back to the manual. "No ambition, I guess."

The truth was that I never made it through high school. I dropped out of P.S. 105 and never looked back. Or forward, I guess. I remember sitting in freshman algebra and watching the teacher's lips flap and not understanding a word he was saying. I turned in worksheets and got Ds every time, even after I redid them. None of the other kids were complaining, though. They just laughed at me when I kept asking him to explain the difference between squaring and doubling variables. You don't have to be Einstein to figure out where you don't belong.

I started piecing my way through the troubleshooting diagrams. No clogs indicated. Go to Mechanics Diagnostics, Volume Three. I picked up the next binder of pages and started flipping. "Anyway, you've got a bad frame of reference. We aren't exactly a bunch of Nobel Prize winners here." I glanced up at Suze's office. "Smart people don't work in dumps like this." Suze was scowling down at me again. I gave her the universal salute. "You see?"

Chee shrugged. "I dunno. I tried reading that manual about twenty times on the john, and it still doesn't make any sense to me. If you weren't around, half the city would be swimming in shit right now."

Another flasher winked on the console: amber, amber, red . . . It stayed red.

"In a couple minutes they're going to be swimming in a lot worse than that. Believe me, buddy, there's lots worse things than shit. Mercati showed me a list once, before he retired. All the things that run through here that the pumps are supposed to clean: polychlorinated biphenyls, bisphenyl-A, estrogen, phlalates, PCBs, heptachlor . . . "

"I got a Super Clean sticker for all that stuff." He lifted his shirt and showed me the one he had stuck to his skin, right below his rib cage. A yellow smiley face sticker a little like the kind I used to get from my grandpa when he was feeling generous. It said SUPER CLEAN on the smiley's forehead.

"You buy those?"

"Sure. Seven bucks for seven. I get 'em every week. I can drink the water straight, now. I'd even drink out of the Hudson." He started scratching his skull again.

I watched him scratch for a second, remembering how zit girl Nora had tried to sell some to Maria before they went swimming. "Well, I'm glad it's working for you." I turned and started keying restart sequences for the pumps. "Now let's see if we can get this sucker started up, and keep all the neighbors who don't buy stickers from having a pack of trogs. Get ready to pull a reboot on my say-so."

Chee went over to clear the data lines and put his hands on the restart levers. "I don't know what difference it makes. I went through the park the other day and you know what I saw? A mama trog and five little baby trogs. What good does it do to keep trogs from getting born to good folks, when you got those ones down in the park making whole litters?"

I looked over at Chee to say something back, but he kind of had a point. The reboot sequences completed and Pump Six's indicators showed primed. "Three . . . two . . . one . . . Primed full," I said. "Go. Go. Go."

Chee threw his levers and the consoles cleared green and somewhere deep down below us, sewage started pumping again.

We climbed the skin of the Kusovic Center, climbing for heaven, climbing for Wicky. Maggie and Nora and Wu and me, worming our way up through stairwell turns, scrambling over rubble, kicking past condom wrappers and scattering Effy packets like autumn leaves. Wicky's synthesized xylophones and Japanese kettledrums thrummed, urging us higher. Trogs and sadsack partiers who didn't have my connections watched jealously as we climbed. Watched and whispered as we passed them by, all of them knowing that Max owed me favors and favors and favors and that I went to the front of the line because I kept the toilets running on time.

The club was perched at the very top of the Kusovic, a bunch of old stockbroker offices. Max had torn down the glass cubicles and the old digital wallscreens that used to track the NYSE and had really opened the space up.

Unfortunately, the club wasn't much good in the winter anymore because we'd all gotten rowdy one night and shoved out the windows. But even if it was too damn breezy half the year, watching those windows falling had been a major high point at the club. A couple years later people were still talking about it, and I could still remember the slow way they came out of their frames and tumbled and sailed through the air. And when they hit bottom, they splashed across the streets like giant buckets of water.

At any rate, the open-air thing worked really good in the summer, with all the rolling brownouts that were always knocking out the A/C.

I got a shot of Effy as we went in the door, and the club rode in on a wave of primal flesh, a tribal gathering of sweaty jumping monkeys in half-torn business suits, all of us going crazy and eyeball wide until our faces were as pale and big as fish wallowing in the bottom of the ocean.

Maggie was smiling at me as we danced and our whole oven fight was completely behind us. I was glad about that, because after our fork-in-the-outlet fight, she acted like it was my fault for a week, even after she said she forgave me. But now, in the dance throb of Wicky, I was her white knight again, and I was glad to be with her, even if it meant dragging Nora along.

All the way up the stairs, I'd tried to not stare at Nora's zit-pocked skin or make fun of her swollen-up face but she knew what I was thinking because she kept giving me dirty looks whenever I warned her to step around places where the stairway was crumbling. Talk about stupid, though. She's about as sharp as a marble. I won't drink or swim in any of the water around here. It comes from working with sewage all the time. You know way too much about everything that goes in and out of the system. People like Nora put a Kali-Mary pendant between their tits or stick a Super Clean smiley to their ass cheek and hope for the best. I drink bottled water and only shower with a filter head. And sometimes I still get creeped out. No pus rashes, though.

The kettledrums throbbed inside my eyeballs. Across the club, Nora was dancing with Wu and now that my Effy was kicking into overdrive, I could see her positive qualities: she danced fast and furious . . . her hair was long and black . . . her zits were the size of breasts.

They looked succulent.

I sidled up to her and tried to apologize for not appreciating her before, but between the noise and my slobbering on her skin, I guess I failed to communicate effectively. She ran away before I could make it up to her and I ended up bouncing alone in Wicky's kettledrum womb while the crowds rode in and out around me and the Effy built up in ocean throbs that ran from my eyeballs to my crotch and back again, bouncing me higher and higher and higher . . .

A girl in torn knee socks and a nun's habit was mewling in the bathroom when Maggie found us and pulled us apart and took me on the floor with people walking around us and trying to use the stainless steel piss troughs, but then Max grabbed me and I couldn't tell if we'd been doing it on the bar and if that was the problem or if I was just taking a leak in the wrong place but Max kept complaining about bubbles in his gin and a riot a riot a RIOT that he was going to have on his hands if these Effy freaks didn't get their liquor and he shoved me down under the bar where tubes come out of vats of gin and tonic and it was like floating inside the guts of an octopus with the waves of the kettledrums booming away above me.

I wanted to sleep down there, maybe hunt for the nun's red panties except that Max kept coming back to me with more Effy and saying we had to find the problem, the bubbly problem the bubbly problem, take some of this it will clear your damn head, find where the bubbles come from, where they fill the gin. No no no! The tonic the tonic the tonic! No bubbles in the tonic. Find the tonic. Stop the RIOT, make it all okay before the gag-gas trucks come and shut us down and dammit what are you sniffing down under there?

Swimming under the bar . . . Swimming long and low . . . eyeballs wide . . . prehistoric fishy amongst giant mossy root-laced eggs, buried under the mist of the swamp, down with the bar rags and the lost spoons and the sticky slime of bar sugar, and these huge dead silver eggs lying under the roots, growing moss and mildew but nothing else, no yolky tonic coming out of these suckers, been sucked dry, sucked full dry by too many thirsty dinosaurs and of course that's the problem. No tonic. None. None at all.

More eggs! More eggs! We need more eggs! More big silver tonic dispensing eggs need to rumble in on handtrucks and roll in on whitejacketed bow-tie bartender backs. More eggs need to take the prod from the long root green sucking tubes and then we can suck the tonic of their yolk out, and Max can keep on making g-and-t's and I'm a hero hey hey hey a hero a goddamn superstar because I know a lot about silver eggs and how to stick in the right tubes and isn't that why Maggie's always pissed at me because my tube is never ready to stick into her eggs, or maybe she's got no eggs to stick or maybe she's got no eggs to stick and we sure as hell aren't going to the doctor to find out she's got no eggs and no replacements either, not a single one coming in on a handtruck and isn't that why she's out in the crowd bouncing in a black corset with a guy licking her feet and giving me the finger?

And isn't that why we're going to have a RIOT now when I beat that trogwad's head in with this chunk of bar that I'm going to get Max to loan me . . . except I'm too far underwater to beat up boot licker. And little smoking piles of Effy keep blooming on the floor, and we're all lapping them up because I'm a goddamn hero a hero a hero, the fixit man of all fixit men, and everyone bows and scrapes and passes me Effy because there isn't going to be a RIOT and we won't get shut down with gag-gas, and we won't do the vomit crawl down the stairwells to the streets.

And then Max shoves me back onto the dance floor with more shots of Effy for Maggie, a big old tray of forgiveness, and forgiveness comes easy when we're all walking on the ceiling of the biggest oldest skyscraper in the sky.

Blue kettle drums and eyeball nuns. Zits and dinner dates. Down the stairs and into the streets.

By the time we stumbled out of Wicky I was finally coming out of the Effy folds but Maggie was still flying, running her hands all over me, touching me, telling me what she was going to do to me when we got home. Nora and Wu were supposed to be with us, but somehow we'd gotten separated. Maggie wasn't interested in waiting around so we headed uptown, stumbling between the big old city towers, winding around sidewalk stink ads for Diabolo and Possession, and dodging fishdog stands with after-bar octopi on a stick.

The night was finally cool, in the sweet spot between end of midnight swelter and beginning of morning smother. There was a blanket of humidity, wet on us, and seductive after the club. Without rain or freezes, I barely had to watch for concrete rain at all.

Maggie ran her hands up and down my arm as we walked, occasionally leaning in close to kiss my cheek and nibble on my ear. "Max says you're amazing. You saved the day."

I shrugged. "It wasn't a big deal."

The whole bar thing was pretty hazy, bubbled-out by all the Effy I'd done. My skin was still singing from it. Mostly what I had was a warm glow right in my crotch and a stuttery view of the dark streets and the long rows of candles in the windows of the towers, but Maggie's hand felt good, and she looked good, and I had some plans of my own for when we got back to the apartment, so I knew I was coming down nice and slow, like falling into a warm featherbed full of helium and tongues.

"Anyone could have figured out his tonic was empty, if we hadn't all been so damn high." I stopped in front of a bank of autovendors. Three of them were sold out, and one was broken open, but there were still a couple drinks in the last one. I dropped my money in and chose a bottle of Blue Vitality for her, and a Sweatshine for me. It was a pleasant surprise when the machine kicked out the bottles.

"Wow!" Maggie beamed at me.

I grinned and fished out her bottle. "Lucky night, I guess: first the bar, now this."

"I don't think the bar thing was luck. I wouldn't have thought of it." She downed her Blue Vitality in two long swallows, and giggled. "And you did it when your eyes were as big as a fish. You were doing handstands on the bar."

I didn't remember that. Bar sugar and red lace bras, I remembered. But not handstands. "I don't see how Max keeps that place going when he can't even remember to restock."

Maggie rubbed up against me. "Wicky's a lot better than most clubs. And anyway, that's why he's got you. A real live hero." She giggled again. "I'm glad we didn't have to fight our way out of another riot. I hate that."

In an alley, some trogs were making it. Clustered bodies, hermaphroditic, climbing on each other and humping, their mouths open, smiling and panting. I glanced at them and kept going, but Maggie grabbed my arm and tugged me back.

The trogs were really going at it, all in a flounder, three of them piled, their skins gleaming with sweat slick and saliva. They looked back at us with yellow eyes and not a bit of shame. They just smiled and got into a heavy groaning rhythm.

"I can't believe how much they *do* it," Maggie whispered. She gripped my arm, pressing against me. "They're like dogs."

"That's about how smart they are."

They changed positions, one crouching as though Maggie's words had inspired them. The others piled on top of him . . . or her. Maggie's hand slid to the front of my pants, fumbled with the zipper and reached inside. "They're so . . . Oh, God." She pulled me close and started working on my belt, almost tearing at it.

"What the hell?" I tried to push her off, but she was all over me, her hands reaching inside my pants, touching me, making me hard. The Effy was still working, that was for sure.

"Let's do it, too. Here. I want you."

"Are you crazy?"

"They don't care. Come on. Maybe this time it'll take. Knock me up." She touched me, her eyes widening at my sudden size. "You're never like this." She touched me again. "Oh God. Please." She pressed herself against me, looking over at the trogs. "Like that. Just like that." She pulled off her shimmersilk blouse, exposing her black corset and the pale skin of her breasts.

I stared at her skin and curves. That beautiful body she'd teased me with all night long. Suddenly I didn't care about the trogs or the few people walking by on the street. We both yanked at my belt. My pants fell down around my ankles. We slammed up against the alley wall, pressing against old concrete and staring into each other's eyes and then she pulled me into her and her lips were on my ear, biting and panting and whispering as we moved against each other.

The trogs just grinned and grinned and watched us with their big yellow eyes as we all shared the alley, and all watched each other.

At five in the morning, Chee called again, his voice coming straight into my head through my earbug. In all the excitement and Effy, I'd forgotten to take it out. Pump Six was down again. "You said I was supposed to call you," he whined.

I groaned and dragged myself out of bed. "Yeah. Yeah. I did. Don't worry about it. You did good. I'll be there."

Maggie rolled over. "Where you going?"

I pulled on my pants and gave her a quick kiss. "Got to go save the world."

"They work you too hard. I don't think you should go."

"And let Chee sort it out? You've got to be kidding. We'd be up to our necks in sludge by dinner time."

"My hero." She smiled sleepily. "See if you can find me some donuts when you come back. I feel pregnant."

She looked so happy and warm and fuzzy I almost climbed back into bed with her, but I fought off the urge and just gave her another kiss. "Will do."

Outside, light was just starting to break in the sky, a slow yellowing of the smog. The streets were almost silent at the early hour. It was hard not to be bitter about being up at this ungodly hungover time, but it was better than having to deal with the sewage backup if Chee hadn't called. I headed downtown and bought a bagel from a girly-faced guy who didn't know how to make change.

The bagel was wrapped in some kind of plastic film that dissolved when I put it in my mouth. It wasn't bad, but it ticked me off that bagel boy got confused with the change and needed me to go into his cash pouch and count out my own money.

It seems like I always end up bailing everyone out. Even dumb bagel guys. Maggie says I'm as compulsive as Chee. She would have just stood there and waited until bagel boy sorted it out, even if it took all day. But I have a damn hard time watching some trogwad drop dollars all over the sidewalk. Sometimes it's just easier to climb out of the oatmeal and do things yourself.

Chee was waiting for me when I got in, practically bouncing up and down. Five pumps down, now.

"It started with just one when I called you, but now there's five. They keep shutting off."

I went into the control room. The troubleshooting database was still down so I grabbed the hardcopy manuals again. Weird how the pumps were all going off-line like that. The control room, normally alive with the hum of the machines, was quieter with half of them down. Around the city, sewage lines were backing up as we failed to cycle waste into the treatment facilities and pump the treated water out into the river.

I thought about Nora with her rash, thanks to swimming in that gunk. It could really make you nervous. Looks clean, makes you rash. And we're at the bottom of the river. It's not just our crap in it. Everyone upstream, too. Our treatment plants pump water up from underground or pipe it in and treat it from lakes upstate. At least that's the theory. I don't really buy it; I've seen the amount of water we move through here and there's no way it's all coming from the lakes. In reality, we've got twenty-million-odd people all sucking water that we don't know where it's coming from or what's in it. Like I said, I drink bottled water even if I have to hike all over the city to find it. Or soda water. Or . . . tonic, even.

I closed my eyes, trying to piece the evening back together. All those empty canisters of tonic under the bar. Travis Alvarez saves the world while flying to the moon on Effy, and two rounds of sex yesterday.

Hell, yeah.

Chee and I brought the PressureDynes up one by one. All of them came back online except Pump Six. It was stubborn. We reprimed it. Fired. Reprimed. Nothing.

Suze came down to backseat drive, dragging Zoo, her secretary, behind her. Suze was completely strung out. Her blouse was half-tucked in, and she had big old fishy Effy eyes that were almost as red as the flashers on the console. But her fishy eyes narrowed when she saw all the flashers. "How come all these pumps went down? It's your job to keep them working."

I just looked at her. Zoned out of her mind at six a.m., romping around with her secretary girlfriend while she tried to crack the whip on the rest of us. Now that's leadership. Suddenly I thought that maybe I needed to get a different job. Or needed to start licking big piles of Effy before I came to work. Anything to take the edge off Suze.

"If you want me to fix it, I'll need you to clear out so I can concentrate."

Suze looked at me like she was chewing on a lemon. "You better get it fixed." She poked my chest with a thick finger. "If you don't, I'm making Chee your boss." She glanced at Zoo. "It's your turn on the couch. Come on." They trooped off.

Chee watched them go. He started picking at his head. "They never do any work," he said.

Another flasher went amber on the console. I flipped through the manual, hunting for a reason. "Who does? A job like this, where nobody gets fired?"

"Yeah, but there ought to be a way to get rid of her, at least. She moved all her home furniture into the office, the other day. She never goes home now. Says she likes the A/C here."

"You shouldn't complain. You're the guy who was throwing t.p. around yesterday."

He looked at me, puzzled. "So?"

I shrugged. "Never mind. Don't worry about Suze. We're the bottom of the pile, Chee. Get used to it. Let's try the reboot again."

It didn't work.

I went back to the manual. Sludge was probably coming up a hundred thousand toilets in the city by now. Weird how all the pumps shut down like that: one, two, three, four. I closed my eyes, thinking. Something about my Effy spree kept tickling the back of my head. Effy flashbacks, for sure. But they kept coming: big old eggs, big old silver eggs, all of them sucked dry by egg-slurping dinosaurs. Wow. That was some kind of weird spree. Nuns and stainless steel eggs. The urinals and Maggie . . . I blinked. Everything clicked. Pieces of the puzzle coming together. Cosmic Effy convergence: Emptied silver eggs. Max forgetting to restock his bar.

I looked up at Chee, then down at the manuals, then back up at Chee. "How long have we been running these pumps?"

"What do you mean?"

"When did they get installed?"

Chee stared at the ceiling, picked his head thoughtfully. "Hell if I know. Before I came on, that's for sure."

"Me too. I've been here nine years. Have we got a computer that would tell us that? A receipt? Something?" I flipped to the front of the manual in my hands. "PressureDyne: Hi-Capacity, Self-Purging, Multi-Platform Pumping Engine. Model 13-44474-888." I frowned. "This manual was printed in 2020."

Chee whistled and leaned over to finger the plasticized pages. "That's pretty damn old."

"Built to last, right? People built things to last, back then."

"More than a hundred years?" He shrugged. "I had a car like that, once. Real solid. Engine hardly had any rust on it at all. And it had both headlights. But too damn old." He picked something out of his scalp and examined it for a second before flicking it onto the floor. "No one works on cars anymore. I can't remember the last time I saw a taxi running."

I looked at him, trying to decide if I wanted to say anything about flicking scalp on the floor, then just gave it up. I flipped through the manual some more until I found the part I wanted: "Individual Reporting Modules: Remote Access, Connectivity Features, and Data Collection." Following the manual's instructions, I opened a new set of diagnostic windows that bypassed the PressureDynes' generalized reports for pump station managers and instead connected directly with the pumps' raw log data. What I got was: "Host source data not found."

Big surprise.

The rest of the error text advised me to check the remote reporting module extension connectors, whatever those were. I closed the manual and tucked it under my arm. "Come on. I think I know what's wrong." I led Chee out of the control room and down into the bowels of the tunnels and plant system. The elevator was busted so we had to take the access stairs.

As we went deeper and deeper, darkness closed in. Grit and dust were everywhere. Rats skittered away from us. Isolated LEDs kept the stairwell visible, but barely. Dust and shadows and moving rats were all you could see in the dim amber. Eventually even the LEDs gave out. Chee found an emergency lantern in a wall socket, blanketed with gray fluffy dust, but it still had a charge. My asthma started to tickle and close in, sitting on my chest from all the crud in the air. I took a hit off my inhaler, and we kept going down. Finally, we hit bottom.

Light from Chee's lantern wavered and disappeared in the cavern's darkness. The metal of the PressureDynes glinted dimly. Chee sneezed. The motion sent his lantern rocking. Shadows shifted crazily until he used a hand to stop it. "You can't see shit down here," he muttered.

"Shut up. I'm thinking."

"I've never been down here."

"I came down, once. When I first came on. When Mercati was still alive."

"No wonder you act like him. He trained you?"

"Sure." I hunted around for the emergency lighting.

Mercati had shown the switches to me when he brought me down, nearly a decade before, and told me about the pumps. He'd been old then, but still working, and I liked the guy. He had a way of paying attention to things. Focused. Not like most people who can barely say hello to you before they start looking at their watch, or planning their party schedule, or complaining about their skin rashes. He used to say my teachers didn't know shit about algebra and that I should have stayed in school. Even knowing that he was just comparing me to Suze, I thought it was a pretty nice thing for him to say.

No one knew the pump systems as well as he did, so even after he got sick and I took over his job, I'd still sneak out to the hospital to ask him questions. He was my secret weapon until the cancer finally took out his guts.

I found the emergency lighting and pulled the switches. Fluorescent lights flickered, and came alive, buzzing. Some bulbs didn't come on, but there were enough.

Chee gasped. "They're huge."

A cathedral of engineering. Overhead, pipes arched through cavern dimness, shimmering under the muted light of the fluorescents, an interconnecting web of iron and shadows that centered in complex rosettes around the ranked loom of the pumps.

They towered over us, gleaming dully, three stories tall, steel dinosaurs. Dust mantled them. Rust blossoms patterned their hides in complex overlays that made them look like they'd been draped in oriental rugs. Pentagonal bolts as big as my hands studded their armored plating and stitched together the vast sectioned pipes that spanned the darkness and shot down black tunnels in every compass direction, reaching for every neighborhood in the city. Moisture jewels gleamed and dripped from ancient joints. The pumps thrummed on. Perfectly designed. Forgotten by everyone in the city above. Beasts working without complaint, loyal despite abandonment.

Except that one of them had now gone silent.

I stifled an urge to get down on my knees and apologize for neglecting them, for betraying these loyal machines that had run for more than a century.

I went over to Pump Six's control panel, and stroked the dinosaur's vast belly where it loomed over me. The control panel was all covered with dust, but it glowed when I ran my hand over it. Amber signals and lime text glowing authoritatively, telling me just what was wrong, telling me and telling me, and never complaining that I hadn't been listening.

Raw data had stopped piping up to the control room at some point, and had instead sat in the dark, waiting for someone to come down and notice it. And the raw data was the answer to all my questions. At the top of the list: Model 13-44474-888, Requires Scheduled Maintenance. 946,080,000 cycles completed.

I ran through the pump diagnostics:

Valve Ring Part# 12-33939, Scheduled for Replacement.
Piston Parts# 232-2, 222-5, 222-6, 222-4-1, Scheduled for Replacement.
Displacement Catch Reservoir, Part# 37-37-375-77, Damaged, Replace.
Emergency Release Trigger Bearing, Part# 810-9, Damaged, Replace.
Valve Kit, Part# 437834-13, Damaged, Replace.
Master Drive Regulator, Part# 39-23-9834959-5, Damaged, Replace.
Priority Maintenance:
Compression Sensors, Part# 49-4, Part# 7777-302, Part# 403-74698
Primary Train, Part# 010303-0
Gurney Belt Valve, Part# 9-0-2 . . .

The list went on. I keyed into the maintenance history. The list opened up, running well into Mercati's tenure and even before, dozens of maintenance triggers and scheduled work requests, all of them blinking down here in the darkness, and ignored. Twenty-five years of neglect.

"Hey!" Chee called. "Check this out! They left magazines down here!"

I glanced over. He'd found a pile of trash someone had stuffed under one of the pumps. He was down on his hands and knees, reaching underneath, rooting things out: magazines, what looked like old food wrappers. I started to tell him to quit messing with stuff, but then I let it go. At least he wasn't breaking anything. I rubbed my eyes and went back to the pump diagnostics.

For the six years I'd been in charge, there were over a dozen errors displayed, but the PressureDynes had just kept going, chugging away as bits and pieces of them rattled away, and now, suddenly this one had given way completely, coming apart at the seams, loyally chugging until it just couldn't go on anymore and the maintenance backlog finally took the sucker down. I went over and started looking at the logs for the nine other pumps.

Every one of them was riddled with neglect: warning dumps, data logs full of error corrections, alarm triggers.

I went back to Pump Six and looked at its logs again. The men who'd built the machines had built them to last, but enough tiny little knives can still kill a big old dinosaur, and this one was beyond dead.

"We'll need to call PressureDyne," I said. "This thing is going to need more help than we can give it."

Chee looked up from a found magazine with a bright yellow car on the cover. "Do they even exist anymore?"

"They better." I grabbed the manual and looked up their customer support number.

It wasn't even in the same format as our numbers. Not a single letter of the alphabet in the whole damn thing.

Not only did PressureDyne not exist, they'd gone bankrupt more than forty years ago, victims of their overly well-designed pump products. They'd killed their own market. The only bright spot was that their technology had slouched into the public domain, and the net was up for once, so I could download schematics of the PressureDynes. There was a ton of information, except I didn't know anyone who could understand any of it. I sure couldn't.

I leaned back in my desk chair, staring at all that information I couldn't use. Like looking at Egyptian hieroglyphs. Something was there, but it sure beat me what I was supposed to do with it. I'd shifted the flows for Pump Six over to the rest of the pumps, and they were handling the new load, but it made me nervous thinking about all those maintenance warnings glowing down there in the dark: Mercury Extender Seal, Part# 5974-30, Damaged, Replace . . . whatever the hell that meant. I downloaded everything about the PressureDynes onto my phone bug, not sure who I'd take it to, but damn sure no one here was going to be able to help.

"What are you doing with that?"

I jumped and looked around. Suze had snuck up on me.

I shrugged. "Dunno. See if I can find someone to help, I guess."

"That's proprietary. You can't take those schematics out of here. Wipe it."

"You're crazy. It's public domain." I got up and popped my phone bug back into my ear. She made a swipe at it, but I dodged and headed for the doors.

She chased after me, a mean mountain of muscle. "I could fire you, you know!"

"Not if I quit first." I yanked open the control room door and ducked out.

"Hey! Get back here! I'm your boss." Her voice followed me down the corridor, getting fainter. "I'm in charge here, dammit. I can fire you! It's in the manual! I found it! You're not the only one who can read! I found it! I can fire you! I will!" Like a little kid, having a fit. She was still yelling when the control room doors finally shut her off.

Outside, in the sunshine, I ended up wandering in the park, watching the trogs, and wondering what I did to piss off God that he stuck me with a nutjob like Suze. I thought about calling Maggie to meet me, but I didn't feel like telling her about work—half the time when I tried to explain stuff to her, she just came up with bad ideas to fix it, or didn't think the things I was talking about were such a big deal—and if I called up halfway through the day she'd definitely wonder why I'd left so early, and what was going on, and then when I didn't take her advice about Suze she'd just get annoyed.

I kept passing trogs humping away and smiling. They waved at me to come over and play. I just waved back. One of them must have been a real girl, because she was distendedly obviously pregnant, bouncing away with a couple of her friends, and I was glad again that Maggie wasn't with me. She had enough pregnancy hang-ups without seeing the trogs breeding.

I wouldn't have minded throwing Suze to the trogs, though. She was about as dumb as one. Christ, I was surrounded by dummies. I needed a new job. Someplace that attracted better talent than sewage work did. I wondered how serious Suze had been about trying to fire me. If there really was something in the manuals that we'd all missed about hiring and firing. And then I wondered how serious I was about quitting. I sure hated Suze. But how did you get a better job when you hadn't finished high school, let alone college?

I stopped short. Sudden enlightenment: College. Columbia. They could help. They'd have some sharpie who could understand all the PressureDyne information. An engineering department, or something. They were even dependent on Pump Six. Talk about leverage.

I headed uptown on the subway with a whole pack of snarly pissed-off commuters, everyone scowling at each other and acting like you were stealing their territory if you sat down next to them. I ended up hanging from a strap and watching two old guys hiss at each other across the car until we broke down at 86th and we all ended up walking.

I kept passing clumps of trogs, lounging around on the sidewalks. A few of the really smart ones were panhandling, but most of them were just humping away. I would have been annoyed at having to shove through the orgy, if I wasn't actually feeling jealous. I kept wondering why the hell was I out here in the sweaty summer smog taking hits off my inhaler while Suze and Chee and Zoo were all hanging around in air-con comfort and basically doing nothing.

What was wrong with me? Why was I the one who always tried to fix things? Mercati had been like that, always taking stuff on and then just getting worked harder and harder until the cancer ate him from the inside out. He was working so hard at the end I think he might have been glad to go, just for the rest.

Maggie always said they worked me too hard, and as I dragged my ass up Broadway, I started thinking she was right. Then again, if I left things to Chee and Suze, I'd be swimming up the Broadway River in a stew of crap and chemicals instead of walking up a street. Maggie would have said that was someone else's problem, but she just thought so because when she flushed the toilet, it still worked. At the end of the day, it seemed like some people just got stuck dealing with the shit, and some people figured out how to have a good time.

A half-hour later, covered with sweat and street grime and holding a half-empty squirt bottle of rehydrating Sweatshine that I'd stolen from an unwary trog, I rolled through Columbia's gates and into the main quad, where I immediately ran into problems.

I kept following signs for the engineering building, but they kept sending me around in circles. I would have asked for directions—I'm not one of those guys who can't—but it's pretty damn embarrassing when you can't even follow a simple sign, so I held off.

And really, who was I going to ask? There were lots of kids out in the quad, all sprawled out and wearing basically nothing and looking like they were starting a trog colony of their own, but I didn't feel like talking to them. I'm not a prude, but you've got to draw the line somewhere.

I ended up wandering around lost, going from one building to the next, stumbling through a jumble of big old Roman- and Ben Franklin-style buildings: lots of columns and brick and patchy green quads—everything looking like it was about to start raining concrete any second—trying to figure out why I couldn't understand any of the signs.

Finally, I sucked it up and asked a couple half-naked kids for directions.

The thing that ticks me off about academic types is that they always act like they're smarter than you. Rich-kid, free-ride, prep-school ones are the worst. I kept asking the best and brightest for directions, trying to get them to take me to the engineering department, or the engineering building, or whatever the hell it was, and they all just looked me up and down and gibbered at me like monkeys, or else laughed through their Effy highs and kept on going. A couple of them gave me a shrug and a "dunno," but that was the best I got.

I gave up on directions, and just kept roaming. I don't know how long I wandered. Eventually I found a big old building off one of the quads, a big square thing with pillars like the Parthenon. A few kids were sprawled out on the steps, soaking up the sun, but it was one of the quietest parts of the campus I'd seen.

The first set of doors I tried was chained, and so was the second, but then I found a set where the chain had been left undone, two heavy lengths of it, dangling with an old open padlock on the end. The kids on the steps were ignoring me, so I yanked open the doors.

Inside, everything was silence and dust. Big old chandeliers hung down from the ceiling, sparkling with orangey light that filtered in through the dirt on the windows. The light made it feel like it was the end of day with the sun starting to set, even though it was only a little past noon. A heavy blanket of dust covered everything; floors and reading tables and chairs and computers all had a thick gray film over them.

"Hello?"

No one answered. My voice echoed and died, like the building had just swallowed up the sound. I started wandering, picking doorways at random: reading rooms, study carrels, more dead computers, but most of all, books. Aisles and aisles with racks full of them. Room after room stuffed with books, all of them covered with thick layers of dust.

A library. A whole damn library in the middle of a university, and not a single person in it. There were tracks on the floor, and a litter of Effy packets, condom wrappers, and liquor bottles where people had come and gone at some point, but even the trash had its own fine layer of dust.

In some rooms, all the books had been yanked off the shelves like a tornado had ripped through. In one, someone had made a bonfire out of them. They lay in a huge heap, completely torched, a pile of ash and pages and backings, a jumble of black ash fossils that crumbled to nothing when I crouched down and touched them. I stood quickly, wiping my hands on my pants. It was like fingering someone's bones.

I kept wandering, running my fingers along shelves and watching the dust cascade like miniature falls of concrete rain. I pulled down a book at random. More dust poured off and puffed up in my face. I coughed. My chest seized and I took a hit off my inhaler. In the dimness, I could barely make out the title: *Post-Liberation America. A Modern Perspective.* When I opened it, its spine cracked.

"What are you doing here?"

I jumped back and dropped the book. Dust puffed around me. An old lady, hunched and witchy, was standing at the end of the aisle. She limped forward. Her voice was sharp as she repeated herself. "What are you doing here?"

"I got lost. I'm trying to find the engineering department."

She was an ugly old dame: Liver spots and lines all over her face. Her skin hung off her bones in loose flaps. She looked a thousand years old, and not in a smart wise way, just in a wrecked moth-eaten way. She had something flat and silvery in her hand. A pistol.

I took another step back.

She raised the gun. "Not that way. Out the way you came." She motioned with the pistol. "Off you go."

I hesitated.

She smiled slightly, showing stumps of missing teeth. "I won't shoot if you don't give me a reason." She waved the gun again. "Go on. You aren't supposed to be here." She herded me back through the library to the main doors with a brisk authority. She pulled them open and waved her pistol at me. "Go on. Get."

"Wait. Please. Can't you at least tell me where the engineering department is?"

"Closed down years ago. Now get out."

"There's got to be one!"

"Not anymore. Go on. Get." She brandished the pistol again. "Get."

I held onto the door. "But you must know someone who can help me." I was talking fast, trying to get all my words out before she used the gun. "I work on the city's sewage pumps. They're breaking, and I don't know how to fix them. I need someone who has engineering experience."

She was shaking her head and starting to wave the gun. I tried again. "Please! You've got to help. No one will talk to me, and you're going to be swimming in crap if I don't find help. Pump Six serves the university and *I don't know how to fix it!*"

She paused. She cocked her head first one way, then the other. "Go on."

I briefly outlined the problems with the PressureDynes. When I finished, she shook her head and turned away. "You've wasted your time. We haven't had an engineering department in over twenty years." She went over to a reading table and took a couple swipes at its dust. Pulled out a chair and did the same with it. She sat, placing her pistol on the table, and motioned me to join her.

Warily, I brushed off my own seat. She laughed at the way my eyes kept going to her pistol. She picked it up and tucked it into a pocket of her moth-eaten sweater. "Don't worry. I won't shoot you now. I just keep it around in case the kids get belligerent. They don't very often, anymore, but you never know . . . " Her voice trailed off, as she looked out at the quad.

"How can you not have an engineering department?"

Her eyes swung back to me. "Same reason I closed the library." She laughed. "We can't have the students running around in here, can we?" She considered me for a moment, thoughtful. "I'm surprised you got in. I'm must be getting old, forgetting to lock up like that."

"You always lock it? Aren't you librarians—"

"I'm not a librarian," she interrupted. "We haven't had a librarian since Herman Hsu died." She laughed. "I'm just an old faculty wife. My husband taught organic chemistry before he died."

"But you're the one who put the chains on the doors?"

"There wasn't anyone else to do it. I just saw the students partying in here and realized something had to be done before they burned the damn place down." She drummed her fingers on the table, raising little dust puffs with her boney digits as she considered me. Finally she said, "If I gave you the library keys, could you learn the things you need to know? About these pumps? Learn how they work? Fix them, maybe?"

"I doubt it. That's why I came here." I pulled out my earbug. "I've got the schematics right here. I just need someone to go over them for me."

"There's no one here who can help you." She smiled tightly. "My degree was in social psychology, not engineering. And really, there's no one else. Unless you count them." She waved at the students beyond the windows, humping in the quad. "Do you think that any of them could read your schematics?"

Through the smudged glass doors I could see the kids on the library steps, stripped down completely. They were humping away, grinning and having a good time. One of the girls saw me through the glass and waved at me to join her. When I shook my head, she shrugged and went back to her humping.

The old lady studied me like a vulture. "See what I mean?"

The girl got into her rhythm. She grinned at me watching, and motioned again for me to come out and play. All she needed were some big yellow eyes, and she would have made a perfect trog.

I closed my eyes and opened them again. Nothing changed. The girl was still there with all of her little play friends. All of them romping around and having a good time.

"The best and the brightest," the old lady murmured.

In the middle of the quad, more of the students were stripping down, none of them caring that they were doing it in the middle of broad daylight, none of them worried about who was watching, or what anyone might think. A couple hundred kids, and not a single one of them had a book, or a notebook, or pens, or paper, or a computer with them.

The old lady laughed. "Don't look so surprised. You can't say someone of your caliber never noticed." She paused, waiting, then peered at me, incredulous. "The trogs? The concrete rain? The reproductive disorders? You never wondered about any of it?" She shook her head. "You're stupider than I guessed."

"But . . . " I cleared my throat. "How could it . . . I mean . . . " I trailed off.

"Chemistry was my husband's field." She squinted at the kids humping on the steps and tangled out in the grass, then shook her head and shrugged. "There are plenty of books on the topic. For a while there were even magazine stories about it. 'Why breast might not be best.' Stuff like that." She waved a hand impatiently. "Rohit and I never really thought about any of it until his students started seeming stupider every year." She cackled briefly. "And then he tested them, and he was right."

"We can't all be turning into trogs." I held up my bottle of Sweatshine. "How could I buy this bottle, or my earbug, or bacon, or anything? Someone has to be making these things."

"You found bacon? Where?" She leaned forward, interested.

"My wife did. Last packet."

She settled back with a sigh. "It doesn't matter. I couldn't chew it anyway." She studied my Sweatshine bottle. "Who knows? Maybe you're right. Maybe it's not so bad. But this is the longest conversation that I've had since Rohit died; most people just don't seem to be able to pay attention to things like they used to." She eyed me. "Maybe your Sweatshine bottle just means there's a factory somewhere that's as good as your sewage pumps used to be. And as long as nothing too complex goes wrong, we all get to keep drinking it."

"It's not that bad."

"Maybe not." She shrugged. "It doesn't matter to me, anymore. I'll kick off pretty soon. After that, it's your problem."

It was night by the time I came out of the university. I had a bag full of books, and no one to know that I'd taken them. The old lady hadn't cared if I checked them out or not, just waved at me to take as many as I liked, and then gave me the keys and told me to lock up when I left.

All of the books were thick with equations and diagrams. I'd picked through them one after another, reading each for a while, before giving up and starting on another. They were all pretty much gibberish. It was like trying to read before you knew your ABCs. Mercati had been right. I should have stayed in school. I probably wouldn't have done any worse than the Columbia kids.

Out on the street, half the buildings were dark. Some kind of brownout that ran all the way down Broadway. One side of the street had electricity, cheerful and bright. The other side had candles glimmering in all the apartment windows, ghost lights flickering in a pretty ambiance.

A crash of concrete rain echoed from a couple blocks away. I couldn't help shivering. Everything had turned creepy. It felt like the old lady was leaning over my shoulder and pointing out broken things everywhere. Empty autovendors. Cars that hadn't moved in years. Cracks in the sidewalk. Piss in the gutters.

What was normal supposed to look like?

I forced myself to look at good things. People were still out and about, walking to their dance clubs, going out to eat, wandering uptown or downtown to see their parents. Kids were on skateboards rolling past and trogs were humping in the alleys. A couple of vendor boxes were full of cellophane bagels, along with a big row of Sweatshine bottles all glowing green under their lights, still all stocked up and ready for sale. Lots of things were still working. Wicky was still a great club, even if Max needed a little help remembering to restock. And Miku and Gabe had their new baby, even if it took them three years to get it. I couldn't let myself wonder if that baby was going to turn out like the college kids in the quad. Not everything was broken.

As if to prove it, the subway ran all the way to my stop for a change. Somewhere on the line, they must have had a couple guys like me, people who could still read a schematic and remember how to show up for work and not throw toilet paper around the control rooms. I wondered who they were. And then I wondered if they ever noticed how hard it was to get anything done.

When I got home, Maggie was already in bed. I gave her a kiss and she woke up a little. She pushed her hair away from her face. "I left out a hotpack burrito for you. The stove's still broke."

"Sorry. I forgot. I'll fix it now."

"No worry." She turned away from me and pulled the sheets up around her neck. For a minute, I thought she'd dozed off, but then she said, "Trav?"

"Yeah?"

"I got my period."

I sat down beside her and started massaging her back. "How you doing with that?"

"S'okay. Maybe next time." She was already dropping back to sleep. "You just got to stay optimistic, right?"

"That's right, baby." I kept rubbing her back. "That's right."

When she was asleep, I went back to the kitchen. I found the hotpack burrito and shook it and tore it open, holding it with the tips of my fingers so I wouldn't burn myself. I took a bite, and decided the burritos were still working just fine. I dumped all the books onto the kitchen table and stared at them, trying to decide where to start.

Through the open kitchen windows, from the direction of the park, I heard another crash of concrete rain. I looked out toward the candleflicker darkness. Not far away, deep underground, nine pumps were chugging away; their little flashers winking in and out with errors, their maintenance logs scrolling repair requests, and all of them running a little harder now that Pump Six was down. But they were still running. The people who'd built them had done a good job. With luck, they'd keep running for a long time yet.

I chose a book at random and started reading.

～

Paolo Bacigalupi's writing has appeared in *Wired Magazine*, *High Country News*, *Salon.com*, *OnEarth Magazine*, *The Magazine of Fantasy and Science Fiction*, and *Asimov's Science Fiction Magazine*. His short fiction has been anthologized in various "Year's Best" collections of short science fiction and fantasy, nominated for three Nebula Awards, four Hugo Awards, and won the Theodore Sturgeon Memorial Award for best sf short story of the year. His short story collection *Pump Six and Other Stories* was a 2008 Locus Award winner for Best Collection and also named a Best Book of the Year by *Publishers Weekly*. His debut novel *The Windup Girl* was named by *Time Magazine* as one of the ten best novels of 2009, and also won the Hugo, Nebula, Locus, Compton Crook, and John W. Campbell Memorial Awards. His debut young adult novel, *Ship Breaker*, was a Micheal L. Printz Award Winner, and a National Book Award Finalist. His most recent novel, *The Drowned Cities*, was a 2012 *Kirkus Reviews* Best of YA Book, a 2012 *VOYA* Perfect Ten Book, and 2012 *Los Angeles Times* Book Prize Finalist. He currently lives in Western Colorado with his wife and son, where he is working on a new novel.

～

Blake Butler's story may or may not be surreal. Why should the End of an irrational world be particularly rational? Why should anyone experience it in easily explicable ways?

• THE DISAPPEARED •
Blake Butler

The year they tested us for scoliosis, I took my shirt off in front of the whole gym. Even the cheerleaders saw my bruises. I'd been scratching in my sleep. Insects were coming in through cracks we couldn't find. There was something on the air. Noises from the attic. My skin was getting pale.

I was the first.

The several gym coaches, with their reflective scalps and high-cut shorts, crowded around me blowing whistles. They made me keep my shirt up over my head while they stood around and poked and pondered. Foul play was suspected. They sent directly for my father. They made him stand in the middle of the gym in front of everyone and shoot free throws to prove he was a man. I didn't have to see to know. I heard the dribble and the inhale. He couldn't even hit the rim.

The police showed up and bent him over and led him by his face out to their car. You could hear him screaming in the lobby. He sounded like a woman.

For weeks after, I was well known. Even bookworms threw me up against the lockers, eyes gleaming. The teachers turned their backs. I swallowed several teeth. The sores kept getting worse. I was sent home and dosed with medication. I massaged cream into my wounds. I was not allowed to sleep alone. My uncle came to stay around me in the evenings. He sat in my mother's chair and watched TV. I told him not to sit there because no one did after Mother. Any day now Dad expected her return. He wanted to keep the smell of her worn inside the cracking leather until then. My uncle did not listen. He ordered porn on my father's cable bill. He turned the volume up and sat watching in his briefs while I stood there knowing I'd be blamed.

Those women had the mark of something brimming in them. Something ruined and old and endless, something gone.

By the third night, I couldn't stand. I slept in fever, soaked in vision. Skin cells showered from my soft scalp. My nostrils gushed with liquid. You could see patterns in my forehead—oblong clods of fat veins, knotted, dim. I crouped and cowed and cringed among the lack of moonlight. I felt my forehead coming off, the ooze of my blood becoming slower, full of glop. I felt surely soon I'd die and there'd be nothing left to dicker. I pulled a tapeworm from my ear.

My uncle sent for surgeons. They measured my neck and graphed my reason. Backed with their charts and smarts and tallies, they said there was nothing they could do. They retested my blood pressure and reflexes for good measure. They said *say ah* and stroked their chins. Then they went into the kitchen with my uncle and stood around drinking beer and cracking jokes.

The verdict on my father's incarceration was changed from abuse to vast neglect, coupled with involuntary impending manslaughter. His sentence was increased. They showed him on the news. On screen he did not look like the man I'd spent my life in rooms nearby. He didn't look like anyone I'd ever known.

The bugs continued to swarm my bedroom. Some had huge eyes. Some had teeth. From my sickbed I learned their patterns. They'd made tunnels through the floor. I watched them devour my winter coat. I watched them carry my drum kit off in pieces.

Another night I dreamed my mother. She had no hair. Her eyes were black. She came in through the window of my bedroom and hovered over. She kissed the crud out from my skin. Her cheeks filled with the throbbing. She filled me up with light.

The next morning my wounds had waned to splotches.

After a week, I was deemed well.

In the mirror my face looked smaller, somehow puckered, shrunken in. My eyes had changed from green to deep blue. The school required seven faxes of clearance before my readmission. Even then, no one came near me. I had to hand in my assignments laminated. I was reseated in far corners, my raised arm unacknowledged. Once I'd had the answers; now I spent the hours fingering the gum under my desk.

On weekends I went to visit Dad in prison. He was now serving twenty-five to life. They made him wear a plastic jumpsuit that enclosed his head to keep the felons' breath from spreading their ideas. Through the visor, my father's eyes were bloodshot, puffy. His teeth were turning brown. His small paunch from years of beer had flattened. He had a number on his arm. He refused to look at me directly. He either shook his head or nodded. This was my fault, I knew he thought. We spent our half-hour grunting, gumming, shrugged.

Each time before I left he asked one question, in sign language: HAS YOUR MOTHER FOUND HER WAY BACK YET?

Each time before I left he slipped me a ten and told me where to go.

At home we had a map of downtown that Dad kept on the kitchen table where we used to eat together. He'd marked with dated dots in fluorescent marker where he thought he'd seen her last. Mom was one of several who'd gone missing in recent weeks. Each night, between commercials, the news showed reams and reams of disappeared—pigtailed teens and Air Force pilots, stockbrokers, grandpas, unwed mothers. Hundreds had gone unaccounted. The missing ads covered milk cartons on every side. The government whispered *terrorism*. On the news they used our nation's other problems as distraction: the wilting trees; the mold-grown buildings, high-rise rooftops clung together; the color shift of oceans; the climaxed death rate of new babies.

The way the shores washed up with blood foam.

How at night you couldn't see the moon.

Before prison, Dad had sat at night with his cell phone on his knee on vibrate, waiting to feel the pulse shoot up his leg and hear her on the other end, alive. His skin would flex at any tremor. The phone rang through the night. The loan folks wanted back their money. Taxes. Electricity. They would not accept Visa or good will. Dad developed a tic and cursed with no control. He believed my mother's return in his heart. His list of sightings riddled the whole map. He thought he'd heard her once in the men's room at the movies. Once he'd seen her standing on the edge of a tobacco billboard, pointing down. He wanted me to keep tabs on all these places. As well, he wanted farther acres combed. Mom had been appearing in his sleep. She would not be hard to find if he truly loved her, he said she whispered. *You should already know by now.* On his skin, while in his cell bed, he made lists of the places where he should have looked: that spot in the ocean where he'd first kissed her; the small plot where they'd meant one day to be buried side by side; behind the moon where they joked they'd live forever; in places no one else could name. He wanted a full handwritten report of each location.

After school, before the sun dunked, I carried the map around the nearer streets in search. Sometimes, as my dad had, I felt mother's hair against my neck. I smelled her sweet sweat somehow pervading even in the heady rush of highway fumes. I heard her whistle no clear tune, the way she had with me inside her and when I was small enough to carry. I used the hours between school's end and draining light. I trolled the grocery, hiked the turnpike, stalked the dressing rooms of several local department stores. I felt that if I focused my effort to the right degree I could bring an end to all this sinking. I'd find her somewhere, lost and listless, lead her home, reteach her name. Newly aligned, she'd argue dad's innocence in court to vast amends, and then there'd be the three of us forever, fixed in the only home we'd ever known.

I did not find her at the creek bed where she'd taught me how to swim via immersion.

I spent several hopeful evenings outside the dry cleaner's where she'd always taken all our clothes.

There were always small pools of buzzed air where I could feel her just behind me, or inside.

My uncle did not go home. He'd taken over my parents' bed and wore Dad's clothing. Through the night he snored so loud you could hear it throughout the house. You could hear as well the insects crawling: their tiny wings and writhing sensors. You could hear the wreathes of spore and fungus. The slither in the ground. It was all over, not just my house. Neighborhood trees hung thick with buzz. House roofs collapsed under heavy weight. Everyone had knives. They ran photo essays in the independent papers. The list of disappeared grew to include news anchors, journalists, and liberal pundits. I stayed awake and kept my hair combed. I tried not to walk in sludge.

I received an email from my father: SHE SAYS THERE'S NOT MUCH TIME.

I committed to further hours. I stayed up at night and blended in. I looked in smaller places, the ones no one else could name: through the sidewalk; in the glare of stoplights; in the mouths of tagless dogs. I avoided major roads for the police. Out-of-town travel had been restricted. They mentioned our best interests. They said recovery begins at home. I marched through the forest with a flashlight, not quite laughing, being careful not to die. Trees fell at random in the black air. Anthills smothered whole backyards. It hadn't rained in half a year. You might start a mile-wide fire with one mislaid cigarette. The corporate news channel spent their hours showing pictures of dolphin babies and furry kittens cuddling in the breeze.

Meanwhile, at school, other people started getting sick. First, several players on the JV wrestling team shared a stage of ringworm—bright white mold growths on their muscles. The reigning captain collapsed in the hot lunch line. They had to cancel future matches. The infestation was blamed on high heat and tight quarters. Days later, Jenny Rise, the head cheerleader grew a massive boil on the left side of her head. It swelled the skin around her eyelids until she couldn't see. She went to the hospital not for the boil itself, but for how she'd tried to stab it out.

The seething moved in small creation through the cramped halls of our school. Popular kids got it. Kids with glasses. Kids in special ed. Teachers called out absent, then their subs did. Sometimes we were left in rooms unmanned for hours. There were so many missing they quit sending people home. Fast rashes rushed from collars. Guys showed up with their eyes puckered in glop. My lab partner, Maria Sanchez, grew a strange mustache. They had to sweep the hallways several times a day.

Instead of our usual assignments, we read manuals on how to better keep our bodies clean. Diagrams were posted in our lockers. Baskets of dental floss and disinfectant were placed in the nurse's office with the condoms. No one really laughed.

Then, one day during my math class, men in military gear barged in. They had batons and air masks with complex reflectors. They made us stand in line with our hands against the wall. We spread and coughed while they roughed us over. They pulled hair samples and drew blood. From certain people they took skin grafts. The screaming filled the halls. They confiscated our cell phones and our book bags. Our class fish, Tommy, was deposed. The walls were doused with yellow powder. Several people fainted or threw up. They put black bags over the windows. The school's exit doors were sealed with putty. A voice that was not the cafeteria lady's came over the loudspeaker and said what was being served. We'd eaten lunch already. We sat at our desks and said the pledge. We sat at our desks with no looking at each other. The sub for our sub was reprimanded for attempting exit. They laid her flat out on the ground.

We were contained this way without explanation. Because of the window bags, we couldn't tell how many days. There was a lot of time and no way to pass it. We were not allowed to talk or use the restroom. We were given crossword puzzles and origami. The PA played Bach and Brahms over the rumble overhead. When the lunchroom ran out of leftovers, we were fed through tubes lowered from the ceiling.

After the first rash of fistfights and paranoia spasms, they locked our wrists with plastic. They turned the heat to high. The veins began to stand out on people's heads. Their skin went red and dented, then bright purple. Their hair fell out. Their teeth and nails grew green and yellow. Their swollen limbs bejeweled with sores. Cysts blew big in new balloons.

I felt fine. I felt an aura, my mother's breath encircling my head.

The costumed men carried the expired elsewhere. Those who weren't sick were crazed. I watched a girl bang her face in on a blackboard. I watched a boy stick out his eyes. The rest of us sat with our hands flat on the desktops, not sure which way to turn.

Soon the power was extinguished. False neon panels were employed. Peals of static began to interrupt the PA's symphonies. A sudden voice squawked through with contraband report. *Look what we've done. Can you imagine? Half the nation under quarantine. The buildings crumpled. The oceans aboil. The President's committed suicide. And now, just a bit too late, we're getting rain.* The men burst in and shot the speaker with a machine gun. They said to assume the duck and cover. One spotty redhead whose glasses had been confiscated refused to get down. She walked around in small circles reaching from desk to desk to guide her way. The men zapped her in the neck with a large prong. She ran straight into a wall. She fell on the floor and bumped her forehead, and it spilled open on the white tile. None of the men would let me help them help her. They carried her out and wrapped our heads in plastic and went into the hall and shut the door. I heard the tumblers clicking in the lock. I saw the hall fill thick with smoke. There were sirens, screech and screaming. Something scraping on the roof. It wasn't long yet until other . . . I didn't try to think of what. Small Susie Wang huddled beside me, praying. She spoke in hyperventilated mumble. She put her hands over her mouth.

I sat on the floor in the neon light with stomach rumbling and sounds of flame and stink of rot. I saw things moving toward me and then gone. I couldn't remember where or why I was. I couldn't find my name writ on my tongue or brain-embedded. I felt a burning in my chest. I fumbled in my pockets for my father's map. I stared and rubbed the paper between my fingers. I read the sightings' dot's dates with my wormed eyes, connecting them in order. There was the first point where my father felt sure he'd seen mother digging in the neighbor's yard across the street. And the second, in the field of power wires where Dad swore he saw her running at full speed.

I connected dots until the first fifteen together formed a nostril.

Dots 16 through 34 became an eye.

Together the whole map made a perfect picture of my missing mother's head.

If I stared into the face, then, and focused on one clear section and let my brain go loose, I saw my mother's eyes come open. I saw her mouth begin to move. Her voice echoed deep inside me, clear and brimming, bright, alive.

She said, "Don't worry, son. I'm fat and happy. They have cake here. My hair is clean."

She said, "The world is slurred and I am sorry."

She said, "You are okay. I have your hand."

Her eyes seemed to swim around me. I felt her fingers in my hair. She whispered things she'd never mentioned. She nuzzled gleamings in my brain. As in: the day I'd drawn her flowers because all the fields were dying. As in: the downed bird we'd cleaned and given a name. Some of our years were wall to wall with wonder, she reminded me. In spite of any absence, we had that.

I thought of my father, alone and elsewhere, his head cradled in his hands. I thought of the day he'd punched a hole straight through the kitchen wall, thinking she'd be tucked away inside. All those places he'd looked and never found her. Inside their mattress. In stained-glass windows. How he'd scoured the carpet for her stray hair and strung them all together with a ribbon; how he'd slept with that one lock swathed across his nostrils, hugging a pillow fitted with her nightshirt. How he'd dug up the backyard, stripped and sweating. How he'd played her favorite album on repeat and loud, a lure. How when we took up the carpet in my bedroom to find her, under the carpet there was wood. Under the wood there was cracked concrete. Under the concrete there was dirt. Under the dirt there was a cavity of water. I swam down into the water with my nose clenched and lungs burning in my chest but I could not find the bottom and I couldn't see a thing.

⌐⌐

Blake Butler is the author of the novella *Ever*, the novel-in-stories *Scorch Atlas* (from which this story is taken), and novels *There Is No Year* and *Sky*

Saw, as well as the memoir *Nothing: A Portrait of Insomnia*. Butler edits the literature blog HTML Giant, and two journals: *Lamination Colony*, and concurrently with co-editor Ken Baumann, *No Colony*. He has published more than one hundred stories in magazine and journals. Butler's story "Insomnia Door" won an &NOW award in 2009 and was published in *The &NOW Awards: The Best Innovative Writing*.

After this End, authoritarianism is not always dystopic. Carrie Vaughn portrays a future society that voluntarily adheres to strict regulation in order for all to survive with most needs filled and some measure of comfort. There are abuses and, of course, not all desires are met. But can't that be said of any social system?

· AMARYLLIS ·
Carrie Vaughn

I never knew my mother, and I never understood why she did what she did. I ought to be grateful that she was crazy enough to cut out her implant so she could get pregnant. But it also meant she was crazy enough to hide the pregnancy until termination wasn't an option, knowing the whole time that she'd never get to keep the baby. That she'd lose everything. That her household would lose everything because of her.

I never understood how she couldn't care. I wondered what her family thought when they learned what she'd done, when their committee split up the household, scattered them—broke them, because of her.

Did she think I was worth it?

It was all about quotas.

"They're using cages up north, I heard. Off shore, anchored," Nina said. "Fifty feet across—twice as much protein grown with half the resources, and we'd never have to touch the wild population again. We could double our quota."

I hadn't really been listening to her. We were resting, just for a moment; she sat with me on the railing at the prow of *Amaryllis* and talked about her big plans.

Wind pulled the sails taut and the fiberglass hull cut through waves without a sound, we sailed so smooth. Garrett and Sun hauled up the nets behind us, dragging in the catch. *Amaryllis* was elegant, a thirty-foot sleek vessel with just enough cabin and cargo space—an antique but more than seaworthy. She was a good boat, with a good crew. The best.

"Marie—" Nina said, pleading.

I sighed and woke up. "We've been over this. We can't just double our quota."

"But if we got authorization—"

"Don't you think we're doing all right as it is?" We had a good crew—we were well fed and not exceeding our quotas; I thought we'd be best off not screwing all that up. Not making waves, so to speak.

Nina's big brown eyes filled with tears—I'd said the wrong thing, because I knew what she was really after, and the status quo wasn't it.

"That's just it," she said. "We've met our quotas and kept everyone healthy for years now. I really think we should try. We can at least ask, can't we?"

The truth was: No, I wasn't sure we deserved it. I wasn't sure that kind of responsibility would be worth it. I didn't want the prestige. Nina didn't even want the prestige—she just wanted the baby.

"It's out of our hands at any rate," I said, looking away because I couldn't bear the intensity of her expression.

Pushing herself off the rail, Nina stomped down *Amaryllis'* port side to join the rest of the crew hauling in the catch. She wasn't old enough to want a baby. She was lithe, fit, and golden, running barefoot on the deck, sun-bleached streaks gleaming in her brown hair. Actually, no, she *was* old enough. She'd been with the house for seven years—she was twenty, now. It hadn't seemed so long.

"Whoa!" Sun called. There was a splash and a thud as something in the net kicked against the hull. He leaned over the side, the muscles along his broad, coppery back flexing as he clung to a net that was about to slide back into the water. Nina, petite next to his strong frame, reached with him. I ran down and grabbed them by the waistbands of their trousers to hold them steady. The fourth of our crew, Garrett, latched a boat hook into the net. Together we hauled the catch onto the deck. We'd caught something big, heavy, and full of powerful muscles.

We had a couple of aggregators—large buoys made of scrap steel and wood—anchored fifty miles or so off the coast. Schooling fish were attracted to the aggregators, and we found the fish—mainly mackerel, sardines, sablefish, and whiting. An occasional shark or marlin found its way into the nets, but those we let go; they were rare and outside our quotas. That was what I expected to see—something unusually large thrashing among the slick silvery mass of smaller fish. This thing was large, yes, as big as Nina—no wonder it had almost pulled them over—but it wasn't the right shape. Sleek and streamlined, a powerful swimmer. Silvery like the rest of the catch.

"What is it?" Nina asked.

"Tuna," I said, by process of elimination. I had never seen one in my life. "Bluefin, I think."

"No one's caught a bluefin in thirty years," Garrett said. Sweat was dripping onto his face despite the bandana tying back his shaggy dark hair.

I was entranced, looking at all that protein. I pressed my hand to the fish's flank, feeling its muscles twitch. "Maybe they're back."

We'd been catching the tuna's food all along, after all. In the old days the aggregators attracted as many tuna as mackerel. But no one had seen one in so long, everyone assumed they were gone.

"Let's put him back," I said, and the others helped me lift the net to the side. It took all of us, and when we finally got the tuna to slide overboard, we lost half the net's catch with it, a wave of silvery scales glittering as they hit the water. But that was okay: Better to be under quota than over.

The tuna splashed its tail and raced away. We packed up the rest of the catch and set sails for home.

The *Californian* crew got their banner last season, and flew its red and green—power and fertility—from the top of the boat's mast for all to see. Elsie of the *Californian* was due to give birth in a matter of weeks. As soon as her pregnancy was confirmed, she stopped sailing and stayed in the household, sheltered and treasured. Loose hands resting atop mountainous belly, she would sometimes come out to greet her household's boat as it arrived. Nina would stare at her. Elsie might have been the first pregnant woman Nina had seen, as least since surviving puberty and developing thoughts of carrying a mountainous belly of her own.

Elsie was there now, an icon cast in bronze before the setting sun, her body canted slightly against the weight in her belly, like a ship leaning away from the wind.

We furled the sails and rowed to the pier beside the scale house. Nina hung over the prow, looking at Elsie, who was waving at *Californian*'s captain, on the deck of the boat. Solid and dashing, everything a captain ought to be, he waved back at her. Their boat was already secured in its home slip, their catch weighed, everything tidy. Nina sighed at the image of a perfect life, and nobody yelled at her for not helping. Best thing to do in a case like this was let her dream until she grew out of it. Might take decades, but still . . .

My *Amaryllis* crew handed crates off to the dockhand, who shifted our catch to the scale house. Beyond that were the processing houses, where onshore crews smoked, canned, and shipped the fish inland. The New Oceanside community provided sixty percent of the protein for the whole region, which was our mark of pride, our reason for existing. Within the community itself, the ten sailing crews were proudest of all. A fishing crew that did its job well and met its quotas kept the whole system running smoothly. I was lucky to even have the *Amaryllis* and be a part of it.

I climbed up to the dock with my folk after securing the boat, and saw that Anders was the scalemaster on duty. The week's trip might as well have been for nothing, then.

Thirty-five years ago, my mother ripped out her implant and broke up her household. Might as well have been yesterday to a man like Anders.

The old man took a nail-biting forty minutes to weigh our catch and add up our numbers, at which point he announced, "You're fifty pounds over quota."

Quotas were the only way to keep the stock healthy, to prevent over-fishing, shortages, and ultimately starvation. The committee based quotas on how much you needed, not how much you could catch. To exceed that—to pretend you needed more than other people—showed so much disrespect to the committee, the community, to the fishing stock.

My knees weak, I almost sat down. I'd gotten it exactly right, I knew I had. I glared at him. Garrett and Sun, a pair of brawny sailors helpless before the scalemaster in his dull gray tunic of authority, glared at him. Some days felt like nothing I did would ever be enough. I'd always be too far one way or the other over the line of "just right." Most days, I'd accept the scalemaster's judgment and walk away, but today, after setting loose the tuna and a dozen pounds of legitimate catch with it, it was too much.

"You're joking," I said. "Fifty pounds?"

"Really," Anders said, marking the penalty on the chalkboard behind him where all the crews could see it. "You ought to know better, an experienced captain like you."

He wouldn't even look at me. Couldn't look me in the eye while telling me I was trash.

"What do you want me to do, throw the surplus overboard? We can eat those fifty pounds. The livestock can eat those fifty pounds."

"It'll get eaten, don't worry. But it's on your record." Then he marked it on his clipboard, as if he thought we'd come along and alter the public record.

"Might as well not sail out at all next week, eh?" I said.

The scalemaster frowned and turned away. A fifty-pound surplus—if it even existed—would go to make up another crew's shortfall, and next week our catch would be needed just as much as it had been this week, however little some folk wanted to admit it. We could get our quota raised like Nina wanted, and we wouldn't have to worry about surpluses at all. No, then we'd worry about shortfalls, and not earning credits to feed the mouths we had, much less the extra one Nina wanted.

Surpluses must be penalized, or everyone would go fishing for surpluses and having spare babies, and then where would we be? Too many mouths, not enough food, no resiliency to survive disaster, and all the disease and starvation that followed. I'd seen the pictures in the archives, of what happened after the big fall.

Just enough and no more. Moderation. But so help me I wasn't going to dump fifty pounds just to keep my record clean.

"We're done here. Thank you, Captain Marie," Anders said, his back to me, like he couldn't stand the sight of me.

When we left, I found Nina at the doorway, staring. I pushed her in front of me, back to the boat, so we could put *Amaryllis* to bed for the night.

"The *Amaryllis'* scales aren't that far off," Garrett grumbled as we rowed to her slip. "Ten pounds, maybe. Not fifty."

"Anders had his foot on the pad, throwing it off. I'd bet on it," Sun said. "Ever notice how we're only ever off when Anders is running the scales?"

We'd all noticed.

"Is that true? But why would he do that?" said Nina, innocent Nina. Everyone looked at me. A weight seemed to settle on us.

"What?" Nina said. "What is it?"

It was the kind of thing no one talked about, and Nina was too young to have grown up knowing. The others had all known what they were getting into, signing on with me. But not Nina.

I shook my head at them. "We'll never prove that Anders has it in for us so there's no good arguing. We'll take our licks and that's the end of it."

Sun said, "Too many black marks like that they'll break up the house."

That was the worry, wasn't it?

"How many black marks?" Nina said. "He can't do that. Can he?"

Garrett smiled and tried to take the weight off. He was the first to sign on with me when I inherited the boat. We'd been through a lot together. "We'll just have to find out Anders' schedule and make sure we come in when someone else is on duty."

But most of the time there were no schedules—just whoever was on duty when a boat came in. I wouldn't be surprised to learn that Anders kept a watch for us, just to be here to rig our weigh-in.

Amaryllis glided into her slip, and I let Garrett and Sun secure the lines. I leaned back against the side, stretching my arms, staring up along the mast. Nina sat nearby, clenching her hands, her lips. Elsie and *Californian*'s captain had gone.

I gave her a pained smile. "You might have a better chance of getting your extra mouth if you went to a different crew. The *Californian*, maybe."

"Are you trying to get rid of me?" Nina said.

Sitting up, I put my arms across her shoulders and pulled her close. Nina came to me a clumsy thirteen-year-old from Bernardino, up the coast. My household had a space for her, and I was happy to get her. She'd grown up smart and eager. She could take my place when I retired, inherit *Amaryllis* in her turn. Not that I'd told her that yet.

"Never. Never ever." She only hesitated a moment before wrapping her arms around me and squeezing back.

Our household was an oasis. We'd worked hard to make it so. I'd inherited the boat, attracted the crew one by one—Garrett and Sun to run the boat, round and bustling Dakota to run the house, and she brought the talented J.J., and we fostered Nina. We'd been assigned fishing rights, and then we earned the land allocation. Ten years of growing, working, sweating, nurturing, living, and the place was gorgeous.

We'd dug into the side of a hill above the docks and built with adobe. In the afternoon sun, the walls gleamed golden. The part of the house projecting out from the hill served as a wall protecting the garden and well. Our path led around the house and into the courtyard. We'd found flat shale to use as flagstones around the cultivated plots, and to line the well, turning it into a spring. A tiny spring, but any open fresh water seemed like a luxury. On the hill above were the windmill and solar panels.

Everyone who wanted their own room had one, but only Sun did—the detached room dug into the hill across the yard. Dakota, J.J., and Nina had pallets in the largest room. Garret and I shared a bed in the smaller room. What wasn't house was garden. We had producing fruit trees, an orange and a lemon, that also shaded the kitchen space. Corn, tomatoes, sunflowers, green beans, peas, carrots, radishes, two kinds of peppers, and anything else we could make grow on a few square feet. A pot full of mint and one of basil. For the most part we fed ourselves and so could use our credits on improving *Amaryllis* and bringing in specialties like rice and honey, or fabric and rope that we couldn't make in quantity. Dakota wanted to start chickens next season, if we could trade for the chicks.

I kept wanting to throw that in the face of people like Anders. It wasn't like I didn't pay attention. I wasn't a burden.

The crew arrived home; J.J. had supper ready. Dakota and J.J. had started out splitting household work evenly, but pretty quickly they were trading chores—turning compost versus hanging laundry, mending the windmill versus cleaning the kitchen—until J.J. did most everything involving the kitchen and living spaces and Dakota did everything with the garden and mechanics.

By J.J.'s sympathetic expression when he gave me my serving—smoked mackerel and vegetables tonight—someone had already told him about the run-in with the scalemaster. Probably to keep him or Dakota from asking how my day went.

I stayed out later than usual making a round of the holding. Not that I expected to find anything wrong. It was for my own peace of mind, looking at what we'd built with my own eyes, putting my hand on the trunk of the windmill, running the leaves of the lemon tree across my palms, ensuring that none of it had vanished, that it wasn't going to. It had become a ritual.

In bed I held tight to Garrett, to give and get comfort, skin against skin, under the sheet, under the warm air coming in through the open skylight above our bed.

"Bad day?" he said.

"Can never be a bad day when the ship and crew come home safe," I said. But my voice was flat.

Garrett shifted, running a hand down my back, arranging his arms to pull me tight against him. Our legs twined together. My nerves settled.

He said, "Nina's right, we can do more. We can support an extra mouth. If we appealed—"

"You really think that'll do any good?" I said. "I think you'd all be better off with a different captain."

He tilted his face toward mine, touched my lips with his, pressed until I responded. A minute of that and we were both smiling.

"You know we all ended up here because we don't get along with anyone else. But you make the rest of us look good."

I squirmed against him in mock outrage, giggling.

"Plenty of crews—plenty of households—don't ever get babies," he said. "It doesn't mean anything."

"I don't care about a baby so much," I said. "I'm just tired of fighting all the time."

It was normal for children to fight with their parents, their households, and even their committees as they grew. But it wasn't fair, for me to feel like I was still fighting with a mother I'd never known.

The next day, when Nina and I went down to do some cleaning on *Amaryllis*, I tried to convince myself it was my imagination that she was avoiding me. Not looking at me. Or pretending not to look, when in fact she was stealing glances. The way she avoided meeting my gaze made my skin crawl a little. She'd decided something. She had a secret.

We caught sight of Elsie again, walking up from the docks, a hundred yards away but her silhouette was unmistakable. That distracted Nina, who stopped to stare.

"Is she really that interesting?" I said, smiling, trying to make it a joke.

Nina looked at me sideways, as if deciding whether she should talk to me. Then she sighed. "I wonder what it's like. Don't you wonder what it's like?"

I thought about it a moment and mostly felt fear rather than interest. All the things that could go wrong, even with a banner of approval flying above you. Nina wouldn't understand that. "Not really."

"Marie, how can you be so . . . so *indifferent*?"

"Because I'm not going to spend the effort worrying about something I can't change. Besides, I'd much rather be captain of a boat than stuck on shore, watching."

I marched past her to the boat, and she followed, head bowed.

We washed the deck, checked the lines, cleaned out the cabin, took inventory, and made a stack of gear that needed to be repaired. We'd take it home and spend the next few days working on it before we went to sea again. Nina was quiet most of the morning, and I kept glancing at her, head bent to her work, biting her lip, wondering what she was thinking on so intently. What she was hiding.

Turned out she was working up the courage.

I handed the last bundle of net to her, then went back to double check that the hatches were closed and the cabin was shut up. When I went to climb off the boat myself, she was sitting at the edge of the dock, her legs hanging over the edge, swinging a little. She looked ten years younger, like she was a kid again, like she had when I first saw her.

I regarded her, brows raised, questioning, until finally she said, "I asked Sun why Anders doesn't like you. Why none of the captains talk to you much."

So that was what had happened. Sun—matter-of-fact and sensible—would have told her without any circumspection. And Nina had been horrified.

Smiling, I sat on the gunwale in front of her. "I'd have thought you'd been here long enough to figure it out on your own."

"I knew something had happened, but I couldn't imagine what. Certainly not—I mean, no one ever talks about it. But . . . what happened to your mother? Her household?"

I shrugged, because it wasn't like I remembered any of it. I'd pieced the story together, made some assumptions. Was told what happened by people who made their own assumptions. Who wanted me to understand exactly what my place in the world was.

"They were scattered over the whole region, I think. Ten of them—it was a big household, successful, until I came along. I don't know where all they ended up. I was brought to New Oceanside, raised up by the first *Amaryllis* crew. Then Zeke and Ann retired, took up pottery, went down the coast, and gave me the ship to start my own household. Happy ending."

"And your mother—they sterilized her? After you were born, I mean."

"I assume so. Like I said, I don't really know."

"Do you suppose she thought it was worth it?"

"I imagine she didn't," I said. "If she wanted a baby, she didn't get one, did she? But maybe she just wanted to be pregnant for a little while."

Nina looked so thoughtful, swinging her feet, staring at the rippling water where it lapped against the hull, she made me nervous. I had to say something.

"You'd better not be thinking of pulling something like that," I said. "They'd split us up, take the house, take *Amaryllis*—"

"Oh no," Nina said, shaking her head quickly, her denial vehement. "I would never do that, I'd never do anything like that."

"Good," I said, relieved. I trusted her and didn't think she would. Then again, my mother's household probably thought that about her too. I hopped over to the dock. We collected up the gear, slinging bags and buckets over our shoulders and starting the hike up to the house.

Halfway there Nina said, "You don't think we'll ever get a banner, because of your mother. That's what you were trying to tell me."

"Yeah." I kept my breathing steady, concentrating on the work at hand.

"But it doesn't change who you are. What you do."

"The old folk still take it out on me."

"It's not fair," she said. She was too old to be saying things like that. But at least now she'd know, and she could better decide if she wanted to find another household.

"If you want to leave, I'll understand," I said. "Any house would be happy to take you."

"No," she said. "No, I'll stay. None of it—it doesn't change who you are."

I could have dropped everything and hugged her for that. We walked awhile longer, until we came in sight of the house. Then I asked, "You have someone in mind to be the father? Hypothetically."

She blushed berry red and looked away. I had to grin—so that was how it stood.

When Garrett greeted us in the courtyard, Nina was still blushing. She avoided him and rushed along to dump her load in the workshop.

Garrett blinked after her. "What's up with her?"

"Nina being Nina."

The next trip on *Amaryllis* went well. We made quota in less time than I expected, which gave us half a day's vacation. We anchored off a deserted bit of shore and went swimming, lay on deck and took in the sun, ate the last of the oranges and dried mackerel that J.J. had sent along with us. It was a good day.

But we had to head back some time and face the scales. I weighed our haul three times with *Amaryllis*' scale, got a different number each time, but all within ten pounds of each other, and more importantly twenty pounds under quota. Not that it would matter. We rowed into the slip at the scale house, and Anders was the scalemaster on duty again. I almost hauled up our sails and turned us around, never to return. I couldn't face him, not after the perfect trip. Nina was right—it wasn't fair that this one man could ruin us with false surpluses and black marks.

Silently, we secured *Amaryllis* to the dock and began handing up our cargo. I managed to keep from even looking at Anders, which probably made me look guilty in his eyes. But we'd already established I could be queen of perfection and he would consider me guilty.

Anders' frown was smug, his gaze judgmental. I could already hear him tell me I was fifty pounds over quota. Another haul like that, he'd say, we'll have to see about yanking your fishing rights. I'd have to punch him. I almost told Garrett to hold me back if I looked like I was going to punch him. But he was already keeping himself between the two of us, as if he thought I might really do it.

If the old scalemaster managed to break up *Amaryllis*, I'd murder him. And wouldn't that be a worse crime than any I might represent?

Anders drew out the moment, looking us all up and down before finally announcing, "Sixty over this time. And you think you're good at this."

My hands tightened into fists. I imagined myself lunging at him. At this point, what could I lose?

"We'd like an audit," Nina said, slipping past Sun, Garrett, and me to stand before the stationmaster, frowning, hands on her hips.

"Excuse me?" Anders said.

"An audit. I think your scale is wrong, and we'd like an audit. Right?" She looked at me.

It was probably better than punching him. "Yes," I said, after a flabbergasted moment. "Yes, we would like an audit."

That set off two hours of chaos in the scale house. Anders protested, hollered at us, threatened us. I sent Sun to the committee house to summon official oversight—he wouldn't try to play nice, and they couldn't brush him off. June and Abe, two senior committee members, arrived, austere in gray and annoyed.

"What's the complaint?" June said.

Everyone looked at me to answer. I almost denied it—that was my first impulse. Don't fight, don't make waves. Because maybe I deserved the trash I got. Or my mother did, but she wasn't here, was she?

But Nina was looking at me with her innocent brown eyes, and this was for her.

I wore a perfectly neutral, business-like expression when I spoke to June and Abe. This wasn't about me, it was about business, quotas, and being fair.

"Scalemaster Anders adjusts the scale's calibration when he sees us coming."

I was amazed when they turned accusing gazes at him and not at me. Anders' mouth worked, trying to stutter a defense, but he had nothing to say.

The committee confirmed that Anders was rigging his scale. They offered us reparations, out of Anders' own rations. I considered—it would mean extra credits, extra food and supplies for the household. We'd been discussing getting another windmill, petitioning for another well. Instead, I recommended that any penalties they wanted to levy should go to community funds. I just wanted *Amaryllis* treated fairly.

And I wanted a meeting, to make one more petition before the committee.

Garrett walked with me to the committee office the next morning.

"I should have been the one to think of requesting an audit," I said.

"Nina isn't as scared of the committee as you are. As you *were*," he said.

"I'm not—" But I stopped, because he was right.

He squeezed my hand. His smile was amused, his gaze warm. He seemed to find the whole thing entertaining. Me—I was relieved, exhausted, giddy, ashamed. Mostly relieved.

We, *Amaryllis*, had done nothing wrong. I had done nothing wrong.

Garrett gave me a long kiss, then waited outside while I went to sit before the committee.

June was in her chair, along with five other committee members, behind their long table with their slate boards, tally sheets, and lists of quotas. I sat across from them, alone, hands clenched in my lap, trying not to tap my feet. Trying to appear as proud and assured as they did. A stray breeze slipped through the open windows and cooled the cinderblock room.

After polite greetings, June said, "You wanted to make a petition?"

"We—the *Amaryllis* crew—would like to request an increase in our quota. Just a small one."

June nodded. "We've already discussed it and we're of a mind to allow an increase. Would that be suitable?"

Suitable as what? As reparation? As an apology? My mouth was dry, my tongue frozen. My eyes stung, wanting to weep, but that would have damaged our chances, as much as just being me did.

"There's one more thing," I managed. "With an increased quota, we can feed another mouth."

It was an arrogant thing to say, but I had no reason to be polite.

They could chastise me, send me away without a word, lecture me on wanting too much when there wasn't enough to go around. Tell me that it was more important to maintain what we had rather than try to expand—expansion was arrogance. We simply had to maintain. But they didn't. They didn't even look shocked at what I had said.

June, so elegant, I thought, with her long gray hair braided and resting over her shoulder, a knitted shawl draped around her, as much for decoration as for warmth, reached into the bag at her feet and retrieved a folded piece of cloth, which she pushed across the table toward me. I didn't want to touch it. I was still afraid, as if I'd reach for it and June would snatch it away at the last moment. I didn't want to unfold it to see the red and green pattern in full, in case it was some other color instead.

But I did, even though my hand shook. And there it was. I clenched the banner in my fist; no one would be able to pry it out.

"Is there anything else you'd like to speak of?" June asked.

"No," I said, my voice a whisper. I stood, nodded at each of them. Held the banner to my chest, and left the room.

Garrett and I discussed it on the way back to the house. The rest of the crew was waiting in the courtyard for us: Dakota in her skirt and tunic, hair in a tangled bun; J.J. with his arms crossed, looking worried; Sun, shirtless, hands on hips, inquiring. And Nina, right there in front, bouncing almost.

I regarded them, trying to be inscrutable, gritting my teeth to keep from bursting into laughter. I held our banner behind my back to hide it. Garrett held my other hand.

"Well?" Nina finally said. "How did it go? What did they say?"

The surprise wasn't going to get any better than this. I shook out the banner and held it up for them to see. And oh, I'd never seen all of them wide-eyed and wondering, mouths gaping like fish, at once.

Nina broke the spell, laughing and running at me, throwing herself into my arms. We nearly fell over.

Then we were all hugging, and Dakota started worrying right off, talking about what we needed to build a crib, all the fabric we'd need for diapers, and how we only had nine months to save up the credits for it.

I recovered enough to hold Nina at arm's length, so I could look her in the eyes when I pressed the banner into her hands. She nearly dropped it at first, skittering from it as if it were fire. So I closed her fingers around the fabric and held them there.

"It's yours," I said. "I want you to have it." I glanced at Garrett to be sure. And yes, he was still smiling.

Staring at me, Nina held it to her chest, much like I had. "But . . . you. It's yours . . . " She started crying. Then so did I, gathering her close and holding her tight while she spoke through tears, "Don't you want to be a mother?"

In fact, I rather thought I already was.

⌒

Carrie Vaughn is the author of the *New York Times* bestselling series of novels about a werewolf named Kitty, the most recent of which is *Kitty Rocks the House*. She's also the author of young adult novels (*Voices of Dragons, Steel*) and contemporary fantasy (*Discord's Apple, After the Golden Age*). A graduate of the Odyssey Fantasy Writing Workshop, she's a contributor to the Wild Cards series of shared world superhero books edited by George R. R. Martin, and her short stories have appeared in numerous magazines and anthologies. An Air Force brat, she survived her nomadic childhood and managed to put down roots in Boulder, Colorado. Visit her at www.carrievaughn.com.

⌒

In the other stories of After the End, *humankind evidently managed to muck up the world entirely on its own. In this one, it seems like we had some outside help. Margo Lanagan posits a disturbing future in which the most essential elements of even being human are forever altered.*

• THE FIFTH STAR IN THE SOUTHERN CROSS •
Margo Lanagan

I had bought half an hour with Malka and I was making the most of it. Lots of Off girls, there's not much goes on, but these Polar City ones, especially if they're fresh off the migration station, they seem to, almost, enjoy it? I don't know if they really do. They don't pitch and moan and fake it up or anything, but they seem to be *there* under you. They're *with* you, you know? They pay attention. It almost doesn't matter about their skin, the feel of it a bit dry and crinkly, and the color. They have the Coolights on all the time to cut that color back, just like butchers put those purply lights over the meat in their shop, to bring up the red.

Anyway, I would say we were about two-thirds the way there—I was starting to let go of everything and be the me I was meant to be. I knew stuff; I meant something; I didn't *givva* what anyone thought of me.

But then she says, "Stop, Mister Cleeyom. Stop a minute."

"What?" I thought for a second she had got too caught up in it, was having too good a time, needed to slow things down a bit. I suppose that shows how far along *I* was.

"Something is coming," she said.

I tensed up, listening for sounds in the hall.

"Coming down."

Which was when I felt it, pushing against the end of me.

I pulled out. I made a face. "What is it? Have I got you up the wrong hole?"

"No, Mister Cl'om. Just a minute. Will not take long."

Too late—I was already withering.

She got up into a squat with one leg out wide. The Coolight at the bedhead showed everything from behind: a glop of something, and then strings of drool. Just right out onto the bedclothes she did it; she didn't scrabble for a towel or a tissue or anything. She wasn't embarrassed. A little noise came up her throat from some clench in her chest, and that clench pushed the thing out below, the main business.

"It's a puppy?" I said, but I thought, *It's a turd?* But the smell wasn't turd; it was live insides, insides that weren't to do with digestion. And turds don't turn over and split their skin, and try to work it off themselves.

"It's just a baby," Malka apologized, with that smile she has, that makes you feel sorry for her, she's trying so hard, and angry at her at the same time. She scooped it up, with its glop. She stepped off the bed and laid it on top of some crumpled crush-velour under the lamp. A white-ish tail dangled between her legs; she turned away from me and gathered that up, and whatever wet thing fell out attached to it.

This was not what I'd had in mind. This was not the treat I'd promised myself as I tweezered HotChips into artificial tulip stalks out at Parramatta Mannafactory all week.

The "baby" lay there working its shoulders in horrible shruggings, almost as if it knew what it was doing. They're not really babies, of course, just as Polar "girls" aren't really girls, although that's something you pay to be made to forget.

Malka laughed at how my faced looked. "You ha'n't seen this before, Mister Sir?"

"Never," I said. "It's disgusting."

"It's a regular," she said. "How you ever going to get yourself new girls for putcha-putcha, if you don't have baby?"

"We shouldn't have to see *that*, to get them."

"You ask special for Malka. You sign the—the thing, say you don't mind to see. I can show you." She waved at the billing unit by the door.

"Well, I didn't know what that meant. Someone should have explained it to me exactly, *all* the details." But I remembered signing. I remembered the hurry I'd been in at the time. It takes you over, you know, a bone. It feels so good just by itself, so warm, silky somehow and shifting, making you shift to give it room, but at the very same time—and this is the crazy-making thing—it nags at you, *Get rid of me! Gawd,* do *something!* And I wouldn't be satisfied with one of those others: Korra is Polar too but she has been here longer and she acts just like an Earth girl, like you're rubbish. And that other one, the yellow-haired one—well, I have had her a couple of times thinking she might come good, but seriously she is on something. A man might as well do it with a Vibro-Missy, or use his own hand. It's not worth the money if she's not going to be real.

The thing on the velour turned over again in an irritated way, or uncomfortable. It spread one of its hands and the Coolight shone among the wrong-shaped fingers, going from little to big, five of them and no thumb. A shiver ran up my neck like a breeze lifting up a dog's fur.

Malka chuckled and touched my chin. "I will make you a drink and then we will get sexy again, hey?"

I tucked myself in and zipped up my pants. "Can't you put it away somewhere? Like, does it have to be there right under the light?"

She put her face between me and it and kissed me. They don't kiss well, any of these Offs. It's not something that comes natural to them. They don't take the time; they don't soften their lips properly. It's like a moth banging into your mouth. "Haff to keep it in sight. It is regulation. For its well-being." Her teeth gleamed in another attempt at smiling. "I turn you on a movie. Something to look away at."

"Can't you give the thing to someone else to take care of?" But she was doing the walk; I was meant to be all sucked in again by the sight of that swinging bottom. They do have pretty good bottoms, Polars, pretty convincing.

"I paid for the full half-hour," I said. "Am I gunna get back that time you spent . . . Do I get extra time at the end?"

But I didn't want extra time. I wanted my money back, and to start again some other time, when I'd forgotten this. But there was no way I was going to get that. The wall bloomed out into palm-trees and floaty music and some rock-hard muscle star and his girlfriend arguing on the beach.

"Turn the sound off!"

Malka did, like a shot, and checked me over her shoulder. I read it in her face clear as anything: *Am I going to get trouble from this one?* Not fear, not a drop of it, just, *Should I call in the big boys?* The workaday look on her face, her eyes smart, her lips a little bit open, underneath the sunlit giant faces mouthing on the wall—there was nothing designed to give Mister Client a bigger downer.

Darlinghurst Road was the same old wreck and I was one loser among many walking along it. It used to be *Sexy Town* here, all nightclubs, back in history, but now it's full of refugees. Down the hill and along the point is where all the fudgepackers had their apartments, before the anti-gay riots. We learned 'em; we told 'em where to stick their bloody feathers and froo-froos. That's all gone now, every pillow burned and every pot of Vaseline smashed—you can't even buy it to grease up handyman tools any more, not around here. Those were good times when I was a bit younger, straightening out the world.

It didn't look pretty when we'd finished, but at least there were no 'packers. Now people like me live here, who'd rather hide in this mess than jump through the hoops you need for a 'factory condominium. And odd Owsians, off-shoots of the ones that are eating up the States from the inside, there are so many there. And a lot of Earth-garbage: Indians and Englanders and Central Europeans. And the odd glamorous Abbo, all gold knuckles and tailoring. It's *colorful*, they tell us; it's got *a polyglot identity that's all its own and very special*. Tourists come here—well, they walk along Darlo Road; they don't explore much either side, where it gets *real* polyglot.

I zigzagged through the lanes towards my place. I was still steaming about my lost money and my wasted bone, steaming at *myself* for having signed that screen and done myself out of what I'd promised myself. There was nothing I could do except go home and take care of myself so I could get some sleep. Then wake up and catch the bike-bus out to Parramatta, pedaling the sun up out of the drowned suburbs behind me.

That EurOwsian beggar-girl was on my step again, a bundle like someone's dumped house-rubbish. She crinkled and rustled as I came up. When she saw my face she'd know not to bother me, I hoped.

But it wasn't her voice at all that said, "Jonah? Yes, it *is* you!"

I backed up against the opposite wall of the entry, my insides gone all slithery. Only bosses called me Jonah, and way back people who were dead now, of my family from the days when people had families. Grandparent-type people.

Out of what I had thought was the beggar girl stood this other one that I didn't know at all, shaven-headed and scabby-lipped. "Fen," those lips said. "Fenella. Last year at the Holidaze."

"Oh!" I almost shouted with the relief of making the connection, although she still didn't click to look at. She put her face more clearly in the way of the gaslight so that I could examine her. "Fen. Oh, yeah." I still couldn't see it, but I knew who she was talking about. "What are you doing in here? I thought you lived up the mountains."

"I know. I'm sorry. But, really, I've got to tell you something."

"What's that?"

She looked around at the empty entry-way, the empty lane. "It's kind of private."

"Oh. You better come up, then." I hoped she wasn't thinking to get in my bed or anything; I could never put myself close to a mouth in that condition.

She followed me up. She wasn't healthy; two flights and she was breathing hard. All the time I'm also, *Fen? But Fen had* hair. *She was very nearly* good-looking. *I remember thinking as we snuck off from the party, Oh, my ship's really come in this time—a normal girl and no payment necessary.*

She didn't go mad and attack me for drug money when I lit the lamp and stood back to hold the door for her. She stepped in and took in the sight of my crap out of some kind of habit. She was a girl with background; she would probably normally say something nice to the host. But she was too distracted, here, by the stuff in her own head. I couldn't even begin to dread what that might be.

"Sit?" In front of the black window my only chair looked like, if you sat there, someone would tie you to it, and scald you with Ersatz, or burn you with beedy-ends.

She shook her head. "It's not as if there's much we can do," she said, "but you had to know, I told myself. I thought, Maybe he can get himself tested and they'll give him some involvement, you never know. Or at least send you the bulletins too."

I tipped my head at her like, *You hear what's coming out your mouth, don't you?* I'd just about had it with women for the night, this one on top of Malka and of Malka's boss with the cream-painted face and the curly smile, all soothing, all understanding, all not-giving-a-centimeter, not giving a cent.

Fen was walking around checking my place out. No, there was nowhere good for us to settle; when I was here on my own I sat in my chair or I lay on my bed, and no one ever visited me. She came and stood facing across me and brought out an envelope that looked just about worn out from her clutching it. She opened it and fingered through the pages folded in there one behind the other. "Here, this one." She took it out and unfolded it, but not so I could see. She looked it up and down, up and down. "Yes. I guess. May as well start at the beginning." She handed it to me. "It's not very clear," she apologized. "I wouldn't keep still for them. They'd arrested me and I was *pissed off.*" She laughed nervously.

It was a bad copy of a bad printout of a bad color scan, but even so, even

I could work it out. Two arms. Two legs. A full, round head. For a second there I felt as if my own brain had come unstuck and slopped into the bottom of my skull.

"It's . . . It's just like the one on the sign," I said, with hardly a voice. I meant the billboard up on Taylor Square—well, they were everywhere, really, but I only biked past the others. People picnicked under the Taylor Square one; people held markets and organized other kinds of deals; I sometimes just went up and sat under it and watched them, for something to do. *Protect Our Future*, it said; it was a government sign, Department of Genetic Protection, I think: a pink-orange baby floating there in its bag like some sleeping water creature, or some being that people might worship—which people kind of did, I guess, with all the fuss about the babies. This was what we were all supposed to be working towards, eh—four proper limbs and a proper-shaped head like every baby's used to be.

Fen looked gleeful as a drugger finding an Ambrosie stash. One of her scabs had split and a bead of blood sat on her lip there.

I went to the chair; it exclaimed in pain and surprise under me. "What else?" I looked at the envelope in her skeleton hands.

She crossed the room and crouched beside me. She showed me three bulletins, because it was two months old. Each had two images, a face and a full-body. The first one gave me another brain-spasm; it was a girl-baby. *The hope of the line*, said the suits in their speeches on the news screen down the Quay; their faces were always working to stop themselves crying by then; they were going for the full drama. *Man's hope is Woman*, they would blubber. *We have done them so wrong, for so long.*

In every picture the baby girl was perfect—no webbing, no cavities, no frills or stumps, and nothing outside that ought to be in. Fen showed me the part where the name was Joannah. She read me the stats and explained them to me. These things, you could tell from the way she said them, they'd been swimming round and around in her head a long time. They came out in a relief, all rushed and robotic like the datadump you get when you ring up about your Billpay account.

When she finished she checked my reaction. My face felt stiff and cold—I had no blood to spare to work it, it was all busy boiling through my brain. "It's something, isn't it?" she said.

"You and me under the cup-maker. It only took a few minutes."

"I know." She beamed and licked away another drop of blood. "Who would've thought?"

I was certainly thinking now. I sat heavily back and tried to see my thoughts against the wall, which was a mass of tags from before they'd secured this building. I needed Fen to go away now—I couldn't make sense of this while she was here watching me, trying to work out what I thought, what I felt. But I couldn't send her away, either; this sort of thing takes a certain amount of time and no less, and there was no point being rude. It takes two to tango, no one knew that better than me.

After a while I said, "I used to walk home behind that Full-Term place."

"Argh," she said, and swayed back into a crouch. "You've got one of those skip stories!"

I nodded. "Mostly it was closed, and I never lifted the lid myself."

"But." She glowered at me.

"If someone had propped it open, with a brick or, once, there was a chair holding it quite wide? Well, then I would go and have a look in. Never to touch anything or anything."

"Errr-her-her-herrr." She sat on my scungey carpet square and rocked her face in her hands, and laughed into them.

"One time—"

"No, no, no!" She was still laughing, but with pain in it.

"One time someone had opened it right the way up—"

"No!" she squeaked, and put her hands over her ears and laughed up at me, then took them off again and waited wide-eyed.

"And taken a whole bunch out—it must've been Ukrainians. They will eat anything," I added, just to make her curl up. "And they'd chucked them all over the place."

"No-no!" She hugged her shins and laughed into her knees. This woman had done it, this scrawny body that I couldn't imagine having ever wanted or wanting again, had brought a perfect baby to nine months. In the old days she would have been the woman who *bore my child*, or even *bore me a child, bore me a daughter*, and while I had to be glad she wasn't, I . . .

Well, to tell you the truth, I didn't know what to think about her, or about myself, or about those loose sheets of paper around her feet, and the face that was Fen's, that was mine, two in the one. Joannah's—my name cobbled together with a girl's. I didn't have a clue.

"It's true," I said. "All these—" I waved at the memory of their disgustingness against the cobbles and the concrete, across the stormwater grille.

"Tell me," she whispered. "It's mostly the heads, isn't it?"

"It was mostly the heads." I nodded. "Like people had hit them, you know, with baseball bats, big . . . hollows out of them, every which side, sometimes the face, sometimes the back. But it was . . . I don't know, it was every kind of . . . Sometimes no legs, sometimes too many. It was, what do you call those meals, like at the Holidaze, where it's all spread out and you get to put whatever you want of it on your plate?"

"A smorgasbord?"

"That's it."

"A smorgasbord of deformities, you reckon?"

"Yeah." *Deformities*, of course—that was what nice people called them. Not *piggies* or *wingies* or *bowlheads*. Not *blobs* for the ones with no heads at all.

"And don't tell me," said Fen, "some of them were still alive."

"Nah, they were dead, all right."

"Some people say, you know? They see them moving?"

I shook my head. My story was over, and hadn't been as interesting as *some people's*, clearly.

"Well," she said, and bent to the papers again, and put them in a pile in order.

"Let me see again." She gave them to me and I looked through them. It was no more believable the second time. "Can I have these?"

"Oh no," she said. "You'll have to go and get tested and take the strips to the Department. Then they'll set you up in the system to get your own copies of everything sent out."

"That'll cost," I said glumly. "The test, and then getting there—that's way up, like, Armidale or somewhere, isn't it? I'd have to get leave."

"Yes, but you'll get it all back, jizzing into their beakers. Get it all back and more, I'd say. It's good for blokes; you have your little factory that only your own body can run. They have to keep paying you. Us girls they can just chop it all out and ripen the eggs in solution. We only get money the once."

"They have to plant it back in you, don't they?"

"They have to plant it back in *someone*, but they've got their own childbearers, that passed all the screenings. I don't look so good beside those; where I come from used to be all dioxins. My sister births nothing but duds, and she's got some . . . mental health issues they don't like the sound of."

"But you brought this one out okay, didn't you, this . . . Joannah?"

"Yeah, but who knows that wasn't a fluke? Besides, I don't want that, for a life. They offered me a trial place there, but I told them they could stick it.

I met some of those incubator girls. The bitchery that went on at that place, you wouldn't believe. Good thing they don't do the actual mothering."

She took the papers from me and we both looked at the top one with its stamp and crest and the baby looking out. Poor little bugger. What did it have to look forward to? Nothing, just growing up to be a girl, and then a woman. Mostly I think that women were put here to make our lives miserable, to tease us and lure us and then not choose us. Or to choose us and then go cold, or toss us aside for the fun of watching us suffer. But you can't think that way about a daughter, can you? How are you *supposed* to think about a daughter?

"Well, good on you, I say." I tried to sound okay with it, but a fair bit of sourness came through. "Good on both of us, eh," I added to cover that up. "It makes us both look good, eh."

She folded the papers. "I guess." She put them away in the envelope. She gave a little laugh. "I hardly know you, you know? There was just that one time, and, you know, it wasn't like we had any kind of *relationship*. I didn't know how you were going to take this. But anyway." She got up, so I did too. She was no taller than me—that was one of the reasons I'd had a chance with her. "Now you know everything, and . . . I don't know what I thought was going to happen after that! But it's done." She spread her hands and turned towards the door.

I believe it used not to be like this, people being parents. Olden days, there would have been that whole business of living together and lies and pressures, the *relationship*, which from what I've heard the women always wanted and the men kind-of gave them for the sake of regular sex. Not now, though; it was all genes and printouts now. Everyone was on their own.

I closed the door after Fen, and went and sat with my new knowledge, with my new status. It was some kind of compensation for the rest of my evening, for not getting Malka properly to myself. What's more, I might end up quite tidily off from this, be able to drop assembly work completely, just sell body fluids. I should feel good; I should feel excited, free and stuff. I should be able to shake off being so annoyed from my poor old withered bone. Some people had simple feelings like that, that could cancel each other out neatly like that.

What I hadn't told Fen, what I wouldn't—her of all people, but I wouldn't tell anyone—was that I used to go home behind the Full Term place because there was always a chance there'd be someone in labor down the back wards there. And the noises they made, for a bloke who didn't have money then, who was saving up his pennies for a Polar girl, the noises were exactly what I wanted to hear out of a woman. No matter I couldn't see or touch them; it was dark, and I could imagine. I could hang onto the bar fence like the rungs of some big brass bedhead and she would be groaning and gasping, panting her little lump of monster out, or—even better—yowling or bellowing with pain; they all did it different. And some nurse or someone, some nun or whatever they had in there, would be telling her what to do. *Oh, what a racket!* she'd say. *You'd think you were birthing an elephant! Now push with this one, Laurie.* And I'd be outside thinking, *Yeah, push, push!* and somewhere in the next yowl or roar I would spoof off through the fence and be done. There was nothing like the night air on your man-parts and the darkness hiding you, and a woman's voice urging you on.

There's always the buttoning, though, isn't there? There's always rearranging your clothes around your damp self and shaky knees, zipping, buttoning, belting. There's always turning from the bed and the girl, or the fence and the yowling and the skip there, and being only you in the lane or hallway, with no one missing you or needing you, having paid your fee. You're tingling all around your edges, and the tingle's fading fast, and that old pretend-you floats back out of wherever it went, like sheets of newspaper, blows and sticks to you, so that then it's always there, scraping and dirty and uncomfortable.

I turned out the lamp and crawled into bed. Now stars filled the window. In the old days of full power and streetlights, Sydneysiders saw bugger-all of those, just the moon and a few of the bigger stars. They say you couldn't see the fifth star of the Cross, even. Now the whole damn constellation throbs there in its blanket of galaxy-swirl. People were lucky, then, not knowing what was out there, worse than a few gays poncing about the place, worse than power cuts and restrictions and all these "dire warnings" and "desperate pleas", worse than the Environment sitting over us like some giant troll or something, whingeing about how we've treated her. Earth must have been cozy then. Who was it, I wonder, decided we wanted to go emitting all over the frickin universe, saying, *Over here, over here! Nice clean planet! Come here and help us fuck her right up.* That was the bloke we should have smashed the place of. The gays, they weren't harming anyone but themselves.

I jerked awake a couple of times on the way down to sleep. *My life is changed! I am a new man! They'll show me proper respect now, when they see that DNA readout.* To get to sleep, I tried to fool myself I'd dreamed Fen visiting. Passing those billboards every day, and Malka's baby this evening—everything had mishmashed together in my unconscious. I would wake up normal tomorrow, with everything the same as usual. Fen's scabby lips, the proper kisses, full and soft, we'd had behind the cupmaker—thinking about those wouldn't do any good. Push them into some squishy, dark corner of forgetting, and let sleep take me.

Margo Lanagan has published five collections of short stories—*White Time, Black Juice, Red Spikes, Yellowcake,* and *Cracklescape*—and two dark fantasy novels, *Tender Morsels* and *The Brides of Rollrock Island* (published as *Sea Hearts* in Australia). She is a four-time World Fantasy Award winner, and her work has also won and been nominated for numerous other awards. Margo lives in Sydney, Australia, maintains a blog at www.amongamidwhile.blogger.com and can be found on Twitter as @margolanagan.

After the End, much of what remains of true civilization inhabits in the now-balmy Arctic and Antarctic circles. Survivors still live in the rest of the world, though—the exploiters and the exploited, and loners like Bear Jessen, who isn't sure why he's still hanging around . . . except for a silent promise made to his dying wife.

· TRUE NORTH ·
M. J. Locke

On the last day of March 2099, on the rocky, parched slopes west of Rexford, Montana, Lewis Behrend Jessen met Patricia de la Montaña Vargas.

Jessen was sixty-seven years old. Everybody who mattered called him Bear. He had been American by birth, back when that sort of thing mattered, and Danish by ancestry. He was so pale his skin had peeled and burned in successive layers over the years, always revealing deeper, ruddier ones. Each layer also added freckles and age spots, too, till now he looked like a ruined patchwork man. His eyes were blue, like a cloudless sky. His hair, when he'd had any, had been red as rubies. His belly, when he'd had one, had hung over his big sterling silver horseshoe belt buckle. (Tacky? Damn straight. It had belonged to his father, as had the Colt .45 revolver with ivory grips. The Browning 9mm, and the shotgun for scaring away the megafauna, he had bought for himself.)

Bear was seven feet tall, broad-shouldered and big-boned. These days he looked more like a giant human walking-stick, ninety percent bones and one hundred percent wrinkles. He lived in an aging ranch-style house he and Orla had built in Rexford back when they moved up here. That was in the late sixties, maybe twenty years before the collapse was officially acknowledged, but by then everybody who had a lick of sense had seen it coming.

Rexford was just south of the Canadian border. A lot of people had moved through over the years, trying to make it across into Canada. Bear and Orla had talked about trying for it themselves. But at first they thought they wouldn't need to, this far north, and later it just seemed as if it were too late to try.

Bear had just celebrated his forty-second anniversary the night before, over a trout he had caught that very evening, at a fire he built in his back lot, on the banks of the stream. Maybe it had been the fire that attracted the girl.

It was a miracle anyway that that seasonal wash could house a living fish, choked as it was with algae and weeds. The fish was certainly an endangered species. But hell; who wasn't, these days?

Here's a curious thing: when Bear cut the fish's belly open he found an aluminum ring, a soda can pop-top. They didn't make soda cans anymore—never mind the kind of pop-tops you can wear. Bear washed the blood off the ring in the stream, kissed it, and put it on his pinkie finger. As he did so he had to shake his head at his foolishness. Orla would have been amused. They had had to barter the real ring away long ago, along with Orla's. The reason had seemed important at the time, and it wasn't as if their marriage had suffered for want of a wedding band or two. Now that she was dead he rather wished he hadn't.

With her gone, truth to tell, Bear didn't mind much whether he lived or died. He'd had his share of living, and was ready to be done with it all.

Orla had not approved of his thoughts of suicide.

"Why?" he had asked. Seeing her on her deathbed (it had been late last fall; lung cancer, Orla believed, though they weren't sure—anyway, it didn't matter, since they had no way to treat it), he had made up his mind. Bear did not want to outlive his wife. He had gotten out his Colt .45 and thumbed cartridges into the cylinder, one by one. "I figure it's better to go out together. Don't you?"

She had wheezed, "Lewis . . . " A pause for air. "Behrend Jessen. Put that . . . thing away." She was glaring at him as fierce as the day they'd wed. "Don't you . . . *fucking* dare."

He eyed the gun with a sigh. Where did she get the energy to pick a fight at a time like this? Damned woman. "Now, Orla, for cry-eye—"

She clutched her mother's blue cross-stitched coverlet that she loved so much. "Don't . . . bullshit me, fool. Put it . . . away."

He started to argue; she coughed up blood. You can't trump bloody gobbets for settling an argument. He put the gun away, intending to get it out later. He was baffled by her obstinacy.

The next night, he held her hand and said again, "Why not?"

She did not answer right away, and he thought maybe that was it, that she was gone. But she squeezed the words out between inhalations. "There's . . . a . . . reason."

He did not reply right away. He felt her implacable gaze, felt her grip on his hand.

"Promise . . . me."

He scowled. "Orla Jessen, you have never believed in God. If you are going to tell me the Lord Almighty has a plan for me, I swear I'll put a bullet in my brain right this minute."

"Reason," she said again. It was quite literally a gasp. And it was her last word. Perhaps an hour later, perhaps two, her breathing ceased.

When he thought about it afterward he figured Orla would have been glad that was her last word. She was an atheist from way back. The reason she spoke of would be logical. Not metaphysical.

Bear still believed in the Protestant God of his youth (he'd been brought up Methodist), but it was not a worshipful relationship. Oh my, no. He was furious with God, who had promised salvation and had delivered hell on earth. Refugees passing through had spoken of the die-offs. Faithful or no, people were dying—had died—by the billions. By the *billions*. God was a big fat eternal asshole, and Bear had stopped caring long before who heard him say so. His pastor, Desmond Marcus, had kicked him out of the church, ten years back, and had said some hurtful things about Orla. That was hard; they had been close friends. Des and Gloria had moved on a few years ago, headed to Seattle, Bear had heard, to apply for entry there, or perhaps north to Victoria, where the summers were still tolerable.

He fingered his Colt, thinking about Des's opinion of suicide. There had been waves of them over the years, and Des had been quite vocal about how we mustn't succumb to despair. The man knew how to inspire you, for sure. How to keep you hanging onto hope. But in the end, Des had given up, too, in his own way. Bear had seen it in his eyes.

This isn't despair, Bear thought. *I'm just done, is all. I'm done.*

Bear could have gone ahead and offed himself then, as Orla lay cooling in their bed. But in the face of her earlier implacability, it seemed too violent. Disrespectful. And after Bear had buried her he lost whatever spark of initiative he had had. That had been four months ago, now.

Truth was, Orla was wrong. There was simply no reason he was still living, when so many had died. Billions meant *thousands of millions*. A hundred New Yorks. Loads of Londons, a plethora of Parises, trainloads of Tokyos, whole basketsful of Beijings, Torontos, Jakartas, Mumbais. If you stacked the bodies, Orla had told him once, they'd reach to the moon and back *four times over.* (She'd always been the one with the head for figures.) All gone. In two short generations human civilization had collapsed under its own weight, the way Ponzi schemes do. Now even the greatest cities were in their death throes. The people out in the big empty middle of the U.S. had been on their own for decades. Last he heard, scientists were saying human population would stabilize at somewhere under a hundred million, worldwide, once the resource wars and genocides died down: most of them within the Arctic and Antarctic circles.

A hundred million starving, miserable people. Of every hundred people, ninety-nine dead, within a hundred years of humanity's apex. Might as well call it extinction and be done with it. No reason *he* should still be hanging around.

Bear fingered the ring. He felt as though he had made his wife a promise, though he had never spoken the words. *Happy goddamn anniversary.*

Orla would only have laughed and kissed him. Eventually, he figured, he'd either get over being mad at her for dying first, or die too, and end the argument that way.

Thanks to the fish with the ring in its belly, hunger didn't wake him early the next morning. And that changed everything.

The morning after the fish dinner he awoke to a cool breeze blowing through the window. The sun was up. The window screen was gone, and a girl was exiting Orla's closet. Bear lay still and observed her through slitted eyes. She had dark, tangled, dirty hair that went down well past her skinny butt. She had pulled on some clothes of Orla's: a shirt, a pair of jeans. They hung off her. She was struggling into a pair of Orla's walking shoes, biting her lip and grimacing. Bear could see the crusted sores on her feet from where he lay. She couldn't have been more than thirteen years old.

Next she moved over to his chest of drawers, not three feet away from the bed. He breathed through his mouth, shallow and quiet.

She must have climbed the dead aspen. He had left the window open to let the breezes in. These days you didn't say no to a cool breeze, not even at night in winter. It was a screened, second-story window on the slope of a steep hill, and the aspen was dead: brittle and as skinny as she was. A difficult climb. Anyone bigger wouldn't have been able to pull it off.

He was not sure why he had awakened. She was quiet as a whisper as she emptied his drawers and pocketed the few items she seemed to find useful. It may have been the stink: she reeked of feces and body odor.

He spoke finally. "You won't find much in there, I'm afraid."

She spun to face him. She had a petite face with big eyes as dark and clear as obsidian. Sunlight glinted on the knife blade in her hand. It was a long blade, a serrated one. A fine hunting knife. It would gut him as easily as he had gutted that trout last night.

"Stay where you are," she said. She stood just beyond arm's length. From her accent he could tell her native language was Spanish. Orla would have known what country she was from. She had been in Central America back in the sixties. *Medecins sans Frontieres*. But the girl's English was sharp and clear as broken glass. "Try anything and I'll kill you."

"Fair enough."

A tense silence ensued. He felt a twinge—it wouldn't be breaking his promise to Orla if someone else did him in. But his intruder, she was just a kid. She did not want to harm him, or she would have killed him at the outset. He didn't want to make a murderer out of her for his own convenience. Besides, she might muff it, and sepsis was an awful, lingering way to go.

"I have provisions downstairs," he said. "I'll show you where I keep them. You look like you could use some, young lady."

She eyed him suspiciously, but the left corner of her mouth twitched at the "young lady." After another long pause, she shrugged. "All right. Get up. Don't get cute."

He swung his legs out of bed and stood. His joints were always stiff in the mornings.

She stared as he stood, and stepped back. *"Usted es un gigante!"* He remembered a little of his college Spanish: *You are a . . .* what? Oh. Of course. *A giant.*

It was true. Even in his current state he could easily have overpowered her. But he did not. He felt a deep pity. A dreadful fate, to be alive so young at the end of the world.

He led her into the kitchen and showed her the hidden door in his pantry. It led down into the cellar. As she stepped over the threshold and headed down the complaining stairs, he shone his flashlight in across the shelves onto Orla's hand-labeled Mason jars.

The entire underside of their ranch house was filled with food. Jars of pickled turnips, potatoes, peppers, carrots, green tomatoes, and a hundred or more different kinds of jams. Sealed carboys, filled with beans, rice, and corn.

It'd been at least two decades since they had had access to groceries shipped from elsewhere, and maybe twelve years since the local open-air market that replaced the grocery store petered out. Since then, he and Orla had lived off wild game, water hand-pumped from their private well, and supplies they had stored up before the collapse. Orla had spent years preparing. All the years of their marriage. She had dedicated herself to their survival—even before it was clear to most that collapse was imminent; well after everyone else had died or moved on. Cured hams and chickens and turkeys hung from the rafters, and a rack held jalapeño jerked beef. Bear figured he had a good three or four years' supplies left, if he continued the way he had. After that it was the bullet, dammit, whether Orla liked it or not.

What caught the girl's eye, he could tell, were the medical supplies. Orla had been an ER doctor till the town had shut down ten years back, and had stocked up on bandages, antibiotics, medicines, and whatnot. All kinds of whatnot. There were vitamins and supplements, cold remedies, and the like. Most of these were post-date by now. After the last and biggest Deflation in '84, even the mercy shipments had stopped coming in.

The girl stood on the bottom step, silhouetted by the light he shone—fists tight little balls, shoulders stiff. Then she turned and darted up the stairs, past him into the kitchen, where she pulled the tablecloth off the table. One of Orla's handmade vases shattered on the floor. Bear looked at it. His vision went red. He roared—grabbed the girl's arm, wrenching it—yanked her off her feet. Her eyes went wide.

"You little shit!" he yelled in her face.

Then he felt the sharp bite of her knife blade in his gut and dropped her. She backed away, knife at the ready, eyes wide, breathing fast. Mentally, he revised her age upward. She was more like eighteen. He lifted his torn, bloodied shirt and checked his belly. Just a scratch. The folds of skin there had protected him.

He ignored the girl—maybe he'd get lucky and she'd slit his throat while his back was turned—and knelt to pick up the pieces of broken vase. These he carried gingerly into the study. He laid the pieces out on the hearth. *Maybe I can glue them back together.* But pain squeezed at his heart and he knew he never would. He just didn't have it in him.

He heard the girl clattering around, and after a few moments he sensed her watching him. He turned. She stood in the kitchen doorway. Orla's tablecloth was slung over her shoulder like a hobo bag. Medical supplies and jars and bags of food stuck out between the hastily tied knots. The burden of living had never been heavier on his shoulders than it was in that instant.

"Sorry," she said finally.

Bear passed a hand over his eyes. "Just go."

She stood there silent for another moment. When he looked back next she was gone.

Two mornings later when he went downstairs, he found the vase glued back together, its cracks all but invisible. It sat on the kitchen table next to his now-empty, second-to-last bottle of Super-Glue, with the now-slightly-soiled tablecloth beneath it.

That week fire season started. The winds came up and lightning storms rolled across the sky. Smoke hung in the air. It clung to the low areas and snaked through the valley below his house. Charred wood smell stank up Bear's clothes and hair and made his eyes burn. Bear spent the two days hiking through the back twenty, scanning the horizons from every angle, checking for fires. From the ridge that stretched along the southern edge of his property, he saw what he had been dreading. A line of smoke and flame snaked along the ridge next door.

He trudged back home. His house perched on a ridge that adjoined the one now aflame, the ridge about a mile or two to the west. Uncleared brush and dying trees filled the valley between the two. If the wind got much stronger, it would carry sparks into the valley and up toward his ridge. Time to chop down the last two trees in range of the house: the dead aspen next to his bedroom window and the big ponderosa by the front porch.

The aspen he didn't care about. But the ponderosa . . . Orla had loved that damn pine, with its widespread branches and needles green and vibrant; its slats of rust-colored bark and the black vertical fissures that separated them.

"She'll outlast both of us," Orla had told Bear once. She called the tree Old Lady, or Old Woman Pine. When it dropped its cones on their roof, they would bounce down on the shingles with a frightful clatter, and drop around the eaves onto a cushion of pine needles so soft you never heard them land. Orla would look up from whatever it was she was doing and smile. "Old Lady's heard from."

He looked up through the branches that morning. "Nothing lasts," he said.

First he brought down the aspen. He used a comealong and an axe. Once he had it down, he was dirty and sweating, and doused himself in the icy well water. Then he chopped the wood into sections, dragged it over near the workshop, and cut it down into firewood. Next day it was time to deal with the ponderosa. He got out his axe and his comealong. He went so far as to lift the axe and give the old lady a whack. The bark shattered where the blade struck, and the wet white living wood beneath splintered. He rested the bit of the blade against the tree's root, rubbed his face, and looked up through the branches.

He couldn't do it. Old Lady Pine had been too much a part of their lives, for too many years. He ran his hand over the gouge he'd made. *If this tree is to be the death of me, so be it.* He put his tools away.

That night Bear woke to find his bedroom on fire. Flames crawled in through the window and across the ceiling. Acrid smoke clawed his sinuses and lungs.

He rolled onto the floor, choking and gagging. Somehow he made it down the stairs. No conscious thought was involved. He returned to himself on the lawn in front of his home, watching flames devour his home. Painful welts bubbled up along his left forearm but he had no memory of how he had gotten them.

The winds were up. The ponderosa whipped to and fro in the grip of the flames devouring it. The roof had already started to cave in. Orange light shone from the upper-story windows. Even from here, the heat scorched his face and the light hurt his eyes. Through the open front door he saw that the staircase banister was alight. And now flames attacked the ceiling beams in the living room.

He looked at the blazing doorframe and a powerful urge gripped him. *I'm going to perdition anyway, for loving Orla more than I ever loved God.* It was as good an end as any.

But in that instant before action followed thought, a yank on his arm threw him off balance. Something—someone—was dragging him away from the flames. The young woman who had broken in before pulled at him now.

"Come on!" she yelled above the noise. "*Venga*! We have to go!"

He looked down at her. She was covered in soot and her gaze was wild with fear.

He looked back at the house. *Orla. Orla.*

Then he saw a troupe of children at the far edge of the lawn. They were skinny as this young woman was, dirty and stiff with terror. The fire hadn't jumped to that copse where they stood, but soon it would. Old Woman

Pine was cracking—splitting—about to go down. When it did, it would tip down the hill toward them. He couldn't run into a fire and leave them with that memory. God knew what else they had already seen. With a grunt of anguish, he ran after the young woman, amid falling branches and billowing smoke. He snatched up a couple of the littlest ones. So did the young woman. The rest fell in around them. Down the hill they went.

They ran far and hard, following the muddy creek. He noticed a youth— the next oldest after the young woman. He carried a younger boy on his back. Others carried toddlers. He glimpsed an infant. Babies saving babies. The young woman yelled at them, dragged them back to their feet when they stumbled, forced them on, away from the burning trees. At least three times she circled back and returned with someone who had stumbled or fallen behind.

They found a mine-tailing pile against a hillside. It was poisoned— lifeless. No brush to betray them by catching fire while they slept. They all huddled on the rocky ground in the predawn chill. Even the littlest ones were too spent to weep.

The fire moved on around them. Bear eventually dozed.

When he awoke, he found himself surrounded by a silent, ragged army of sleeping children. He sat up in the predawn gray, gazing around in wonder. They ranged in age from infants to preteens. Most of them looked to be maybe between five and eight years old. There must have been twenty or so: girls and boys, about evenly mixed, best he could tell. Some of the older ones had weapons: knives, clubs, sticks. All had sticklike arms and legs; several had distended bellies, including the one infant, who hung limp in the arms of one of the five-year-olds, clearly too weak to cry.

It was a boy—he had no diaper—and lay limp in a foul, brown-stained blanket in the lap of one of the younger girls. The corners of his eyes crawled with flies.

The young woman soon came into view dragging a heap wrapped in a filthy blanket. Bear recognized the blanket: it had come from the house. She was covered in soot and had swaddled her head in an old torn T-shirt. She had a military-issue rifle on her shoulder. She dumped the bundle at the feet of the youth, and gave him a good, hard shove with her foot.

"Tomás," she said. Her tone was sharp. "Get them up."

The boy groaned, gave her a sullen look, and sat up rubbing his arm. "All right."

"Get them fed. Get Vanessa to help you. I need everyone to meet me at this man's house *tan rápido que posible. Bueno?"* As quickly as possible. The boy blinked and nodded. He shook the girl next to her, who stirred. They two began waking the others.

"You." The young woman gestured at Bear. "Come with me."

He raised his eyebrows and leaned his elbows on his knees. "Try again," he said.

She grimaced. He spotted impatience and regret. "I need your help," she said. "We need supplies. Your—*¿como se dice?—su bodega."* She wiped at her eyes and he could see her exhaustion. "I'm sorry. Usually my English is better. Under your house—the food. *La medicina.* It is still there. We need it. The children need it." A pause. "Please."

He stood. He couldn't help it; he towered over her. She stepped back and half-raised her rifle. But Bear simply extended his hand. "Lewis Behrend Jessen. Pleased to meet you."

She looked at his hand as if she had forgotten what the gesture meant. Then she blinked, lowered her weapon, and took his hand in a brief, strong grip. "Patricia de la Montaña Vargas," she replied. "Call me Patty."

"I'm Bear."

While they hiked back along the streambed, he asked, "Where are you from?"

"Mexico City. My parents were *profesores.* Professors. At the university."

She said nothing else. He didn't pry, but clearly there was a lot more to tell. How had she made it so far, across the thousands of war-torn miles between there and here? Where did the children come from? Where were they all headed? And why?

As they came up over the rise, he saw the smoking ruins of his home. The fires appeared to have burned themselves out. The air was still and cool.

Old Lady Pine rose above the rubble: a blackened, ruined post. Everything but the barn had burned to the ground. His hundred-acre wood was now nothing but ash and char. The sun rose, swollen and red as a warning, over the eastern ridge.

As Patty had said, the larder was mostly intact. In another stroke of luck, though the barn roof had caved in on one side thanks to a fallen tree, the walls still stood. So they had shelter.

It took them three full days to extract the supplies. Bear insisted on doing it right, pulling out the debris and shoring up the cellar infrastructure as they went. He had been a mine worker in his college days, before he got his engineering degree.

Patty paced across the ridge with the crook of her rifle in her arm, watching the horizons, while Bear organized his tools, built the supporting structures, and directed the children to carry the timber and debris out of the way.

By the first evening they had extracted enough rations for a decent meal. They camped out in the shell of the barn, exhausted. A soft rain started and the temperature dropped sharply. They huddled, shivering, under the portions that had a roof. Still, Bear was grateful for the rain. He persuaded Patty that it would be safe to have a fire in a barrel for cooking, light, and warmth.

"No one will see the flames behind these walls," he said. "And with all the fires right now, the smoke means nothing."

"A fire would be nice," she replied, and sent the children to the unburned areas below to gather firewood.

By the end of the second day they had most of the supplies out of the cellar. He found the gun safe. The children cheered when he brought out his Colt and shotgun, and all the boxes of ammo. He felt better for having his Colt—not least because of what the children had told him the night before.

There were twenty-three, including Patty. Bear set about trying to learn all their names. He kept asking over dinner that first night, and they kept telling him, but their names rolled off his old brain. They were all so dirty and bony and so quicksilver fast he couldn't tell them apart. For now, he settled for remembering Tommy (Patty called him Tomás, but he was of Asian ancestry and told Bear his name was Tommy Chang) and Vanessa (a freckled girl of Northern European ancestry, with curly red hair and a lisp, who didn't know her last name). They were the next oldest after Patty. Tommy didn't know how old he was but thought he might be thirteen. Vanessa said she was twelve. They told her that Patty had rescued them from a work camp down in Denver, two months before.

"There's a man chasing us," Tommy said. "The man who ran the camp in Denver. The colonel, they called him."

"That's why she's so worried," Vanessa added in a whisper, glancing over her shoulder at Patty, who was pacing at the edge of the camp. "She's scared he's going to catch us."

Bear laid a hand on the butt of his shotgun and wondered how real the danger was.

The first and second days they worked till there was no more light. But when the sun was low in the sky on the third day, Patty called a halt to the preparations and clapped her hands. "Time for school!"

School?

Patty chose a slope facing the sun. The children jostled each other as they sat down in a rough semicircle on the hillside. She used a stick to draw letters, pronounce them, and had the children repeat the work with a stick at their own feet. Then she spelled some simple words. After this she drew numbers and tried to teach the older ones how to add.

She walked around checking their work: encouraging, cajoling, and scolding. She had a hard time keeping their attention, though. The older kids spent most of their time taking turns with the infant, who whimpered incessantly, or chasing toddlers and keeping them from putting things in their mouths that they shouldn't. The toddlers ran around, naked from the waist down, giggling, scuffing up the students' work.

Tom and Vanessa paced behind the students while Patty talked, and occasionally gave the rowdier students a whack across the shoulders to make them be quiet. It was Keystone Elementary. Bear rubbed his face, unsure whether to laugh or cry. *Well*, he thought, *points for trying.*

He sat a short ways up the hillside at the class's back; now he stood up and walked over to Tom, who had raised his stick to strike seven-year-old Jonas. The younger boy had not seen Tom coming. He was giggling after kicking dirt over little Hannah's work and she cried and rubbed her eyes with her knuckles. Bear caught the stick and gave Tom a warning head shake. He pressed a finger to his lips, then caught hold of Jonas and lifted him back over to his own spot, as easily as someone else might lift a doll.

"That'll be quite enough of that," he told Jonas. "Do your numbers like your teacher says."

He said it rather mildly, he thought, but with a look that brooked no back talk. The little boy's reaction shocked him: he stared at Bear in sheer terror, sat right down, and started sketching in the dirt with a shaking hand. His sketch came out looking more like a tree than the numeral *9*. Urine spread on the ground behind the boy's seat.

Bear understood, and felt sick.

He sat next to Jonas. "It's all right, son," Bear said. "It's all right. I won't hurt you."

The boy leaned away from Bear, trembling like an aspen leaf.

Nothing I say or do will make this better. Bear stood up, brushed the dirt off, and went over to Patty to put in a quiet word about what had happened. She gazed at him and gave a nod.

"Class is over," Patty announced. "Now Bear is going to tell a story."

While Bear distracted the other kids with "The Three Little Pigs," Patty led Jonas over to get washed up and changed, before the other children noticed and teased him.

By that third evening he had learned the names of most of the children, but couldn't put them to the right faces with one hundred percent accuracy. (As an engineer, accuracy was very important to him.) They were all so somber. He'd never seen children so silent. To cheer them up he told them the story of "Jack and the Beanstalk," and acted out all the parts. They listened raptly, even the two Patty had told to take the first night shift, standing guard. They went still when he stomped about, acting out the part of the giant: *Fee! Fi! Fo! Fum!* When Jack chopped down the beanstalk and the giant fell to his death, they all cheered.

Later Patty sat beside Bear, next to the fire. She handed him a picture, half burned, of him and Orla. "I found it in the debris."

"Thank you." He rubbed a thumb over it, rubbing the charring off Orla's face. He tucked it into his wallet.

"*Fee, fi, fo, fum* . . . " She wore a smile. "I like the magic beans, and the golden eggs."

"Do you know the story?"

She shook her head. "But my mother used to tell me a different story about a giant. *El Secréto del Gigante.* The giant's secret. Do you know it?"

It was Bear's turn to shake his head.

"This giant too had a magical egg. It held his soul, and so the giant could not be killed. The hero had to find and destroy the egg. There was a maiden, of course, and a happily-ever-after." She pulled her knees to her chest and her gaze grew distant and sad.

To distract her, Bear asked, "Where did you find all these kids?" He gestured at the children now setting down to sleep around them.

She shook her head. "The past doesn't matter. Only the future does."

Bear had to smile. "Okay, so . . . where are you taking them?"

She hesitated for a long time and her eyes glinted in the flames' light as she studied him. "North," she said finally. "As far north as we can go."

She fell silent, but Bear saw how she bunched her blanket between her fists. She was holding onto something big. He sat quiet, watching the flames dance through the holes they had cut in the barrel. If she trusted him enough, she would tell him. Finally she got up and threw another log onto the fire. Then she sat next to him and leaned over her rifle, lowering her voice. He had to strain to hear.

"My parents were part of—how do you say, *una expedicion?*" she asked.
"An expedition?"

"*Sí.* It was a secret. A group of thinkers. Academics? Is that the word? And others who saw. They gathered all books, all data, *todo el conocimiento* —literature, art, science, and technical books. Like you with your food, only knowledge instead. They gathered from all over the world. They worked for many years, since the twenty-twenties, my father told me. No one knew, not even heads of government. They didn't trust them. Instead they took money from their grants, their salaries. Just little bits, here, there. You understand?" Bear nodded. "They hid it away, combined it, and bought land up there. Up north." She gestured vaguely northward. "They built a secret network. Peer-to-peer, my father told me. *Escondido*—concealed, you call it?

"It happened over so many years. You can't imagine. My grandfather, Papa Chu, was a founder. Thousands of people all over the world collected and stored the knowledge. When the collapse came, they would take their families and start anew. It's on the shores of the Arctic Ocean. It's called Hoku Pa'a. That means the North Star in Hawaiian."

Bear eyed her, a queasy feeling in his belly. *Stuff and nonsense.* More folk tales—fantasies—to keep a child from being afraid to sleep at night. But when all you have is fairy tales, it's a cruel man who steals those from you. So he said nothing.

She read it in his expression anyway, and shrugged. "You can believe me or not. But I know it is there. My mother told me how to find it, before she and my father left for the last time." She tapped her head. "I'm taking the children to Hoku Pa'a."

"How will you cross the border?" he asked. "Canada has guards at all the major roads, and the warlords cover the land in between."

"We will find a way."

The campfire was dying down; only the dullest glow issued from the old cut-down barrel. "Tomorrow we will prepare," she said softly, "The next day we leave. We will head up Highway 93. You must help us get across the border."

Bear had known this moment would come but his heart leapt like a frightened jackrabbit. He had watched them this afternoon: They had rigged harnesses for themselves out of some rope, and had attached them to the flatbed. He shuddered to think of those kids tied to that trailer, straining to pull it along. They'd be easy targets for the warlords, who kept watch in the hills approaching the border. Yet there was no way they could afford to abandon such a cache of food, water, goods, and ammunition.

He said, "It'd be better to hole up somewhere nearby, you know, find a well-defended place to put down roots. It gets hot as blazes in the summer here now, but it's dry enough you can survive it. Not like the Wet-Bulb Die-Offs in the southeast."

She shook her head. "And do what? This food won't last us all through next winter and the land is too dry and rocky for crops. No, Bear. No. We have to go somewhere else, where we can grow food, raise livestock. Where we have a chance to survive and make a better life. We must find Hoku Pa'a. You have to help us."

Bear sighed. "Patty, this is madness. It's over two thousand miles to the Arctic Ocean from here. What are you going to do, *walk* all the way?"

A smile curved her lips. "Why not? I've walked over two thousand miles here from *La Ciudad de México*"

"I don't think you understand. Canada has been inundated with refugees; they have a full deportation policy now. And even they have lost control of their unpopulated territory. They don't have the resources to keep the warlords under control."

"And I don't think *you* understand," she said. "Nothing has stopped us yet and nothing will."

Bear eyed her with deep reluctance.

Truth was, for these kids, the chances were not so good no matter which way you cut it. Sometime soon they'd starve, or be cut down by a warlord's snipers. Or get murdered, thrown into a work camp, or made into sex slaves. Bear and Orla had survived so long because they had kept low—stayed out of sight. That suited him much better than a journey off into the unknown, where you didn't know the terrain or who was patrolling it. Patty might have an unstoppable will, but even she couldn't fend off with her bare hands the bullets and hatchets, that barehanded violence that would befall these kids once they stepped onto the roads.

But Patty was right that there was not much point in staying here. And their chances of making it someplace safe were even worse without him. He knew the area; he was a decent shot and a good hunter. His many years of life experience could come in handy. And Canada was the only nation in this hemisphere whose lands had remained partially arable, and whose cities were mostly still viable. If they could get the kids across the border, maybe someone in authority somewhere would have pity on them. It was their best chance to survive. Edmonton, perhaps, or Calgary.

And if they were going to try for Canada, Highway 93 was better than

I-15 or US 287. Refugees who traveled those two roads were not long for the world.

Anyway, he thought, *death by Good Samaritanism isn't such a bad way to go.*

"All righty, then," he said, and slapped his thighs. "I'm in."

As they were preparing their bedrolls, Sarah, the girl whose turn it was to care for the baby, came to Patty. She held the infant out. He hung limp in her hands. The little girl said, "He won't wake up."

Patty took the baby in her lap and examined him. Her expression told Bear everything he needed to know. "Thank you, Sarah. Go get ready for bed now."

"Gone?" Bear asked softly.

She nodded, lips thin. "He had diarrhea. Day after day. We tried. Nothing worked." Her eyes glittered in the dim light of the fire and she passed her hands over them. After a silence she said, "The day he was born, it was the day his mother died. I promised her. I said I would take him, that I would protect him. But I knew even then. I knew it would be too much. No food. No water for days, till we got here. And the food was not right for him. I had hope, when we found *la medicina. Pero no le ayudó.*"

She stroked the infant's head, looking at Bear. "If I had cared for him only, and a few others, he might have survived. I hoped the children could do it . . ."

"Sounds like you had to make a tough call," he said.

She nodded and wiped tears away. Then she swaddled the infant's body in a clean blanket and set it on the floor away from the others. She grabbed a shovel but Bear took it. "Let me." Tom and Vanessa jumped up to help, too.

She took it back, and yelled at all of them, "Go to bed! You need your rest," and strode out into the dark.

"Mind the little ones," Bear told them. He grabbed his pickaxe and went outside. The moon had just risen, a pale lopsided knob beyond distant veils of smoke. Patty was nowhere to be seen. He made his way to the grove where he had buried Orla.

"You see?" he told the stone that covered her grave. "You see? This is exactly why I should not have listened to you."

He took out his anger on the unforgiving ground: He pummeled it with his pickaxe, blow after jarring blow. After a while, he noticed Patty standing at the hole. She picked up the shovel and dug out the soil and rocks he had loosened. Neither of them said anything. They worked hard and long, till Bear's back ached and his lungs screamed for mercy. When they finished, the moon was touching the western peaks of the Grand Tetons, and the stars in the east were starting to fade. They returned to the barn trembling with exhaustion, and pumped well water for each other to rinse off the dirt.

Patty finally said, "Thank you."

"No trouble," he mumbled. Damn stubborn woman.

Bear did not wake till well after sunup. Not even the children's noisy morning preparations fully awakened him. Finally Vanessa shook him and called his name. She handed him a cup of bitter black coffee and a handful of dried apples. The barn was empty but for the two of them. The infant's wrapped body was gone.

"Patty says you need to wake up now. It's time to bury Pablo."

He gulped down the tepid coffee and ate the apples. Then he followed Vanessa along the hillside to Orla's grove. Everyone else had gathered there, around the deep hole Bear and Patty had dug. Patty stood at the head of the grave. They all held little handfuls of wildflowers and grasses and twigs. Bear and Vanessa took their places among the mourners. Bear saw that the infant's body had been laid in the hole.

"Pablito," Patty said, "You were very brave." Her voice quavered. "We will always remember you." She threw a flower into the grave and the others followed suit. "I know Pablo is with his mother now," she told the others, and said the Lord's Prayer in Spanish.

"Amen," Bear said, out of courtesy, though the days were long gone when he could take comfort from prayer.

They rested that afternoon, and went to bed early that night. The children were all subdued. For a change they didn't beg him for a story. But Bear sensed that this was not the first death they had seen. They had shown a quiet competence today. They knew how to say goodbye to the dead.

After breakfast the next morning, Patty insisted that everyone take a bath. Bear said, "I thought you were in a hurry." Tom and Vanessa thought it was a waste of water. "We're just going to get dirty again," the younger girl pointed out.

"I don't care!" Patty said. "It's not healthy to be dirty all the time. When we can, we wash. So don't argue." To Bear she pointed out, "We'll have a better chance at the border if we don't look dirty."

The kids lined up and took turns bathing and washing their clothes, using water from Bear's well, and soap and shampoo from Bear's supplies.

They ran a bucket brigade and set up a tarp near the well, so the kids could have a little privacy. Bubbles slowly spread from under the tarp, and shrieks, laughter, and splashing sounds issued forth. Patty went last. The relief on her face as she exited, combing her soaked hair with her fingers, spoke louder than a shout. The littlest ones, of course, were already dirty again, and Patty scolded them, and made them clean up again. She made them all brush their teeth, too. Everyone groaned and complained.

"You want all your teeth to fall out? You'll look like this!" She made gumming faces at them with her lips.

Next they checked the kids' wounds and sores, and treated them with Betadine and bandages. It was mostly their feet that needed attention. Bear used his hunting knife to rig sandals from the tires of his old Ford and leather bridle straps from the days they had kept horses. It took them all day. Patty didn't want to lose another day, but when she got a look at the first pair he made, she agreed it was a good tradeoff.

Vanessa, Patty, and Tom helped. Bear taught them how to measure and cut the rubber, how to weave in the leather straps and lace them up. They were all hot and sweaty again by the time they finished, and the kids were scattered about the meadow, running about and admiring their new shoes.

"Time to go," Patty said. Everyone lined up. The fourteen kids who were big enough (the kids who looked to be between six and nine) would pull the tarped load. The eldest four would walk alongside with their weapons. The six littlest ones would ride in the front of the trailer. Of these, four were perhaps four or five years old. Patty put them in charge of the two toddlers. Patty told the elder four, "You mind those babies! If they get hurt and it's your fault, I'll leave you by the roadside!"

They stared at her and sucked their fists. They knew she meant it.

Bear had argued with her over his own role. He had insisted on taking the front position at the harness but she said no; she needed him to keep watch. "You have to trust me, Bear. They are strong! They can do it."

"How are we different than the slavers, then?" he asked.

She gasped in outrage. "Because we *feed* them every day, and teach them their letters, and make sure they bathe. We are trying to save them—not rape them, not make them kill their mothers and fathers, their sisters and brothers!"

She turned away, fists clenched, breathing hard.

"I'm sorry," he said.

She turned back. "Bear, you hurt me very badly with your words. I wish they could have had the years I had and you had, of being a child without so many worries and so much hurt. But those times are gone.

"Mira." She shook her rifle. "We have this. Now a shotgun, thanks to you. And two *pistoles,* and plenty of bullets. That's good, yes? We need all the weapons we can against *los caudillos."* The warlords. "Now look around and tell me. Besides you, me, Tomás, and Vanessa, who should handle such a weapon?"

He looked across at the children's faces and sighed. *Babies,* he thought. *An army of babies, Orla.*

They set off shortly before sunset, down the rough gravel road of Bear's driveway toward a farm-to-market road that fed onto Highway 93 about a mile and a half to the west.

Everyone pushed, to start out. Once the wheels were rolling, the oldest four took their positions: Bear in front, Patty in the rear, and Tom and Vanessa flanking them.

Privately Bear had thought that Patty's plans were far too ambitious. The children would surely give up and she would have to stop. But he was wrong. The children strained and hurled themselves against the harness, time and again, till he thought his heart would burst with pride and anguish. They pulled the trailer over the bumpy road, up and down the hills, but no one uttered a sound, other than grunts as they struggled over the cracks and potholes in the asphalt. Even the infant and toddlers were silent (perhaps they slept).

They'd reach 93 by twilight. Bear knew the road so well he could walk it with his eyes closed. And it was a good thing: Tonight would be a dark night. The moon, half full, would not be up till well after midnight.

They paused for a rest. Sunlight's last vestiges made a mauve smudge above the western peaks and a night breeze cooled their sweat. Patty gave Tommy Bear's night-vision binoculars and sent him and Vanessa ahead into the hills, to scout for criminals and warlords. Then they got moving again. Bear walked ahead with Jonah and Margaritte, who led the team pulling the wagon. Despite Patty's instructions, he helped haul. It was a clear, cool night, and the starlight gave them just enough light once their eyes had adapted to avoid the worst of the cracks and potholes.

They reached 93, maybe three miles from the border. There they paused for dinner and a rest. The aurora borealis put on quite a show while they ate. Luminous purple and green veils of light rippled across the Milky Way's pale white band of stars. The children gasped and Patty grabbed Bear's arm.

"What is that? It's so beautiful." Bear explained about the Earth's magnetic field and how it created these lights. She said, "I've heard of these. But I think also it is a sign. We are very close!"

They got going again. Soon, Tommy and Vanessa emerged from the trees and joined Bear and Patty, out of breath.

"We found bandits," Vanessa said. "Two men." Tommy added, "On the hills above the highway. About a mile north of here."

Bear stood. "I'll take care of it." He handed Patty his shotgun. He stuck his Colt into the belt at his back and his hunting knife into his left boot, and then pulled a bottle of Jack Daniel's Black Label out of the trailer. "Stay here till you hear from me or until you hear gunfire. If you hear weapons, hide the kids and the trailer. Gunfire echoes far among these hills, and lots of unsavory sorts might come around to investigate. Okay?"

"Be careful," she said. "Tomás, you show Bear where."

Bear had to give Tommy credit: He knew how to move quietly. They walked along the hill's shoulder a good long ways, then crept up a slope at an angle. Soon they observed two men squatting on an outcropping that overlooked Highway 93.

Bear recognized them. They were Lona and Gene's sons, Arden and Zach. The Hallorhans had left Rexford ten years ago. Apparently they hadn't gone far. Or at least, the boys hadn't. They were in their twenties now: big strapping men who weren't hurting for a meal. A two-way radio Zach wore spat occasional chatter.

Bear and Tommy listened for a while. Most of their talk was about people they both knew, including a man they called the colonel, and grumbling about their rations and duties. Bear wondered if he was the same as Patty's *el coronel.* He feared it was. They both had automatic weapons and belts heavy with ammo.

Arden said with a heavy sigh, "Man, *nobody's* ever going to come by."

"Yeah, I bet Marco and Jay got I-15 watch. They get all the big hauls."

They started joking about things they had seen and done to refugee convoys that made Bear feel ill. *Enough of this.* He looked at Tommy and pressed a finger to his lips. Tommy nodded. Bear pried the cork out of the whiskey bottle with his teeth. He swished a mouthful of liquor around to foul his breath, and sprinkled more on his clothes. Then he staggered noisily into their campsite. They came half to their feet, then saw his face.

"I know you . . . " Arden said, and Zach said, "It's Bear Jessen."

"Hey, Ardie—hey, Zach," he said, slurring his words a bit. "Thought I heard somebody in the woods out here." He sat down next to them and took a fake gulp of whiskey. "Didn't even know you boys were still around! How are your parents?"

The two young men looked at each other. Zach was the elder brother, and Bear guessed, the tougher. He was gazing at Bear with a puzzled expression that could quickly pivot to suspicion. "I didn't know you were still around these parts."

"Oh, yeah. Hell, yeah. Orla and me, we didn't really have any place to go. Figured we'd stock up and do for ourselves, once everybody left."

At *stock up*, he sensed both young men's attention sharpen.

"Back at your place?" Arden asked.

"Yup. Thass right."

"Orla there now?" Zach asked.

"Yup. Bet she'd make you boys a proper meal. Wanna pay a visit?"

The two young men exchanged a glance. "I'm up for it," Zach said.

"Me, too," Arden said. They stood, and started down toward the road.

Bear said, "Nah, it's quicker to take the trail over the ridge. Come on."

He led them up to the trail, and on the way he pretended to drink. The young men had military-issue flashlights. Bear walked in front and avoided looking at the lights, to keep his night vision. To deaden theirs, he offered them the bottle, and both young men partook heavily. Soon their own steps on the trail grew uncertain and their words grew slurred.

By this point Bear's house stood out against the ridge, a faint black shape in the distance. The house's shape was wrong. He doubted Zach and Arden would notice.

Bear ducked off the trail at a turn and moved behind a boulder. He pulled the knife from his boot and flanked them silently. The flashlight beams bounced around as the two brothers stumbled on, boots scraping against stone. Then they slowed to an uncertain halt.

He thought, *I'm nowhere near as agile as them, and not as strong as I used to be. Need to make this quick.*

"Bear?" they called. "Hey, old man!—Hello!"

"We lost him," Zach said softly. "Probably fell onto his drunk old ass."

"Shit," Arden replied. "He's onto us."

"Shut up, you idiot," Zach said, but apparently decided the same thing. "Listen here, you old fucker! Come out now or I'll cap your ass! Or I'll do your old lady and then cap *her.*"

Bear moved up from behind a boulder, pulled Zach backward off his feet, and slit his throat. Sticky, warm fluid washed over his face, neck, and arms. He got a mouthful of blood.

Arden came around the rock and shone the light in Bear's face.

"What the—?"

He opened his mouth in a scream of rage and raised his automatic. Then he toppled and fell over his brother's corpse with a hatchet jutting from his upper spine. He twitched. Little Tommy stood behind him, a silhouette against the stars.

Bear suppressed his gorge, looking down at his neighbor's sons. When they were little, they'd climbed Old Lady Pine and picked wild strawberries on the back twenty.

War makes us all monsters, he thought, and slapped Tommy's back. "Quick thinking. Let's strip them of their weapons and supplies. We'll get cleaned up in the stream and catch up with the others."

It was all for naught. They crossed the border unharmed but were stopped by the Mounties the next morning, about five miles in. The Canadians were not cruel, but they said little. They confiscated the trailer—all their food and water and medicines. Bear complained and the soldiers only shrugged. They locked them in a windowless warehouse at their border station, along with dozens of other refugees: people of all nationalities, all religions, all races. The world's detritus, tossed up against a nation's borders. Bear tried to doze on the hard concrete. His tailbone ached and the burn on his arm hurt like hell.

They were there for about six days. They were fed, but the cramped and uncomfortable quarters and their own low spirits made time drag. Late one afternoon—or so Bear guessed from the slant of the sun's rays on the wall—he heard noises outside. After a while, the guards brought them out into the sunlight, where a convoy of big military trucks waited. A Canadian officer turned them over to a group of men in a hodgepodge of American uniforms. Patty gripped Bear's arm so tight she nearly broke the skin.

"You know them?" Bear asked.

She nodded. "I recognize that one." She gestured with her chin at the officer who spoke to the Canadians. "He is *el coronets* number-three man." Her skin had gone pallid. "The man whose camp we escaped in Denver."

She faded back among the others and kept her head down as the first lieutenant walked past. He wore Air Force insignia. The man stopped and looked Bear over.

"Name?" he asked.

"Bear Jessen. Lately of Rexford."

The lieutenant shouted over his shoulder, "Load them up!"

They were hustled toward the trucks. They tried to stay together, but the trucks only held twelve or so. This did not bode well.

Bear towered above the rest. He caught Patty's gaze, and then Tommy's and Vanessa's. Somehow, they all understood what needed to happen—they each gathered the children nearest them, whispering, passing the word. Bear took the youngest six, the five-and-under set. Bear and his kids sat near the back of the open transport, across from a young soldier with a rifle across his knees. Land passed by; Bear recognized the road, and the miles and miles of wind power generators. They were headed over the Grand Tetons, toward Spokane.

Penelope and Paul, the toddler twins, cried inconsolably. Bear pulled them onto his lap and bounced them on his knee making shushing sounds. The other little ones sat looking out at the scenery, to all appearances unafraid.

That night they reached a military base. The sign by the road said FAIRCHILD AIR FORCE BASE. They passed a munitions dump and an enormous hangar, and rows and rows of military barracks. The trucks came to a halt at a roundabout in the middle of the camp. Soldiers unloaded them all from the trucks. Floodlights lit the concrete pad they stood on. They gathered the refugees in a circle. Two officers came out of the nearby barracks. One of them spoke to the lieutenant. Bear knew instantly he was the colonel.

The colonel was a big man, perhaps six-foot-four. He wore a gun at his belt and Air Force insignia. He was no true military man, though: His hair was long and unkempt and he wore a bushy beard.

"We need to resolve some questions," the colonel said. He looked them all over, then walked up to Bear. "I understand that it was your group that had these . . . " He had one of his men spread out on the ground the weapons and supplies Bear and Tommy had taken from Zach and Arden. "I think you must be the leader. I want to know who the members of your group are, and what happened to my two men."

Bear merely looked at him. The colonel pulled out his gun and shot one of the other refugees in the head, a young man Patty's age. Bear cried out. He couldn't help himself. *Not one of ours,* he thought, heart pounding. *Not one of ours.* He felt shame that that mattered.

"What kind of sick bastard are you?"

"I do my duty," the colonel replied. "And I look after my men. Anyone who harms them has to account for it. You people"—he gestured at Bear and the rest of the refugees—"may be useful to me. But only up to a point."

Bear opened his mouth to tell the man exactly where he could stuff his duty. That would no doubt have been the end of him. But Patty stepped out and spoke up.

"He is not the leader," she said. "I am."

Recognition bloomed on the colonel's face.

"Patricia," he said. "Is it really you? Somehow I'm not surprised to find you mixed up with the disappearance of my men. Lieutenant, get her cleaned up and take her to my quarters. I want to question her personally. Take the rest of the refugees to be processed."

Another man strode up, saying "Excuse me, Colonel. Colonel!"

Bear recognized that voice. He turned to stare. His old pastor!

Des had aged. He looked as healthy as ever, though; even rotund. He wore his reverend's collar and a cross. The military man watched Des greet Bear. Then Des turned to the colonel. "Colonel O'Neal, I can personally vouch for this man. He was part of my congregation for years. He doesn't belong with them." Des waved a hand at the rest of the refugees. He said more quietly, "He's an engineer."

The colonel gave Bear a penetrating look, then shrugged.

"Very well. If he's of use . . . But I believe he is mixed up with the disappearance of some of my men. I'll want to question him. Meanwhile, I'll hold you responsible for him, Reverend." He waved them away. Bear felt Patty's gaze burning into the back of his neck, as he let himself be led away by his old friend.

"Thank the Lord you are still alive," Des said as he showed him through the darkened camp. "I've wondered about you over the years. Gloria will be so happy to see you. Orla?"

Bear shook his head. "Lost her," he said. "Lung disease. Cancer, we think."

Des looked up at Bear and laid a hand on his arm. "She's with God now."

Bear's molars ground together. But he tried to take the words as Des intended: as comfort.

"Don't worry about the colonel," Des said. "Just keep your head down. You'll do fine."

"Hard for me to do," Bear replied, "keeping my head down." Des seemed to think he was joking, and chuckled. "How did you end up here?"

"Gloria and I never made it to Seattle. Fortunately we found this refuge. We joined Colonel O'Neal's company a long time since, and we have been here doing the Lord's work, helping to comfort the soldiers and succor the refugees."

Succor? Was that what they were calling it now?

"Colonel O'Neal is building an army," Des went on. "He is working with others across the US to rebuild and reclaim our country. It's a great endeavor! You must join us. We need you." He showed Bear the barracks, the "soldiers" doing drills, the fuel and military vehicles. Obviously O'Neal had big plans.

"The man doesn't look very military."

"Well . . . technically, he's not." In fact, the remaining few US military battalions had been disbanded twelve years ago. There might be a few companies here and there, in the major cities, but they reported up no chain of command. "But that's going to change soon. He wants to reconstitute the US: reunite the entire northern portion of the country."

He went on like this for a while. Bear fell silent. Des eventually seemed to notice. He stopped and turned. "I know we parted on less-than-friendly terms, Bear, but that's all behind us. I hope you know that. It's a sign from God that you are here. I'm so thankful to see you."

Bear said, "Pastor, we were friends once, and I'm grateful for your help just now. But I have no intention of joining Colonel O'Neal in these escapades. I simply want to take my kids and go."

"Kids?" Pastor Des seemed confused. "You and Orla never had kids."

"I mean the kids I came in with. The refugees. I made a promise. I mean to keep it."

Des got a horrified look. "Oh, no, no, no. You have to let that go, Bear. There's nothing you can do for them now. They're destined for a munitions factory in Denver. We need all the hands we can get, to help us prepare for war."

"What?"

"This is God's plan! To make America great. We're going to invade Canada."

Now it was Bear's turn to stare, horrified. "Des . . . that's insane."

"I thought so too, at first. But it's a good plan. Let me show you."

He had brought Bear to a giant hangar. The hangar had big radioactivity warning signs on it, and Authorized Personnel Only. A guard stood outside. He glowered at them, but Desmond gave him a stern look and he let them through. Des must be in good with the colonel. Or he had something on him.

Inside the hangar was a blimp—the largest airship Bear had ever seen. It was lit by floodlights. People, ant-size against its flanks, swarmed around working on it. Beneath its belly was a cabin the size of a 757, and numerous missiles. Nuclear weapons.

"It's nearly ready," Des said. "It's one of five military blimps that were built in the thirties and forties. Four are still in good repair. They've been moved to our northern border and are being outfitted for battle. The colonel is coordinating with other military commanders west of the Great Lakes." You mean warlords, Bear thought. "We've uncovered this cache of nuclear warheads, and are going to use our blimp to deliver them to the other airships soon. I'm told they are even getting orders from *Washington*," he said in a hushed voice tinged with awe. Unlikely, Bear thought, unless a tin pot dictator had set up shop in the White House. Which since Washington, D.C., was uninhabitable in the summer, like most of the US south of about forty degrees north latitude, did not make sense.

Des went on, "We're shorthanded. We need engineers who can help keep equipment in repair. Here's a chance for you to show your worth. The colonel will reward you."

Bear stared at his old friend. They stood beneath one of the few lights in the camp that was not burned out. Words wouldn't come. Nuke Canada? The sheer delusional magnitude of the plan overwhelmed thought.

Des misinterpreted his silence. "Impressive, isn't it? Our glory days are ahead."

Bear rubbed his mouth. "I'm a railroad engineer, Des. I know nothing about aeronautics. Never mind airship technology. Or nuclear weapons."

"A machine is a machine. You'll figure it out."

Des took Bear to his place, where Gloria made him a late dinner. They served a meal the likes of which he had not had in years: bread with real butter, roast chicken, yams, and asparagus, with a glass of '82 Merlot.

"Impressive provisions," he remarked. Des beamed. "Yes. The colonel has his connections."

"I'll get the cheesecake," Gloria said, laying her napkin on the chair. She shared a look with Bear that told him a great deal about Des, Gloria, and the choices they had made.

Des swirled his wine in his glass. "Too bad you didn't find us earlier, Bear. Maybe they could have treated Orla's cancer."

Really, he shouldn't have mentioned Orla. "You never much cared for her, did you, though?" Bear asked.

"Aw, Bear. That's water under the bridge."

But something about deciding he was ready to die made all this a lot easier for Bear. The church held no more power over him. And he found he had a lot of things to say. "I seem to recall you hated her for her defiance of the church."

Des's face grew stiff. "It was not for me to judge her. That's God's job."

A knock came at the door. Gloria answered, looking anxious. An enlisted man stood there. "The colonel wants to talk to Mr. Jessen."

Bear shook his head. "You still spin such amazing bullshit out of your own hot air."

Des's lips went thin. He stood and threw his napkin on his chair. "You want to know what I think? God punished your wife for her defiance. It's too late for her. But *you* have a chance to repent. Jesus welcomes you with open arms. Come to me when you are ready."

"I don't think so." Bear stood. *Orla, he shouldn't have implied that, about your cancer being God's punishment.* At the door, he turned. "I'm done with your God and I don't think we have anything more to say to each other."

The airman took Bear to a room at the command barracks, where Colonel O'Neal and his second-in-command waited. Two armed men stood outside the door. They made him sit in the room's only chair.

"Now it's time for you to tell us what happened to my men out on Highway 93," the colonel said.

What the hell, Bear thought. "All right. I killed your men myself. I'd do it again if I had the chance. They were about to slaughter a group of innocent children."

They stared at him as if he had grown two heads. The colonel said, "I didn't think we'd have it out of you so quickly."

Bear shrugged. Death by firing squad seemed an okay way to go. Death by torture, not so much.

"They weren't necessarily going to kill them," the colonel said. "We need strong arms and backs for our war effort. Of course I give my troops broad discretion. We have an agreement with the Canadians. We help protect their borders and they give us any refugees who make it across."

"Ironic, that, since you are using those refugees to build ammunition to attack the Canadians."

The colonel looked at him thoughtfully. "Yes." He paced for a moment.

The major stood by the door, silent. "Ordinarily I would have you executed, Mr. Jessen. But we are in sore need of engineers. So Major Stedtler and I"—he gestured at the other officer—"have decided to give you a reprieve. If we can count on your cooperation, we will keep the children you traveled with here, and not send them off to the factory."

Hostages, Bear thought. "How do I know I can trust you?"

"I'm a man of my word, Mr. Jessen."

The hell you are. "What about Patty?"

"No, you can't have Patricia. I have other plans for her."

At that, Bear caught a fleeting shadow in the major's eyes. Disgust? Anger? Or envy?

"I want to see the children now."

The colonel studied Bear. "All right. Fair enough. But I have my limits. For every stunt you pull, one of your kids gets a bullet. Clear?"

"As crystal."

Bear might be old. He might not be as massive as he once was, and his joints in the morning were stiff. But he was still plenty big and plenty strong. And he wasn't afraid of dying anymore. He surged at the colonel and picked him up by the neck. His hand encircled the colonel's neck as easily as a normal-sized adult's hand might encircle a child's. He plucked the gun from the colonel's holster with his other hand. To Bear's joy, it turned out to be his own Colt .45.

The colonel flailed in his grip, pinned with his back against Bear's massive chest. Bear put the colonel between himself and the major and eased his grip on the colonel's throat, just enough to let air through. As he did so, the two armed men burst in and aimed their weapons at him. Colonel O'Neal made wheezing noises but couldn't speak. Bear said, "Drop your guns on the floor. Kick them over to me. Then lie on the floor with your hands on your heads"

The men did so. The major said, "You'll never make it out of here."

"You let me worry about that part," Bear said.

He got the information he needed from the major, and left him trussed up and gagged in the interrogation room, secured to a pipe. Each of the colonel's two guards he left in their own little rooms, also securely tied and gagged. He wasn't a big fan of shooting people out of turn, but couldn't have them alerting the camp. He tied and gagged the colonel, too, and carried him out over his shoulder, like a sack of grain. He crossed the camp in darkness to the building Des had pointed out to him as the colonel's quarters. He knocked several times before Patty's face appeared at the window.

Her eyes widened. She gestured and shouted. He could barely hear her. "It's locked! I can't get out!" So Bear kicked the door in.

He came inside and dumped the colonel on the carpet. The room was dark other than the light streaming in through the door. Patty gazed at the colonel with contempt. She was wearing a flimsy nightgown. She gave him a good, hard kick in the testicles. Colonel O'Neal curled up with a moan.

"Let me get dressed," she said.

"Hurry."

When she came back in, she was wearing her clothes from before, Orla's jeans and sneakers and a T-shirt, and was tying her long hair into a bun. "What are we going to do with him?" she asked, gesturing at the colonel.

Bear hadn't wanted to kill the colonel. But after seeing Patty in the nightgown, he had changed his mind. He raised his gun but Patty put her hand on the barrel. "No. We may need him." She pulled Bear out of the colonel's earshot. "We can rescue the children and steal a vehicle."

"And I know *exactly* which vehicle to steal," Bear said, thinking of the airship. "Do you know where the kids are?"

"I do. They are in a big building," Patty said. "A room with benches where people watch sports. What do you call it?"

"A gymnasium?" Bear asked.

"Yes. A gymnasium." She pronounced it *hymn-nauseum*. "All right, then. We're getting out of here. We're headed to Hoku Pa'a."

Amusement glinted in her gaze. "I thought you didn't believe in Hoku Pa'a."

"If it doesn't exist yet, it will when we get there."

She smiled.

The best-guarded place in camp was the hangar with the nuke-encrusted blimp. He glanced at his watch. It was midnight. They needed to be out of here before dawn and there was too much to do before then. He looked at Patty, so fierce a woman, so tiny—barely more than a child herself. He grimaced. *Dammit, Orla; she's given me something to care about.* He handed her an automatic weapon. "Can you rescue the children on your own?"

"I can."

"You sure? It's important, Patty. Don't say yes if you don't mean it."

"I saw only two guards guarding the gymnasium as we passed by, and they were both drunk." She glowered. "You have to trust me, Bear. I know what I am doing."

"All right. I'm going to need time to rig a diversion. It'll take most of the night." He took her to the kitchen, and gestured at Des and Gloria's place. A light shone in their window. "I want you to take the kids *there.*" He pointed. "Hide the kids. Take Desmond—the man—hostage. Tell him you need to talk to his wife. When she comes out, you bring out the kids out. Her name's Gloria. You tell her Bear said they needed a good meal and a decent night's sleep. She'll make sure they are taken care of.

"But you have to watch Des, the pastor. The man. You understand? He's afraid of *him*"—he gestured at O'Neal, who glared at them from the carpeting—"and he'll turn you in or raise the alarm, if he gets a chance. Also, don't let Desmond get Gloria alone, or he will bully her into doing what he wants. Got that?"

"Yes, I understand."

"At six a.m., bring the children and meet me near the airship hangar. You can't miss it—it's the giant building at the base of the hills. That way." He pointed out the window, at the black hills that blotted out the starlight to the southeast. "Don't be late."

Two guards were at the munitions shack. They were both asleep when he found them, and stank of booze. He took their flashlights and other equipment, tied them up with electrical cord, and left them a safe distance from the shed. In the munitions shack he found everything he needed. Bear might not know nukes, but as a former railroad man, he knew explosives. He spent the next several hours prepping charges and setting up a radio detonator.

Then Bear went back for O'Neal. The warlord (Bear refused to think of him as true military) had managed to worm his way from the middle of his living room carpet to the kitchen and was on his knees by the kitchen counter . . . presumably trying to get a knife out of the drawer. Bear slung him over his shoulder and headed out toward the blimp hangar. It was almost six a.m.

The sky was still dark as pitch. Patty was waiting for him, and so were the rest of the kids. The children swarmed around Bear and greeted him. They were all there, miraculously, in one piece, along with a few other people Bear didn't recognize. "They needed help too," Patty said.

Bear dumped O'Neal on the ground and cut the bonds on his ankles. He ungagged him. O'Neal spat, and gazed at Bear with the requisite fear and loathing.

"Don't much like being on the receiving end, do you, son?" Bear asked.

"There's no way you can escape."

Bear put his Colt under the man's chin, finger on the trigger. "You're only alive because *she*"—he gestured in Patty's direction—"reminded me you might be useful. Mind your manners."

Patty edged over. "What now?" she asked in a low voice. "Fireworks," Bear said. "Make sure the kids are behind the dumpsters."

Patty did so, and gave him the okay signal. He blew the munitions dump. The response was gratifying. It made a very big boom. Everyone in the entire camp, it seemed like, went running to help put out the fire.

"Follow me," Bear told Patty. "Bring the kids." He carried O'Neal over and set the man down between himself and the soldier standing guard at the hangar door.

"Don't make me hurt you, son," Bear said. The soldier stood there for a moment staring first at the gun and then up at Bear. Then he threw down his own weapon and ran.

And so did they all run—Bear and Patty and Vanessa and Tommy, and Nabil and Margaritte and Phyllis and Angelique and Jonah and Katie and Earl and Janette and Frankie and George and Bill and Jess, and Teresa and Mimi and Sandra and Lin—except of course, the three littlest ones, Penelope and Paul and Latoya, who were carried—for the blimp.

O'Neal's second-in-command, Stedtler, stepped out from behind the airship as they neared it. He had with him a handful of large, well-armed men. He gestured at the rafters, where more soldiers crouched, aiming weapons at them. Desmond stood there, too, hands clasped before him and a grim, worried look on his face. Bear realized Des must have found and freed the major.

Des, Bear thought, sad. *At least you could have stayed home.*

"I should have shot you when I had the chance," Bear told Stedtler, who gave him a gallows grin. Bear looked around for Patty. She and the children had all moved to a spot between the containers and the airship cabin, mostly out of range of snipers. Bear put his weapon against the joint of O'Neal's jaw. "Tell your men to put down their weapons."

Stedtler stared hard at O'Neal. "Do it," O'Neal said. Stedtler gestured to his men and they lowered their guns. Bear waved Patty and the children into the airship cabin.

"I want all the weapons on the floor," Bear said. None complied. By now the last of the refugees were scrambling up the ramp. Bear did a quick calculation, and started edging toward the ramp himself. The soldiers began raising their weapons again. Bear stopped moving. He felt the ramp's rim against his right heel.

O'Neal tried to look over his shoulder at Bear. "We can't let you take our nukes."

"Nobody needs nukes," Bear replied. He kept his grip around O'Neal's chest as firmly as he could, but it had been a long night without sleep, and weariness was creeping in around the edges.

"Give up this foolishness," Des said. "Be a patriot, Bear. Let go of the colonel and I can guarantee you no one will be hurt."

Bear gave his old friend an incredulous look. Did he really believe that? "The US is *gone,* Des. Long gone. These men are nothing but bullies and warlords who use fairy tales to get people to listen to their ravings. The last thing our Canuck neighbors need is crazy people like O'Neal dropping nuclear weapons on their heads."

O'Neal gave a sudden lurch while Bear was talking and managed to break Bear's grip. The two men wrestled for Bear's Colt. Bear tripped on the edge of the ramp and went down on his tailbone. O'Neal pointed the gun at him, but a shot struck him in the forehead and he fell backward, looking surprised. Bear's Colt skittered across the hangar floor. Bear bade it goodbye. Bullets started to fly—he scrambled up the ramp with hands and feet.

Patty dragged him into the blimp and hit the switch to close the cabin door. He lay down. "You shot the colonel, didn't you?" he asked. "Good work."

She was pressing her hands against his diaphragm. Blood was leaking out of him from somewhere and he realized he was going into shock. "He's been hit," Patty said to someone Bear couldn't see, as she faded away.

Damn shame, Bear thought. *Just when I'd about decided to live.*

Orla came to him in a dream. There was nothing consequential—nothing he remembered later. Just that she was standing with him, smiling. Somehow their love outlived her, and he thought it might even outlive him as well, as something he passed along to Patty and the little ones. It pleased him to think so, anyway.

He woke up in the airship infirmary. A woman there identified herself as Dr. Maribeth Zedrosky. "You missed a bit of excitement," she said, fiddling with his bandages.

"How long have I been out?"

"Four days, just about." He gaped. It didn't seem possible.

"How do you feel?"

He felt like a crap sandwich with a side of crap. "I'll live." He sat up with a grunt. His midriff and neck were swathed in bandages, and his calf was in a cast.

"What happened?"

"You were shot. Three times. We had to operate to remove a bullet in your lung. Another struck your ankle, fracturing it, and a third one grazed your carotid. Luckily for you, we are well stocked with medical supplies. This airship was designed to be a field hospital, among other things."

"No. I mean, what happened to my friends? Are we safe? Did we escape O'Neal and his crew?"

The woman gave him a big smile. "We are safe."

He blinked. He felt groggy and couldn't think clearly. "How?"

"Once your young friend Patty dragged you inside and sealed the cabin, O'Neal's men tried to scale the blimp and steal the warheads. We blew a hole in the hangar door and floated away on a breeze."

"You're not with them, I take it," he said. The warlords, he meant.

She made a rude noise. "Not by a long shot. They've held five of us here for months. They've been forcing us to work on the airship. When we didn't cooperate, they would start killing the other prisoners. Right now," she said, "we are about three miles up, heading northwest toward the Arctic Ocean. We're nearly there. You should come see."

She helped Bear along the corridor and down a spiral stair to a lounge that hung at the bottom of the airship, below the pilot's bridge.

The lounge was big enough for a whole platoon, Bear thought. Near the rear were the tables and the mess. Some of the children were there. Three adults Bear did not know were teaching some of the older children how to play cards. The little ones were tottering around in makeshift diapers. Near the front sat Patty on the floor, legs curled under her, looking at maps and out at the terrain. She wore a worried look and looked out the floor-to-ceiling windows that lined the front and sides of the lounge.

Beyond the glass, the air was a dark, intense blue strung with piles of cumulus. The early spring sun shone behind them, casting their shadow ahead of them onto a nearby cloud. Far below lay a swatch of brilliant green. Livestock and herds of wild caribou dotted the landscape, and rivers snaked through sodden marshes that had once been tundra. The sun shone over across the Arctic Sea to the north. Islands jutted up from the sea, and their peaks cast long shadows across the choppy water.

When Patty spotted Bear, she gave a happy shriek, bounced over the couch, and hugged him. It sent shooting pains down his side and he groaned.

"I'm so sorry!" she said, and released him.

The children came up too, nine or ten of them. They jumped up and down and all wanted a hug.

"Careful, please—careful!" Patty scolded. She grabbed his hand in a tight grip. "Bear, thank God you are all right. You nearly died! Your lung collapsed and they had to do an emergency surgery—what do you call it?" she asked Dr. Zedrosky, who stood at the stair up to the main deck, arms folded, looking amused. "Oh, never mind. You are here now," she said to Bear. "That is what matters."

He looked over her head toward the others. Tom was there, and Jonah, and perhaps another six of the children. "Vanessa?" he asked. "Where is she? Where are the others?" A spasm of fear gripped him.

"No, no—don't worry. She is fine. They are all fine. No one was hurt. Vanessa is learning to fly the blimp."

"It's not fair!" Tom told Patty. "I have to watch the twins and Latoya," he said, turning to Bear. "I wanted to go first."

Patty said, "Be patient, Tomás. You always nag!"

Bear laid a hand on Tom's shoulder. "You'll have your turn soon."

Patty introduced Bear to the other scientists at the table near the back.

"Thank you," Bear told them. "Thanks for rescuing us."

A man about his age replied, "You're the ones who rescued *us.*" They shook hands all around.

"Excuse me," Patty said, "but I need to talk to Bear." She pulled him over to the front of the lounge. "I'm very worried. Come see." She set him up in a cushioned seat with pillows propping up his ankle, and laid a set of maps across his lap. It'd been a long time since he'd seen working smartpaper. He wondered whom O'Neal had stolen it from.

"I've plugged in my parents' coordinates," she said. "But they aren't right. I just don't understand." She pointed out features below and before them on a mountain range. "Those peaks are right, but look out there. Where we are going, it is not supposed to be an island. My parents made me memorize, and this is wrong. What happened?"

"The seas have risen," he told her, "since the maps were made."

At the location where Patty's coordinates said they should land, they began their descent, slow as a soap bubble, into a mountain valley lush and green. Bear should not have been surprised, but he was, when they peered at the ground through their instruments and what appeared to be ground cover was revealed to be camo netting.

Patty could hardly stand still. She paced like a cat in the lounge, and glanced over at him with an expression that said, *See? What did I tell you?*

The "fifteen minutes to touchdown" alert sounded. Patty dropped into a seat next to Bear's. "How has it come to this?" she asked.

She meant, *Why?* She meant, his generation, and all those before them. Why had nothing been done, while there had still been time to act?

Because of men like O'Neal, he wanted to say, and the people who are afraid, and want him to tell them what to do.

There was perhaps truth in that. But it was also a lie.

We carry the past with us, he thought. *The living and the dead, and all our past choices.* No one person, no one nation, even, could have saved the planet alone. And we were incapable of working together. We were too greedy—too hungry, too afraid. Too distracted. Orla would have pointed out that there had been numerous extinctions before. *We're just clever monkeys, after all.* Smart mammals, social chimps. Just not . . . quite . . . social enough.

In the end, he just shrugged and gave her a hug.

The entire population of the blimp crowded around the hatch when the airship alighted. The door went up and light streamed in. Bear was among the last to exit. Patty helped him down the ramp but she was wound as taut as a coiled spring.

"Go!" he said grumpily. "I'm not a child." With a grateful glance, she raced ahead.

The ground was spongy and the morning air was chilly. Bear found himself wanting a jacket during daytime, for the first time in, oh, forty years.

A group of people came out of long, low buildings. Patty cried out. A man and woman who resembled her picked her up and hugged her close. They spoke together in rapid-fire Spanish. Patty sobbed. The woman cradled her and made crooning noises. Bear had never seen Patty cry till this moment.

The man came over to Bear. "Jesus de la Montaña."

"Bear Jessen." Bear shook his hand.

"You have returned our daughter to us. The *soldados* attacked and when we came back for her she was gone. We feared the worse. *Gracias. Mil gracias.* How can we ever repay you?"

"Your daughter" Bear replied, "is a remarkable young woman." He looked around. "This is Hoku Pa'a?"

"It is. Welcome. Make yourself at home."

"Is it true what Patty said? You've stored the world's knowledge?"

270 · True North

"We have tried. Much is lost. But not all. And we have ideas for how to remove carbon from the atmosphere, how to restore and rebuild. It will be the work of many lifetimes. Perhaps next time we will do a better job of caring for the world."

"And each other," Bear said.

"De verdad," Patty's father said.

Bear watched the Hoku Pa'ans welcome the travelers. They viewed the children with surprise and delight. He watched the little ones spread out across the green valley—running, skipping, shrieking— giddy with joy.

"Fee! Fi! Fo! Fum!" Jonah yelled. "I'm a giant!"

"No you're not," Angelique said. "You're a midget. Bear is the giant!" "Am too a giant!" "Are not!" "Tag, you're it!" Off they went.

Bear thought at Orla, *Oh, fine. You win. There* was *a reason. I'll carry on for the young ones' sake. But I'm still not ready to let you off the hook for dying first. Damn you.* He glared at his pop-top ring. Then he kissed it. Of course, Orla would laugh and kiss him and call him a fool.

⌣

Laura J. Mixon wrote YA novel *Astropilots;* the Avatars Dance trilogy: *Glass Houses, Proxies,* and *Burning the Ice;* and, as M. J. Locke, *Up Against It,* the first book of the Wave series. Her work has appeared in *Analog,* George R. R. Martin's shared-world Wild Cards series, and *Asimov's,* as well as anthologies *Worldmakers* and *Welcome to the Greenhouse.* An environmental engineer and information management specialist, she attended Clarion in 1981, then spent two years in the Peace Corps in Kenya. She has taught regularly at Viable Paradise, an SF and fantasy genre workshop on Martha's Vineyard. She lives in New Mexico with spouse Steven Gould and their two daughters.

⌣

Border skirmishes, food shortages, riots, and martial law probably played a part in this apocalypse, but it is nuclear bombs that actually bring the End. This story of the immediate post-bomb future concentrates on a few isolated individuals.

• HORSES •
Livia Llewellyn

Thunder
Conquest
White

. . . clouds drift overhead, faint strands against the cobalt blue of night. Missile Facilities Technician Angela Kingston presses her nose to the cool glass. Cirrostratus. They'll burn off before morning, she's sure of that. If anything, Kingston knows the rising eastern sun, knows the searing heat that coats the dead-brown scablands of Washington. In ten hours, deep orange will bleed from the horizon, as day rips itself once more from a star-studded womb.

Kingston turns away from the window. Across the room, her face floats in the mirror under a cap of dark brown hair, pixie-neat against her skull. She looks like a teenager, not a woman pushing forty. Below the mirror, a rectangle of plastic balances upright on her dresser, revealing a pink line bisecting a circle of white. The alchemical wedding of urine and litmus have combined to create the line—the closest thing to marriage she'll ever know. It's proof that two missed periods are more than the product of stress from the looming war, the constant fear that the next twin turn of the launch keys won't be a test, but—like that faint pink line—the real thing.

The watch at her wrist beeps. With absolute economy of movement, sculpted by a year-old routine, Kingston inspects the apartment. She couldn't bear to leave it for good, knowing it was a mess. In the bathroom, she slips a small plastic vial into her pants pocket, next to the stick. It contains a powerful abortive drug, military issue. In the next twenty-four hours, she'll take the pill, or a bullet. Which one it will be, she cannot say.

Outside, gravel crunches under tires—her ride to silo 7-4 is here. Kingston hoists a duffle bag over her shoulder, and grabs a photo before locking the front door behind her. It's part of her routine, so much so that she doesn't notice pausing to caress its scalloped sepia edges. The photo is of a young man in uniform, a grim-faced cavalry officer astride a large pale horse. The rider's a distant relative, whose name on the back, scribbled in fading brown ink, is "Ensley." That's all she knows of him. Why he rides, what it is he and his horse race toward, is lost.

"Keep me safe, Ensley," she mutters as she starts down the stairs. "Just one more day."

Sanders, the Deputy Crew Commander, drives Kingston's crew of four to the silo without speaking. He keeps the radio in his hummer tuned to the news station. Border skirmishes, food shortages, riots, and martial law—it's their country newscasters speak of. Public figures scramble, civilians protest and pray for a second chance at peace, but Kingston and her crew know it's too late. The only negotiations going on now are over the best hour to begin the war.

Beside Kingston, Ballistic Missile Analyst Cabrera slumps in light sleep. Up in the front next to Sanders, Major Hewitt talks into his phone—his wife calls every morning. All the men on the team are married, and they all have children. Kingston stares out the window at the flat farmlands. She thinks about the apartment, how the sun will soon shine into rooms that look like no one ever lived there. She wanted to be an astronaut when she was little. She wanted to fly to the moon, or maybe Mars. Instead, she's headed to a Titan-class missile silo, where her crew will stand on alert for twenty-four hours, waiting for the order to push a button. She's proud of what she's doing to defend her country, proud of eighteen years served. Sometimes, though, at night, she cradles a phantom weight as she slips into uneasy dreams . . .

Hewitt whispers "I love you" into the phone. Kingston closes her eyes, concentrates on the news.

Their shift passes in half-hours of systems checks and double-checks. Wing Command Post calls every hour with the same message: launch in one hour. Each hour passes with no launch. In the short calm between false alarms, Kingston stares at Sander's neck, his shoulders hunched over cold coffee and clipboards, jotting words down—a letter to his wife, his last farewell? "Useless," Kingston mutters. Sanders looks up. Kingston reaches for a report, her face like stone.

At 03:29, Kingston glances at the clock's second hand. The latest message was for 03:30 launch. Her hands press against her pants, fingering the pregnancy stick and plastic vial. They feel heavier than her sidearm. Is this continual, low-grade fear imprinting on the fetus? Maybe the lack of fear is worse, the low-grade irritation that they haven't yet released Black Beauty from her shackles. 03:29:30. Kingston wishes she had some gum, or a Lifesaver, anything to get the aftertaste of the MRI out of her mouth. Maybe she should take the capsule now. Her fetus and the missile, shooting out of the gate on the very same day. Thoughts like that don't shock her. They never did.

03:29:55. Kingston mouths the seconds down to 03:30.

Silence.

03:30:01.

"Goddamnit, here we go again," Cabrera says. His lips form the words, but Kingston can't hear his voice: the alarm is wailing. Kingston feels herself heart stop, and all emotions bleed away. Black Beauty is a go.

Kingston and Sanders scan their equipment panels while Hewitt and Cabrera verify the authenticity of the SAC message coming through. No more nerves or baby thoughts or boredom, only buttons and switches at her fingertips—she's the missile now. She always has been. Above ground, rotating beacons will be flashing red warnings as sirens howl. Hewitt is asking if they're ready to launch, and Kingston's voice gives a distant affirmative. All throughout the complex, systems shut down as they rout electricity and power to Black Beauty. Kingston licks her lips. The taste in her mouth has mutated into an unnamed desire.

By 03:41, Hewitt has verified target selection. It's one of two possibilities, neither of which has been revealed to the team. Kingston will never know where Black Beauty and her multiple warheads are headed, and she doesn't care. Trans-Pacific fallout will ensure that the winds bring it all right back to America. Sanders and Hewitt have their keys out. They break the seals off the launch commit covers. It sounds like the snapping of spines.

" . . . three, two, one, mark."

Both keys turn. The LAUNCH ENABLE light glows. They have nothing left to do but sit, and wait.

Out in the dark earth, the Titan powers up, gathering every single bit of energy into herself, readying for birth. Kingston's hands creep over her belly. The man was Nez Pierce, like her grandpa's family on her mother's side. He told her his name, but she doesn't remember it. She didn't care. His skin was dark, hot. Black beauty.

The SILO SOFT lights wink on. Above, the great doors are sliding open, spreading apart like a woman's willing legs.

FIRE IN THE ENGINE.

Lights in the control room fade. They hunch in the dark, waiting for release. The tick of the fans, the thump of her heart, the race horse rasp of her breath: she's at the starting gate, straining against metal bars. Kingston snaps open the leather casing holding her side arm. This is how it must be. They have a new type of ICBM across the ocean, a hydra-headed destroyer of nations. This whole planet is fucked. And she deserves life least of all, because she had the audacity to conceive it. That taste in her mouth: she knows what it is. She aches for the taste of the gun.

Klaxons wail out one shrill warning after another. Kingston slides her weapon out, cocks the trigger. But it remains on her thigh, pointed away. *Lift it. Lift it up, you spineless cunt.* Her whole body shakes, but she can't tell if it's nerves or the colossal springs under the cement hollow of the control center, keeping them from cracking apart. "*WE HAVE LIFTOFF,*" Hewitt shouts over the last of the klaxons, and a low, long rush of air thunders through the complex as Black Beauty's engines reach full speed: she lifts. Kingston clutches her stomach, bites her tongue. The heartbeat of some ancient god of war drills into them like jackhammers, wave after quaking wave setting their bones to ring like funeral bells . . .

. . . and now it fades: a reprieve back to silence, as Black Beauty arcs into cold skies. Panel lights wink on and off, but Kingston ignores them. Hewitt is on the phone, confirming what they already suspect: other launches, from every silo in the nation. And in two hours time, another missile will slam back into the complex, filling the void. A constellation is soaring across the ocean, right back into their arms.

"Officer. Hand over your weapon." Hewitt's voice is calm. He's staring at the drawn weapon pressed at her thigh.

"No, sir, I cannot," Kingston says. "I'm getting out." She raises her arm, moving the barrel to her head.

"Well," Cabrera says as he pulls his weapon, "good-fucking-bye to you, too."

From all directions, bullets fly. Guess they're all getting out of the silo, one way or another. Kingston turns the barrel and blindly fires out as she drops to the floor, tucking herself into the space between her console and the wall. Cabrera slams against his chair, leaving behind a black slick as he falls to the floor. Kingston sets her sights and shoots, nailing Hewitt in the chest. Blood pumps from his shirt, staining the floor around him in an uneven circle.

"Kingston, drop your weapon!" Sanders, somewhere in the dark.

Kingston checks her clip, touches her belly. Suddenly, surprisingly, she wants to stay alive. Down in the empty silo, smoke and flame is roiling—the afterbirth of the engines. They'd put it out, if it had been a test. Now they can let it burn.

Kingston stands up, weapon pointed.

"I was going to kill myself, you stupid motherfucker. You should have left me alone." From across the room, Sanders mimics her stance, even with his shot-up arm. Overhead, clocks tick away the seconds they have left.

"It doesn't have to be like this," Sanders finally speaks. "I know a place—an underground shelter. I can take you there."

Kingston keeps calm.

"A bomb shelter?"

"No, a real habitat—a place to live, not just survive."

What does he care if she lives or dies? "You're lying," Kingston says. "You need me to let you go."

"I swear on my fucking life I'm telling the truth." Sanders lowers his weapon a touch. "We've been planning it for years."

"We?"

"People—military, civilian. People who knew this was coming. My wife and son are already there." He's babbling. "It's got everything, we can live there for a year or more."

"And they'll let you bring some stranger in? An extra mouth eating your food, stealing your air?"

"Jesus Christ, Kingston, why are we arguing? We're out of time!"

Kingston looks down. Hewitt stares at the ceiling as he bleeds out. He might still be alive in two hours, when the warhead hits. He was a good commander.

Kingston puts a bullet in his head.

"Let's go," she says. Her lips taste like blood, and she licks them clean. Yeah, she's going to hell.

Damned if she'll go there alone.

Fire
War
Red

. . . footprints trail behind them as Kingston and Sanders drag several large duffel bags back through the blast doors, up smoky stairs to the surface. Together they'd stripped Hewitt and Cabrera of their weapons, then proceeded to take anything else that might be of use. Sanders insisted on taking their dog tags, with the launch keys threaded onto the chains. "We owe it to them," he said as he lowered Hewitt's tags over her head. It's a sentimental gesture, one that repels Kingston. She'll take them off later, when there's time.

The sky is black, blazing with stars. The guards have disappeared—no one stops them as they cram the bags into the already packed hummer.

"You're driving," Sanders says, holding out the keys.

"I don't know where the shelter is. Wouldn't it be easier for you to drive?"

Sanders nods at his wounds. "I can't shift, and I'll barely be able to grip the wheel. I need you to drive."

"This is why you're taking me, isn't it?"

Sanders says nothing, but she sees the affirmation in his eyes. She's dead to him. Once she drives him to safety, it won't be hard for him to finish the job.

She takes the keys.

Driving the huge machine gives her focus. She rolls down the window, letting the night air rush in as 904 slips past in a ribbon of slick blacktop. Several campers and trucks loaded with boxes and luggage barrel past her in both directions. This is military country—they know. An ancient Volkswagen camper draws up, and for a moment they race side by side down the empty stretch, each bathed in the other's lights. In the passenger seat, a woman with a tear-streaked face shoots her a baleful glare. Kingston realizes that the woman sees her uniform. The woman leans toward the glass, and lips spit out two angry words.

FUCK YOU.

Kingston presses down on the gas. She shoots ahead, away from the woman's accusing face. "We did it for you, you fucking bitch," Kingston mutters. "You paid us to."

"What?" Sanders' head lolls up. "Problem?"

"No."

"What time is it?"

"04:47. Sunrise should start around 05:15. We'll be past the town by then."

Sanders falls silent again. Kingston takes the exit, navigates the quiet streets. Small ramblers and faded Victorians sit under trees, crowned by telephone wires and stars. Everyone asleep, unaware that everything in their lives has changed, and they're alone. The town dribbles down into isolated trailers, abandoned shacks. Overhead, the sky grows light blue, with bands of pink and purple pushing up from the horizon. Cloudless, so far. Kingston keeps her eyes fixed on the low brown hills ahead.

"Time to get off the road," Sanders says. "You're going to get off to the left—there's no road, but it's drivable. Just past the bend." As Kingston steers the hummer over the blacktop and into the brush, Sanders flips the radio on. Static fills the space. Kingston waits for a recognizable sound. Nothing. Sanders flicks the radio off.

Sunrise comes early in this flat part of the world, yet on the western side the sky is still speckled with stars. Kingston steers in sweeping curves between night and day, through the rough and gaping wounds of the scablands, reminders of the glaciers and floods that once scoured the land. Every hill and shallow looks the same, but Sanders never falters in his directions. At 05:40, he leads her up one of the larger mounds, and she cuts the engine. After close to two hours of driving, the silence is shocking.

"How's the arm."

"It's fine. Get out."

Is this it? Kingston's mouth dries up as she walks to the front of the hummer.

"Where's the shelter?" She might as well ask, though she knows there won't be an answer.

"The large barrow over there." Sanders gestures southwest. In the morning haze, Kingston makes out a stretch of barrow-like hills at the horizon, dark green with scrub and brush. A couple hundred miles away, but a straight shot through flat land. Easy to get to with just one arm at the wheel.

"Which larger one? They all look the same from here."

No answer.

"We need to keep moving. Let's go." Kingston turns, but Sanders only points at the far horizon, in the direction they came from. To the north and east, dappled patterns of farmlands and towns all lay in peaceful quiet, and birds circle overhead in lazy loops. Another beautiful morning has begun.

Kingston's heart slows. She knows what he's looking for. She looks for it, too.

They wait.

The horizon erupts in brilliant white light: this is what they wanted, needed to see. Too many to count, in too many places to see—voluptuous jets of lightning-shot ziggurats unfurling past the cloud line. A metropolis of death, created in an instant. Deep, low booms wash over them, like the thunder of incoming storms. Kingston presses her hand against her chest. They're safe here. This place is too desolate to destroy.

The cloud columns keep pluming, faster and higher than any she's ever seen. "Tsars, maybe—fifty megatons, at least," Sanders speculates. "Multiple warheads. We did the right thing. They would have done it anyway."

Sanders' hand creeps down to his holster.

"We need to go," Kingston says, turning away.

She turns again.

Two shots ring out. Hawks wheel and scatter away.

Sanders' weapon hits his foot with a thud. Blood blossoms in the center of his chest. He looks at her, confused. Behind him, the distant clouds spread higher, drift apart. "Bitch." Blood drivels out of his mouth. "I would have let you go—"

Another shot rips the air, echoing over the scabby hills.

"No," she says. "You couldn't."

Grimacing, she holsters her weapon. He clipped her right thigh, a nice deep slice that'll keep her limping for weeks. There's no time for the pain, though. Not today. She puts his tags around her neck with the rest. They smell of hot metal and desperation. As she steers the hummer off the hill, Kingston doesn't look back at his body. He's dead, she tells herself. Things won't get any worse.

An hour later, when the engine sputters to a halt, Kingston remembers her words. Her cracked lips form a parody of a smile, and bits of dried blood flake down her chin and neck. Did Sanders lie about the shelter, too? She pulls everything out of the back, looking for any clue of where it might be. Not one fucking map or drawing. There's bottled water and MRIs, but the rest is weapons and medicine. And a small stuffed bear—for his kid? Kingston runs her fingers over the bear's soft head. Maybe this is proof enough. He was a cautious man, a planner. He wouldn't forget to store extra gas. Maybe she ran out when she did, because this is where she's supposed to be. It's just a hunch, and a shitty one at that, but it's all she has left to go on.

Kinston loads two duffle bags, tucking the bear next to the boxes of ammo. She takes the keys, but leaves the windows open. The winds will come, then the rains. Radiation will eat the rest.

Two hours walking puts her in a small shallow leading to the hills Sanders had pointed to—massive mounds, sitting like beached leviathans, petrified and lost to time. It's there that she sees a glint of metal halfway up the longer mound—an air intake valve, or exhaust vent. Thick clouds roll overhead, and the winds have picked up speed. Kingston stops, and fishes out a small plastic bottle of KI tablets. She swallows two with a gulp of water, then tosses the bottle back in the bag. As she zips it up, she remembers: and pats at the ripped fabric of her pants, where the bullet tore its path. Her fingers feel the pregnancy stick, wedged in what's left of the pocket, but the abortion pill is gone. No matter. There are other, older methods. No fucking way is she bringing a child into this world. Not now. Not ever.

Kingston hoists the bags up again, and limps forward, her face contorted with the weight and pain, with the heat pressing down from above. Big fucking deal, she tells herself. She's walked down this road of pain before, in other years, for lesser reasons. She can make this one. Never mind the bile burning a trail up your throat, the piss trickling down your legs, the blisters and battered bones. Never mind the dark presence riding up behind you, the whip of fear spurring you on. Take one more step, bitch. No one's going to help you. You're alone. Take another.

Take another.

Take . . .

Kingston stands, legs trembling, on the concrete lip of the bunker entrance. "What," she says, realizing she's repeating herself. Dark spots dance in her eyes, and she blinks. How much time did she lose?

"A man," an older woman says. "We were expecting a man." Her face is worn and leathery, but her eyes are bright blue—intelligent, wary. *Farmer, or rancher*, Kingston thinks. *A survivor.* Can she be like this woman? Her hand slides into her pocket, a cautious movement under the gaze of the woman and her rifle. Kingston pulls out the pregnancy stick and holds it up. Why not make that unborn bit of flesh work for her survival, just like everyone else.

"Help me," she says. "Help *us*."

The woman shakes her head. "We corresponded with a military man—"

"Sanders. He knew me."

"I don't know you from jack shit."

"But his wife and son should be here." Kingston peers past the woman—all she can see is an industrial-sized conveyor belt leading down into darkness. "Ask her, she'll know my name."

"Really."

"We were crew members at Fairchild. He died on the way here." Kingston points to the duffel bags. "His ID and papers are in there. And I brought weapons, medicine."

"We already have weapons and medicine. We weren't expecting a pregnant woman. This isn't a hospital or a spa."

Kingston bristles. "I'm a technician—a mechanic. I can work with anything you have down there—generators, water, air, electrical systems. You need me."

"She can fix things." A man behind the woman moves forward, speaking up for the first time. "We can use her."

"We don't need a baby." The woman is emphatic.

Above their heads, dark clouds roll in an unbroken wave, blotting out the sun. This is her last chance. Kingston keeps her voice devoid of emotion, even though she's swimming in despair. She thought she couldn't go lower, deeper, but she can. She always will.

"Neither do I."

The woman doesn't blink. She's harder than the ground.

"All right," Kingston says. "But you know you can't just let me walk away. Take me in or fucking shoot me. It's what I'd do."

Kingston and the woman stare at each other. Wind rattles against the entrance, rolling bits of gravel down the ramp. Particles of radiation already float around them, nestling into cells, blooming like flowers in their bones. How surprised they'll be when they reach her heart, and find it's already gone.

The man moves forward, whispers something in the woman's ear. She sniffs and pulls a frown. "Give him all your weapons," she says, "then get inside. Hurry."

Kingston disarms, handing the four weapons and both duffel bags over to a young Hispanic man. The older man pats her down. Kingston's breath catches in her throat as the man finds the photo. He steps aside, his dirt-creased fingers still caressing its worn edges. She walks into the corridor, turning to watch as they push the thick door shut. Slowly day fades, reduces to a single line of hot white light, the wind to a thin scream.

"Why's he running," the man says.

"What?"

The man holds out the photo. "What was coming after him? He's riding for his motherfucking life."

Kingston takes the photo. And she sees.

"Oh god," Kingston says over the screech of metal slamming tight, to the sun, the wind, the world. At her fingertips, the officer rides his pale horse into the unknown.

Desolation
Famine
Black

. . . bugs flutter in loops around the ceiling light. They dip and dive away, return and dance again. Kingston watches them from her cot, amazed to see proof that beyond the concrete walls and press of earth, there's still life in the world. What lies sleeping beside her is too horrible a joke to be proof enough.

As if reading her thoughts, one tiny hand uncurls and reaches out. Kingston recoils, then tucks the arm back under the blanket—an unkind gesture. The stale air is stifling hot. But Kingston can't stand to be touched. Especially by the child.

"Knock, knock." It's Ephraim, behind the curtain. There aren't any doors down here, except on cages and lockers that hold medicine, weapons, and electrical equipment. The rest is all open corridors and rooms, constructed from fifty gutted school buses that were lowered into a hole and covered with concrete. This is the shelter Sanders had spoken of with hope: half-finished, filled with faulty plumbing and wiring, and silence. Sometimes it's so quiet, Kingston hears the land shift about the ceilings. She hears the far-off boom of thunderstorms, the sifting of metal as it rusts and flakes away. She hears herself grow old.

And that thing they cut out of her womb, that creature, grows old with her.

"Come in," Kingston whispers as she sits up. Loud noises and swift movements horrify the girl, send her into fits that last for hours. Not that Kingston has the strength to yell or move quickly, nowadays. Neither of them do. They're on strict rations, semi-starvation amounts, with most of it going to the girl, at Ephraim's insistence.

Kingston watches Ephraim slip his satchel off a bone-thin frame. His hands shake more than usual as he pulls out a carton of soy milk. It's the one thing they had in abundance—cloying, vanilla soy. Despite her howling stomach, the thought of that taste in her mouth makes Kingston's gorge rise. She stopped drinking it months ago. Just as well. There's almost none left.

"Alice, Uncle Ephraim's going to stay with you for a while, while Mommy goes for a walk."

"Stop calling her that. Stop calling me 'Mommy.' "

"Sorry, I forgot. Alice, your monster is going for a walk."

"Whatever."

Their voices are flat, monotonous. Is this the first or fiftieth time they've had this fight? It doesn't matter. It always ends the same.

"And I told you, she doesn't have a name."

"She's your daughter, she's almost three. She needs a name."

"She came out of me. That doesn't make her my daughter."

"That's exactly why she's your daughter: she came out of *you*." Ephraim's voice catches. "She *is* you."

"Shit comes out of me, too."

Ephraim turns away.

Kingston watches the girl rub her eyes and yawn. Does she understand a word? Her face, as always, is a luminous cipher, her mind a mystery. She made a beautiful baby, that's for sure, her and that Nez Perce. And all fucked up inside, just like her mom.

"Something funny?" Ephraim glares at her.

"No." Kingston turns away, biting her tongue. He doesn't know she lied to him. She did give the child a name, one she's never said out loud. It's what she sees every time she looks at the child, what she wants to draw over her, a sign for the world to remove its mistake. She calls her Ex.

"Get her off the bed. I need my jacket." She doesn't like to touch Ex, if she can help it.

"Fine." Despite his diminished strength, Ephraim lifts Ex easily, handing her the teddy bear. As always, Kingston feels a momentary imbalance whenever she watches Ephraim hold Ex, as if some vital part of her has fallen away, never to be found again. She doesn't know what that feeling is, and it frightens her.

"Which areas did you check?" Kingston asks as she slips her jacket on, willing the feeling away.

"Most of the middle section. I gave up after the toilet. I just don't—"
Ephraim breaks off. He's young enough to be her son, and he's wrinkled
and aged, with sunken eyes. "I'm tired," he finishes. He sounds just like the
woman sounded, after her husband died. Whatever's eating away at them
gnaws at Ephraim more quickly than Kingston. Radiation poisoning, no
doubt, although the defective dosimeters can't confirm it. She knew they
couldn't escape it, even down here.

"We're all tired." Kingston pulls her satchel strap over her shoulders, and
a wave of dizzy nausea hits her—low grade, nothing new, she can take it.
"Take a nap. You don't look so good."

"You're no beauty queen."

"Never was." She smiles—a tight-lipped grin that hides the holes left by
those loose teeth of long ago. No matter. It's been months since she's felt
sorrow or self-pity. Years.

Ephraim sings a Spanish lullaby as Kingston limps into the corridor.
Almost immediately, a weight drops from her thin shoulders. Looking in
the girl's face is like looking in a mirror held by a cruel god. After the woman
hacked Ex out of Kingston, silent and swollen, Kingston had hobbled out
of the room without so much as a glance back, dragging placenta and
bloody strands behind her. It wasn't her fault. Four months in, she knew
it was wrong, but the man wouldn't let her abort it. He'd kept her under
close watch, him and the teenage Ephraim, who they'd found wandering
the scablands on their way to the shelter. Maybe it'd have been different, if
Sanders' wife and child had showed up. The man wouldn't have fixated on
that lump in her stomach, "our future" as he put it once. Then again, maybe
they did show up. Kingston heard knocking, once, maybe . . .

But maybe that was just a machine—in all the years they've been down
here, no one's broken through those steel doors. Now, in every hour of this
endless night, Kingston prays that someone will. Because no matter what
she's tried, she can't break out. The keys are missing, secreted away by that
old country bitch in a fit of grief after her husband died. Maybe she figured
if her man could never leave the shelter, none of them would. Whatever her
reasoning, she damned them all.

Kingston walks into the library—a few crates of books stacked next to
a moldering upholstered chair. Kingston points her flashlight at the first
crate, and pulls out a large photo album. Has she checked this before? The
pages crackle with age as she opens them. The album is old, but some of
the photos are recent—picnics and holidays, births and weddings. Kingston

sighs. Tables laden with Kodachrome-colored meals. Children, radiant and laughing in sunny rooms. Thick-furred dogs, plump cattle, glossy mares—

The album slips from her hands. Quick, before the thought races from her head like a horse slipping its reins. She lopes into the hallway, heading to the farthest end of the shelter, where the storage rooms sit. Several times she pauses, hands trembling against crumbling walls. She took a journey like this, once before. All she's ever done is race down empty highways, with no destination in sight.

In the last room, next to a half-dug exit tunnel, the man lays on a cot, dead almost two years now from the cancer that ate him down to nubs. The last time Kingston was down here, the woman's weapon had just fallen from her mouth. She'd refused food and water for days, just sat there in silence after he'd died. Kingston had left her alone, figured she'd stop mourning eventually. She couldn't. A bullet did it for her.

Kingston's fingers feel for the light switch, click it back and forth several times. The bulb must have burned out long ago. Kingston gives her flashlight several shakes to reactivate the cells. A circle of faint blue pops onto an empty chair.

"Shit." Kingston falls back against the door. "No fucking way." Steadying her hand, she points the beam over the man's desiccated body, then moves it down. The light hits a pair of withered feet.

A shaky laugh erupts from her mouth. The body slid off the chair onto the floor, that's all. No ghosts or ghouls here. Kingston pushes the chair aside, then kicks the body with her boot. It rolls back, revealing a wizened face, empty eye sockets, and a broken nose to compliment the teeth.

"I hope you're in hell." Kingston kicks the body again as she turns to the man—skeletal and crippled, with a face locked in pain. She and Ephraim had listened to his screaming for days. Oddly, the sounds hadn't upset Ex at all. She'd been the most well-behaved she'd ever been. Kingston should have recorded his death howls, to play them back for her as lullabies.

Kingston pats him down. "Please let it be here," she says, as she pushes his body over and rips the stiff fabric from his flesh. The old photo of her relative—Kingston had hidden it away in her room, but it vanished not long after. She told herself he'd stolen it, an easy lie to live with. Easier than thinking she'd lost the one thing that meant more to her than anything else in the world.

"No." It wasn't anywhere on him. And this was the only place she hadn't searched. Kingston sits on the edge of the bed, her shoulders slumping as she runs the light over the woman. She stares at the weapon. The woman's finger still laces through the trigger—one brown digit has separated from the hand, pointing to the woman's head like a twiggy arrow. Kingston reaches down, and the flashlight catches the glint of the barrel, a silver filling, and—

No, not a filling. A beaded chain—two, created for one purpose: to hold something.

Like keys.

"You swallowed them. You shot them into yourself."

Kingston tugs at the chains. They run deep into her head, where the bullet rammed them. She hears the faint clink of metal, and a strange rasp—she'd swear the woman was choking even now. Well, fuck her. Kingston pulls, hard. The woman's head lifts, and inside, cartilage and tendons crack. It sounds like the saltwater taffy pulls her mother used to buy for her at the fair, the ones that broke in sharp pieces if you whacked them just the right way. Kingston lets go of the chains. All that hot metal and blood and brains have fused into a single stubborn mass.

Not a problem.

Kingston brings her boot down, hard. A satisfying crunch fills the room as bones and tissue grind beneath her heel. "Someone walking on your grave, bitch?" She raises her foot, and stomps on the head again. A loud *crack*: the entire jaw breaks off, and the rest of the face caves inward. Kingston smiles.

Her boot comes down again. The head is pulp now, a sticky-dry mash of brain and bone slivers. The woman's hair lies on the floor like silver-threaded silk, beaded with ivory teeth. Kingston admires it as she reaches down.

This time, the chains lift freely, clusters of keys swinging from looped ends. Most will open electrical lockers, weapon and drug caches—keys Ephraim and Kingston already have duplicates of. But six of them should unlock the entrance door. Kingston runs a ragged fingertip over serrated edges. She thinks of the town she and Sanders drove through, the sleepy houses and the soft sound of leaves rustling in the cool night air.

Maybe it's not too late.

Kingston's halfway back to her room when she stops. Flakes of concrete crinkle onto her face as she listens. At the end of the hall, Ephraim sits behind the curtain, holding that thing she birthed. She hear snatches of words and phrases, and an occasional squeal or grunt as Ex replies as best she can.

Kingston's fingers steal up to the tangle of dog tags and launch keys resting between her flat breasts. They've rubbed the skin down to red cuts and rashes, thumping at her chest every time she breathes or moves. A vision of the girl as she might have been hovers next to them, staining her soul. She's always there, inescapable.

Unless . . .

Before she has a chance to ask herself *could I?* her feet are backtracking away from Ephraim, away from—Away. Kingston glides in quiet steps past the decontamination rooms, past a reception area that's never received anything other than dust, and up the conveyer belt ramp to the thick metal door. After so many years, this is it. She's free.

The locks are dusty, but undamaged. Kingston picks out the cleanest key, trying to work it into the lower lock. It doesn't fit the first keyhole, or any of the others. She moves to the next key, slightly bent but intact. It fits the fourth lock. Kingston turns the key and the sound of the tumblers clicking fills her with such joy that she almost passes out. One down, five to go.

And then the rest of the keys, and then—

She doesn't know how long she's been leaning against the door, sweat dribbling into her boots. She only knows that at some point, the only keys left are the mangled lumps of metal that the bullet destroyed. If she could rip the bones from the woman's body and whittle them into the two missing keys she needs—but, it's no use. They're here now till they die, and long after.

Kingston she slides to the floor. The thought of walking back into that maze, back to that child, of spending her final days trapped in the earth—she can't do it. Kingston wraps the chains tight around her fingers until they turn blue. She stares at them, blinking hard.

"Two door keys on each chain. Two chains."

She pauses, the headache dissolving.

"There should be three chains, each with two keys. One for the man. One for the woman. And—" Kingston stands.

"And one."

Decay
Death
Pale

. . . skin floats up through the dark, as if a swimmer is breaking the surface of the ocean. Kingston tightens her grip on her weapon. Hold onto that, she thinks, don't go away again. There's nothing for her in that mindless black.

Ephraim stands before her, stripped bare, skeletal. Black and purple bruises smudge his decaying skin. He's at the end.

"Satisfied?" Tears trickle down his face, but his voice is calm. At his feet, Ex clings to her bear. "I told you, the keys aren't on me. Or in me."

"But you have them."

"I had them."

"If you had them, what the fuck where you pretending to look for all this time?"

"It doesn't matter. There's nothing for us out there."

"That's not the point."

"Then what is the point? All we'll do out there is die."

"But we'll die *outside*, under the sky—we'll be free!"

"We stopped being free the day a bunch of assholes in uniform dropped the bomb."

Kingston's finger jumps against the trigger.

"Fine. You and that—" she points to Ex "—can stay here as long as you like. Give me the keys."

A peaceful look steals over Ephraim's face, giving him an almost sculptural beauty. He's preparing himself. She can tell.

"No."

"You tell me where those motherfucking keys are or I'll kill you, you fucking fag piece of shit!"

The girl begins crying, howls that make Kingston cringe. Something hot and hard burns in Kingston. Columns of smoke and flame, pluming up—

"No."

"Tell me!"

"No."

It's like he's already gone, and she's still stuck inside the rotting cunt of the world. Kingston points the weapon up, and fires. Sparks shower over them like fireworks. Ex convulses against Ephraim's leg.

"*TELL ME!*"

Silence, then:

"All right."

Kingston feels a cold finger press against her soul.

"I'll tell you on one condition." Ephraim touches Ex's head.

"Give your daughter a name."

Kingston opens her mouth.

"Give your daughter a name, and I'll give you the keys."

Nothing comes out.

"You won't," Ephraim says. "But you don't need them anyway. You're already dead, Angela. You've always been dead."

Ephraim leans in, smiling.

"*Pale rider.*"

Kingston slams the weapon handle into Ephraim's head, and he hits the floor with a wet crack. A crimson crown surrounds his head, expanding like the corona of the summer sun. Kingston drops onto his chest, crouched like an animal. His eyes are open, but she knows what they see are not in this room or world.

"Where are the keys? Where are they, you bastard!" She slaps his face, but only the faint traces of a last breath slip from his lips, then nothing more. He's gone.

"Get up, you son of a bitch. Get up, don't leave me here alone!" Ex begins to cry again, and Kingston whips around. "Shut up, just shut the fuck up and let me think for one goddamn second!"

The girl's mouth opens wider. That noise, that fucking noise—

Kingston grabs Ex hard, fingers clenching down on flesh and bone. "SHUT UP YOU FUCKING PIECE OF SHIT I NEVER WANTED YOU I NEVER WANTED YOU—"

Ex's eyes roll back, body going hard. Her face is a bright cherry of broken blood vessels and puffed flesh. And she doesn't stop howling—

Kingston screams. Again and again, colossal screams lurch out of her like the limbs of some primeval monster unfurling from the dead void inside. She sits before Ex, hands reaching out, grasping for something incomprehensible, something beyond the sorrow, beyond the pain. Ex raises her hands as she rages in reply, but Kingston's fingers stretch past her, only holding empty air like reins.

But this fire can't rage forever, can't feed itself. Kingston feels it wilting, falling away. She can't say what is happening—she's never had the words for things like this. She's always avoided things like this. Ex chokes, gasping. Half-fallen against Ephraim's body, glossy ringlets of black hair soaked with sweat, her head barely rises from his gray flesh. Kingston stares, the sounds fading in her throat. In Ex's sorrowful face, she sees the faint memory of summer, the sounds of leafy night sifting through the screens. Her mother smelled like fresh bread, and it lingered on Kingston's skin long after she'd left the room. Kingston would drift to sleep with her nose in her palms, safe in the dark. The feeling was in that smell.

Exhausted. She can't go on like this anymore. Kingston wraps her hands around the girl's trembling body and pulls her close. The girl's shit herself, it runs down her legs in stinking clumps. Kingston ignores it. Still howling, almost singing the sobs in one mournful note, Ex shivers, but doesn't draw away. Kingston buries her face in Ex's wet hair, breathing deep. Sweat, shit and soy, traces of hard soap and metallic water, and—

And.

Tears gush from Kingston's swollen eyes: it's there, soft and delicate, the scent that tells her that, no matter how hard she denies it, how far she tries to run, this child has always been, will always be, her daughter.

"Ensley," Kingston whispers into her hair, letting the word wash over the girl.

"Your name is Ensley."

Kingston sits in the shower stall, stripping her daughter's clothes off her tiny body. When she pulls the shift over her head, revealing a braided yarn necklace holding a soft felt pouch, Kingston doesn't need to open it to know what's inside. If she'd held her daughter just once all these years, she would have known. Ephraim's final gift, perhaps, his faith that she would do one right thing, someday. Kingston runs bits of yellow soap over Ensley's limbs, careful not to get it in her eyes. Ensley sleeps most of the time, but sometimes her eyes flutter open, and she stares into Kingston's face with a look of dazed wonder. Each time, Kingston steels herself, waits for Ensley to realize that she isn't Ephraim, to recoil in fear from the monster. Instead, she only curls back into her mother's arms, as if she'd been doing this all her short life.

Long after the last of the water runs out, Kingston sits in the stall, listening to the slow beat of her daughter's heart. They can't go on like this. She can't go on. There's no place for them, below or above. Even after all that's happened in this small pocket of time, she'll never be a good mother. A monster cannot change what she was born to be.

It is too late, after all.

Kingston carries Ensley back to the room. She leaves the two keys behind. Ephraim's body lies under a blanket—he'd want to stay close to them, right up to the end. She dresses Ensley in a T-shirt for a nightgown, smoothing it past her naked rear. Diaper—she's never put one on a child in her entire life. How did Ephraim do it? Where did he get them? It doesn't matter. In a few hours, nothing will.

The lock to the medicine room is broken, and there's not much left inside. Kingston inspects each bottle label, searching for the right combination to toss in the box she cradles, empty except for a carton of vanilla soy. She thinks about the pill that Sanders shot away, as the skies erupted around them. She should have dropped to her knees, scoured the earth for it. Well, she'll make do. It's the most compassionate she can be for the both of them. Then again, if it doesn't work—she stops in the weapons room on the way back to reload her side arm. She can be both quick and dead, if she has to.

As she places the side arm back in its holster, a thin screech rolls down the corridor like a sigh, followed by a massive crash—metal being bent and torn apart. Every hair on the back of Kingston's neck prickles. She pulls out her weapon, and takes another from the cabinet. Maybe it's a machine breaking down, the generators are long past falling apart. She glides down the hallway, knowing it's not that at all.

At the junction where the conveyor belts lead to the loading ramp, Kingston stops. Goosebumps erupt on her arms. She takes a deep breath.

Night air.

The door is open.

Kingston creeps up the hall, hugging the conveyor belt as she rounds the corner, raises her weapon and fires a warning shot into the florescent tube overhead. Ahead, several figures halt in the doorway, their silhouettes outlined by the cobalt of an early morning sky.

The sky.

"Hey!" A man's voice calls out. "We're unarmed, don't shoot!"

Kingston points her weapons out, starts up the ramp. "I *am* armed, so don't move—one step closer and you're dead."

"Sure, fine—we just—"

"Who are you and what do you want?"

One of the men drops a massive pry bar to the ground with a clang as he steps forward. She sees a hard, thin face, desperate eyes. Is that what she looks like to him?

"We've been traveling; we need a place to stay. We didn't think anyone lived here."

"The door was bolted and locked."

"We didn't see any signs of life. Listen, we just need shelter, a little food and water." He points at the men behind him. All men, no women. "Hard times, right?"

"There's nothing here. You have to leave."

The man takes another step down the ramp, his hands raised as if in peace. He smiles, a yellow-fanged Stonehenge rising up from scablands of skin. "Well, maybe we can just rest a while, away from the sun. Gonna be another scorcher today."

Kingston doesn't move. "Look at me," she snarls, "does it look like I have anything? Come back in a week when I'm dead."

His smile fades. "Put down the guns, honey. Ten of us, one of you. No need to die. Not just yet, that is."

Overhead, stars wink. She sees them now, clear and high, calling to her like beacons in a storm.

"Is it—how is it, out there?" She has to ask. "Did we win? The radiation, did it kill everything? Is this still America?"

Silence: and then, something she hasn't heard in years. Laughter. Loud mocking laughter as the men repeat her questions, *jesus christ did we win is this still America*, wiping tears from their eyes. As they bend over in hysterics, Kingston spies someone at the far end of the loading ramp, a small figure in rags peering down at her in the gloom. A girl. She fingers a large chain running between small breasts, attached to a thick collar at her neck. Kingston starts, and the girl does the same, eyes widening under shanks of greasy hair before slinking away from the ramp.

Two weapons, twenty-nine bullets—against ten men, all of them armed. She's weak, she's tired. But she's angry. And she was always the best.

"Keep sleeping, Ensley," she whispers, as she opens fire. "I won't leave you alo—"

She doesn't know how many she kills: the first bullet back gets her right in the gut, and two more clip her as she slams against the wall and crashes onto the ground. The weapons fall from her hands, spinning down the ramp.

And, so, that's it. This is the end.

It's so banal.

The men say nothing as they walk down the ramp, dragging their dead as they pass. Kingston lays with her legs pointing to the surface, and her head in the dark, neither outside in the world or within it. A herd of scuffed boots pushes past, and then three pairs of brown, delicate feet shuffle after the men. They're heavily chained and scarred, stained with dried shit and blood.

Tears bead down her face. They'll find Ensley. The things they'll do to her, and she won't understand. Or worse, she will, and she'll never have the words for her pain.

For the first time in her life, Kingston truly weeps.

⌐

. . . sun beats down on her face, searing her pale skin. Noon. Kingston gasps, forces a swollen tongue over lips split and bleeding. The shots to her arms, they're painful, but nothing compared to the one in her stomach. Slow death, those gut shots. Yeah, like she deserved better. Always quick to kill and walk away. It felt good. It was clean. But shouldn't she have called her sister to say goodbye? Her name . . . Kingston cries again, a feeble whine. She can't remember her sister's name . . .

. . . found her, they found her, and the men so large and rough, so desperate, and Ensley the angel of the underground, all soft black curls and pale skin. She's screaming. Kingston tries to rise, and can't. Her right hand presses against her stomach, as more blood and bile dribbles out. Pages and papers, little notes roll up the ramp, float away. They're trashing everything. Laughter, deep voices, footsteps, all fading. Ensley's screams sink into the pitch-black void, where Kingston cannot follow. Only her blood makes the effort, snaking in thin streams down the ramp, reaching out one last time before succumbing, before giving in . . .

. . . shadows flicker against the walls. The sun is setting. Kingston drifts, each dip into the dark a bit longer than before. Somewhere deep, wherever her daughter now lies, wind whistles through thin cracks, and the mournful song filters back through the tunnels. Kingston's heart thumps painfully as little threads of electricity fire in her head before winking out forever: evergreens tossing in blue skies and high winds over a little yellow house, a woman in a flowered dress throwing a red plastic ball up up up, the scent of cut grass and daffodils. A summer scene from her childhood? Her mother? Or maybe a dream of what might have been, in a peaceful world. No matter. There will never be a summer like that again . . .

. . . and now there is only wind, the rattle of gravel down the ramp, the flapping edge of a photo as the currents dance it closer to her. Fear bolts through Kingston, and her body jerks. Blood spurts from her lips, and some hidden warhead of pain finally explodes as she grasps the scalloped edges. She sees, oh god she sees . . .

. . . it's the image of a young man, a pale-faced rider astride on a paler horse, lunging into a future yet unknown. Kingston sees that future now. It's behind the photo, the gaping maw of darkness that creeps closer as the sun gallops across the sky. Galloping like the rider, galloping like the arrhythmic apocalypse traveling through her bones, throwing her body into painful curves, her mouth snarling open in a soundless cry. Her fingers spasm, and the photo flies up and away, the pale rider thunders into the dark . . .

. . . and she is the pale rider, grasping the neck of the lunging beast as they begin the final ride through eternal night.

And for one sliver of a moment, Kingston remembers a name that rends her soul. There is someone she must look for here in this wasteland, someone she must find. But the horse does not slow, and the night does not end, and her memories sink into the land with the western sun. There is no one else beside her, behind her or ahead. Five billion people, five billion pale thundering horses, all looking for lovers, daughters, sons. All of them, each of them, alone . . .

There is only Kingston.

There is only the pale rider, hurtling into the void.

There is only the void.

Livia Llewellyn is a writer of horror, dark fantasy, and erotica. A graduate of Clarion 2006, her fiction has appeared in *ChiZine, Subterranean, Sybil's Garage, PseudoPod, Apex, Postscripts, Nightmare*, and numerous anthologies. Her first collection, *Engines of Desire: Tales of Love & Other Horrors*, was published in 2011 by Lethe Press. It received a nomination for the Shirley Jackson Award for Best Collection, and "Omphalos" received a Best Novelette nomination. She's currently working on a series of novellas for her next collection. You can find her online at liviallewellyn.com.

Among this band of six inadvertent survivors of an End that may or may not have happened—although chances are it has—three cling to the belief they are just part of a television reality show and the world outside is fine, one is mad, one doesn't buy the prevalent theory, and one doesn't really have an opinion.

• THE CECILIA PARADOX •
John Mantooth

We've been underground for one hundred ninety-three days when Henry sends his only begotten son, Ralph, to save us.

Ralph's like eighteen and wears two big, diamond studs in each ear. He's got a beard and long Jesus hair. His breath reeks of tuna fish, and don't let him touch you because his hands smell like they've been places hands are not necessarily meant to go. Once, when I made the mistake of giving him a high five after my team won the New World Relay Race for a Better Tomorrow, my hand smelled like ass for hours.

There are only six of us. Survivors, that is. Or dumbasses. Sometimes it's hard to tell the difference. In order of how much I like them, they are:

Cecilia

Theresa

Frank

Theo

Marjorie.

I hate Marjorie.

All of us signed up for some government survey. It paid one thousand dollars, which is pretty good money, or was pretty good money. Now money is something you wipe your ass with when Dominic forgets to refill the toilet paper dispenser. Oh yeah, Dominic's the custodian/muscle down here.

So Ralph trots around all day, speaking in parables and turning water into wine—"You have to use your imagination!" he says when Theresa points out it still looks like water after he's muttered some mumbo jumbo over it—and raising little roaches from the dead. The roach thing is almost cool. After touching them with some holy water, he slides them across the concrete floor, and it's almost as if they scurry, but their legs aren't moving.

"So when's the big man going to show?" Frank wants to know. I like Frank all right, but he's a man, so I have to rate Cecilia and Theresa in front of him. Frank is the vocal leader of a group who believes this is all fake and we're on a reality show.

"But how can it be a reality show if it's all fake?" I ask.

"Exactly," he says. "One day one of us is going out that door and when we do, we'll see that everybody in the real world has got their damned TV's tuned to channel 3, laughing their asses off."

The others either pretty much agree with him (Theo, Theresa, and Marjorie) or pretty much think the whole concept is bogus (me). Cecilia doesn't really have an opinion.

She just likes to sleep around.

I love Cecilia.

So what do you do when you go to an underground room that smells like an abandoned whorehouse/methlab and a screen comes down showing you footage of your family dying from some airborne disease? What do you do when the screen switches and shows people all over the place dying the same way? What do you do when it looks real? More real than any of the movies? What do you do when a disembodied voice named Henry—who tells you right up front you should call him God—announces the old world is over and the new one has just begun? What do you do when he tells you, anyone may leave at anytime, the door is unlocked, but by doing so, you will be sacrificing his free gift of salvation and you will choke to death like the rest of the world he has chosen to forsake? What then?

Long answer: you agonize about the door, the world outside, the family that may or may not be dead, depending on how much technology this asshole has. You debate the merits of worshipping Henry (he is after all the man in charge) versus raging against him, and end up with a passive-aggressive stance, much like how a surly seventh grader would treat his pre-algebra teacher. You try to hook up with the girls. You fail. You meet Cecilia. You screw her twice before you find out she did Dominic four times and Theo (he's missing an arm) once. You fall into an emotional abyss, driven to the depths by grief and guilt. Cecilia comes by and makes you feel better with a blowjob. You love Cecilia and think how you and she will run away through that door together someday and whatever is there—good, bad, ugly—you'll find it together.

Short answer: nothing.

Originally there were eight of us. Sharon died when Henry showed her the footage of her son gagging on a pocket of bad air. His eyes popped out of his head and landed in his cereal. Sharon must have had a heart attack or something because she screamed once, swooned to the floor and died.

Then there was Freddie. Freddie's like the antichrist around here. We all worship him, but Henry tells us he's a false god and following him will lead to destruction and pain and our eyes popping out from all the bad air up there.

On the third day, Freddie rose from his tomb, amen. He asked me if I wanted to go with him. I told him I'd think about it. He promised to come back for us.

One-hundred-ninety days later and no Freddie.

Marjorie asks me if I'm going to the Crucifixion later this evening.

"You're kidding, right?"

"No, Adam. Henry's serious about this. I think this may be the season climax."

"There's no one watching, Marjorie."

She twists her long black hair and looks at me with those stupid, pouty eyes. Getting caught down here is probably the greatest thing that ever happened to her.

"Then leave," she says.

"That doesn't make sense," I say. "If I think there is no TV show, it means I think there really was an airborne disease that killed everybody else in the world except us. It means I believe Henry is some kind of God or at least history's greatest scientist."

"Believe what you want. I don't care. Like I said, you should just leave if you're going to be so miserable. Go be like that idiot Freddie. I'll bet everybody's laughing at him right now."

"Bitch."

"Stupid fuck."

I snarl, about to say something else nasty when the fire alarm goes off.

Fire alarm?

Henry's voice booms over the loudspeaker: "This is not a drill. Report to the north exit immediately."

I look at Marjorie. She shrugs. "Maybe it's a ratings sweep."

We gather at the north exit, near the same brown door Freddie left by, months ago. Dominic hands out gas masks. I have to go to the bathroom.

"Hold it," Dominic says.

I smell smoke. We line up. Frank's behind me, saying he heard Ralph went nuts when Henry told him he was really going to crucify him and started a fire in the rec area.

"Henry told him he was really going to crucify him?"

Frank laughs. "Yeah. Henry is fucked up in the head. He really thinks he's God."

"And you really think this is a TV show?"

"No fucking question."

Dominic reaches for the door, resting his hand on the silver handle. "Get your masks on, you two," he says, gesturing at me and Frank. He pulls his own mask over his nose and mouth, adjusting the valve.

"I want to see Henry," I say.

"Not possible," Dominic says.

"He's staying inside, then? With the fire?"

"He's the big man," Dominic says. "He calls the shots. Not you."

And that's that. I slide on my gas mask, Dominic opens the door. We shuffle out into the outside world. First time in one hundred ninety-three days.

They blindfolded us when they brought us to the survey. Top-secret government bullshit. Just give me my check. I didn't care. Blindfold? Sure. You still paying me one thousand dollars at the end?

I've got a new perspective now. Like a man might have after being in prison for a long time. What's money? Shit. Money's just paper or plastic. I want the air, the solid ground beneath my feet. I want the sun. These are the things that are real.

We're behind a pockmarked brick building with no windows in a little alley. It's dark out. I look up and see not a star in the sky, which would make sense considering all the bad air. Or it could just be cloud cover. The agony of not knowing is the worst.

Dominic looks like one of those guys you see in movies about World War I, holed up in his trench, waiting for the gas, waiting for the end.

"Face the building," he says.

"Eyes in front of you," he says.

"Keep those masks on. Stay together," he says.

"This is all a big fucking joke," he says. "But not, I repeat, not a reality show."

Okay, he doesn't really say those last two parts.

I'm trying to look around for something, anything that suggests people are still alive in the world. One good sign: I don't see Freddie's dead body anywhere. If he'd come out this door—which he did—his body would be somewhere over there by the end of the building. Hey, there is something over there. I crane my neck a little more for a better look and then WHAM. A big hand slaps the side of my face.

"Eyes in front. Face the building," Dominic says.

But what was that thing I saw?

The rumors are true. Ralph started the fire when he used one of his cigarettes to light a roll of toilet paper in the john. Funny thing is, he was taking a dump at the time, the dumbass, and after the toilet paper burned down to nothing, he couldn't even wipe.

This is our Messiah.

Henry announces it is time for the Crucifixion. We gather in the rec room wide-eyed and eager for some entertainment. Dominic stands, arms crossed by the double doors that lead into Henry's lair, aka Heaven, aka the promised land, aka some dumpy office with black construction paper shrouding the windows so none of us can see in.

"I Walk the Line" by Johnny Cash comes on over the loudspeaker. Henry is a devout old-time country fan. We get treated to all the old timers: Hank Williams, Patsy Cline, Marty Robbins, and Willie Nelson before he discovered pot.

The volume is louder than usual, and we can tell Henry is trying to MAKE A STATEMENT. The doors next to Dominic fly open and Ralph comes out, dragging his cross on his back. He's wearing a pair of gym shorts but otherwise naked. Dark red lashes run the length of his thin frame, and this almost startles me a little.

"So he really lashed him," Frank mutters. "I wonder how much they're paying Ralph to do this." He whistles. "You think Henry spanked Ralph as a kid?"

There are so many responses I have for this question that my mind goes swimmy and I can't say any of them, so I simply shrug and watch Ralph drag what looks like a cardboard cross.

"You'd think with all the CGI effects they used on the videos of our loved ones dying, they'd be able to afford more than a cardboard cross," Marjorie says. "Very disappointing."

Johnny Cash reminds us it's because "you're mine" that he walks the line, and Marjorie shoves me out of the way when Ralph passes by. Dominic is behind him. Marjorie believes the TV camera is hidden somewhere on Dominic's massive body.

I drift to the back of our little group, where Cecilia puffs on a cigarette. She smiles at me. She looks hot. She's got on my favourite gray mini and the red sweater that makes her breasts kind of perky and pendulous at the same time. Her hair is pulled back and her forehead shines with a sheen of sweat.

"Hey," I say.

"Hey," she says, and it's a hey with possibilities in the tone, a hey that suggests another blowjob could be in the cards as long as I play mine right.

"You know," I say, "this Jesus stuff just isn't the same when his hands smell like ass."

"Fully God, fully man," Cecilia says cryptically. That's the other thing about Cecilia, the thing you forget about her because she's hot and capable of mind-altering blow-jobs: she's really kind of smart. Maybe too smart to be here with the rest of us doofuses. Maybe Freddie smart.

"So what's that mean?"

She shrugs as Ralph climbs onto a stage Dominic constructed last week and lays his cross down on a chair. He looks dazed.

"Drugged," Frank says. He's in front of me and Cecilia. "He's been drugged."

"Fully God, fully man. It's Biblical," Cecilia says. "The Bible says Jesus was a paradox. Fully God and fully man at the same time."

Dominic is nailing the cardboard cross to the wall. Ralph watches him, red-eyed and stoned.

Cecilia takes my hand. "I don't want to see this," she whispers.

"Nah," I say. "Crucifixions bore me."

We head to our spot, the third stall in the men's restroom. It's one of those handicap deals, so there's extra room and a bar for Cecilia to hang on to when I'm doing her from behind.

She locks the door and gets right to work, unbuttoning my pants and breathing all heavy.

When it's over, we both lay on the floor, exhausted.

Cecilia speaks first. "I really hate myself sometimes."

"Me too," I say, not catching the edge of seriousness in her voice, well at least not at first, not until it is too late.

Luckily she ignores me. "This sex stuff. It's an addiction, you know."

This time, I stay quiet and wait for more. She's quiet too. Finally, she sits up and pulls her sweater back on, sans bra which is still laying where I dropped it, on the back of the toilet. "He's probably dead by now, you know."

"Who?"

"Ralph. The Son of Man. Whatever you want to call him. He's probably already bled to death on the cross for nobody's sins but Henry's."

"Do you think Henry really killed him?"

She moves to the toilet where she sits to pee. "I know he really killed him. He's been talking about it for weeks."

"You talk to Henry?"

She tears some toilet paper off the roll and smirks. "Do you really think Henry's God, Adam? Of course, I talk to him. He's a man. You're a man. Think about it. As a man, would you not talk to me?"

I start to form an answer, but my mind is moving too slowly, trying to put it together. Cecilia and Henry. Henry and Cecilia.

She keeps talking instead of waiting for me to answer: "And me? I'm a sex addict. That's why I don't mind this place so much. All these men, young and old. No wives to get in the way." She pouts and pulls her panties and miniskirt up. "I hate myself."

"Why?"

She frowns, her brown eyes going serious and sad. "You're just like the rest of them. You only want me for the sex. You don't even listen to me when I talk."

"No, Cecilia." I stand up, amazed a little by the intensity in my voice. It must catch Cecilia off guard as well, because she tilts her head to the side as if seeing me new for the first time.

"I do care about you. I want out of this place. Am I the only one who wants out? Do you want out?"

"I don't know what I want. I thought I wanted to have sex anytime I wanted it, with any man I wanted. I've got that now, sort of. You, Henry, Dominic, Theo. Frank."

"Frank? He's like seventy."

"I don't discriminate. Besides, he's a freak of nature."

"Come again?"

"Never mind."

I don't get mad. Not exactly. Just frustrated. Disappointed. Here I am thinking this girl likes me, but all she's concerned about is finding the next dick.

"I knew you'd get mad," she says. "If it makes you feel any better, I hate myself for being this way. I really do. And another thing. What we just did. Just a minute ago. It was special. More than just my addiction. I like you, Adam."

This is maddening. Maddening because I want to hate her but when she says something like this I can't hate her. In fact, I think I love her.

"You know what," I say, my voice rising. "You're a paradox. Fully slut and fully . . ." I hesitate, not knowing how to end it. From the look on her face, she is not hurt by the *fully slut* remark, so I reach for something else, some extreme that will satisfy both ends of her paradox, and settle on " . . . Fully slut and fully angel." It comes out silly sounding and sentimental, but she doesn't seem to mind. She softens, brown eyes doing this little flash before going all sweet.

She comes over and hugs me. "That's the nicest thing anybody ever said to me, Adam." She holds me, not letting go and there is no sex vibe in this embrace, a first in all my encounters with Cecilia. She whispers in my ear. "You're different."

I whisper back, "I saw something outside. The day of the fire. I think it might have been a body."

They've killed him. Nailed him to the wall. He's still hanging there now. I would worry more about who is going to be next, but I think Henry has made his point. Today at lunch, he called for mandatory prayer time. Communing with Him, he said. We were supposed to lay prone on the floor and repeat some stupid mantra. I refused. Everybody else went down, the bloody spectre of Ralph hanging over them like a reminder that we may not serve God, but we serve Henry, and Henry is a vengeful, well, Henry.

Dominic comes over and grabs me by the scruff of my neck, nearly lifting me out of my seat at the table. I didn't even know I had a scruff on my neck, but Dominic obviously does.

"Get down like the rest," He shoves me hard to the ground, but instead of lying prone like the others, I bounce back to my feet.

"Leave him, Dominic," Henry's deep voice intones. "I would like to see him in my celestial office."

"Sure thing," Dominic says, cracking a big grin that suggests he knows what is about to happen to me and he finds it immensely pleasing.

Me? I'm scared shitless. I'm going to meet the only God I've ever known, and he's a loser named Henry who gets his kicks watching us squirm.

On the way back to that dark cubicle that is his celestial office, three thoughts run through my mind. The door to the outside, unlocked, beckoning is one of them. This is followed by a memory, just a flash, from the other day when Dominic had been shouting at us, telling us to face the building and I'd seen something by the corner of the building . . . what had it been? I try hard to pull a picture up, to rewind to that fleeting glimpse, but I can't. It was too fast. All I can remember is the sensation, the sudden gripping of my insides, a dizzy feeling in my head that whatever it was had mattered.

The third thought that enters my head on the way to Henry's idea of heaven is unrelated to the other two. Or . . . maybe it isn't. I can't tell. It is the realization that once again, Cecilia had not been among us.

Surprisingly, the door is unlocked. I walk right in. The room is bare except for a desk with a chair behind it and two chairs in front. The only other item of note is a long black curtain covering the back wall. Cecilia sits in one of the chairs, her legs crossed beneath her pink mini skirt, her hands folded in her lap. Despite this posture, her face tells a different story. Flushed cheeks, damp brow, languid eyes; she's been fucking Henry again. She looks at me and smiles and starts to speak, maybe to say sorry, maybe something else, when a voice comes from behind a curtain.

"Please sit, Adam."

I laugh, resisting the sudden urge to rush the curtain, peel back the veil and throttle Henry.

"Would you like to share your laughter with me, Adam?"

"Not particularly." I take the seat next to Cecilia and try to look relaxed. Now that I'm here, I can't decide if I'm afraid or simply amused.

"My son," Henry begins, and the curtain billows a little. I wonder if he's puffing it out for effect. "My son died on the cross for all of you, yesterday. I saved you from the Apocalypse. I fed you." His voice trembles with emotion. "I love you. Yet. Yet, you both dishonor me. You both choose to rut in the bathroom instead of witness the greatest event in the new history of your lives. Not that there is anything inherently wrong with rutting in the bathroom. That is one of the things I would like you to understand about the new history. The old God? He was a God of rules and of sin. That's not me. I actually encourage rutting. I need you folks to make babies if this new world is to survive. What I do demand is respect and fear. I demand you kneel when it is time to kneel. Or, if you don't like it, damnation, the new damnation awaits, ironically, above us now." The curtains shift, and I can almost picture a little bald man back there chuckling and scratching his ass. Anger boils inside me. I start out of my chair, but Cecilia puts her hand on my arm and I sit back down.

"Adam, my beloved, Adam," Henry says. "The door is unlocked. Please, if you would like to join Freddie in eternal damnation, go."

Cecilia's hand tightens on my arm.

"Well?" Henry says. "What will you do?"

Long answer: I see myself get up, go into the room where the rest of the idiots are still prone on the floor worshiping a man who doesn't have the courage to show his face. I tell them this is hell and I hope they're happy in it. I shout, "I hope you enjoy your reality show!" and dash for the steps, taking them two at a fucking time as I head up to the brown door. I wait, just an instant, just long enough to breathe a good gulp of air, long enough to feel it pour into my lungs. Long enough to know I've made the right decision, win, lose, or die. Then I turn the handle and step into a world without precedent, a world where it could all be true or a world where it could all be false. And I am not afraid.

Short answer: My imagination has balls, but I don't.

After we are dismissed, Cecilia and I go back to the others and assume the posture. My rebelliousness is gone, replaced by an apathy so profound I'm not sure I care about anything anymore. If the real God, the one who unfortunately has been as inscrutable as Henry in my own life, deems this to be my fate, then so be it.

The floor smells like sweat and piss and mildew, and I wonder if it has been cleaned since Ralph used to slide those half-smashed roaches across it. I try to think if I've ever seen Dominic with a mop before, and before I know it, I am asleep.

The dream is a simple one. Me, above ground, on a windswept piece of brown earth. There is nothing. Nothing at all around me except the same dull brown earth, hard packed and unforgiving.

The world is gone or appears to be. I'm left alone to wander this bleak landscape. But then I see it out of the corner of my left eye, a fleck of contrast, almost blinding in the drabness. I whirl and see a human body. It lays in the unnatural posture of death. I go over to it and am not surprised to see Cecilia, her face serene except for the deep cavities where her eyeballs used to belong.

I touch her skin, noting the smoothness, the soft texture, like velvet. I touch a strand of hair, moving it over one of the brooding caverns.

I sit beside her body for a very long time.

"We need to go now."

The wind keeps blowing. It's something. Better than nothing. And the body. Something about her body doesn't make sense. It's on the tip of my tongue.

"Now, Adam. We have to go, now."

Her skin is so new. The eyeballs are gone. Who took them? Her skin is so new, even in death.

The wind is clawing at me, pulling my shirt tight against my neck.

"Wake up, damn it."

And then I am awake. Eyes open, I see I am still on the floor, but the others have gone. I look up into Cecilia's face.

"Your eyes," I say. "They're still th—" But I trail off, assimilating the dream with what passes for reality these days. "Never mind," I add.

She stares at me, her eyes wide and earnest. She looks lovely. Not just sexy, but pretty, the kind of girl you fall in love with and leave underground shelters to face an apocalypse that may or may not have ever happened with.

"I know where the masks are. Do you want to go up? We could go look at what you saw. We could maybe learn something about the truth." She smiles. "You know, reality show or the end of the world. One or the other. Can't be both."

I smile. "Sure it can. If it's a paradox."

She takes my hand and helps me to my feet.

"What about Henry? And Dominic?"

"Taken care of. Even the Gods and their henchman must sleep, especially after a bottle of wine and a killer blowjob."

She says this last part without the least trace of shame, and I know now her addiction is separate from what we have, like an alcoholic who must get drunk, but still loves his wife. I decide I can deal with her addiction if it means I get to have her love. Besides, if things work out, it could be just the two of us in a new world, far above this godforsaken place. And for the first time, I realize my acceptance—no, my resignation—to the idea that the world is gone, and we are the last. I allow my mind to imagine, in detail, Cecilia and I rediscovering the world, mile by mile. The mountains, the oceans, the sky. I shudder with pleasure as a new possibility strikes me: we would not only rediscover the planet, we would repopulate it. Post-apocalyptic Adam and, er, Cecilia.

"Coming?" she says. She's standing at the steps that lead up to the outside world.

"I'd follow you anywhere," I say. I am there when I realize it's true. I really would follow Cecilia anywhere.

As we prepare to leave the shelter, I say a prayer. Not to Henry's lame ass. Instead I set my sights higher, to someone or something more ancient than the earth, a master Creator who saw fit to let all us humans loose upon his sublime creation so we could fuck it up and fuck each other and fuck each other up. Perhaps I should be angry at Him for making us like we are. Putting us in a situation where our needs outpace our interests, where sex-addicted angels like Cecilia are the nearest some of us will ever get to a prophet or a minister or even a person capable of true love. But I'm not angry. I'm only tense. Wound up with excitement of what could be, of what my life, so fucked up before, might offer around the next bend, outside the shelter, underneath a sky that just might have been made by a real, genuine God who loves us enough to suffer us, whether we be sex addicts or child-murdering pseudogods.

"It's a paradox," I say, talking in a low calm voice that, strangely, is completely representative of the way I feel, despite the possibility the world outside this door is gone and all that exists is the bleak landscape of my dream.

"What is?" Cecilia asks.

"I met the false god Henry and an angelslut named Cecilia. And now, I believe in God. You made me realize that. He's a paradox. Fully man, fully God. Once you've got that, everything else seems simple. Kind of like this whole experience being fully terrible and fully wonderful. Kind of like Henry being fully genius and fully insane. A paradox." I laugh with the joy of it all, thinking how there's one more paradox I haven't considered. What if the world is gone? Yeah. That would suck. But what if it's not? What if the thing I saw is a corpse, but a corpse that has eyes and died some other way than the disease? What if the world is still ticking along just the way it always has, unaware of Henry and his God games? Cecilia won't stay with me. There's no way. Out there in the real world, a girl like Cecilia, a sex freak, won't give me the time of day. I take her hand in mine. I want to leave, but I want to stay; I want the world, but I want it gone, leveled by the eyeball-popping disease and wiped clean. I want to wander the bare, unpopulated earth with Cecilia, but I also want to stay right here in this moment, one hand in hers, the other on the door, a world of possibility on the other side.

"Are you sure about this?" she asks, as rain begins to fall outside the door. It sounds wonderful, and I wonder if it is cleansing the earth, washing away the disease, the hurt, the addictions. And I wonder if it will cleanse us as well, so no matter what is on the other side, we will be better than we were before.

"I'm not sure about anything," I say, "but that's why we've got to do this."

She nods. "If the world still exists, I'm going to do you like you've never been done before."

"And if it doesn't?"

She tightens her hand on mine. "If it doesn't, I'll do you in the middle of Times Square."

"Slut."

"Angelslut. Get it right."

"I love you," I say and open the door.

⌒

John Mantooth is an award-winning author, middle school teacher, former school bus driver, and basketball junkie. His first novel, *The Year of the Storm*, was published by Berkley in 2013, and his collection, *Shoebox Train Wreck*, was published in 2012. He lives in Alabama with his wife and children.

⌒

War, disease, madness, those left alive killing one another . . . but, slowly,
after the End, those who do survive start forming communities. But
does human nature change? Do humans? Brian Evenson contemplates
a terrifyingly bleak future through the eyes of a unique character.

· THE ADJUDICATOR ·
Brian Evenson

We have been some time putting our community back into some semblance
of body and shape, and longer still sifting the living from the dead. There
are so many who seem as alive as you and I (if I may be so bold as to
number you, with myself, among the living) but who already are all but
dead. Much has been done that would not be done in better times, and I
too in desperation have committed what I ought not have, and indeed may
well do so again.

I have become too accustomed to the signs and tokens of death. I meet
them both in the faces of the living and in the remnants I have encountered
in my daily round: the blackened arm my plough turned up and which I
just as quickly turned back under again; the bloody marks smeared deep
into the grain of the wood of my door and which I have not the fortitude to
scrub away; the man who lies dying in the ditch between my farm and my
neighbor's, and who, long dying, somehow still is not altogether dead.

Shall I start at the beginning? No, the end. Here am I, waiting for this same
beditched man to either die or lurch to his feet and return to claw again at
my door. I have no crops, my entire harvest having been pilfered or razed
because of all I have witnessed and done and refused to do. If I am to make
it alive to the next harvest, I must carefully pace the consumption of my few
remaining stores. I must catch and eat what maggots and voles and vermin I
can, glean and forage a little, beg mercy of my neighbors if any are still wont
to deliver mercy to the likes of me. And then, if I am lucky, I shall sit here

and starve for months, but perhaps not enough to die. No, let us have the beginning after all: the end is too much with me, its breath already warm and damp on the nape of my neck.

At first there are wars and rumors of wars, then comes a light so bright that it shines through flesh and bone. Then a conflagration, the landscape peeled off and away, and nearly everyone dies. Those who do not die directly find themselves subject to suddenly erupting into pustules and bleeding from every pore and then falling dead. Most of the remainder are subject to a slow madness, their brains softened so as to slosh within their skulls. All but dead, these set about killing those who remain alive. The few who survive unscathed are those in shelters underground or swaddled deep within a strong house. Or, simply, those who, like myself, seem not to have been afflicted for reasons no one can explain. Everything slides into nothingness and collapse, and for several years we all live like animals or worse, and then slowly we find our footing again. Soon some of us, maybe a few dozen, have banded together into this new order despite the disorder still raging in all quarters. We appoint a leader, a man named Rasmus. We begin to grow our scraggled crops. We form a pact to defend one another unto death.

At times I was approached by those who, having heard that I had been left unscathed in the midst of conflagration, believed I might provide some dark help to them. Others were more wary, keeping their distance as if from one cursed. Most, however, felt neither one thing nor the other, but saw me merely as a member of their community, a comrade-in-arms.

This, then, the fluid state of the world when, of a sudden, everything changed for me in the form of a delegation of men approaching my house. From a distance, I watched them come. The severed arm, having surged up under the sharp prow of the plough, was lying there, its palm open in appeal. Uncertain how they would feel about it, I quickly worked to have it buried again before they arrived.

I watched them come. One of them hallooed me when he saw me watching, and I waved back, then simply stood watching them come. I had grown somberly philosophical by this time, and was not distant enough from the conflagration ever to feel at ease. I still in fact carried a hatchet with me everywhere I went, and even slept with it beside me on the pillow. And it was upon this hatchet that Rasmus's eyes first alighted once the delegation had approached close enough to form a half-circle about me, and upon the way my hand rested steady on the haft.

"No need for that," he said. "Today will not be the day you hack me to bits."

This remark, perhaps lighthearted enough, based no doubt on the rumors of my past and meaning nothing, or at least little, drew my thoughts to the arm buried beneath my feet. I was glad, indeed, that I had again inhumed it.

"Gentlemen," I said, "to what do I owe this pleasure?" and I opened my pouch to them and offered them of my tobacco.

For a moment we were all of us engaged in stuffing and lighting our pipes, and then sucking them slowly down to ash, Rasmus keeping one finger raised to hold my question in abeyance. When he finished, he knocked the pipe out against the heel of his boot and turned fully toward me.

"We have an assignment for you," he said.

"The hell you have," I said.

Or at least wanted to say.

I do not know how to tell a story, a real one, or at least tell it well. Reading back over these pages, I see I have done nothing to give a sense of how it felt to have these determined men looming over me, their eyes strangely steady. Nor of Rasmus, with his wispy beard and red-pocked face. Why did we choose him as a leader? Because he was little good for anything else?

So, a large man, ruddy, looming over me, stabbing the air between us with a thick finger, nail yellow and cracking. Minions to either side of him.

What I said was not *The hell you have*, but "And it takes six of you to tell me?" Perhaps not, in retrospect, the wisest utterance, and certainly not taken exceptionally well. Not, to be blunt, in the proper community spirit. But once I was started down this path, I had difficulty arresting my career.

He tightened his lips, and drew himself up a little, stiff now.

"What," he asked, "was your profession?"

"I have always been a farmer," I said. "As you yourself know."

"No," he said. "Before the conflagration, I mean."

"You know very well what I was before the conflagration," I said.

"I want to hear you say it," he said.

But I would not say it. Instead, I filled my pipe again as they regarded me. Then lit and smoked it. And he, for whatever reason, did not push his point.

"There are rumors about you," he claimed. "Are they true?"

"For the purposes of this conversation," I said, not knowing what he was talking about, which rumors, "you should assume they are all true."

"Paper," he said, and one of the others came forward, held out a folded sheet of paper. I stared at it a long time, finally took it.

"We have an understanding then," said Rasmus, and, before I could answer, started off. Soon, he and his company were lost to me.

After they had gone, I dug the arm up again and examined it, trying to determine how long it had been rotting and whether I had been the one to lop it free. In the end, I found myself no closer to an answer than in the beginning. Finally I could think to do nothing but plough it back under again.

The matter of my former profession amounts to this: I had no former profession. I was dissolute, poisonous to myself in any and all ways. At a certain moment, I reached the point where I would have done anything at all to have what I wanted, and indeed I often did. Many of the particulars have faded or vanished from my memory or been pushed deeper down until they can no longer be felt. There was one person, someone I was, in my own way, deeply in love with, whom I betrayed. Someone else, of a different gender, whose self I stripped away nerve by nerve.

When the conflagration came, it was nearly sweet relief for me. And, to be honest, what I did to survive, largely with the hatchet I still carry, is little worse, and perhaps better, than what I had done beforehand.

But for Rasmus before the conflagration I had been a jack-of-all-trades, someone with little enough regard to take on any business, no matter how raucous or how bloody.

How much easier, I think now, *had I just raised my hatchet then and there with Rasmus and his crew and started laying into them. And then simply sewed their bits wide about my field and ploughed them in deep.*

There are other things I should tell, and perhaps still others forgotten that I shall never work my way back to. There are the rumors he had mentioned, asking if they were true. I cannot say one way or the other what he thought they were. Some people, as I have said, believe me charmed because of my aboveground survival, others believe me cursed. I am, I probably should have said before, completely devoid of hair—the only long-term consequence I suffered from the conflagration—and as such look to some homuncular, though not fully formed. I also heal, I have found, much faster than most, and it is, fortunately, somewhat difficult to inflict permanent damage upon me. It could be this that Rasmus had been referring to, which has become a rumor that I cannot die: a rumor that may well be disproved this winter. Or perhaps it was something else, something involving the past I have just elucidated above, or something touching on my deadly skill with the hatchet with which I live affectionately, as if it were a spouse. Who can say? Certainly not I.

The piece of paper, once unfolded and spread flat, read as follows:

In two days' time a man will approach your door. You will invite him in and greet him. You will share with him of your tobacco. You will converse with him. And then, when he stands to leave, you will lay into him with your hatchet until he is dead. This is the wish of the community, and we call upon you as a man of the community and one who has often proved himself capable.

There was, as one would have expected, no signature. The words themselves were simple and blocky, anonymous. I screwed the note into a twist and then lit one end of it, used it to ignite my pipe, discarded it in the fire, watched it become its own incandescent ghost and then flinder and flake away into nothingness.

How much shall I tell you about myself? Do I have anything to fear from you? How much can I tell you before I lose hope of holding, by whatever tenuous grasp, your sympathy? Or have I already gone too far?

I have no strong moral objection to murder pure and simple, nor, for that matter, to anything else. Why this is so, I cannot say. And yet I derive no pleasure from murder, have no taste for it. I was as content—and perhaps more content—being a simple farmer as I had ever been in my earlier, dissolute life. I felt as if most of my old self had been slowly torn free of the rest of me, and I was not eager to have it pressed back against me again.

True, I had, on the occasions when our community had been afflicted by swarms of the dead or dying, done my part and done it well. After a particular effort, standing blood-spattered over the remains of one of the afflicted who had refused to stop moving, I had sometimes seen the fear in the eyes of those who had observed my deeds. But I did not like Rasmus's quick slide from witnessing my having dispatched the dead to his assuming I would do the same without reluctance to the living. Not, again, that I had any reservations about the act of murder, only that I did not care to be taken for granted. And I knew from my past that, having been asked once, I would be asked again and again.

Still, there are sacrifices to be made when one has the privilege of living in a community. I could see no way around making this particular one, even if I was not, technically speaking, the one being sacrificed.

I spent the rest of the day at work on my house, replacing the shingling of the room where the wood had grown gaunt and had been bleached by wind and sun. The next day it was back to the fields, with ploughing and planting to finish and the ditch to be diverted until the near field was a soppy patch that glimmered in the sunset. A pipe at evening as always, and early the next morning a walk two farms away for some more tobacco, trading for it a few handfuls of dried corn from the dwindling stores of the previous year's harvest. Then a careful survey of the property, the dark, loamy earth of the still damp fields.

He came late in the day, just before sunset. Had I not known he was coming, I might well have been reluctant to swing wide the door, or at least would have opened it with hatchet raised and cocked back for the swing. He was a large man in broad-brimmed hat and long coat, wearing what once would have been called driving gloves.

"I have been sent to you," he said. "They claimed perhaps you could help me."

And so I ushered him in. I gestured to a chair near the fire. I placed my tobacco pipe and pouch within easy reach. I invited him to remove his gloves, his coat, his hat.

To this point there had been a certain inexorability to the proceedings, each moment a tiny and inevitable step toward the time when I would, without either fear or rage, raise my hatchet and make an end of the fellow. And yet, when he was freed of hat and coat and gloves and I saw the bare flesh of his hands, his arms, his face, I suddenly found everything grown complex. What I had seen as a simple deathbound progression now became a sequence of events whose ending I could not foresee, one in which, from instant to instant, I could not begin to divine what would happen next.

What was it that had thrown me into such uncertainty? Had I, as in the dead art of a dead past, glimpsed in the lines and the contours of his visage the face of a long-lost brother? A long-lost lover? No, nothing as simple or as clever as that. Rather, it was the fact that his hands and arms, his face and skull, had been completely epilated. Like me, he had lost all his hair. Had he been a brother or a lover, it would not have been enough to confuse me. But this, somehow, was.

He came in, he sat. His hat and coat I hung from a hook beside my door. His gloves he paired and smoothed and laid gently over his knee once he had sat. His name was Halber, he claimed.

"And who was it sent you?" I asked, though I knew the answer.

Your leader, he claimed. Who had said that I would adjudicate for him.

"Adjudicate?" I said.

Yes, he claimed, since that was my role in the community, or so he had been told by Rasmus.

I nodded for him to go on.

The story he unraveled was one of the utmost wrongheadedness. He had once, it seemed, so he claimed, owned all of this property, but when the conflagration had come he had traveled quickly and hurriedly to try to throw his body in the path of his parents' death. He had of course misthrown himself; they had died despite him, his mother going mad so that in the end he had had to be the one to kill her, and his father simply having his skin slough off until the bone was showing. Upon which he thought to return, but the world being as it was, he had spent many months just keeping alive, and only now had he begun to manage.

What he wanted, he stated, was not to reclaim his land. He understood well enough the degree to which everything had transformed. All he wanted was to be given a small plot of land and be allowed to farm it, so he could be back in a place that he knew, and to be accepted into the community. He had said this to Rasmus and the council, and they had deliberated for three days as he awaited their decision. At last they had sent him to me, the adjudicator.

Adjudicator, I thought. *Well, that's one name for it.*

I thought, too, with sudden insight, *Normally they would kill him themselves, and perhaps have done so with others in times past. But because, like me, he is hairless, they have sent him to me. They are frightened.*

And this made me think, too, of what they must have thought of me, and why they had chosen to admit me into the community. And I could not but think it was out of fear or because I was already there, and perhaps it was only because there were those among them who believed I was charmed or cursed and could not die. And perhaps soon, once I had done away with Halber and proved that a man like myself could be killed, they would see no reason not to do away with me as well.

"Please tell them," I said, "that I have thought carefully and have adjudicated in your favor. You shall join us."

He stood and awkwardly embraced me, an operation I suffered only with great reluctance. And then after gathering his things he departed, leaving me to ponder why I had done what I had done, and what would be its dark consequence.

I was not to wonder long. Late that night I heard shouts and, as I roused myself, a banging had begun at my door. "It's Halber!" a man was screaming, his screams enough to curdle the blood. "It's Halb! Let me in!"

And indeed I almost did. I might well have, had I not heard the other voices and sounds that followed, the grunts and indifferent, dull sounds of metal slipping into flesh, and heard the pounding suddenly stop. I climbed onto the bed and looked down through the high window. In the pale moonlight I saw him, dying and staring, being dragged away by the legs. Had it been only a pack of the dead and the dying, I would have perhaps opened the door and commenced to lay about me with my hatchet, as I had done in the past when the dead came for the living. But as it was, seeing that the faces were those of the living, Rasmus's face among them, I hesitated just long enough to feel that it was too late.

And perhaps it is there that the story should have ended. Perhaps, had I said nothing, done nothing, kept to my house, then my reputation, the myths surrounding me, would have been enough for Rasmus and his council to decide to let me be. Perhaps they would have grudgingly levied a fine, remembered my usefulness in other ways, and life would have gone much as usual, if anything can be described as usual in these days. But we both of us made mistakes that made this impossible.

The mistake I made was in not staying to my house for a few days, deciding instead to tend to my crops, to go about the business that needed to be attended to on my farm. This, under most circumstances, would not be considered a dire mistake. Or, to be frank, in most conditions, even a mistake at all.

Their mistakes were more severe. Tired of dragging the body, they abandoned it in a ditch halfway between my and my neighbor's farms. And instead of tearing the head free of the corpse and incinerating it, they left the hairless Halber lacerated but more or less intact.

With every disaster, I have come to believe for my own personal reasons, comes a compensation, a certain balancing of the accounts—not spread evenly about but clumped here and there, of benefit to very few. I heal, as I said, very quickly—or at least I do now; before the conflagration I did not. There are rumors I cannot die. Not having died, I can neither confirm nor deny these rumors, nor am I curious enough to uncover the truth that I feel compelled to slit my own throat. But from what I have seen of what is happening to Halber, I fear these rumors might well be true, and hardly in the way one would hope.

So, we have reached the day after Halber was hauled away, my door clawed and scratched on the outside, the bloody marks of his dying smeared there and on the threshold. I stare at the door a moment, checking to see whether my hatchet is with me. Outside, there are always things to attend to, things to do to keep the farm going. I do them, wondering all the while when, if ever, the little poultry and livestock remaining in the area will start to breed again and if I will ever be able to afford my own chickens. I irrigate my fields again, just enough, then sit on a stone near the border of the field, and smoke.

That is when I begin to hear it, a slow and distant whistle, a soft wind. At first I think nothing of it. But when it persists, I become afflicted with the disease of curiosity.

I stand, trying to ascertain where it is coming from. I follow it in one direction, then another. It slowly becomes louder, just a little louder, just a little louder, a moan now.

It is some time still before I make my way all the way out to the road and follow it a little way down and find him there, Halber, bloody in the ditch, grievously wounded—by all rights he should be dead.

What do I do? One look is enough to tell me he should be dead. I have dealt often enough with the living turned dead to be leery, but he struck me as something different, as a new thing. He was, in any case, too hurt to be moved. I went back to the house, brought back a blanket and some water. I wrapped him in the former and dribbled the latter into his mouth. He was delirious and hardly conscious. He would, it seemed to me, soon be dead.

And so I stayed there beside him, waiting for him to die.

Only he did not die. His body seemed unable to let go but also unable to heal itself, and so he struggled there between life and death. I thought for a moment to kill him, but what if he did heal himself? I wondered. Was he not like me? Would he not eventually heal himself?

In the end I left him and went home to sleep.

That night I dreamt of him, lying there in his ditch, slowly dying but never dead, breathing in his shallow way but breathing despite everything, never stopping. And then, his breathing no less shallow, he managed over the course of long, painful moments to make it to his feet and shuffle forward, like the walking dead. I watched him coming. Later, much later, in my head, I heard a knocking and a dim, inarticulate cry and knew him—suddenly and with, for once, a certain measure of terror—to be knocking on my door.

When I came back the next morning, I found my blanket was gone, stolen. Some creature had eaten most of one of his hands and the finer portion of his face. But he was still, somehow, alive. And so I slit his throat and watched the blood gurgle out, and then went back to get on with my work.

This seemed to me sufficient, and I must confess that I did not think about him through the course of my day. There were fences to be attended to, wood to be chopped, brush to be cleared. A corner of the field had become too soggy and I found myself cutting a makeshift drainage channel, thinking up its course as I went. By the end of the day I was mud-spattered, my bones and muscles aching.

And still, as the sun set, I found my thoughts returning to Halber. I could not stop myself from going to see him.

There are strange things that happen that I cannot explain, and this is one of them. He was as I had left him, but still alive. His throat, I saw, had filmed over, the veins not reconnecting exactly but blood moving there, pulsing back and forth within the film in a kind of delicate bag of blood and nascent tissue, pus-like. I watched it beat red, then beat pale, in the gap where his throat had been. At that sight I nearly severed his head from his shoulders, but I was too terrified of what would happen inside of me if I removed his head, and somehow, despite this, he still refused to die. So instead I went home and sharpened my hatchet.

What can I say about the night that followed, when I chose to become the one who would judge who lived and who died? I have no apologies for what I did, nor any justification, either. I did it simply because I could think of nothing else to do. I am neither proud of my actions nor regretful.

I sharpened the hatchet until it had a fine and impossible edge, and then in the dark I set out. Perhaps if I had met some of the dying and the afflicted, some of those made vicious and deranged by the conflagration, I would have been satisfied. But the only one I met in my path was Halber, and I gave the fellow a wide berth.

What need is there to pursue in detail what followed next? I did unto Rasmus as might be expected. A single blow of the hatchet and I was through his door. I caught him on his way out of bed as he moved down the hall and went after his gun, the hatchet cutting through his back and ribs and puncturing one lung so that it hissed. He went down in a heap, groaning and breathing out a mist of blood, and I severed first one forearm, then the other, and, as his eyes rolled back, lopped off his head. His wife arose screaming from the bed and rushed to the window and tried to hurl herself through. I struck her on the back of the skull with the cronge of the handle, meaning only to silence her screams, but it was clear from the way she fell and the puddle of blood that soon spread from her head that perhaps I had struck too hard. Then I approached Rasmus again and very delicately, with the sharpest part of the blade, peeled off his face.

The other five who had earlier come with him to see me now suffered the same fate, though I killed them more swiftly, with a single blow, and did not disjoint or decorticate them as I had their leader. There is no need to say more than that, I suppose. In the end, I was sodden with blood and gore, and made my way back to my farmhouse, past the still dying Halber, and slept the sleep of the truly dead.

I awoke to the smell of burning, saw when I burst open the door that they had set my fences afire. My fields, too, had been trampled apart, then the ditch redirected and trenches dug to wash away the topsoil. Had my house not been stone, they would have burnt that, too. I stared at the flames a moment and then, not knowing what else to do, went back to bed.

It was a week before I could bring myself to leave the house. Finally I stripped off my gory clothing, the blood now gone black, and burnt it in the fireplace. Then I took water from the irrigation canal and washed in it and dressed myself in my town clothes and set off for my neighbor's farm. I do not know what I expected. At the very least I expected, I suppose, for Halber to be dead. But he was still alive, still feebly dying in the ditch. I chose not to get close to him. My neighbor was at his farm, his crops just starting to sprout. When he saw me coming, he rushed inside, came out with his rifle.

"Not another step," he said.

I stopped. "Do you think your gun can stop me?" I asked him.

"I don't know," he said, "but if you come any closer we shall find out."

"I have no grudge against you," I said. "I only want those who destroyed my crops."

"Then you want me," he said. "You want all of us, the community."

"But why?"

"Can you possibly ask?"

And I suppose in good conscience I could not, though I thought my neighbor had at least a right to know why I had done what I had done. So I sat on the ground and kept my hand far away from the hatchet and, rifle trained on me, recounted to him, just as I have recounted to you, all that had occurred.

When I was finished, he shook his head. "We have all been through much," he said, "and you have made us go through more. None of us are perfect men, but you are less perfect than most."

Then he gestured with his gun. "Come with me," he said.

He led me back to the road and toward my farm, to the place in the ditch where the dying man was to be found.

"Is this the man you meant?" he asked. "A man who when he was alive he was not hairless but in fact replete with hair. Please," he said, "go away and do not come back."

But I could not see it. Indeed, to me he still appeared as hairless as a baby and, though dying, still alive. I wondered to myself as to what my neighbor was trying to do to me. Had he not had his gun trained upon me, I would have turned upon him and laid into him with my hatchet. Instead, I simply turned away from him and returned to my house.

Where I have been ever since. I do not know if what is wrong is wrong with me or wrong with the world. Perhaps there is a little of both. I find it difficult to face the man dying in the ditch, and it is clear that my neighbors and I no longer live in altogether the same worlds.

It seems strange to think that after all this, after my years of dissolution and then the hard years after the conflagration, I might die here alone, might slowly starve to death. Assuming it is true that I can in fact die.

I will make do as long as I can and then when my straits are indeed dire I shall leave my house and beg mercy from my neighbors. Perhaps they will show mercy, even if only out of fear, or perhaps they will kill me. Either way, it cannot be but a relief.

As for now, though, I shall sit here and write and very slowly starve, waiting part in anticipation and part in fear for the moment when the dying man who so greatly resembles me shall drag himself to his feet and leave his ditch and come again to knock at my door.

This time I shall be ready for him. This time I shall know what to do.

Brian Evenson is the author of a dozen works of fiction, most recently *Immobility* (Tor, 2012) and *Windeye* (Coffee House Press, 2012). His novel *Last Days* won the American Library Association's Award for Best Horror Novel of 2009, his story collection *The Wavering Knife* won an International Horror Guild Award, and his novel *The Open Curtain* was a finalist for an Edgar Award. He lives in Providence, Rhode Island where he works at the university on which Lovecraft's Miskatonic University is based.

Robotic "bugs" that devour metal—and anything else that happens to come between them and their meal, including human flesh and bone—have left portions of the Earth relatively unscathed or at least somewhat recovered. But in the devastated zones that are still infested, various micro-cultures have arisen.

• A STORY, WITH BEANS •
Steven Gould

Kimball crouched in the shade of the mesquite trees, which, because of the spring, were trees instead of their usual ground-hugging scrub. He was answering a question asked by one of the sunburned tourists, who was sprawled by the water, leaning against his expensive carbon-framed backpack.

"It takes about a foot of dirt," Kimball said. "I mean, if there isn't anything electrical going on. Then you'll need more, depending on the current levels and the strength of the EMF. You may need to be underground a good ten feet otherwise.

"But it's a foot, minimum. Once saw a noob find a silver dollar that he'd dug up at one of the old truck stops west of Albuquerque. 'Throw it away!' we yelled at him. Why did he think they replaced his fillings before he entered the territory? But he said it was a rare coin and worth a fortune. The idiot swallowed it.

"We could have buried him. Kept his face clear but put a good foot of dirt over him. That could've worked, but there were bugs right there, eating those massive hydraulic cylinders buried in the concrete floor of the maintenance bays, the ones that drove the lifts.

"We scattered. He ran, too, but they were all around and they rose up like bees and then he stepped on one and it was all over. They went for the coin like it was a chewy caramel center."

There were three college-aged tourists—two men and a girl—a pair of

Pueblo khaki-dressed mounted territorial rangers that Kimball knew, and Mendez, the spring keeper. There was also a camel caravan camped below the spring, where the livestock were allowed to drink from the runoff, but the drovers, after filling their water bags, stayed close to their camels.

There were predators out here, both animal and human.

"What happened to the noob?" the tourist asked.

"He swallowed the coin. It was in his abdomen."

"What do you mean?"

"Christ, Robert," the girl said. "Didn't you listen to the entrance briefing? He died. The bugs would just go right through him, to the metal. There aren't any trauma centers out here, you know?"

One of the rangers, silent until now, said, "That's right, miss." He slid the sleeve of his khaki shirt up displaying a scarred furrow across the top of his forearm. "Bug did this. Was helping to dig a new kiva at Pojoaque and didn't see I'd uncovered the base of an old metal fencepost. Not until the pain hit. There weren't many bugs around, but they came buzzing after that first one tasted steel and broadcast the call. I was able to roll away, under the incoming ones."

"Why are you visiting the zone?" asked Mendez, the spring keeper. He sat apart, keeping an eye on the tourists. The woman had asked about bathing earlier and the rangers explained that you could get a bath in town and there was sometimes water in the Rio Puerco, but you didn't swim in the only drinking water between Red Cliff and the Territorial Capital.

"You can bathe without soap in the runoff, down the hill above where the cattle drink. Wouldn't do it below," Mendez had elaborated. "You can carry a bit of water off into the brush if you want to soap 'n' rinse."

Kimball thought Mendez was still sitting there just in case she did decide to bathe. Strictly as a public service, no doubt, keeping a wary eye out for, uh, tan lines.

The woman tourist said, "We're here for Cultural Anthropology 305. Field study. We meet our prof at his camp on the Rio Puerco."

"Ah," said Kimball, "Matt Peabody."

"Oh. You know him?"

"Sure. His camp is just downstream from the Duncan ford. He likes to interview the people who pass through."

"Right. He's published some fascinating papers on the distribution of micro-cultures here in the zone."

"Micro-cultures. Huh," said Kimball. "Give me an example."

"Oh, some of the religious or political groups who form small communities out here. Do you know what I mean?"

"I do." Kimball, his face still, exchanged a glance with the two rangers.

As the woman showed no sign of imminent hygiene, Mendez climbed to his feet, groaning, and returned to his one room adobe-faced dugout, up the hill.

The woman student became more enthusiastic. "I think it's so cool how the zone has ended up being this great nursery for widely diverse ways of life! I'm so excited to be able to see it."

Kimball stood up abruptly and, taking a shallow basket off of his cart, walked downstream where the cattle watered. He filled the basket with dried dung: some camel, horse, and a bit of cow. He didn't walk back until his breathing had calmed and his face was still. When he returned to the spring, one of the rangers had a pile of dried grass and pine needles ready in the communal fire pit and the other one was skinning a long, thin desert hare.

Kimball had a crock of beans that'd been soaking in water since he'd left Red Cliff that morning. Getting it out of the cart, he added more water, a chunk of salt pork, pepper, and fresh rosemary, then wedged it in the fire with the lid, weighted down by a handy rock.

"What do you do, out here?" the woman tourist asked him. Kimball smiled lazily and, despite her earlier words, thought about offering her some beans.

"Bit of this, bit of that. Right now, I sell things."

"A peddler? Shouldn't you be in school?"

Kimball decided he wasn't going to offer her any of his beans after all. He shrugged. "I've done the required." In fact, he had his GED, but he didn't advertise that. "It's different out here."

"How old are you?" she asked.

"How old are *you*?"

She grinned. "Personal question, eh? Okay. I'm nineteen."

"I'm sixteen. Sweet, never been kissed."

She cocked her head sideways. "Yeah, right."

"Kimball," one of the rangers called from across the fire-pit. "A quarter of the hare for some beans."

"Maybe. Any *buwa*, Di-you-wi?" Kimball asked.

"Of course there's *buwa*."

"*Buwa* and a haunch."

The two rangers discussed this in Tewa, then Di-you-wi said, "*Buwa* and a haunch. Don't stint the beans."

They warmed the *buwa*, rolled up blue-corn flatbread, on a rock beside the fire. Kim added a salad of wide-leaf flame-flower and purslane that he'd harvested along the trail. The rangers spoke thanks in Tewa and Kimball didn't touch his food until they were finished.

The woman watched out of the corner of her eyes, fascinated.

The tourists ate their radiation-sterilized ration packs that didn't spoil and didn't have to be cooked and weren't likely to give them the runs. But the smell of the hare and beans wafted through the clearing and the smell of the packaged food didn't spread at all.

"That sure smells good," the girl said.

Kimball tore off a bit of *buwa* and wrapped it around a spoonful of beans and a bit of the hare. He stretched out his arm. "See what you think."

She licked her lips and hesitated.

"Christ, Jennifer, that rabbit had ticks all over it," said the sunburned man. "Who knows what parasites they—uh, it had."

The rangers exchanged glances and laughed quietly.

Jennifer frowned and stood up, stepping over sunburn boy, and crouched down on her heels by the fire, next to Kimball. With a defiant look at her two companions, she took the offered morsel and popped it into her mouth. The look of defiance melted into surprised pleasure. "Oh, wow. So *buwe* is cornbread?"

"*Buwa*. Tewa wafer bread—made with blue corn. The Hopi make it too, but they call it *piki*."

"The beans are wonderful. Thought they'd be harder."

"I started them soaking this morning, before I started out from Red Cliff."

"Ah," she lowered her voice. "What did they call you earlier?"

"Kimball."

She blinked. "Is that your name?"

"First name. I'm Kimball. Kimball . . . Creighton."

Di-you-wi laughed. Kimball glared at him.

"I'm Jennifer Frauenfelder." She settled beside him.

"Frauenfelder." Kimball said it slowly, like he was rolling it around in his mouth. "German?"

"Yes. It means field-of-women."

Di-you-wi blinked at this and said something in Tewa to his partner, who responded, "Huh. Reminds me of someone I knew who was called Left-for-dead."

Kimball rubbed his forehead and looked at his feet but Jennifer said, "Left-for-dead? That's an odd name. Did they have it from birth or did something happen?"

"Oh," said Di-you-wi, "something happened all right." He sat up straight and spoke in a deeper voice, more formal.

"*Owei humbeyô.*"

(His partner whispered, almost as if to himself, "Once upon a time and long ago.")

"Left-for-dead came to a village in the Jornada del Muerto on the edge of the territory of the City of God, where the People of the Book reside." Di-you-wi glanced at Jennifer and added, "It was a 'nursery of diverse beliefs."

"Left-for-dead was selling books, Bibles mostly, but also almanacs and practical guides to gardening and the keeping of goats and sheep and cattle.

"But he had other books as well, books not approved by the Elders—the plays of Shakespeare, books of stories, health education, Darwin.

"And he stole the virtue of Sharon—"

The two male tourists sat up at that and the sunburned one smacked his lips. "The dawg!"

Di-you-wi frowned at the interruption, cleared his throat, and went on. "And Left-for-dead stole the virtue of Sharon, the daughter of a Reader of the Book by trading her a reading primer and a book on women's health."

"What did she trade?" asked the leering one.

"There was an apple pie," said Di-you-wi. "Also a kiss."

Jennifer said, "And that's how she lost her virtue?"

"It was more the primer. The women of the People of the Book are not allowed to read," added his partner.

"Ironic, that," said Kimball.

"Or kiss," said Di-you-wi said with a quelling glance. He raised his voice. "They burned his books and beat him and imprisoned him in the stocks and called on the people of the village to pelt him but Sharon, the daughter of the Reader, burned the leather hinges from the stocks in the dusk and they ran, northwest, into the malpaís where the lava is heated by the sun until you can cook *buwa* on the stones and when the rain falls in the afternoon it sizzles like water falling on coals.

"The Elders chased them on horseback but the malpaís is even harder on horses than men and they had to send the horses back and then they chased them on foot but the rocks leave no prints."

"But the water in the malpaís is scarce to none and Left-for-dead and the girl were in a bad way even though they hid by day and traveled by night. Once, in desperation, Left-for-dead snuck back and stole a water gourd from the men who chased them, while they lay sleeping, but in doing so he put them back on the trail.

"Two days later, Sharon misstepped and went down in a crack in the rock and broke both bones in her lower leg. Left-for-dead splinted the leg, made a smoke fire, and left her there. The People of the Book found her and took her back, dragged on a travois, screaming with every bump and jar.

"They discussed chasing Left-for-dead and then they prayed and the Reader said God would punish the transgressor, and they went back to their village and spread the story far and wide, to discourage the weak and the tempted.

"Left-for-dead walked another day to the north, hoping to reach the water at Marble Tanks, but he had been beaten badly in the stocks and his strength failed him. When he could go no further he rolled into a crevice in the lava where there was a bit of shade and got ready to die. His tongue began to swell and he passed in and out of darkness and death had his hand on him."

Here Di-you-wi paused dramatically, taking a moment to chase the last of his beans around the bowl with a bit of *buwa*.

Jennifer leaned forward. "And?"

"And then it rained. A short, heavy summer thunderstorm. The water dripped down onto Left-for-dead's face and he drank, and awoke drinking and coughing. And then drank some more. He crawled out onto the face of the malpaís and drank from the puddles in the rock and was able to fill the water gourd he'd stolen from the Reader's men, but he didn't have to drink from it until the next day when the last of the rain evaporated from the pockets in the lava.

"He made it to Marble Tanks, and then east to some seeps on the edge of the lava flows, and hence to the Territorial Capital."

"Because the incident with Left-for-dead was just the latest of many, a territorial judge was sent out with a squad of rangers to hold hearings. The City of God sent their militia, one hundred strong, and killed the judge and most of the rangers.

"When the two surviving rangers reported back, the territorial governor flashed a message beyond the curtain and a single plane came in answer, flying up where the air is so thin that the bugs' wings can't catch, and they dropped the leaflets, the notice of reclamation—the revocation of the city's charter."

"That's it?" said Jennifer. "They dropped a bunch of leaflets?"

"The first day. The second day it wasn't leaflets."

Jennifer held her hand to her mouth. "Bombs?"

"Worse. Chaff pods of copper and aluminum shavings that burst five hundred feet above the ground. I heard tell that the roofs and ground glittered in the sunlight like jewels."

The sunburned man laughed. "That's it? Metal shavings?"

"I can't believe they let you through the curtain," Jennifer said to him. "Didn't you listen at all?" She turned back to Di-you-wi. "How many died?"

"Many left when they saw the leaflets. But not the most devout and not the women who couldn't read. The Speaker of the Word said that their faith would prevail. Perhaps they deserved their fate . . . but not the children.

"The last thing the plane dropped was a screamer—an electromagnetic spike trailing an antennae wire several hundred feet long. They say the bugs rose into the air and blotted the sun like locusts."

Jennifer shuddered.

Di-you-wi relented a little. "Many more got out when they saw the cloud. I mean, it was like one of the ten plagues of the first chapter of their book, after all. If they made it outside the chaff pattern and kept to the low ground, they made it. But those who stayed and prayed?" He paused dramatically. "The adobe houses of the City of God are mud and dust and weeds, and the great Cathedral is a low pile of stones and bones."

"*Owei humbeyô.*" Once upon a time and long ago.

Everyone was quiet for a moment though Jennifer's mouth worked as if to ask something, but no sound came out. Kimball added the last of the gathered fuel to the fire, banged the dust out of his basket, and flipped it, like a Frisbee, to land in his rickshaw-style handcart. He took the empty stoneware bean crock and filled it from the stream and put at the edge of the coals, to soak before he cleaned it.

"What happened to Sharon?" Jennifer finally asked into the silence.

Di-you-wi shook his head. "I don't know. You would have to ask Left-for-dead."

Jennifer: "Oh, thanks a lot. Very helpful."

Di-you-wi and his partner exchanged glances and his partner opened his mouth as if to speak, but Di-you-wi shook his head.

Kimball hadn't meant to speak, but he found the words spilling out anyway, unbidden. "I would like to say that Sharon's leg still hurts her. That it didn't heal straight, and she limps. But that she teaches others to read now down in New Roswell. That I had seen her recently and sold her school some primers just last month."

Jennifer frowned, "You would like to say that?"

"It was a bad break and I set it as best I could, but they bounced her over the lava on their way home and trusted to God for further treatment. She couldn't even walk, much less run, when the metal fell."

Jennifer's mouth was open but she couldn't speak for a moment.

"Huh," said Di-you-wi. "Hadn't heard that part, Left-for-dead."

Kimball could see him reorganizing the tale in his head, incorporating the added details. "Got it from her sister. After I recovered."

Jennifer stood and walked over to Kimball's cart and flipped up the tarp. The books were arranged spine out, paperbacks mostly, some from behind the Porcelain Wall, newish with plasticized covers, some yellowed and cracking from before the bugs came, like anything that didn't contain metal or electronics, salvaged, and a small selection of leather-bound books from New Santa Fe, the territorial capital, hand-set with ceramic type and hand-bound—mostly practical, how-to books.

"Peddler. Book seller."

Kimball shrugged. "Varies. I've got other stuff, too. Plastic sewing-needles, ceramic blades, antibiotics, condoms. Mostly books."

Finally she asked, "And her father? The Elder who put you in the stocks?"

"He lives. His faith wasn't strong enough when it came to that final test. He lost an arm, though."

"Is he in New Roswell, too?"

"No. He's doing time in the territorial prison farm in Nuevo Belen. He preaches there, to a very small congregation. The People of the Book don't do well if they can't isolate their members—if they can't control what information they get. They're not the People of the Books, after all.

"If she'd lived, Sharon would probably have made him a part of her life . . . but he's forbidden the speaking of her name. He would've struck her name from the leaves of the family Bible, but the bugs took care of that."

Di-you-wi shook his head on hearing this. "And who does this hurt? I think he is a stupid man."

Kimball shrugged. "It's not him I feel sorry for."

Jennifer's eyes glinted brightly in the light of the fire. She said, "It's not fair, is it?"

And there was nothing to be said to that.

⌒

Steven Gould is the author of the frequently banned book *Jumper,* as well as *Wildside, Helm, Blind Waves, Reflex, Jumper: Griffin's Story, 7th Sigma,* and *Impulse.* He has had several short stories published in *Analog, Asimov's,* and *Amazing,* and other magazines and anthologies. *Wildside* won the Hal Clement Young Adult Award for Science Fiction and was nominated for the Prometheus Award. He has been on the Hugo ballot twice and the Nebula ballot once for his short fiction. *Jumper* was made into the 2008 feature film of the same name with Samuel L. Jackson, Jamie Bell, Rachel Bilson, and Hayden Christensen. Steve lives in New Mexico with his wife, writer Laura J. Mixon (M. J. Locke) and their two daughters, where he keeps chickens and falls down a great deal. He just returned from Doha, Qatar where he discussed writing and science fiction with Qatari college students.

⌒

Tokyo has been annihilated by a crude North Korean nuclear bomb. The quality of everyday life in Japan after the End, has, however, been restored. But the island of Tsushima is haunted by bombs, illegal narcotics, and pirates.

• GODDESS OF MERCY •
Bruce Sterling

Miss Sato left the hostage compound. Her liaison was waiting in a rusty Toyota pickup.

Miss Sato's guide in Tsushima was the star reporter of a local broadsheet called *Truth Dawn*. Yoshida was a gangling twenty-two-year-old with a broad bamboo hat, a dirty undershirt, cargo shorts, Brazilian flip-flop sandals, and a pet terrier.

Yoshida helped Miss Sato into the back of the truck as the frisky dog barked a greeting. "So, how's the old woman doing?"

"The 'old woman' looks twenty years older from her sufferings," Miss Sato declared. She knotted a scarf on her head and grabbed the pickup's roll bar. "She used to look so pretty on television. I campaigned for Mrs. Mieko Nagai, you know. That was part of my political awakening."

Yoshida removed his big conical hat, examined the bright autumn sky, thought better of the exposure to surveillance, and put the hat back on. "You campaigned for the hostage? That's an interesting angle to your story."

The Toyota jounced along the crumbling roadbed. Miss Sato and Yoshida had to ride standing because a bulky Russian antiaircraft gun took up most of the room in the truck bed.

This rugged Russian gun had arrived on Tsushima with two Russians, bored young mercenaries from Kamchatka. Bumper stickers on their truck made the absurd claim that Tsushima was a Russian island, but since the stickers were in Cyrillic, nobody noticed or cared.

Yoshida spoke up over his terrier's excited yapping. "I hope you assured

Mrs. Nagai that my newspaper's party line is firmly against hostage-taking. Mrs. Nagai does read my work, right? *Truth Dawn* offers free subscriptions to all political prisoners."

"Where are we going?" Miss Sato hedged. She had seen a land-mine crater scarring the road ahead.

Miss Sato had experienced close calls on Tsushima, but thanks to due caution and her steady alertness, she had never been blown up. Miss Sato had learned to read the wreckage on Tsushima the way one might read tealeaves. The neat round holes in roofs and walls were American naval artillery. The shattered palm trees and big dirt craters were aircraft bombs from the mainland provisional government. All the other bombs had been built and exploded on Tsushima itself.

The pirate island of Tsushima had wireless belt-bombs and miniature pocket grenades. Tsushima had head-breaker cell-phone bombs. Leg-breaker land mines. Car-breaker bike bombs. House-breaker car bombs. Every once in a while, in particular fits of malignant frenzy, Tsushima had truck bombs that could demolish a city block.

The center of this story, the Gojira of this transformation, was "The Bomb." That half-forgotten monster of Japanese history, "The Bomb." "The Bomb" had entirely smashed Tokyo. "The Bomb" remade Japanese history. Even when The Bomb was just a crude, barely ballistic, North Korean bomb.

With Tokyo in ruins from the North Korean sneak attack, Nagoya became the emergency center of southern Japan. Northern Japan rallied around Sapporo. In the chaos, the obscure rural island of Tsushima had been abandoned to its own devices. Its esoteric, electronic devices.

The first pirates to settle in Tsushima came from North Korea. These wretches were starving North Korean refugees, Asia's latest boat people, fleeing the vast, searing, vengeful blast zones of the many American hydrogen bombs. The North Korean refugees had quickly overwhelmed what passed for law and order on the sleepy little tourist island.

In the wake of the Korean invasion came all of Asia's waterborne criminals: Taiwanese arms dealers, South Korean drug merchants, and Hong Kong triads. Even the Russian mafia drifted south from the Kuril Islands. These network-savvy global marauders shared a single goal. They all came to rob Japan, a land without a government or a capital, the world's richest and newest "failed state."

The Americans observed this development with grave concern—because the Americans had already much seen the like in Iraq, Somalia, Afghanistan,

Colombia, Mexico, Pakistan, and Nigeria. "Boots on the ground" rarely triumphed against "global guerrillas." The insurgents merely scattered, regrouped, and left their roadside bombs to kill soldiers.

The Americans, much overstretched in Korea, Iran, and elsewhere, could not invade and pacify the rugged pirate island of Tsushima. But the Americans did possess tremendous air power and precision satellite targeting. So the Americans pounded Tsushima. They pulverized the island's harbors, bridges, power plants, and telecom towers.

A great and lasting silence and darkness descended on the island. A silence broken only by bombs.

That was what always impressed Miss Sato about her life in Tsushima: not the bombs, but that deep, lasting darkness. Mainland Japan was not dark. North Japan and South Japan had restored their shares of the broken power grid. Everyday life in post-atomic Japan was about as bright and busy as life in Argentina. But Tsushima was dark to its core.

Tsushima's darkness was damp, dense, and mystical. No neon, no traffic. No electrical power, and no Internet. No light, no heat. No banks, no credit cards. No passports. The pirates of Tsushima were stateless, anarchic, gun-toting marauders from all over the world. They had no documents, no official identities. No marriage, no religion. No police and no priests. No running water. They didn't even have clocks.

Tsushima was haunted by bombs and by a head-bending swoon of illegal narcotics. The ragged coasts swarmed with fast, small boats full of hard, scarred men of every shape, size, and language. They rushed ashore to raid the fat and peaceful coastal villages of Japan, and they ran off with anything and anyone they could grab.

Tsushima had newfangled global crimes that hadn't been named yet. This was Miss Sato's island of Tsushima. She spent much more of her life here than she ever did in her cheerless little relief office in Nagoya.

"So, what can you tell me," said Miss Sato to Yoshida, as the war-truck squeaked and rattled, "about a blind man, some kind of pilgrim or gambler, who visits the Mechatronic Visionary Center?"

"Oh, that poor old guy's not news to anybody." Yoshida grabbed the rusty roll bar welded to the Toyota's roof. "He's like the Mechatronic janitor. They let him in and out because he's blind and he can't steal the precious hardware stored there. He used to live in there, before the Tokyo Bomb."

Miss Sato grew alert at this intelligence. "What kind of role did he have in that laboratory?"

"The role of some helpless blind man, I guess," Yoshida said with a shrug. "That 'Visionary Center' was supposed to be the research lab for a Japanese camera company. We all knew that was just the cover story. So many weird people coming in and out of that place . . . Foreign scientists, the military, politicians, bankers . . . spies, yakuza gangsters. They were up to no good in there, and every weekend, we Tsushima people had to get them drunk and find them women. And we did that for them too. But was that news story ever in the mainland Japanese media? Never! Not at all! Not one word!"

"The women's movement knew about the military lab on Tsushima," Miss Sato objected. "We women were aware that the Japanese Self-Defense Forces were contravening the Constitution. They were reacting with covert violence to the pirate attacks on Japanese shipping in Somalia. They used offshore, deniable proxies."

Yoshida scowled. "That's the problem with you peacenik feminists: you have no ideological insight! Pirate, anti-pirate, that is just pure dialectic! A covert War on Terror is the same as the Terror itself. It all becomes the same in the long run! Once you abandon the quest for social justice, it just becomes a matter of market price."

Miss Sato tactfully overlooked this Marxist tirade. "I'm sure your readers agree with you, so, then, may I ask, can you please introduce me to this Zeta One? I need to talk to him. Mrs. Nagai says that whenever he visits the labs there, he always brings the hostages steamed buns and pickles. He can't be that bad a person if he feels such pity for other human beings."

Yoshida nodded impatiently, his bamboo hat wobbling. "Yes, I interviewed your Mrs. Nagai. You know what? She has Stockholm Syndrome. She's gone crazy in her head."

"It isn't crazy that Mrs. Nagai sympathizes with her pirate oppressors."

Yoshida bent down and unclipped his dog's leash. "Yes it is. She's in chains, but she spends all her time crying about pirates in prisons on the mainland! What a joke!"

"Mrs. Nagai wants to arrange a prisoner exchange. She wants to go home to her family. She wants all this mutual suffering to end. Tsushima should be at peace with Nagoya. We're all Japanese, even if we have no capital city anymore."

"Well, that's just not going to happen," said Yoshida, grinning with conviction. "If Nagoya ever released those pirates, they'd just jump back into their speedboats and seize more Nagoya politicians, just like they grabbed her. No government is that stupid—not even your sorry little emergency government."

"It's true that our hostage negotiations have progressed rather slowly to date," said Miss Sato, restraining herself. "But progress might go very quickly if I could find an authority who could release Mrs. Nagai."

"Forget that," scoffed Yoshida. "If there was anyone in charge here, the Americans would kill him with a drone bomb. That's what they always do."

"Well, since this blind pirate is allowed inside the prison with the hostages, he must have some political influence. Maybe he can lead me to Khadra the Pirate Queen. I've received certain signals that Khadra the Pirate Queen would respond positively to my peace initiatives."

"I can't believe you've been in Tsushima this long and you still have such harebrained ideas," Yoshida said. "Zeta One is useless! Half his head and both his eyes were blown off by a mobile-phone bomb. Zeta One is poor, he's in rags, and he's a drunk. Plus, he smells. And Khadra is not the 'queen' of anything. Nobody's seen Khadra for months. She'd hiding or she's dead. So, forget all about them. Zeta One is not a story, and today I got a hot new lead on a great story. We're going to find a buried treasure today!"

The Toyota rambled past a motley mess of black-market shacks. These shabby hovels had been built to blow over, in storms, or fires, or car bombs, or drone strikes. The pirates who manned them looked just as makeshift and temporary as their shacks.

The Tsushima pirate shacks featured a great many cardboard signs, hand-daubed in English, Korean, Japanese, Chinese, even Tagalog, Malay, and Filipino. They offered the various products of a boat people's theft-based economy.

Used clothing appeared in ragged heaps, with plenty of used Chinese shoes. Also beans, dried tofu, dried fish, bark, roots, seeds, fried insects, anything remotely edible: seaweed, boiled taro stems, acorns scrubbed with soap. Big "wood ear" mushrooms were growing from clear plastic bottles stuffed with wet sawdust.

Also, hand-forged bicycle parts, useless power tools all gone to bright red rust, hand-woven bamboo baskets, rusty radish graters, little clay stoves with tall chimneys. Gloomy pirate molls and their ragged pirate children had some bundled stacks of fuel for sale: straw, reeds, and twigs.

Then, in bursts of relative prosperity, came whitewashed concrete-block hovels, which sold all kinds of things made from dismantled Japanese cars.

These long-dead vehicles yielded chairs, big glass windows, mirrors, wire jewelry, engine-block anvils, and muffler oil lamps.

The truck began weaving back and forth uphill.

Gripping the Toyota's roll bar in the crook of his bare arm, Yoshida unfolded a yellowing sheet of old-fashioned notebook graph paper. "You're good at reading English, right? Kindly read this pirate treasure map for me."

The folded graph paper held a map of the city of Tsushima, a modest village that stretched along the island's eastern coastline. This fiendishly detailed diagram was spotted and dotted all over with bomb craters, skulls, and furious hand-scribbled notes in the English language.

"Maps are always so complicated," said Miss Sato, squinting in dismay. "I can read some names of dead men and the dates when they died . . . This says 'whacko,' in English. Here it says 'wacko,' which is a different English spelling. Also, here it says 'wako,' but that word is in Japanese."

"Yes, a computer-vision genius drew that map," said Yoshida aloud, tapping the side of his close-cropped noggin under the hat. "Computer hackers love puns! When there's no electricity, and their computers are all dead, programmers get touched in the head. My source used to snort Korean speed and stay up for days drawing this map. With nothing but paper and a pencil!"

The Toyota loudly crunched over a broad scattering of bricks and shattered glass. "So is this truly a real map of pirate treasure?" Miss Sato said. "It certainly looks mysterious!"

"Well, this map is mine now, but I'm bad with English," Yoshida said.

"But what does it mean, this map?"

"Well, any treasure map is always news to my readers. I believe this map leads to the sniper death-robot of Boss Takenaka. Boss Takenaka was a 'King of the Pirates' for a while. Takenaka is dead now, of course. A drone strike wiped out his whole gang with one blast, just slaughtered everybody. But three years ago, Boss Takenaka was the scariest gangster this island ever saw."

Yoshida shook his treasure map triumphantly. "My job today is to write the last big news story of Boss Takenaka's career. Everybody's going to read my great scoop too. I'll sell out that whole issue all by myself." Yoshida tucked the folded map in his wallet and rubbed his hands with anticipation.

"Can you stop this truck, please? I need to find this blind pilgrim pirate person. Can you tell me the real name of Zeta One? Where does he live?"

"Look, Zeta One is so brain-damaged that he doesn't remember his name! Nobody on Tsushima has any legal identity. Nobody, never! My real name's not even Yoshida."

Miss Sato was hurt. "Your name isn't Yoshida?"

"I had a legal identity once, but I'm a Tsushima native. The Americans blew up our city halls and destroyed all our legal records."

"Why do they call him 'Zeta Number One'? A name that strange must mean something."

"It's a pun. It's a pirate pun. The Zetas were Mexican drug cops who turned into Mexican drug crooks. Pirates here love that idea, of being a pirate, but also a state privateer. All the biggest pirates in history had some state support. Every pirate thinks he's a master criminal, but he also thinks he's some kind of superspy cop."

Miss Sato wasn't entirely surprised to hear this. She read every issue of *Truth Dawn*, and the newspaper always featured splashy glamour stories about Tsushima's wickedest pirates. Since the tabloid lacked any cameras, the stories were always illustrated with woodcuts.

"Just remember Osama bin Laden," Yoshida said, "the world's most-wanted criminal, living in his mansion as a rich Pakistani spy. This Tsushima story is really an Osama bin Laden story. This is Osama's world now, and the rest of us just live in it."

"I'm getting confused," Miss Sato admitted.

Yoshida nodded as he caught a flea with his thumbnails. "You should read this very important pamphlet that I wrote about the 'Global Pirate Heritage.' My nonfiction pamphlet is full of revealing facts and figures on the subject. I'm gonna write a whole book someday: 'Inside Global Piracy.' Because that's my ticket out of here. My pirate book will make me world famous someday because, unlike most soft sissies who just write about piracy, I'm a skilled reporter who has really been there where piracy happens."

Miss Sato bounced bruisingly from the cab of the Toyota as the wheels hit a fresh patch of rubble. "I can't afford to buy your 'important pamphlet on pirate heritage.' Can you loan it to me?"

"No! Absolutely not! You have to pay! No sharing and no stealing! My pamphlet is totally analog, a privately printed limited edition! It's published only here on Tsushima, with a metal press and handmade local paper! My pamphlet is a precious cultural artifact! Now, if you told your sponsors back in Nagoya to give me a mainland bank account, like I said before . . . "

"My relief society does not engage in any offshore money laundering."

Yoshida sighed. "I keep thinking you'll 'wise up' someday, but you sure are a 'pill' and a 'stick-in-the-mud.' Never mind—that's pirate slang. You wouldn't understand."

The Toyota was climbing uphill. The slopes on the spine of the island were treacherous, precipitous, rocky, and commonly mined. Little terraced patches thick with the weeds of neglect, here and there. Feral fruit trees burst through the tumbledown walls of dead vacation homes.

"When will we return to Tsushima City?" said Miss Sato at last.

"Well, my story deadline for *Truth Dawn* is Wednesday. But I could push that to Thursday morning if I'm willing to set type myself."

"But I have much more important things to do than hunt for some pirate treasure!"

"What are you, crazy? There's nothing more important than treasure! Besides, Boss Takenaka was ten times more important than your stupid female politician hostage from Nagoya. Takenaka was the pirate captain who grabbed your hostage in the first place! Takenaka was a major kingpin—a criminal millionaire warlord wanted in twenty different countries. He was bigger than Chapo Guzman."

"What are you talking about?"

Yoshida sighed. "After they killed Osama bin Laden, Chapo Guzman was the world's second biggest pirate. Since you haven't read my famous pamphlet, you just have no sense of heritage. Boss Takenaka became the warlord of Tsushima, just like bin Laden in Afghanistan and Guzman in Sinaloa. And you know how Takenaka did that? With Japanese high technology. With an augmented computer-vision system from the Mechatronic Visionary Center. That's how he did it."

Yoshida retrieved the paper map from his wallet and passed it over. "Look at all these lines and angles and geometric viewpoints. That's what computer vision looks like when you draw it with a paper and pencil. Takenaka had high-tech killer hardware; he stole it and he deployed it here. And this map shows where it still is. Buried on Tsushima. Just waiting to be dug up."

Miss Sato glanced reluctantly. The patient fanatic who had hand-drawn the map, annotating it with icons, Japglish puns, and at least ten thousand geometric lines, was obviously out of his mind. What could drive a person to such fits of unnatural intensity? Revenge.

Yoshida scratched his whining terrier behind the ears. "So many dead men in this story already—and not one of them dead on Takenaka's own turf. That was my best clue, see? That's how I broke this story wide open.

Listen! Everybody thought that the Americans were killing those pirates with drones. Just more Americans shooting more terrorists with their robot airplanes. That was a lousy story for Truth Dawn because that story's so boring, so old-fashioned, so obvious to everyone. Nobody would want to read about that, trust me."

Yoshida drew a breath. "But—it turns out—and this treasure map proves it—that story's not even true! The truth is, Boss Takenaka had a Japanese robot-vision system. He stole it from the Mechatronic Center and hot-wired it to a machine gun. Then, Takenaka planted that killer thing up in the hills, and that robot vision just watched for pirates, all day and night, like a security camera. So if you carried a gun or a rocket grenade, anything that made you look piratical—pow! Bang! A fifty-caliber round right through the center of your silhouette."

"But why would a pirate like Boss Takenaka kill the other pirates?"

"Because that system was anti-pirate technology. He stole that from the Mechatronic Center, he didn't invent it himself! Pirates are stupid, they can never understand high technology! It's the journalists like me who are smart and always on top of these trends."

"Oh."

"Takenaka wiped out his competition by remote control. That machine gave him a really good alibi too because he was never around when they died. Boss Takenaka used to go to their funerals with big heaps of flowers, that yakuza hypocrite. We even published his eulogies in Truth Dawn, but I finally figured out the truth about Takenaka, and today, I'm going to prove it! I'll inform every subscriber! That's what my career as a trusted newsman is all about."

"Some very smart man must have given you that map," Miss Sato concluded.

"Oh no, don't you dare try that with me," said Yoshida airily, pulling a Korean candy bar from the baggy pocket of his army-surplus shorts. "I will never betray a source." He broke the bar and tossed a sugared morsel to the terrier. "Me and the pup here are gonna sniff out the robot of death! We'll bring it back into town as our trophy. An exclusive scoop! Think how great a machine gun will look next to our big mechanical printing press. Now you see why this matters so much, don't you? Military high tech is always a fantastic story!"

Miss Sato was meekly quiet for a while. Distant thunder rumbled to the west—a big storm brewing over mainland Korea, or possibly Korean artillery. "Yoshida, can I wait for you back in your newspaper office? It sounds like you might be some time."

Yoshida stared at her. "What urgent task do you have now—taking bento boxes to your jailbirds? You'll never understand Tsushima if you don't go up into the hills. Sea pirates may seem strange, but wait till you meet those Afghan misty-mountain monsters up in their opium patches."

Miss Sato smiled politely at this bluster. She was older than Yoshida. Furthermore, she had seen stranger things than the blue shores and green hills of his little island. Miss Sato had worked with salvage crews in the ruins of Tokyo. She had even seen what the furious Americans had done to North Korea in their vengeance for Tokyo.

That was why Miss Sato was not afraid of the pirates of Tsushima. Everyone back in Nagoya assumed that she must be very brave to do her relief work among savage pirates. But pirates were merely people, evil people, and evil was a weakness. Miss Sato feared no evil, but she did fear the righteous wrath of the just. Pirates merely robbed and then fled. The vengeance of the just lasted seven generations.

The Russian Toyota forged from a steep track onto an abandoned parking lot, all thigh-high weeds. Up here at the makeshift rendezvous, some hapless pirate drug trucks had been surprised by American missiles. To judge by the shiny bits of scattered high technology, the bombs had cost ten times as much as the trucks.

Miss Sato endured a further hour of smelly engine-gunning, scary skidding, drunken maneuvering, and much cursing in Russian. The precipitous slopes were daubed with feeble lines of mildewed cardboard and spray-bombed graffiti tags. These were long-departed pirate gangs, ferociously warning other dead marauders never to cross the line.

Then a more serious boundary appeared: a kind of pirate Chinese Wall. This barricade was all cheap cement and poorly stacked concrete cinder blocks, but it was as tall as a man could reach and topped with razor wire. There were guardhouses too. Once upon a time, someone had clear-cut the forest to create clean lines of fire along the wall. Now crooked weed trees were engulfing all of that.

The Russian driver carefully unfolded an ancient paper map of Tsushima Island. He conferred with his colleague, a scarred and helmeted global guerrilla who was even drunker than he was.

"We're lost," said Yoshida with relish. This was an exotic, pirate-island thing to say, because people in the rest of the world never got "lost." The rest of the world featured smartphones and tower antennas and satellite locators. But not dark little Tsushima, where all such things had been bombed back to dust and mud.

"Takenaka's walls aren't on any maps," said Yoshida. "Look what he did to that precious old-growth forest, that rascal. You know what? I'm gonna get my Russian friends here to level a chunk of this wall with their antiaircraft gun. Then we can just drive through it."

"Maybe there are mines in that death strip," said Miss Sato.

"You're always carrying on about mines. Takenaka's smart mines ran out of batteries long ago. Why do you think Truth Dawn hires these Russian guys? Takenaka's long dead, nobody's gonna mind. Let them limber up the Russian artillery there, this will look great in my story."

Yoshida engaged in some pidgin shout-and-gesture with his mercenaries. The Russians, who were no older or wiser than Yoshida, had no trouble catching on to his idea. They were very proud of their big gun. They whooped with glee as each deafening round punched a massive hole in the pirate barricade.

Every bang from the jolting gun blew through Miss Sato's scarfed head. It made the very hills ring. From somewhere in the sullen hills came answering blasts. Protest? Celebration?

Yoshida's terrier leapt from the back of the Toyota. The dog bulleted off through the weeds, his furry legs a blur. He disappeared through a freshly blasted hole in the pirate wall.

Yoshida reached down and hooked up a stack of his newspapers, bound with a thick hemp string. "Now we follow the dog," he said, dismounting from the truck.

"Why?"

"Because he's my dog. You want to stay here breaking bricks with Yuri and Leonid? Give them my best!"

Miss Sato followed Yoshida as he pursued the eager dog. They ducked through the fresh rubble of the blasted barricade. No human foot had stepped here in years. The three of them were in utter wilderness, snagged by briars, scratched by weeds, and bitten by whining mosquitoes.

"You told me once you could get me an audience with the Pirate Queen," Miss Sato called out, groping at damp boughs and stepping over wet nettles. "Khadra may be 'hiding underground,' but that doesn't mean that she can hide from you. Not if you really want to find her."

"Look, you need to stop trying to be clever," said Yoshida absently.

"Khadra is just a gangster moll. Khadra's boyfriend Takenaka was a 'King of the Pirates,' but he got blown to bits. Khadra's just a Somalian hooker. She takes her men as they come along, and there's always some new one."

Miss Sato ignored this impropriety. "But the Americans, the Chinese, the Koreans, they uniformly agree—she's the 'Pirate Queen of Tsushima.' They all agree that if an act of mercy can resolve my hostage crisis, then Khadra would be the key actor."

"That's the lying mainstream media! They just say that for their own political advantage. Khadra doesn't rule this island, she is just some pretty Somali girl who got mixed up with pirates! Every man she ever kissed gets killed. And I'll tell you why—it's because Khadra is a police informant. She rats out her lovers to the Chinese, or the Koreans, or the Americans— whoever pays her most."

Miss Sato considered this assertion. She and Yoshida were both lost in the tall grass.

"Doesn't anyone in this world have any sense of decency?" Miss Sato said at last.

"It's the truth! Think about it. Once you're a pirate's woman, you can't just divorce your pirate and walk away. He's evil, he's a killer, and to be free of him you have to have him killed." Yoshida insistently stamped a path through some windblown, rotten bamboo. "It was Khadra who betrayed Boss Takenaka. Khadra got him blown to bits, eighty men dead in one night. A real massacre. Someday I'll find the proof that Khadra herself did that. Then I'll write that story and publish it. People will be totally amazed!"

"Maybe Khadra isn't a pirate queen or a police spy or a hooker or a gangster moll, or any of those cruel things you say about her," Miss Sato offered. "Maybe Khadra's just a refugee woman who is cruelly exploited by violent men. At least, Khadra would know what that means to a woman. And why that oppression should end."

"Oh no, Khadra's evil, all right," said Yoshida. "But I'm not in any hurry to denounce Khadra. That's because Khadra is such great copy. Hot news stories about exotic, promiscuous pirate beauties will practically write themselves. Hey, hey, wait, look at this, look what my dog just found here! Good boy!" Yoshida fell to his bare knees in his cargo shorts. "This is Tsushima ginseng! Still growing up here in the good old mountain wilderness, imagine that! Wild ginseng is as rare as a Tsushima wildcat! This must be my lucky day."

"You could sell that ginseng to a rich Korean," Miss Sato said, "if there were any rich Koreans to eat ginseng anymore."

"That was a joke of yours, wasn't it?" asked Yoshida, rising to his feet with a scowl. "Ginseng is Tsushima's truest buried treasure. I could dig up this root right now if I had a shovel instead of my newspapers. Ginseng roots are shaped just like buried men, you know. They're full of mystical vitamins."

Miss Sato reached into her woven handbag and produced a half-empty bottle of multivitamin pills. "You don't need any dark, ancient roots."

Yoshida wiped wet dirt from his hands and dry-gulped a vitamin. "Well, let's dig up one pirate treasure at a time. Boss Takenaka's robot gun is buried somewhere on this hill. My map says we're standing near it right now." Yoshida waved his hands around the rugged woods, which had a commanding view of the island's eastern slopes. "This was Takenaka's favorite turf. He wanted to dig in deep, up here, with secret forts and pillboxes. Dig in and fight it out to the bitter end, Pacific-War style. Just like the kamikazes from World War II, a hundred years ago."

"The kamikazes flew airplanes," Miss Sato corrected him. "They didn't dig any secret forts in hills."

"Well," said Yoshida, offended, "I meant to say the original kamikazes—the samurai who fought Mongols here on my island, one thousand years ago."

"Weeds are pirates, while pirates spread like weeds."

"That's pretty clever," said Yoshida.

"I read that in your newspaper."

"I've got a real way with words," Yoshida agreed. He gazed around, alertly smiling. "It's incredible how fast the weeds grow during climate change. Turn your back, and the weeds just take over the world! Post-atomic Tokyo is one huge vacant lot now, a vast dead city full of weeds. Fukushima has mutant trees ten meters high!"

"Fukushima is not so bad as that," Miss Sato said. "I've been to Fukushima. Fukushima is very peaceful and pretty. Fukushima has no people, but it is full of wildlife."

Yoshida scowled. "What kind of wildlife is in Fukushima? Glowing, three-eyed dolphin mutants?"

"Whales are in Fukushima. Siberian cranes. Wild monkeys even." Miss Sato laughed. "Monkeys are so funny. Monkeys are much kinder to each other than people are."

Yoshida glanced up at the clouding sky and shifted his bundle of newspapers. "Now it's trying to rain on us. All you have to do is talk about the 'sacred wind,' and here it comes to get you, the kamikaze! Did you ever notice that, when you speak the words 'climate change,' the weather will actually change?"

Miss Sato nodded. "Oh yes. Everybody says that nowadays. Even on the mainland."

"I spotted some roofs on the far side of that ravine," said Yoshida. He picked up his dog in one arm and hefted his newspapers in the other. "So I bet there's a village where I can deliver my newspapers. We'll be uphill of the sniper nest too. So maybe we can see it by looking down at it from a position of vantage."

Yoshida was young and energetic rather than reasonable, but his thrashing through the tall weeds was soon rewarded. He led her from the choking, tangled overgrowth into a clearer area.

Boss Takenaka had built a concealed guardhouse here to defend his mountainside drug farms. Faded warnings of land mines were nailed to the larger trees.

A warm, sticky drizzle began to fall. It was the premonition of much worse weather to come.

"Land mines," Miss Sato murmured.

"Those signs are probably lying," Yoshida advised. He scampered forward along with his yapping terrier. Miss Sato followed, treading with care in his footsteps.

The pirate guardhouse was almost invisible, built to fool aerial surveillance by military drones. The big hut was roofed with a dense thatch, thoroughly smeared with mud and festooned with flourishing gourd vines. Crooked sniper holes allowed a few rays of daylight.

The yawning door was hung all over with lucky pirate amulets. Superstitions had arrived here from all over the planet: wreathed anchors, topless mermaids, see-no-evil monkeys, marijuana leaves, hooded skeletons. Crossed revolvers, hypodermics, bloody dice, Taoist yin-yangs, lightning bolts, ninja masks . . .

Inside the guardhouse were three stone steps leading downward. Dried herbs and spider webs dangled from the rafters. The uneven floor of the hut—just simple, damp, pounded earth—was strewn with rotting tatami mats.

The terrier trotted down the steps and barked at a pile of damp hay in the hut's darkest corner. The hay-pile sat up. It revealed itself as a slumbering derelict under a thick straw raincoat.

"Nice dog," the blind man said mildly, grasping at a long stick. "I know your voice, doggie! If you are here, then your master, that journalist, must be nearby."

"That's right," Yoshida admitted, "and fancy meeting you in here, Zeta One."

"The sacred wind always makes me sleepy," said Zeta One. He crowned his dented head with a rain hat. His conical hat was the size of a bicycle wheel and, from above, made him resemble some harmless patch of weedy island sod.

Zeta One sniffed aloud. "So, what brings you to this lonely place, with your pretty female friend, who is standing there? Should I ask that?"

"She is not my girlfriend," said Yoshida. "She is Miss Sato from the Federation of Nine Relief Societies. She's a peace activist from the mainland."

"So then you're from Nagoya, Miss Sato," said Zeta One, fingering his pilgrim's sacred cane. "I can tell that by the way you talk."

"But I haven't said a word," Miss Sato said.

"See, you really are from Nagoya."

"Are you living inside this shack these days?" asked Yoshida. "I haven't seen you in Tsushima City lately. At least, not since that gambling house exploded. The casino that kicked you out."

"Ah, well then," said Zeta One, smiling blindly into the dim air lit by sniper holes, "a fine young gentleman like yourself doesn't frequent the brothels and gambling dens where a reprobate like me passes his time."

"Well, yes, being a journalist, I do spend my time in there, actually. I was lucky not to get killed."

"We keep different hours," said Zeta One. "Poor, blind wretch that I am, I can't tell any difference between night and day. It's only due to the kindness of strangers that I get by on humble charity bowls of sweet-potato porridge."

A flicker of irritation crossed Yoshida's youthful face. "So—what exactly are you doing in here?"

"I am sleeping the big storm away," said the blind man with a tender, confiding smile. "I can't see the lightning, so the lightning might kill me. The sound of thunder on my poor blind ears, that always makes me jump with fear."

"I don't believe a word of that," Yoshida objected. "Miss Sato and I were just discussing you, not one hour ago. And yet here you are, 'like the daughter-in-law who ate the autumn eggplants.' "

"No one believes in your old proverbs anymore."

"My old proverbs have nothing to do with it! Obviously you knew that we were coming here! You were lurking in here, waiting for us."

"You're such nice people," said Zeta One, "that this must be a blessing from the Goddess of Mercy. You see, in penance for the many past sins of my wretched former life, I have vowed to visit all six temples of the Kannon on Tsushima. Now that I'm on my sacred pilgrimage to the east, west, north, and south of this island. Meeting you is how the Goddess rewards me for my piety."

"What a sweet thing to say," Miss Sato interrupted. "I'm glad to hear of such a blessing! Because I've been searching for you, Mr. Zeta One. I bring you some personal greetings from Mrs. Mieko Nagai. Mrs. Nagai is an unfortunate hostage who is held captive in chains, as you know. And she told me you were kind to her. That's the truth, isn't it?"

"Well, that's all for you to judge, miss," said Zeta One, adjusting a twisted leather thong on his huge rain hat. "This poor old bean of mine took quite a pounding in the old days. So I'm afraid I don't remember any Mrs. Michiko what's-her-name . . . Never saw one glimpse of that lady, can't remember what I don't see, please forgive me." He briefly bowed where he sat.

"Oh stop all that," Yoshida objected. "You wouldn't fool a ten-year-old child!"

Zeta One meekly and silently rubbed at his long cane.

"You got that cane from the Mechatronic Visionary Center," said Yoshida. "You did, didn't you?"

Zeta One chuckled. "What, a poor blind wanderer like me, who can't even read a computer screen? Whatever would I know of your fancy technology?"

"You're in and out of that damn lab all the time, you big faker! You wrapped that metal antenna in leather, and you smeared it with dirt, but that thing's packed with circuitry. That cane has got some kind of radar."

Alarmed by the anger in his master's voice, the terrier began barking furiously at a spider. The spider, disturbed by the rain, was inching up the timber of a ridgepole.

Without looking at the spider—without listening, without even turning his much-battered head—Zeta One hefted his staff, reached out, and precisely mashed the spider into paste.

"You shouldn't scold a blind man about his cane, Mr. Yoshida," said Miss Sato, in the rising patter of rain. "That isn't decent."

"I can tell by your sweet voice that you're a kindhearted lady, Miss Sato," said Zeta One as he levered himself to his huge, callused, straw-sandaled, and malodorous feet. "Not like this nosy young man with his Communist scandal sheet. I'll be on my way to the local temple of mercy. No one cares if an old blind man is soaked to the skin by the typhoon."

"You're not leaving until you tell us why you were waiting here for us," Yoshida said.

"Who, me? But I want nothing from you!" said Zeta One. He shook a leather bag on a belt under his shaggy raincoat. "Unless you want to give me a few gold coins to gamble away at the dice house. That's my only amusement—to listen to the rattle of the dice and the cries of the yakuza gamblers."

"I'll go with you to the temple," said Miss Sato at once.

Yoshida was scandalized. "You can't wander off with this sleazy character! You can't trust him. How can a blind man gamble with dice? He can't even see the spots!"

"You might as well ask why this pirate island has gold coins!" Miss Sato shouted. "Nobody wants Tsushima's stupid coins. Mint all the fake treasure you want, your gold has no legal value with any government! Pirate gold is worse than trash!"

Zeta One rumbled with laughter. "I do so enjoy the witty chatter of clever people. Sadly, since my brain was damaged, I can't keep up with the likes of you. Goodbye." He tapped his way toward the stairs of the guardhouse.

Yoshida blocked his way. The two men confronted one another for a moment, Yoshida glaring and Zeta One mildly turning his ravaged face to the dirt floor. Then, reluctantly, Yoshida stepped aside.

Zeta One found the yawning door of the hut with the tip of his stick. Then he left.

Miss Sato followed him. The forest trail was a sinister maze of briars, loose rocks, and rain-slick muddy slopes. Also, it was raining. But Zeta One moved at quite a brisk pace, setting his huge, sandaled feet with firm decision, like a man placing go stones.

"I'd appreciate it if you stopped following me," Zeta One said at last, stopping but not turning to face her.

"Now that I've finally found you," said Miss Sato meekly, "I'm so afraid to lose you."

"Maybe you're falling in love with me." Zeta One chortled. "Young ladies often do that, you know."

"I might do that," said Miss Sato. "Because I'm a woman with so many troubles, and you're such an interesting man."

The sun emerged from between two swirling fronts of the oncoming storm. Birds sang out in relief, and the trees dripped. "There are land mines all around us here," said Zeta One. "Even your dainty little feet can set one off."

"Oh, that's quite all right. I'm not afraid when you're here. I'll just come along with you."

"Maybe you'd like it if I sang you a song as we walk through these land mines."

"A song? That might be nice."

"Yes, I know an old song from old Tsushima. When it was just an innocent island, long before any satellite positioning or any bomb-targeting maps. You see, my girl, back in the good old days on Tsushima, the trails in this island's great forests were dark even at midday. So every Tsushima boy, and most every girl, knew a song of all the roadmarks. That's what I sing to myself as I make my pilgrimage."

The blind man sang in time with his sandaled steps. Every dozen paces, he would whirl the cane above his head. He poked it about from one side to the other, tilted his rain-hatted head this way and that, sniffed at the air, muttered, and sang. The Korean-flavored, Japanese island dialect was impossible to understand.

"How did you learn such songs?" Miss Sato said at last.

"From old wind-up Victrolas," Zeta One said. "Those old songs were collected by Mr. Miyamoto Tsunekazu, for whom they made the famous Daffodil Festival. But of course stupid old island songs are of no interest to a fine Nagoya girl like yourself."

"I can sing," Miss Sato volunteered.

"That would be a kindness, since we blind men are so appreciative of music. What songs do you sing?"

"I sing protest songs," said Miss Sato. "Peace songs, resistance songs, nuclear disarmament songs, and civil rights songs. Also, many personal singer-songwriter songs about how difficult it is to be a contemporary Japanese woman."

Zeta One cocked his head. "Don't you know any happy songs?"

"You mean children's songs? Yes, I still remember a few."

Zeta One reached under his baggy straw cape and grubbed around through a set of pockets on a bandolier. He munched a brown handful of shredded squid. "Would you like some?"

"Yes," said Miss Sato, plucking the tangled mess out of his hand but not eating it.

"I want you to do something for me."

"What is that?"

"There are solar panels concealed somewhere near here. Those are great treasures because they have power . . . but I can't remember where I put them. The panels are hung high up in the trees. People never look up when they search for pirate treasure. They always think it must be under the ground." He chuckled.

"How can a blind man climb a tree?"

"I'd like you better if you didn't ask questions," Zeta One said simply.

Miss Sato obediently gazed at the tops of the forest trees. It took a while, but she was patient and persistent. At length she spotted a gleam in the canopy. Two solar panels were visible. A monkey couldn't have carried them any higher. A man of Zeta One's bulk, and blind, clambering so high up there while carrying solar panels? Incredible.

However, she asked no more questions. She guided Zeta One to the tree trunk.

The power cable's plastic sheath was dappled with forest camouflage. It had been hidden with devious cunning—writhing through leaf litter, ducking under thorn bushes.

This power cable led, dodging and wriggling, to a spider hole buried in the hill-slope. This cunningly hidden death trap was all vine-covered sandbags, with just one wide leafy slit, like a mouth in an eyeless skull.

The vision-slit commanded an impressive view over the bay of Tsushima City, a splendid vista of East China Sea blue, with a lacy, roiling storm front stretching toward distant Japan.

The spider hole smelled of damp earth and ruin. Inside it squatted a stark mechanism, a long muzzle with legs, cogs, and exposed wiring. The rains and island damp had been at the robot machine gun. It had rusted to junk.

"You built this," said Miss Sato. "You knew it was here, so you're the one who built it."

"I don't remember about that," said Zeta One, "but it would be a good idea if it wasn't here anymore. It would bad if someone sullied the memory of Boss Takenaka, that yakuza man-of-honor. Also, Boss Murai; Murai was killed too, so one shouldn't speak ill of him. Boss Shosuke was never a friendly man, but after the way he perished, it's better to say nothing about that."

Zeta One heaved and pried at the heavy sandbags. After much grunting, hand-groping, and ripping of snarled vines, he hauled the sniper gun from its camouflaged lair. He patted the lethal mechanism from stem to stern, muttering to himself.

Then he briskly dismantled the big, rusty gun, like a sushi chef boning a tuna.

Miss Sato spoke up. "My friend, the journalist, says that this robot gun killed many pirates. They died in the streets of Tsushima City, far away, far downhill there. Farther than a human eye can see."

"I wouldn't know about that," said Zeta One, "as I was never here or there when that happened. I'm always far away when bad men come to bad ends." He bundled up the gun's stripped components, wrapping them with rotten strips of sandbag. "Now, I need some deep water. Even a blind man knows that water always runs downhill . . . " He chuckled to himself. "But I can't carry this gun because I need my staff to walk."

"I'll carry the gun for you," Miss Sato volunteered. "Getting rid of guns is always a good thing to do."

"Don't carry the muzzle like that," he said, gripping her hand. "If you show any silhouette with a heavy weapon, we might both be struck by a drone. Stay below the ridges, because your body might be outlined to a flying robot. Don't walk like a human being walks. The flying machines know what that gait is like. Bend down. Walk like an animal."

Miss Sato's clumsy efforts to skulk didn't please him. He unknotted his shaggy straw cape and wrapped her up in that disguise. His cape reeked of sweat and mildew.

Beneath his cape Zeta One wore crossed webbing bandoliers. Most patches on the bandoliers were empty, and others smelled like rotting squid, yet among this derelict jumble was a personal belt-bomb. A clipped-together set of wires, a battery pack, and seven little cartons of plastique.

She knew better than to ask him about that.

The two of them lurked and skulked downhill until she spotted the slumped ruins of a vacation house. "I can see a big swimming pool over there," she told him. "It's full of mosquitoes and mud."

"When it comes to buried treasure, mud is even better than dirt," said Zeta One. "I'm sure a dainty lady like you doesn't want to touch any filthy mud. But if you will kindly help me into that smelly morass and give me that robot gun, then I'll wallow about a bit and bury it."

Zeta One carefully leaned his long cane at the rim of the dead swimming pool. Then, splashing and snorting like a walrus, Zeta One buried the ruined weapon. He trampled it deep into the all-obscuring muck.

"Can you see anything of the treasure now?" he asked her at last.

"No. No one could possibly see it."

"You're sure," he said. He slapped at a few hungry mosquitoes.

"I'm sure. You are waist-deep in that mud, and the robot monster is deep under your big feet. No one will ever see."

"It's always good to hear," said Zeta One, "that everyone else is just as blind as me." He chuckled. "That means that everyone will forget. My work here is done, and now I have to get out of this mud. For a tired old man like myself, that's not so easy." He stretched out one mud-caked hand.

"I can't reach you," said Miss Sato.

"Why not? Where are you?"

"If I get any closer, I'll get stuck in there myself."

"Just reach out to me with my staff."

"I don't believe I can see your staff," Miss Sato said, picking it up. "It's gone. I can't remember where you left it."

Zeta One stirred about in the wallow of mud. He removed his straw hat and threw it outside the swimming pool. His skull was curiously scarred and thin gray hair grew in patches.

"This situation is so very much like the sad fate of Mrs. Nagai," Miss Sato remarked brightly. "For four years, I've been promising to release her from that jail. She is an elected official of my government, and I helped to elect her. When I visited her, this time, and she told me about you and how kind you are, well, I swore I wouldn't leave the island. Not unless I can take her home with me."

Zeta One muttered in disbelief.

"That was my sacred vow," Miss Sato said casually.

"Your friends in Nagoya can solve your hostage problem," Zeta One said. "It's always foolish for a government to be trapped by sentimental feelings for the innocent. Tell them to bomb the hostage compound. Kill them all, and level the Mechatronic Visionary Center to the ground."

"I'm sure there's some better plan that's rather less cruel."

"I don't make strategic plans." Zeta One shrugged. "Living from day to day as I do. You should listen when I tell you to destroy my own home. That's where they put me when they brought me back from Somalia. They stitched me back together in there. They did amazing things to me. They were cruel things, but I volunteered for the cruelty."

"I volunteered for all this too," said Miss Sato. "That's why, unfortunately, you're not getting free unless Mrs. Nagai also gets free."

Time passed after this declaration. Zeta One struggled to extricate himself from the clutching mud. He made some small progress, but he had to pause periodically to ward off the mosquitoes. Their fierce, annoying whine seemed to bother him far more than their bites.

Miss Sato shared the bites of the mosquitoes. They were painful and possibly infectious.

"I have another plan," said Zeta One at last. "Visit the hostage and leave her a metal file. She could saw the chain off her leg. Then, one dark stormy night, a friend throws a rope ladder over the wall. The escaped captive would use standard escape-and-evasion techniques to reach Teppu Point at the southern tip of Tsushima. Then, swim to the Australian navy base on Naiin Island."

"Mrs. Nagai isn't a global commando. Mrs. Nagai is a sixty-year-old female socialist politician."

"It's a pity my tactics are so inadequate," said Zeta One as he killed another mosquito. "It seems I'm doomed to drown in mud."

"It's bad enough that we have an Australian naval base in Japanese waters!" said Miss Sato, slapping her own mosquito-bitten cheek. "Where is your pride? Where is your decency and honor? All we have to do is liberate one innocent Japanese woman from a terrible situation, and you're carrying on like that's the end of the world! Do we all have to blow ourselves up?"

Miss Sato paced back and forth, rapping the rim of the swimming pool with his heavy cane. "When I think of all the money we Japanese wasted on our soldiery, you men who should have been our roof tiles and instead cost us more than jewels. And for what? What safety and security did you soldiers ever bring us? After all your strutting and boasting and shouting through megaphones and waving of your big, striped, fascist flags, we lost our own capital to a sneak attack! Now we're beset by bandits, and the more we bomb them, the crazier they get!"

"Japan was a pirate island," rumbled Zeta One. "Tsushima was the biggest pirate island in the world for three hundred years. When the pirates ruled Tsushima, there was no Japan, just warlords who killed each other every spring. Evil men came here to rob Asia from as far away as Portugal."

"You sound proud of these evil, wandering men."

"Proud of them? I'm one of them."

A white terrier leapt over a tumbledown wall and began yapping in frenzy.

"I should have blown up that kid's stupid newspaper a long time ago," Zeta One said. "No target is softer than a reporter . . . But since he was born here on Tsushima, well, none of this was really his fault. Yes, yes, I feel true regret for his native family."

Miss Sato watched as the terrier scampered back and forth, yapping till it drooled in sharp distress. "I hate all dogs, but there's something quite wrong with this dog's behavior. I think he wants us to help his master."

"Who, us? How?"

Pirates arrived. They were mountain pirates, the creatures of the backwoods. There were forty of them, and their mood was evident by the fact that they had the severed heads of the two Russian drivers, Yuri and Leonid, stuck onto two sharp steel poles.

These mountain pirates were mostly teenagers, fearless youth who had never spent a day in school. To judge by their angry, pidgin jabber, they had no language in common either. They had only three great commonalities among them: scars and bad tattoos were two of them.

Fresh, bloody wounds were also common because Yuri and Leonid, being Russians, had battled to their last breath.

A few older pirates lurked among the bloodstained crowd of feral teens, veterans of thirty who looked about sixty. They were jittery, twitchy, red-eyed, heavily armed, and very high on drugs. No pirate gang was a family, so these were not motherly, fatherly, older people. The older pirates had the timeworn look of prison trustees, bad people grimly burdened with the task of keeping even worse people in line.

The Toyota's antiaircraft gun was their latest trophy, lashed to a shoulder-borne tote pole. The same fate had befallen Yoshida. The captured journalist had been lashed to a pole with leather thongs at his wrists and ankles.

"Don't you worry, Miss Sato!" Yoshida called out. "I sold all my newspapers!"

Miss Sato picked up Zeta One's metal staff and threw it to the blind man. This quick gesture made little sense, but she knew they would steal the cane from her, and she didn't want that to be her fault.

Irritated by this gesture of defiance, the pirates fell upon Miss Sato and beat her up. Miss Sato limply dropped to the damp earth and offered no resistance. They kicked her, punched her, dragged her around by the hair, tore her clothes off, crudely tied her arms and legs, urinated on her, shouted many insults, and threw mud in her face.

Miss Sato shouted with pain at appropriate times and guarded her vital organs from the blows. Being young people, they soon grew bored with the trouble.

The pirates dumped Yoshida next to her, bound hand and foot. Yoshida rolled in the mud to face her. "My newspaper has comic strips," Yoshida confided. "They can't read the words, but even illiterates love comics."

Miss Sato searched with her tongue for any broken teeth.

"Modern global pirates are a simple people at heart," said Yoshida.

These backwoods Tsushima pirates were studying Zeta One, who was mired in his mud but clutching his cane alertly. They were genuinely puzzled about what to do about him. He was too poor to have anything they wanted to steal, and nobody wanted to jump in the mud and attempt to haul him out. Likely they had noticed his mud-smeared personal belt-bomb.

"What are they going to do to him?" said Miss Sato to Yoshida.

"Well," said Yoshida, "they could shoot him and leave him there."

"If they shoot him, he's going to explode. I'm sure his belt-bomb has a dead-man's switch. He likely has a hidden second bomb, timed to go off when rescuers come to investigate the first bomb. That is rather standard."

"You know," said Yoshida, craning his neck to investigate her bound and naked body, "for a feminist peace campaigner, you're a lot tougher than you look. Where did you get all those scars on your body? You've got more scars than some of these pirates do."

"These pirates never did any salvage work in Tokyo. Skyscrapers fell down in Tokyo. Buildings that big, they fall down even long after they fall down."

"You'll rebuild your Tokyo someday, I suppose."

"No, Tokyo is over. But Japan isn't. Pay attention now. If they shoot him, he will explode. You and I will be deafened and wounded by the blast. But these pirates will all be dead because they're standing up. They're in blast range."

Yoshida's terrier arrived. It tenderly licked Yoshida's face as he lay there bound hand and foot. "Stop briefing me about bombs," Yoshida complained. "I know all about bombs. I wrote a hundred bomb atrocity stories for *Truth Dawn*, and they're always just the same."

The pirates fell silent at the rumble of an approaching jeep. This ex-military American Humvee was a psychedelic wonder of feathers and fronds, all fuchsia, hot pink, magenta, and vermilion. It bore a large and silent uniformed driver and, in the back, a statuesque, very pregnant African woman.

Khadra the Pirate Queen dressed as if a treasure chest had been emptied on her gravid body. She wore necklaces, bangles, rings, hammered gold badges, ropes of pearls, a towering crown of leather and feathers half a meter high, and not much else.

"Stop here," Khadra told her driver in Japanese. She studied the scene before her. "Well! What a good opportunity to get rid of three trespassers and put their bones in this mud pit."

"So, what's new with you, Khadra?" the journalist called out. "Who's the new father?"

"If I wanted you to know about my lovers," said the gorgeous Queen of Pirates, "I wouldn't be living underground. Yoshida, who is this ugly, naked, skinny woman?"

"Miss Sato is a peace activist from the mainland. She is a hostage negotiator."

"Well, well," said the pirate queen, "another mainland captive, that's so nice. Why isn't she chained in the compound with the others? Take her there right away. Wait—untie her and put some clothes on her first, she looks ugly. Also, pull those severed heads off those poles. Those always look vulgar. Can you talk?"

"Yes," said Miss Sato, standing up shakily as four or five pirates gripped her bruised limbs. "Yes, I can talk to you."

"Are you from North Japan, or are you from South Japan?"

"I came here to Tsushima from Nagoya."

"That's really too bad for you," said the pirate queen serenely. "If you'd been one of my dear friends from North Japan, then I would have released you now with all courtesies. And even given you rich gifts of gold and silk and exotic drugs. Whatever you like. But since you're an aggressive corporate criminal who comes from evil South Japan, then I must charge you with overfishing in Tsushima's territorial waters. Also, you are guilty of abusing our beautiful island republic as your toxic waste dump. That's why you're my hostage. You understand that? All right? Good! Now! How much do you think your family would pay for you? In American dollars."

"Khadra," Yoshida protested, "Miss Sato can't be your hostage. She's an official hostage negotiator from the Nagoya regime. It's because of her that the people in South Japan know that we still hold hostages here. See, that's all been settled. That was all printed in the newspaper."

Yoshida's terrier yapped triumphantly.

"Untie that journalist," Khadra said. "We can't shoot a journalist. We need his newspaper to publish our demands and communiques. Also, all the foreign intelligence agencies read his newspaper. He's valuable. That's a cute dog."

An obedient teenager sawed through Yoshida's leather bonds. "Thanks," Yoshida said, rubbing his skinned wrists.

"Now shoot the cute dog," Khadra commanded. Her burly driver pulled out a chromed sidearm and put a round through the terrier. Galvanized with a final spastic fit of animal vitality, the dog ran shrieking in a tight circle and died coughing blood.

"Now throw that bloody dead dog into that dirty mud pit. Dead dogs are so disgusting. You there, big dirty blind man, yes, you, stuck in that mud like a hippopotamus. Bury that dog in the mud for me now. I don't like the way that dog looks."

"I can't see any dog," said Zeta One reasonably. "I'm a blind man."

"Blind man, what are you doing there, stuck in that mud?"

"Your highness, ma'am, your great and beautiful ladyship, I'm on a pilgrimage to the six sacred shrines of the Goddess of Mercy," declared Zeta One. "I seek forgiveness for my many past crimes. But I'm so blind, so stupid and clumsy, that I slipped and fell in here. In my pitiful efforts to thrash my way out, I just sank in deeper and deeper, until, well, I almost lost my cane. If you would graciously help me out of this predicament, I would pray for you until my last days."

"I love this blind man," Khadra said. "I always loved him, because he has the proper humble attitude. All of you should be more like him. He's sweet. Jump in there now and pull him out of that muck."

None of the pirates showed any signs of obeying Khadra on the issue of the mud. They'd been a little startled by the pirate queen's sudden advent in her jeep festooned with seashells, fake pearls, and rhinestone jewels, but they had rapidly lost interest in her. The pirates were a shell-shocked people by nature. They were up to the things that any very ill-organized crowd would do when lost in the woods. They were swatting mosquitoes, aimlessly gathering firewood, scrounging for edible herbs, crouching pantsless behind trees, and so forth.

Miss Sato realized that she was not going to be immediately killed. Although she had been stripped and beaten, she was neither surprised nor afraid. "I'm proud to meet the Queen of the Pirates," she called out in a loud, even voice. "Because I've asked to meet you many times! People often spoke to me of your good temper, your good sense, and your sincerity, and now I can see why."

"Are you talking to me now, you ugly, skinny old woman?"

"Of course! I want to ask you a favor."

"Well, you're not allowed to talk to me in your disgusting condition! Somebody put some clothes on the ugly peacenik witch there. You there, yes, you, the girl with bones in your dreadlocks. Take all your clothes off, put them on the hostage, you're the right size. Yes, your shoes too, especially your shoes, and the rest of you, stop fooling around! It's important when the Queen of the Pirates negotiates with organized governments! You should pay attention to my maneuvers—you'll learn something. Now, hostage, or hostage negotiator, whatever, how many hostages do you want to buy from me? What treasure did you bring me? You didn't bring me very much, unless someone else already robbed you."

Miss Sato knotted a dirty straw skirt around her waist. Then she slipped her bare arms into the girl-pirate's rough canvas coat. "I'd hoped," she said, "that a leader of your great qualities would release one innocent woman for me as an important moral gesture."

"Oh, right, you're one of those, are you?" said the Queen of the Pirates. "You think I've never met your kind before? I know all about you people and your 'moral gestures.' Well, listen to this, bitch: I didn't capture those hostages. I didn't grab them any more than I blew out the eyes of this poor blind man here. It's not my fault that they have to be kept there so that you won't destroy our precious high-tech cultural compound."

"The Federation of Nine Relief Societies never blows up anyone."

"Yes you do. You are dropping bombs on innocent women and children here just like that man Guernica and his painting of Picasso. I should have that beautiful painting tattooed on your ugly, skinny back, you penniless hypocrite. If you want this woman released, why don't you agree to take her place yourself? Ha!"

"I already agreed to take the place of Mrs. Nagai," said Miss Sato. "I agreed to that condition four years ago. Let's do that right now. Let Mrs. Nagai go home, and I will stay in her place."

"Oh my God, how boring!" protested the Queen of Pirates. "What a bother to have to put up with this crazy, ugly woman when that poor blind man there is almost drowning in his mud! Every week I'm harassed by arrogant demands from you stinking mainland bureaucrats, when the loyal subjects of my island, like the blind man there, suffer your oppression." She turned to her enormous, mute brute of a driver. "I want him out of there. Get the big towing chain."

Miss Sato turned her attention to Yoshida. "Well," she began, "we're making some good progress here," and then she broke off because, to her surprise, Yoshida was racked with silent sobs.

"What's wrong?" she said.

"The pirate queen killed my dog," Yoshida choked out.

"What? But you're a journalist in a conflict zone. You see bodies every week!"

"He was my best friend," said Yoshida, writhing with woe and shaking like a leaf.

A pirate approached and slapped Yoshida on the back. "Don't take that so hard," he urged in English. Miss Sato hadn't spotted this English-speaking pirate among the group before—he was dressed with particular oddity.

This new interloper was dressed in land mine-removal armor. He wore the big ceramic helmet with its platelike tinted blast shield, which gave his hidden head an angular, turtleish appearance. He also wore big blast-sloping epaulets that guarded his neck and shoulders, samurai-style. Ridged overlapping plates nestled around his back and belly, but this peculiar gear simply ended at his skinny ass. He wore ragged shorts and rubber wading boots.

"Where's the damn robot gun?" he demanded from Yoshida in English. "You were supposed to fetch down that machine gun for me today."

"I can't talk English to you," Yoshida said in Japanese. "I'm too upset!"

"What the hell good are you, then?" said the faceless man in the armor. "I gave you this important news leak on a plate! All you had to do was dig that circuitry out of its hole and bring it back to me."

"I don't know where your robot gun is," said Yoshida in anguish. "Leave me alone."

Everyone was leaving the interloper alone. This seemed odd for a group of aggressive pirates. Then Miss Sato noticed that, along with his de-mining gear, the stranger was carrying a muddy satchel full of freshly grubbed-up land mines. He had disinterred these treasures somehow and now carried them around like so many daikon radishes.

"I know where your robot gun is," said Miss Sato to the faceless man in English. "Who are you?"

The faceless man casually waved his bare left hand, which was missing the tips of three fingers. "I am in deep background, lady," he said. "I am strictly off the record in this story of yours. You never saw me around here. In fact, you are not even talking to me."

"You must have some kind of name," said Miss Sato practically.

"Look," said the faceless man, "you're Japanese, right? So, did you ever see Noh drama? Where there are all these, like, brave samurai and ghosts and lords and ladies being all super-traditional Japanese? Then there are these other black guys in black costumes. Guys so deep-black they make ninja look too obvious. Well, that's me. I was one of those deep background guys of yours."

"You're his confidential source," Miss Sato concluded. "You made that treasure map for him. You're a hacker from the Mechatronic Visionary Center."

"Yeah, but I haven't been in there in years," the faceless hacker said. "My lab is boarded shut and full of your chained-up dorks from the mainland. That's a dirty shame too, because that place was so perfect. We had creative freedom in there. We had our freedom to build anything we could dream up."

"I have a hostage friend in there who also longs for freedom," said Miss Sato at once.

"What, you want some kind of deal from me then?" scoffed the faceless man. "You, a no-budget peacenik who hangs out at the fringes of a provisional government? What are you gonna do for me, write me a trillion-yen personal check to 'Mickey Tronic'? You have no idea what we accomplished in there. We were fantastic. We were beyond your world."

"I know that you were top secret."

"No, no! First, we were top secret. Then, second, we were war-on-terror secret. Third, we were anti-nuclear-missile-proliferation secret. And then the whole lab was officially run by a sleazy private contractor—a crooked Japanese camera company in hock to the yakuza to keep its stock price up! They just paid our bills and never asked a word. That's how great my situation was. Then some North Korean secret bomb-lab morons had to ruin the whole arrangement."

"My hostage is still a hostage," said Miss Sato patiently, "and she still has a shackle on her leg. Nothing you said has changed that."

"We pulled in cool mil-spec hackers from every garage in the world," said Mickey Tronic mournfully. "Most of us couldn't speak a word of Japanese. I still can't speak any Japanese. '*Yoroshiku onegai itashimasu*,' that's about it."

"That is a good thing to say to me," Miss Sato admitted. "But the prisoner is still in chains, even though you say that to me."

"Just check out that guy stuck in the mud pit over there," said Mickey Tronic. "He was one of us! Terrific guy, never knew his real name, of course, but he was our ideal lab subject. Imagine building a tactile, augmented interface for a blind soldier. An interface so he can literally feel every centimeter, practically every cubic micron of the 3-D spaces around him . . . Do you know what 'proprioception' is?"

"No," said Miss Sato, gazing at the stir of pirates reluctantly gathering around Zeta One. "I don't know that. I do know that they'll never pull him out of there with that chain."

"Yeah, he's pretty well mired in there like a water buffalo," Mickey Tronic admitted. "That's a shame, because once that guy was a true Japanese Special Forces ninja. Superb martial artist, totally dedicated, complete devotion to the Japanese nation—if Tokyo existed, he'd still be saluting his emperor. I have to say, I always liked him."

"I should admit that too," said Miss Sato. "I like him myself."

"That brave guy—he lost everything that mattered to him in two bomb blasts, but he never says one word about his past. He just lives for the now. Very Zen. He wanders this island, pretending to pray—hell, he's probably really praying—and whenever people annoy him, they blow up. This whole section of the island is painted in infrared targeting lasers, right now. These cannibal Peter Pan children can't see that, but they'd be stone-dead if he twitched a finger."

"Is that true?"

"Isn't it obvious? The guy is the one-man focus of death from above. The thing that's great is that, after he liquidates the bad guys, he never attempts to assert any law and order on the ground! He's too soulful for that! That's what I love about him, that's why I never . . . you know . . . put a land mine under his tatami mat. There's something rare and magnificent about him. It'd be like poaching a tiger."

"If there's going to be an airstrike on these coordinates," said Miss Sato, "then we should leave right away."

"What is your hurry? I need my machine-gun robot back," Mickey Tronic said. "I mean, I don't need the gun itself, I'm happy if this weepy clown here mounts that gun in the office of his commie rag. But I need the visual coding for the microcontroller of the gun. Five of us worked on that project for three years, and we were so busy that we never commented the code! You know how much hard work that is, computer-vision coding? No, you don't get that, do you?" Mickey Tronic sighed within his blast helmet. "Why am I talking to you?"

"If you had the software code you want so much," said Miss Sato, "could you get a prisoner released from that computer lab of yours?"

"Let me share the big secret with you here," said Mickey Tronic. "Your hostage, Mrs. Nagai, she doesn't have any jailer. All her jailers are dead. They all got wiped out by mud-pit boy there. That's why you never got anywhere around here, and you're never going to get anywhere. It's not in the interests of anybody anywhere to straighten your situation out."

"So that's it," said Miss Sato. "Then the truth is, I am facing anarchy."

"Not really," said Mickey Tronic. "I'm an anarchist, but your problem is red tape. A setup like yours is just very Japanese. Everybody just ignores your uncomfortable problem till it turns impolite to mention it."

"Well, I am Japanese," said Miss Sato, "and if nobody talks about Mrs. Nagai staying in the prison, then nobody will talk about her if she leaves."

Mickey Tronic shrugged beneath his plate armor. "Go ahead, be all Japanese like that, I never said any different. Be Japanese, just let me have my true hacker freedom, all right? That's all I wanted. Freedom. Not 'free as in beer,' not 'free like free speech.' I mean total hacker freedom, like, completely free of any obligation to any other person, ever. And that's what I've got here on Tsushima. Still." He sighed. "Even when I'm down to a goddamn paper and pencil."

"If you give my treasure—Mrs. Nagai—to me, then I promise that, in return, I'll give your treasure to you."

Drizzle was falling again. Mickey Tronic wiped the smoked glass of his faceplate. "I'm supposed to believe that strange promise of yours?"

"Yes," said Miss Sato, "because I am an honest woman of moral principle, and when I make a promise, I never lie."

"Every tough guy thinks he's bulletproof," said Mickey Tronic, "just like every honest woman thinks she'll never be a whore. But the truth is, people break. They break whenever life gets hard enough. The only guy who will never break is that guy stuck in the mud over there, and that's why he's not human." He sighed. "I didn't even mention all that cyber-stuff we installed in his brain. That was just technical."

"So, do we have an arrangement?" said Miss Sato. "Because you won't see the last of me on Tsushima until I get what I want."

"Yeah, well, you never saw me in Tsushima in the first place. I'm so deep-black budget that I don't even exist. Nobody sees me at all."

"All right," said Miss Sato.

"Then we might, actually, have some kind of deal," admitted Mickey Tronic. "Just, don't ever try to find me. Because, believe me, I can easily locate you."

The Queen of Pirates suddenly loomed upon them in her furious majesty. At close range, her headdress towered over them like a feathered gun turret. The pirate queen had golden rings, silver bracelets, pearl buttons, and spangled, sequined sashes wrapping her grand, pregnant belly.

The pirate queen shouted at Mickey Tronic in very broken English. "Why you talk to this woman so much like that? You betray me now?"

Mickey Tronic gave an indifferent tilt to his smoked-glass faceplate. "Look, lady, don't try to boss me around. If you're the Queen of Pirates, then I'm the Witch Doctor of Pirates. I got your stepping razors, your whipping sticks, I got tech voodoo that would scare you so bad your grandchild will be born two-headed. So back off."

"I never understand this stupid computer man," said the pirate queen to Miss Sato, her regal face wrinkled with dismay. "Why does he speak English to me like that?" She pointed east, with a rattling clatter of bangles. "Does he think that is England over there? That is Japan!"

"Tell the Third World mother-of-eight here," said Mickey Tronic, "that I don't need any geolocation lessons. Tell her to get lost. Tell her that the ninja in the mud pit there is about to liquidate her the same way he did to pirate boyfriends one, two, and three."

"I'm a woman of honor! I hate disrespect!" shrieked the Pirate Queen. "A quick death is too good for this no-face turtle man! I will kill him now in such an awful, terrifying way that everyone will be impressed! Tell me, you, peace woman, you're always crying about the people suffering! What is the very worst thing in the world that ever happened to anyone? Tell me that! Tell him I'll do that to him."

"She claims she's going to torture you," said Miss Sato in English.

"Hell, this is Japan," shrugged Mickey Tronic. "Her torture's no good around here. Tell her I'll commit an agonizing hara-kiri just to spite her."

Miss Sato wisely said nothing.

The pirate queen glanced behind her, where half-hearted attempts to haul the blind man from his mud were getting nowhere. "Talk to him in English and make him scared of me, and I'll reward you richly. Don't make that face, because I'll give you back your real clothes. You'll be just like you were before we beat you. I will, you'll see, I'll do that now."

The pirate queen turned and raised her voice to harangue her scattered minions, but a rolling peal of typhoon thunder blotted out her commands.

This was the season of the sacred winds, and a huge storm front was rolling in from continental Asia. The kamikaze was serious, world-scale weather, a storm front big and black and presumably radioactive. The kamikaze was full of tainted rain from the city-sized craters of North Korea. A tremendous rain was coming, the kind of rain that would scatter a horde of Mongols the way Mongols scattered civilized nations.

"Oh what a bother," said the pirate queen. Gathering her robes in the patter of thumb-sized raindrops, she waddled to her jeep and fled the downpour.

The tempest bent the trees. Howling, ship-killing winds roared across Tsushima with salvo after salvo of thunder.

No one could remain in rain of this kind, so everyone simply left the scene.

Miss Sato and Yoshida found some shelter under the leaning roof of a dead vacation home. This stately family mansion had died not long after Tokyo had perished, as a collateral casualty. The house had suffered a fuel shortage, a water shortage, an electrical blackout, abandonment, a fire . . .

The beautiful island house had just fallen over in that strange mysterious way a civilization decays when nobody champions it. The dead house was a filthy mulch of fire-blackened memorabilia, wise books, tasteful paintings, meaningful photographs, important and civilized things.

These civilized things were so entirely gone now, so entirely flaked to nothingness and debris, that they lacked even the *mono no aware* of a cherry blossom. They were like an entire cherry orchard blown flat by a giant storm. With a loss of such scale, one could not even start over. One could not even vow to persist. One could only, in some halting but seismic fashion, come to identify with the storm winds.

Winds lashed and rain fell in buckets for four hours. When the tempest finally faded, the island landscape was foggy, silent, dark, and very cold. The swimming pool had flooded to its brim. When the evening sun flashed on it, it looked pretty and sweet again, a place of leisure and pleasure.

Zeta One had vanished. A blind aircraft had ditched in his swimming pool. It was perfect and sleek, pearl-white above and, from below, as blue as a sunlit sky.

～

Bruce Sterling is a science fiction novelist and technology blogger who unites his time between Austin, Turin, and Belgrade. His most recent book is a short story collection, *Gothic High-Tech*.

～

*The End, at least for North America, came from the "Aggression Factor,"
which altered the "wiring" of the brain. Come within nineteen paces of
another human and you both become psychotic killers. No one knows
where it came from, but, surely, it will, somehow, go away, wear off,
mutate again . . . surely?*

· ISOLATION POINT, CALIFORNIA ·
John Shirley

Gage pushed the door of his cabin open with his booted foot, as he always
did, peering inside, right and left, without going in, to make sure no one
was hiding there waiting for him. He looked around, saw only his single
bunk, neatly made up, with the solar-powered lamp on a small stand beside
it, glowing faintly in the overcast, late afternoon gloom. Faces did stare back
at him: the old magazine photos of smiling people, mostly girls, on the wall
over his bunk. The wooden chair stood just where he'd left it, pulled back
slightly from the metal table with its two coffee cups, long bereft of coffee,
and his collection of pens, stacks of spiral notebooks, the radio. Above the
table were the shelves of random books, many of them blackened at the
edges, foraged from a burned library in Sweetbite. The axe leaned on the
stack of firewood beside the river-stone fireplace, opposite the old wood
stove, with its two pots.

It was tedious, having to stop and look around in the cabin and the
outhouse, before going in, day after day. But as he went inside, he told
himself that the first time he neglected to do it, someone would be there to
brain him with his own ax.

He closed and barred the door behind him, saw that the fire was out, but
went immediately to the desk and stood there, looking out the window. It
was nailed shut and curtained—a risk having a window at all—but he could
see the light was dimming, the clouds shrugging together for rain. The charge
on the lamp was low, so he plugged it into the socket that connected to the

solar-collection panel on the roof, and the lamp's charge meter bobbed to near full. He dialed up the light, and looked at the radio but decided not to try it. He was usually depressed for a while after listening to the radio and didn't want to ruin his hopeful mood.

He leaned his shotgun against the wall, within reach, put the binoculars on a stack of notebooks, and sat down at the table. He adjusted the shim under the short table leg to minimize the wobbling, picked up a pen, and wrote his newest journal entry. His fingers were stiff with the chill but he wanted to tell his journal what had happened more than he wanted to stoke up the fire.

November 1st, 2023

I saw her again this afternoon, about forty-five minutes ago. She was standing on what was left of the old marina, coming out from all those burned-out buildings along San Andreas Spit, across the river's mouth from me. She was standing right where the river meets the tidal push from the ocean. That always seemed suggestive to me, the river flowing into the ocean; the ocean pushing back, the two kind of mingling. "Here's some silt" and "Here's some salt back at you." Silt and salt, never noticed how close the words were before now.

I looked at her in the binoculars, and when she saw I was doing that, she spread her arms and smiled as if to say, "Check me out!" Not that I could see much of her under all those clothes. It's pretty brisk out now, Northern coast this time of year, wind off the sea, and she was wearing a big bulky green ski jacket, and a watch cap, and jeans and boots. She had a 30.06 bolt-action deer rifle leaned against a rock. She never went far from it. She's got long wavy chestnut hair, and her face, what I could make out, seemed kind of pleasant. She's not tall. Taking into account the silhouette of her legs, she seems slim. Not that there's anyone obese left, not on this continent, anyway. She seemed energetic, confident. I wonder if she found a new supply drop somewhere? If she found it first, she could be doing well. Another reason to make contact.

But who knows what she's up to? She could be talking to men at a safe distance all over the county. Getting them to leave her gifts or something. But that'd be risky. They'll kill her eventually. Unless someone finds a cure for the AggFac soon. Not very goddamn likely.

Anyway it felt good talking to her. Shouting back and forth, really. I got pretty hoarse, since of course she was several hundred feet from me. Said she was from San Francisco. Got out just in time. Told her I was from Sacramento. She laughed when I told her this little peninsula of mine is called "Isolation

Point." Had to swear and cross my heart it was always called that. She said she used to be a high school English teacher. Told her, "Hey that's amazing, I used to be a high school student!" She laughed. I can just barely hear her laugh across the river.

She asked what did I used to do. Said I managed some restaurants. Wanted to be a journalist, write about America. Big story came, no one to tell it to. She said I could still write. I said for who? She said for people—you leave the writing in places and other people find it. "I'd read it!" she said. I said okay. Thinking that writing for one person at a time wasn't what I had in mind, but you scale down your dreams now. Way down.

I was running out of breath and my voice was going with all the yelling back and forth so I asked her name. Told her mine. Our ages too, me 43, she 34. I tried to think of some way to ask her to come closer, maybe at the fence. To ask her without scaring her. But I couldn't think of any way and then she waved and picked up her rifle and walked off.

Her name's Brenda.

I was hiking back to the cabin going, "Brennnn-da! Brennnn-da!" over and over like an idiot. Like I'm twelve. Not surprising after two years alone here, I guess. It was good just to see someone who isn't trying to kill me.

Wish the dog would come back. Someone probably ate him, though. I need to check the fence again. Going to do it now. It might rain. Might get dark before I'm back. Might be someone there. I've got the shotgun. Not that I can afford to use the shells. The sight of the gun keeps people back, though, if they stay beyond The Nineteen. Going now. Should stay here . . . Too antsy . . .

Gage put the pen down and picked up his shotgun. "That's right," he said aloud. "Put down the pen, pick up the gun." He had to talk aloud, fairly often, just to hear a human voice. Brenda's was the first he'd heard, except for the warning noise, for three months. "That's how it is," he said, hearing the hoarseness in his voice from all that shouting. Bad time to get laryngitis. Bad time to get anything—he'd almost died of pneumonia that once. No pharmacies anymore. You ran into a doctor, he'd try to kill you. He'd be sorry afterwards but that didn't do you any good.

Gage unbarred the door, and went out, closing the door carefully behind him. There was still some light. He walked out to the edge of the trees to take a quick look out at the Pacific, beyond the edge of the cliff, fifty yards away. It was steely under the clouds. He was looking for boats and hoping he wouldn't see one. Nothing out there, except maybe that slick black oblong, appearing and disappearing—a whale. At least the animals were doing better now.

He'd chosen this little finger of land, with its single intact cabin, partly because there was no easy way to land a boat. Mostly the sea was too rough around it. You could maybe come in from the sea up into the mouth of the river, clamber onto the big slippery wet crab-twitchy rocks that edged the river bank, if you could secure your boat so it didn't float away, but the current was strong there and no one had tried it that he knew of. His cabin was pretty well hidden in the trees, after all, and it didn't look like much was here. And of course, they were as scared of him as he was of them. But then, that's what his father had told him about rattlesnakes.

He turned and tramped through the pine trees toward the fence, a quarter mile back, noticing, for the first time in a year or more, the smell of the pine needles mingling with the living scent of the sea. Funny how you see a girl, you start to wake up and notice things around you again. To care about how things smell and look and feel.

The wind off the sea keened between the trees and made the hackles rise on the back of his neck. He buttoned the collar of his thick, blue REI snowline jacket with his left hand, the other keeping the Remington twelve-gauge tucked up under his right armpit, pressed against him, the breach-block cupped in his palm. He was good at getting the Remington popped fast to his shoulder for firing. So far nobody had noticed what a lame shot he was. The two guys he'd killed since coming to the area—killed four months apart—had both got it at close to point-blank range. That was the AggFac for you. If people sniped at you, it was out of desperation, not because of the AggFac.

He felt the wind tugging at his streaked beard, his long sandy hair. "I must be getting pretty shaggy," he said to a red squirrel, looking beadily down from a low branch. "But the only thing I've got left to cut it with is a knife and it's so dull . . . I'm down to my last cake of soap. Half a cake really . . . " For two years, cognizant that no one on the continent was making soap anymore, he'd only washed when he could no longer bear his own smell.

The squirrel clicked its claws up the tree, looking for a place to curl up out of the wind, and Gage continued, five minutes later cutting the old deer path he took to the fence. Another ten minutes and he was there: a twenty-five foot hurricane fence with antipersonnel wire across the top in a Y-frame. The fence and the place at the river where he got the fish and the crabs were two of the main reasons he'd chosen this spot. There was no gate in the fence—they'd used a chopper landing pad of cracked asphalt, near the edge of the cliff on the south side of the cape. There'd been some kind of military satellite monitoring station, here, once, and the fence, he figured, had been put up to keep people away from it. It kept bears and wolves out too. The post building had crumbled into the sea after a bad storm—you could see the satellite dish sticking up out of the water at low tide, all rusty; the cabin was all that was left. There was forage, if you knew where to look; there was river water to filter; there was a way he knew to get around the fence, underneath its southern end, when he was willing to try his luck checking the crossroads at Sweetbite Point for supply drops. But he hadn't been out to the crossroads in seven months. Previous time, someone had almost gotten him. So he stayed out here as long as he could. It was a great spot to survive in, if you wanted to survive. He'd almost stopped wanting to.

The fence looked perfectly upright, unbreached, so far as he could see from here, no more rusted than last time. Of course, a determined man could get over it—or around it, if you didn't mind clambering over a sheer drop—but it was rare for anyone to come out onto the cape. There weren't many left to come.

He walked along the fence a ways south, wondering what'd brought him here. He had a sort of instinct, especially sharp post-AggFac, that kept him alive—and usually it had its reasons for things.

There it was. The sound of a dog barking. He hoped it was Gassie.

"Hey Gassie!" he shouted, beginning to trot along the fence. "Yo, dog!" Be a great day, meeting a woman . . . sort of . . . and getting his dog back too. "Gassie!"

Then it occurred to him to wonder who the dog was barking at. Maybe a raccoon. Maybe not.

He bit off another shout, annoyed with himself for getting carried away. Shouting. Letting people know where he was.

He circled a lichen-yellowed boulder that hulked up to his own height, and came upon Gassie and the stranger—who was just a few steps beyond The Nineteen. Gassie was this side of the fence, the man on the other side, staring, mouth agape, at the hole the dog had dug under the fence to get in . . .

Despite the dangerous presence of the stranger, Gage shook his head in admiration at the dog's handiwork. It was the same spot he'd gotten out at—some critter, raccoon or skunk, had dug a hole under the fence where the ground was soft, and the dog had widened it and gotten out and wandered off, more than a month ago. Gage had waited a week, then decided he had to fill the hole in. Here he was, Gassie, his ribs sticking out, limping a little, but scarcely the worse for wear—a brown-speckled tongue-drooping mix of pit bull, with his wedge-shaped head, and some other breed Gage had never been sure of.

The stranger—a gawky, emaciated man in the tatters of an Army uniform, who'd let his hair fall into accidental dreadlocks—goggled stupidly at the hole, then jerked his head up as Gage approached the dog.

Gage reckoned the stranger, carrying an altered ax handle, at twenty-one paces away, with the fence between them. Not at The Nineteen yet. Everyone alive on this continent was good at judging distances instantly. Nineteen paces, for most people, was the AggFac warning distance. It was possible to remain this side of psychotic—like this side of the fence—beyond nineteen paces from another human being. Nineteen paces or less, you'd go for them, with everything you had, to kill them; and they'd go at you just the same. Which was why most people in North America had died over the past few years. A couple of phrases from one of the first—and last—newspaper articles came into his mind: *The very wiring of the brain altered from within . . . That portion of the brain so different victims become another species . . .*

"You're outside the margin, dude," Gage said. "You can still back up."

He knew he should probably kill the guy whether he backed up or not, on general principle. For one thing, the guy was probably planning to kill and eat his dog. For another, now that the son of a bitch knew there was someone camped on the other side of the fence, he'd come over to forage and kill—or rather, to kill and forage.

But you clung to what dignity you could. Gage did, anyway. Killing people when you didn't absolutely have to lacked dignity, in Gage's view.

"Don't come no closer," the man said. He hefted the ax-handle warningly. It was missing its ax blade but he'd found a stiff blade from a kitchen knife somewhere and he'd pushed it into a crack at one end of the handle and wrapped it in place with black electric tape.

"You were a soldier," Gage observed. "Where's your weapon?"

"I got it, real close," the man said. After thinking laboriously a moment, he said, "My partner's got it trained on your ass right now."

Gage laughed. "No one's got a partner. I saw some people try it, before I came here—watched from a roof for two days. They tried partnering by staying twenty feet away from each other. But eventually they would fuck that up, get too close—and you know what happened. Every time. You haven't got a partner—or a gun."

The man shrugged. He wasn't going to waste his breath on any more lies. He looked at the dog, licking his lips. Finally he said, "You knock that dog in the head, push it where I can get it, I'll go away for good."

"That dog's worth ten like you," Gage said. He made up his mind. It'd be pretty ironic if the AggFac had worn off, finally, and he and Brenda were staying out of reach for no reason. Of course, there was no reason to think it ever wore off. But everyone, as far as he knew, hoped it would, eventually. They didn't know what caused it, exactly—there were lots of theories— so maybe it'd wear off as mysteriously as it came. For no good reason, the brain would revert to normal.

Yeah right. But for Brenda's sake he stepped closer to the stranger, within The Nineteen, to see if the AggFac was still there in him.

He felt it immediately. The clutching up feeling, the hot geysering from the back of his skull, the heat spreading to his face, his arms. The tightening of his hands, his jaws, the background humming; the tight focus on His Enemy. And the change in the way things look—going almost colorless. Not black and white, but sickly sepia and gray, with shadows all deep and inky.

Since Gage had come within The Nineteen, the stranger was seized by the AggFac too, and his face went beet red, the veins at his temples popping up. As if propelled from behind he came rushing at Gage, stopped only by the fence, hammering at the chain links with his ax handle, making that *Eeeeee* sound in the back of his throat they all made—the sound Gage might've been making himself, he could never tell somehow. Hammering the ax handle to splinters as Gage shoved the barrel of the shotgun through a fence link and pulled the trigger at point blank range . . .

The stranger fell away, gasping and dying. The AggFac ebbed. Color seeped back into the world.

Gage heard the dog barking, and saw it start for the hole in the fence. Wanting to get at the stranger's body.

"No, Gassie," Gage said, feeling tired and empty and half-dead himself. He grabbed the dog by its short tail, pulled it back before it was quite through the hole. It snarled at him but let him do it. He blocked up the hole with rocks, then started toward the end of the fence, where it projected over the cliff. He'd have to go down by the rocks, about fifty feet south of the fence's end, thread the path, climb the other cliff, to get the body, drag it to the sea. A lot of work.

But he didn't want to leave the bloody corpse there for Brenda to find. He wanted her to come to the fence . . .

So he trudged off toward the cliffs.

November 2nd, 2023
My face hurts from scraping at it with that knife. Used up a lot of soap in place of shaving cream. Hope the contusions go down before she sees me up close. Not too close, of course.

Will she come? She'd be foolish to come. She doesn't know me. She can see the fence from across the river but she doesn't know if it'll keep her safe from me. I might have a gate for all she knows. She's never been out to the point.

She says she's coming. We agreed on high noon. She's got a longer-range weapon than me. She doesn't seem stupid. She'll be smart about it. She'll get close enough to take stock of the situation, with that gun right up against her shoulder, but not so close I could rush her.

I think she does understand that outside the AggFac I'm not some thug, some rapist. But she may decide not to take the chance. Or someone may kill her before she gets here. I think it's almost noon . . .

"Hi! Can you see me okay?" Gage called, spreading his hands so she could see he didn't have the shotgun. She was still about a hundred feet off, on the other side of the fence, assessing the situation from cover, like he'd figured she would, the rifle propped on the top of a big tree stump and pointed right at him.

Dangerous, not to bring the shotgun. But it was meaningful. They both knew that. Not carrying your gun was like, in the old days, bringing a bouquet of flowers.

Still, this could be a setup. She could be after his goods. She could want his cabin, maybe. She could shoot him, and Gassie, if she had the ammo. Shoot him from safety where she was. Nothing to stop her. A couple of rounds, one'd get through that fence. Down he'd go . . .

He kept his arms spread. Standing in the open, a little clearing with just rock-strewn dirt on the ground, so she could see he didn't have the shotgun anywhere near—like, hidden behind a rock close to him. His gun could be somewhere in the brush, of course. But at least it wasn't in easy reach.

Slowly, she got out from behind the stump and walked toward him.

She glanced right and left now and then. Looked at the dog, sitting there wagging its tail, beside him. She smiled.

"Hi Brenda," he said, when she got to about twenty-one paces, and stopped. Slowly, she lowered the gun, holding it cradled in her arms.

Then she sat down, her legs crossed, deciding to trust him that much. He sat down too, on his side of the fence. The dog put his head on Gage's lap.

"I'm embarrassed to tell you his name," Gage said, patting the dog. "It's Gassie."

"Gassie!" She laughed. "After Lassie, right?" She had all of her teeth, which was unusual in itself. Her face had lots of roundness to it, but she wasn't pie-faced. Her eyes were dark brown, he saw, and the shape of them suggested she had some American Indian blood. She'd put her hair up, in a simple kind of way, and she seemed clean.

"What now?" he asked, as mildly, as casually, as much without pressure as he could.

"I don't know," she said. "I just needed to see someone up close as I could, and you seemed nice." She shrugged. "As much as anyone can be, with the—you know."

He nodded, deciding he needed to be as completely honest with her as possible. "I tried it, yesterday, when a stranger came up to the fence. I deliberately stepped closer, just to see. I always hope it might go away some time."

"I've never heard of it going away."

"No. Reports on the radio say it never has for anyone. Kids don't outgrow it, old people don't get over it. It hit me the same as always."

She nodded, not having to ask what'd happened.

"I don't feel too bad," he added. "Guy was trying to eat my dog."

She nodded again. That she understood too, both sides. "You fish?"

"Sure." They talked a long time about practical things like that. He told her about his water filter, the crabs, the fish, the wild plants he knew—she knew them too—and about the forays to the food drops.

"They'll drop food to us sometimes, the foreign people," she said, "but they seem to have just . . . given up on curing it. Unless—you said you had a radio? You heard anything?"

He shook his head. "Nothing new. One guy—hard to get the signal, I think it was from the Virgin Islands, I had to move the radio around—he said the Japanese thought it was some kind of nanotech-creation that got out of hand, like an artificial virus, supposed to alter your brain wiring in a good way, does it in a bad way instead, jumps from person to person. Then there's the biowarfare theory, the mutated virus theory . . . "

"The one I liked was about the schizophrenia virus. Back in the twentieth century some people thought a lot of mental illness is caused by a virus that gets in the brain. They think this is a mutation of the schizophrenia virus. They thought schizophrenia was something you could get from cat shit, once."

"I always knew there was some reason I didn't like cats."

She laughed.

"Whatever it is," he went on, venting, "you'd think someone would make some damn progress by now. No vaccines, nothing. It is like they're just waiting for us to die. Won't let anybody come to their perfect little countries. That blockade in Panama, shoot down our planes . . . "

"Can you blame them?" she asked.

He knew what she meant. The world had watched, as the "Aggression Factor" rolled over a hemisphere; as millions of people had killed one another: people in North America and Mexico, all the way to the geo-quarantine at the Panama Canal; the world had watched as millions of longtime neighbors had killed one another; watched as an unthinkable number of husbands had killed their wives, and wives their husbands; as unspeakable quantities of children were murdered by parents, by siblings, by friends; as others murdered their parents. As women throttled babies freshly plucked from the womb—and then wept in utter bafflement. He remembered a boy walking through the ruins of Sacramento, weeping, "Why did I kill my mom? Why did I kill my mom?" And then the boy had come within nineteen steps and . . . without meaning to, Gage had put him out of his misery.

"Nah. I don't blame them. I just . . . " He didn't have to say it. She smiled sadly and they understood one another.

"Nice not to have to shout."

"Yeah. I . . . have some dried fish for you, if you need it. I'll leave it at the fence. I thought maybe I'd loan you my solar radio, too, if you wanted. The dog dug a hole under the fence a ways down. I could push it under there . . . leave it for you to get later. You can see me walking a good quarter mile off from there."

"That's so sweet. You look like you carved your face up a bit . . ."

"Best I could do with what I had."

"You're still a nice looking guy."

Probably not when the AggFac hits, he thought. But he said only, "Thanks."

"I'll borrow the radio, I promise to bring it back . . . "

November 6, 2023

I've seen her every day but yesterday—I was really worried yesterday when she didn't come but she had to duck a guy who had gotten wind of her. He was stalking her. She finally managed to lure him up to a hill she knew real well and she shot him from cover. Smart, cool-headed girl. I'm crazy about her. Of course, I can't get within nineteen steps of her but . . . I'm still crazy about her.

She told me about a girl who'd lived down the street from her, they talked from rooftops, sometimes. The girl would trade a look at her naked body to guys who'd come around, look at her naked up on a second floor balcony. She had a gun up there in case they started up. They'd leave her food and stuff and they'd look at her naked and masturbate. It worked for awhile but of course some predator got wind of it, some guy who was always more or less AggFac, even before it came along, and he busted in and jumped her. Killed her, of course, the AggFac won't be denied, but I figure her body was still warm afterwards. Lot of bodies get raped now.

Why did Brenda tell me this story? Maybe suggesting we trusted each other enough to get naked, if only from a distance? I'm too embarrassed to masturbate even if she's doing it too. That desperate I'm not.

I wrote her some poetry I'm going to leave for her. She might blow me off for good after she reads it, if she's got any taste . . .

"Feels like it might snow," Brenda said, hugging herself against the morning mist, the occasional gusts of cold wind.

"Kind of cold. I could go back, get you a blanket, toss it over." They were sitting in their usual spot, fence between them.

"Oh, it'd probably get stuck on the wire," she said.

"I could send Gassie over again to keep you warm."

"Last time he came over he humped my leg."

"He did? I didn't see that." He was only momentarily tempted to say, I don't blame him. Even now he could be slicker than that.

"There's something I wanted to talk to you about," she said. She chewed her lip for a moment, then went on, "Look—you ever hear about someone being cured of, like, a phobia, before the AggFac, by getting used to whatever they were scared of, little by little? Scared of flying, they made you go to airports, sit in a plane, but then get off the plane before it flies, look at pictures taken out a plane window, till you're ready to fly . . . all that kind of thing. You know?"

"Yeah, I forget what they call that. But . . . you don't think the AggFac would work that way. It's not a phobia."

"No it isn't. But it's a kind of compulsive aversion for people . . . when they get physically close. Right? What if a person could sort of inure themselves to the presence of another person within nineteen steps—by slow degrees? Make the brain accustomed to the other person . . . the wiring of the brain itself acclimated to them."

"How? It's so powerful that even if your eyes are shut and you can't see the person, soon as you know they're close, the AggFac hits and you kill them. Whatever you do, the murder reflex comes out. I mean—I could probably find a way to restrain myself, somehow, for awhile, so I couldn't get loose too easily. So you could get close—but then, let's face it, *you'd* kill *me*. I mean, mothers killed children they loved all their lives . . . "

"Sure. But . . . suppose we both restrain ourselves somewhat. With rope, whatever, the weapons off somewhere, we keep the fence between us at first, but we're basically within reach. I don't think I could even bite you through those links. But we could have some contact . . . "

The idea made him breathless. His blood raced as he thought about it. But then he shook his head. "Even if we didn't hurt one another—we'd hate one another, within The Nineteen. There'd be no pleasure in it—just rage."

"Our brains would feel that way—at first. But our bodies! Our bodies would . . . I think they'd respond. It'd be a kind of . . . counter force in the brain. Maybe enough, after awhile, to . . . Oh, Gage, I can't take this distance from people much longer. I'm . . . I've got skin hunger. It's bad. I have to try something."

"Hey. Me too. And I really, really like you. I'd have liked you before all this stuff, I swear it. But—even if we couldn't hurt each other, how would the encounter ever end? We'd be smashing at each other through the fence!"

"That's the risk. There has to be some risk. There always was some risk. But Gage—I want to try. I think that . . . if I'm starting to hurt myself against the fence, I'll finally manage to back off and the AggFac'll go away. Then we can try again. We can *inure*. We can *accustom*. We can . . . acclimate. Maybe you'll stop seeing me as . . . the other. Maybe I'll be, like, an extension of you, after awhile, so the AggFac won't come any more, at least when it's me."

"You mean . . . you want to get naked, on either side of the fence . . . "

"Yeah. Well, I'll keep my coat on, and some boots. Won't look too elegant but . . . I'm burning to touch you. I want to love you. I want you to love me . . ."

She was crying now. Finally he said yes.

November 11, 2023
The weather cleared up some, and, partly naked, we tried it. We each had our guns put way out of reach but where the other could see it. She had some rope, left some for me—she'd pushed it through the mesh, inch by inch, while she was waiting for me. We took turns, measuring it out carefully. The rope went from a tree behind me to the fence, just enough so I could press against it, but restraining me so I couldn't start to climb over it easily. My arms were tied to my sides. That was tricky. Had to work with our teeth, use a fork in a tree to pull a knot taut, stuff like that. Laughing a lot back and forth as we worked out how to do it, all alone, each on their side of the fence. Of course we knew it was still possible to get out of the rope but it would take time and the other could get away or get their gun . . . We thought maybe we'd be too frenzied with kill lust or the other kind to really work out how to attack the other person with all that stuff in the way. The AggFac isn't about thinking or planning, god knows.

I used up the last of my soap, getting ready for this. She had cleaned herself up too.

We came close, the fence between us, the rope restraining us. The AggFac hit and there was no remembering how we'd said we'd loved each other, there was no remembering how we wanted to trust.

He tried to nap at her nose through the mesh, envisioned tearing it off in his teeth, but couldn't reach her. She tried to bite into his chin, couldn't reach it.

But their skin touched, through the links, *and he did get a hard-on under the rope*—it was roped to his belly, no way it was going to be free to go through that fence, she'd bite it off for sure. They writhed and snapped and snarled and then she managed to back away.

Still, I swear something did get through the AggFac, some other feeling—it really did get through. Just enough.

We both got bloody on the fence but we're going to try again. We have a plan, a way to try it in the cabin.

⌒

His heart was slamming in his chest, so loud he could hear it in the quiet of the cabin. He just lay there on his bunk listening to his heart thudding, trying the ropes, hoping the self-restraint system he'd worked up was going to hold him long enough. He could get out of the ropes, afterward, but it'd take time. The dog was tied up in the woods. He was ready for her to come. Maybe she wouldn't show up. He'd lie here like an idiot and some son of a bitch would climb over the fence and find him here, before he got loose, and he'd be helpless. Then dead.

Big risk, trying it in the cabin this way. Risk from her too. She said she was getting some control over the AggFac, but how long would it last, in close proximity?

He knew he couldn't bear it if he killed her. If she killed him, well, it wouldn't matter.

The door opened and he looked up and saw her there, inside The Nineteen, almost naked. Her hands were all muffled, tied together and smothered in big thick home-made boxing gloves, and her mouth was gagged, she'd gagged it herself, to try to keep her from biting him.

The color drained from the room. The *Eeeee* was building up in the back of his throat; was trying to get out of her too. He could see her struggling to keep it back. But the other thing, the distance from the AggFac, that they'd worked on, built up through the fence, that was there too. He was able to look at her, like a man close to the sheet of flames in a forest fire—feeling the heat painfully but not quite so close he was burned yet.

She waited there for a moment, looking at his ropes. Then she started toward him. He tried to hold onto the memory of her touch, through the fence, the desire he felt for her, but the AggFac rose up. He writhed against the ropes.

She rushed him, her face reddening with AggFac, leaped on him, straddled him . . .

It was funny how the two feelings were there, right close, so distinct. Kill. Love. Almost intertwined. But not combined. Like, alternating. I just kept trying to drag my mind back to the love feeling. I looked in her eyes, saw her doing the same thing. Whole moments of close, intimate sanity, each one of those moments—impossible to explain how precious they were. Impossible.

The AggFac WAS still there but somehow, for a few moments, they were in a kind of blessed state of between-ness. She was there, so close, her breath on his cheek, the feeling of her closeness like a hot meal after a week of hunger.

Something in him, something that went to sleep during the Aggression Factor, quivered awake and brought color back to the room. Their eyes locked . . . hers cleared. She stopped shaking.

She stopped pounding at him . . . and slipped him into her, pumped her hips, working the gag out of her mouth, chewing the gloves off her hands so she could touch him.

There was intimacy; after so much privation, there was rapid mutual orgasm. Then he drew away from her, instinctively, as he came, and the AggFac returned, and he started thrashing against the ropes, trying to kill her, and her own Aggression broke free in response, and she started clawing at his eyes, snapping at his throat. She bit hard, she tore, his blood began to flow . . .

Some of his rope gave way. Enough.

He seized her by the throat and—just to get her hands from his eyes—threw her off him, to the floor. He tore loose as she scrambled to her feet, turned snarling to face him. He reached out with one hand, scooped up the chair, threw it at her—it felt light as cardboard to him in that moment. It struck her on the side of the head and she fell backwards, crying out. He still had ropes around his ankles and jerked them loose, looking for another weapon to kill her with. Stunned, confused, she crawled to the door . . .

She turned and stared dazedly at him. He hunkered, ready to spring at her. Panting, they stared at one another. She was within Nineteen. He wanted to kill her. But a second passed and he didn't spring. Neither did she. The between-ness was in her eyes. But it wouldn't last, not now.

"Run!" he managed, huskily.

But she hesitated . . .

And then the moment passed.

February 2, 2024.

I've met someone else. Her name is Elise. Pretty soon I'm going to tell her about the fence and the process. I'm going to try again. I have to try again.

There was that one second, when I was free, and didn't attack. Seeing the humanness in her eyes, too, for a moment. It gave me hope. That one second could telescope out to a lifetime of forbearance.

Some day I'll get control of it, and then I can be honest with Elise. And show her Brenda's grave.

John Shirley is a prolific writer who has published over thirty novels and ten short-fiction collections. His most recent novel is *Everything is Broken*; his seminal cyberpunk A Song Called Youth trilogy of *Eclipse*, *Eclipse Penumbra*, and *Eclipse Corona* was re-released as an omnibus in 2012. Shirley's collections include the Bram Stoker and International Horror Guild Award-winning *Black Butterflies* and, most recently, *In Extremis: The Most Extreme Stories of John Shirley*. He also writes for screen (*The Crow*) and television. As a musician Shirley has fronted his own bands and written lyrics for Blue Öyster Cult and others.

Acknowledgements

Special thanks to Paul Tremblay for some great suggestions and, as always, to the editors who first published these stories.

"Pump Six" by Paolo Bacigalupi © 2008 Paolo Bacigalupi. First publication: *Pump Six and Other Stories* (Night Shade Books).

"The Books" by Kage Baker © 2010 Kage Baker. First publication: *The Mammoth Book of Apocalyptic SF*, ed. Mike Ashley (Robinson).

"Chislehurst Messiah" by Lauren Beukes © 2011 Lauren Beukes. First publication: *Pandemonium: Stories of the Apocalypse*, eds. Anne C. Perry & Jared (Jurassic London).

"The Disappeared" by Blake Butler © 2008 Blake Butler. First publication: *New Ohio Review, Issue 3*, Spring 2008.

"Beat Me Daddy (Eight to the Bar)" by Cory Doctorow © 2002 CorDoc-Co, Ltd. First publication: *Black Gate*, Summer 2002.

"The Adjudicator" by Brian Evenson © 2009 Brian Evenson. First publication: *Fugue State* (Coffee House Press).

"A Story, With Beans" by Steven Gould © 2009 Steven Gould. First publication: *Analog*, May 2009.

"The Fifth Star in the Southern Cross" by Margo Lanagan © 2008 Margo Lanagan. First publication: *Dreaming Again*, ed. Jack Dann (HarperCollins Publications).

"Horses" by Livia Llewellyn © 2009 Livia Llewellyn. First publication: *Postscripts #18*.